A HEART *So* HAUNTED

A HEART *So* HAUNTED

a novel

HOLLIE NELSON

Published in the United States by Alcove Press, an imprint of The Quick Brown Fox & Company LLC.

Alcove Press and its logo are trademarks of The Quick Brown Fox & Company LLC.

Library of Congress Catalog-in-Publication data available upon request.

ISBN (hardcover): 979-8-89242-339-7
ISBN (paperback): 979-8-89242-340-3
ISBN (ebook): 979-8-89242-341-0

Cover design by Colin Verdi

Printed in the United States.

www.alcovepress.com

Alcove Press
34 West 27th St., 10th Floor
New York, NY 10001

First Edition: October 2025

The authorized representative in the EU for product safety and compliance is eucomply OÜPärnu mnt 139b-14, 11317 Tallinn, Estonia, hello@eucompliancepartner.com, +33757690241

10 9 8 7 6 5 4 3 2 1

For the younger me, who begged to go to the bookstore after getting her wisdom teeth out. And, with puffy cheeks, said that she'd have a book on the shelf one day.

We did it.

Author's Note

This novel contains serious topics that might be triggering to some readers. Please proceed with caution if subjects of depression, death of a loved one (off page), insinuations of self-harm, deep self-hatred, eating disorders, tumultuous parental relationships, child abuse (emotional, on page; physical abuse/assault, lightly described), drug addiction, addictive tendencies, or suicidal ideation make you uncomfortable.

Before

The house wanted to eat the child. Swallow her whole, keep her near, like a sock flitting from the clothesline in an unexpected breeze.

Keep keep keep.

She'd come back. The very floorboards of the house expanded when her mother had dropped her off. Could the little girl feel it, like it could? Surely, if she was here, that *meant* something.

"Get in the car, Landry!" the woman called. The woman, the house knew, was the child's mother. Harthwait never deigned her worth remembering.

"We're gonna be late!" The girl's mother stood with a cigarette between two fingers by a rickety sedan. A back tire sat deflated, the rear windshield marred by a large crack. It slithered from the upper right corner, to the bottom crease where carpet interior met glass. She tapped a cherry nail on the crack, like she might tempt fate, then pushed herself up from the trunk lid.

The house felt the girl. Her pink shoes on the front porch step, hesitant. Hovering. Staring up at Cadence with one hand fisted in the fabric of her dress. Her little knuckles whitened to snowcapped mountains. On her shoes were daisies. One hung crooked, a petal missing, dried and rinsed and repeated from her bout with the mud pit in the backyard.

She wiggled in place, jumped. Almost lost her balance.

"Why can't I stay with you, Aunt Denny?" the little girl asked. She clutched the porch railing with her free hand. "You promised we'd finish the puzzle."

Cadence looked at Landry like one might examine an adult. The girl stood taller, puffed out her lip, furrowed her brow. Cadence stepped through the front door, onto the porch, as if she might humor the child.

She wouldn't.

Still, Harthwait couldn't complain about Cadence. She fixed what was needed. Kept the windows greased. Replaced the roof a few years ago. Children, however, were not as easy to manage.

"Because my house isn't pretty after dark," Cadence said.

Maybe it would complain after all.

"Mommy's house isn't pretty, either. There are bugs. I wanna stay with you," the girl urged. A damp, soon-to-be summer breeze tickled the hem of her dress, caressed the house's siding.

"Landry!" the woman, who drooped over the back of the car, called again. She exhaled a long stream of smoke. It twirled around her nostrils, her ears. The house could have sworn even the tree branches recoiled.

Aunt Cadence sighed.

"Please? Please, *please*? I'll be good, I promise! I won't—"

Upstairs, a door slammed shut. Cadence flinched, but the child didn't. She was too focused on Cadence, on the way her jaw *ticked ticked ticked* like the grandfather clock in the foyer, how her eyes wavered between the mother, who now stomped out the cigarette in the driveway gravel, to the little girl with doe eyes and a massed tangle of red hair.

"Lanny. Honey. Your momma makes the decisions. You know this."

The girl slumped. "But you said no last time and that maybe this time I could—"

"Keep your head up, chickpea." Cadence bent down to her niece, both hands landing on the girl's shoulders. Bony, pointy little things. "I'll come pick you up tomorrow," she assured her. The girl looked like she could jump into Cadence's words—right off the top of the bridge and into the water below.

"But tomorrow is too late. You'll finish the puzzle without me," she whispered. "*Please.*"

"Landry!"

Cadence's spine curled in. "It'll be fine. Promise. Won't even touch what you left. I'll keep it on that very table you were using in the library, okay?"

The sun heated Harthwait's roof. Warmed it, straight to its bones. But there was something in Cadence's voice that wobbled. Like a lie. Like there lay finality in her words.

That couldn't be, though. The little girl would come back, she'd stay one day—at the very least, return for a moment or two.

Harthwait's floorboards contracted a bit, irritated.

She *had* to come back.

"You promise?"

"It'll be waiting for you. Cross my heart," Cadence said before giving her niece one final hug. When Landry pulled away, Cadence's fingers lingered in the space where the little girl had stood. Then the girl slunk off the porch, shoulders drooped, her little pink shoes clip-clopping over the cobbled path toward her mother.

A window jerked open.

Another.

No. No, no, this child—she had it, she *could*—

The girl's mother muttered something under her breath—something even the wind didn't toss back for Harthwait to hear—and climbed into the driver's seat without so much as a glance at Landry.

The child hauled herself into her own booster seat, snapped her own seat belt, and rolled down her window. She leaned out when the car jerked into reverse, fingers hooked over the window lip, and waved as the car sputtered farther and farther away.

Cadence watched, waited. Until the last of the dirt plume kicked up by the car's wheels faded, the little girl along with it.

She rubbed both hands over her face. Her skin had fallen in the last couple of years, though Harthwait would bet she wasn't much over the age of forty. Not much older than he was, nestled in the walls.

"I swear," Cadence muttered. She pressed down the flyaway hairs, straightened her shirt. Started to talk to herself like she always did, especially when she wanted to ignore the noises at night. Because she always ignored the noises. "Nothing you can do, Denny. She's not yours, and this place isn't good for her, either."

Harthwait bristled. Of course, Cadence would put it off—what was the saying about pulling the wool over the eyes?

The house relaxed, if only a little, as Cadence started locking doors, pulling down windows. The birds hadn't yet stopped singing for the evening. Cadence circled through the next floor, room after room. She plucked the last of the scattered toys from the old playroom floor. Tossed them in the bins, then waltzed into the hall.

But there sat an empty pit where the little girl had been. Like a hunger, it crawled between the stairs, inside the door hinges, beneath the shingles. An ache that sat suppressed for too many years, stretched its arms and legs and unfurled from the concentrated place it had been curled. Like a starving man, unable to recall the scent of smoked venison—until one day, a hunter in the distance started a spit. The aroma drifted downwind, and then the starving man knew a hunger like never before. The pain snaked down to his marrow, and all he could think of was the venison, the possibilities. The need.

That was this child.

And this woman had sent her *away*.

Above the toy bin, a window jerked open. Only a hair's breadth.

The birds still sang.

She wouldn't notice.

Cadence made it to her bedroom and locked the door behind herself. Every once in a while, she would stop and listen. She did so now. Glanced about the space—*her* space. No wayward breeze glided in through cracked windows. No settling of the foundation.

She shuffled through baskets of thimbles and twine, old sewing needle containers and crotchet hooks. Until it emerged from the bottom—the radio remote, the two and the four so worn that the numbers were nearly illegible.

Cadence turned the radio up until the birds quieted outside. Even the birds—it couldn't even have the birds anymore—

One by one, the spare bedroom windows slammed open. One after another, curtains billowing, breeze rustling. If she wanted to do this, then fine. It could wait.

But the radio vibrated through the walls, so obnoxious and loud, Cadence never heard a thing. Not even when the attic door ripped open, just after midnight.

Chapter One

I peeked through the front door's sidelights and watched the woman hobble down the cobblestone path. If she turned around now, she'd see me with my nose pressed to the glass, counting down the seconds until she reached her car. The thought made me pull back—or at least until I was looking out the window at an angle.

She teetered onto the driveway, and only once she opened the driver's side door did I let the stained-glass window covers clatter back into place.

I glared down at the covered dish in my hands. How many meals did someone need? I understood the sentiment—the instinct to provide when someone was in need or experiencing a loss. But this . . . This was too much.

There was no reason for me to find room for another casserole dish in Aunt Cadence's—no, *my*—refrigerator that wasn't going to get eaten, anyway.

"Why does it smell like that?" Sayer muttered. I turned beside the grandfather clock to find my friend leaning against the stair railing, the neck of his penny tee pulled over his nose while he stared at his phone. A search engine reflected in his glasses. *Realtors in Colleton County*, it probably read.

I lifted the aluminum foil with a cringe. "Because it's broccoli." I crunched it back in place. "And cheese."

"Not enough cheese, apparently," he said, voice muffled. "That's absolutely putrid."

"It's the thought that counts, right?" My words were flat, even to my own ears. Sayer's gaze flitted up to me, then back to his phone.

"Right." He nodded to the floor. "I think she dropped something."

I glanced at the entry rug. A little folded slip of paper lay half-open, like a duck bill, an inch from the doorframe. I bent down, dish balanced in one hand, and made a mental note to vacuum up the family of dust bunnies that were huddled by the baseboards later.

"What is it, a ransom note? *Give me your house or I'll get the historical society to revoke it from you?*" he teased, brows scrunched.

"You watch too much true crime."

"Blackmail and hiding a body are two completely different things."

I unfolded the paper, expecting another *Our condolences on your loss* message. Instead, it read, *Haven't heard from you! But I found something! Let me know.*

I frowned. "Sorry to report, but it's not a threat." I crumpled the paper and stuffed it in my pocket. "It was probably—"

A crash echoed from another room.

Both Sayer and I stopped breathing.

Upstairs, a set of heels paused. "Ms. Frederick?"

The realtor. At that moment, I wanted to lean against the closest wall, squeeze my eyes shut, and evaporate into thin air. Today wasn't my day.

But today *had* to be the day she did a walk-through. Time was of the essence. And I had little enough patience as it was—with wills and deed transfers and debt payoffs running out of my ears, the last thing I needed to tack onto my list was hunting down another realtor.

Hence: The sooner the better.

Now, however, I regretted my past self's choices.

Sayer and I stared at each other. I shook my head. Talking to anyone outside my clientele circle didn't usually make my wrists sweat, but this woman intimidated me. "What do I say? Do you think she heard that?"

"Don't look at me! I didn't do anything." He splayed both hands with wide eyes, phone face up. It did, in fact, have another realtor website pulled up.

"I didn't either," I whisper-hissed.

"Tell her something."

My eyes widened. "Me? You brought her here."

"You said you needed an experienced realtor to look at the place! My mom recommended her!"

I gestured with the casserole dish toward the stairs in a poor attempt to point, as if to say, *Help me.*

Sayer shook his head.

My mouth pursed. I narrowed my eyes, stepped closer, and whispered, "You owe me for this."

"You said you need the house sold," he said, forehead crinkled. "You owe *me*."

I sighed. I inched closer to the bottom of the mahogany stairs. "Yes?" I called.

I didn't remember the woman's name. It was something elegant with multiple syllables that started with an E—Evanescence or Evangelina, maybe—but I had as much experience handling a realtor as I did with roofing. My clients dealt with the realtors; I dealt with the paint colors and fixtures and anything not requiring a permit.

"What was that? I thought you said there was no road noise," she called down. Her words sounded nasally and traveled from the left side of the second-floor landing. I tried not to picture her in Aunt Cadence's room or one of the multiple guest rooms, examining my aunt's things, trying to get an idea of the square footage of the house and what might look marketable.

"Sayer closed a door, no worries!" I swallowed around a sandy lump in my throat.

Without a response, her steps faded away. Farther into the second floor. Deeper, peeling away at my childhood memories, marking floorboards and rooms with a price.

Another bang.

It sounded like the heel of a palm against a wall. Or a locked door that made hinges rattle.

I whirled. Sayer stood stick straight now, both hands clutching his phone. The tendons in his forearms stood taut.

"I know you heard that," he whispered. "That was not me. Obviously."

Obviously not. But if it wasn't either of us, and no one else was in the house—

I glared at the foyer floor, waiting. Maybe it would come again?

The stained-glass coverings, which hung over the sidelight panes on either side of the front door, cast ribbons of color onto the rug. A draft brushed over the baby hairs at my temple, the back of my neck, hot and soupy. Typical of Lowcountry, even this early in the summer season.

"Don't lie," he urged.

I squeezed my eyes shut. The draft—that had to be it. It must have caught momentum when it slipped through a window and shut a door that hadn't been latched.

"But what if—" I started.

"Landry." Sayer's mouth pinched. "You heard it. You told me nothing would happen. You *promised* you haven't seen anything weird. You know how I feel about this kind of . . . stuff."

"Okay, okay, I heard it," I whispered. Still, I didn't move. As much as I didn't want to admit it, Sayer was right. I'd promised him as much—he wouldn't have agreed to help me otherwise.

Suddenly, I was ten again, unwinding the balls of yarn in Aunt Denny's room, asking why she didn't let me stay at night.

"Are there ghosts? Amber at school says ghosts live in old houses like this one. She had one in her grandma's house and didn't wanna stay at night. Said that if this one's haunted, you wouldn't let me stay, either," I blurted, swinging the unspooled yarn in two clenched fists.

Aunt Denny folded clothes at the foot of her bed. Every so often, she'd glance to the door, then at me. "Is that why I can't stay? I can handle ghosts. What if they're friendly? Would that make it okay for me to stay?"

"There are no ghosts, Lan."

"Then why can't I stay?" I whined. The yarn drooped at my sides.

"Because your momma wouldn't be happy with me. And you have school."

"But I'm on break and there's nothing to do and I only see you *sometimes* and what if the ghosts need—"

Her eyes grew hard; the T-shirt she held up crinkled at the shoulders, all around her fingers. "Have you seen anything here, Lanny? Anything like that?"

This had made me pause. Seen anything? No. Sometimes the birds perched by the breakfast table in the little windows. The sill was extra wide and I liked to watch them there. Their shadows curved over the glass and the table and sometimes it was like those shadows moved on their own, but never anything else.

"No. Don't think so."

"See? No ghosts."

Sometimes the floors creaked, but Aunt Denny said old houses did that. So I believed her.

"But that story you told me, could it be real? Have you seen anyth—"

She shot me a look down the bridge of her nose. "I have not. You know the nursery rhyme is simply that—a rhyme. For eager little minds and imaginations. Now pick out your yarn so we can make those potholders before your momma comes back."

She'd promised me. And there had never been any reason not to believe her.

I didn't realize tears had started to burn the backs of my eyes until Sayer's voice reeled me to the surface.

"Shouldn't you . . . go look?"

I blinked them away. Inhaled a shaky breath. Sayer was gangly, stuck in a perpetual state of adult-adolescence, despite being on the eve of thirty-one and a long-since graduate of USC's MFA program.

"Don't tell me all those horror novels finally caught up with you," he said, looking at me over the frames of his glasses. Still, a tinge of wariness—like I might crack—crinkled around his eyes. I drew my shoulders back and garnered my only line of defense: sarcasm.

"At least I'm well read in all genres," I said.

"Is that supposed to be an insult? Like I don't read?"

"No, I'm saying your true crime documentary experience makes you better equipped for the situation."

Sayer took the casserole dish out of my slowly warming hands and pushed it onto the entryway table. It'd gradually become the catch-all spot. Cards perched in a cluster on one side—all sage-greens and muted blues, wishing love, sympathies, and anything else that might sound remotely comforting.

They weren't.

"And if it's not someone trying to break open a door?" he tried. "You would really leave me to deal with an angry ghost?"

"So, you'll send *me* instead?"

"It's *your* house."

The words shouldn't have stung, because he was only telling the truth, but they did. "So what, you're a believer now?" I said, the edges of my words serrated.

"There's a reason I couldn't watch cartoons with ghosts in them as a kid, you know." I felt Sayer's eyes weigh me, like a percentage chart or a fates calculator. As if he were debating the value of an argument right now.

"Fine." I wiped my hands on my dress with a sudden flood of urgency. I just needed to get this over with—to prove there was nothing to be scared about. An old house did not mean it was haunted. Aunt Cadence said so.

An old house, with a lot of rooms, with a lot of empty space, just like I'd always wanted. Still, the irony of Aunt Cadence passing in order for me to get my wish, hurt. And now the one woman that could have proved the house was normal was gone.

Before I lost any courage, I pivoted in the middle of the foyer and banked into the living room, off to the right.

"Don't leave me here!"

I rolled my eyes and muttered to myself. Of course he'd be too scared to wait alone. But, to my surprise, he didn't follow.

The living area was just as Aunt Cadence left it—hand-me-down furniture, thrifted art on the walls, and two large, ornate rugs that were nothing more than swirls of beiges and burgundies to hide the stains from when Donald The Chihuahua had potty-training incidents as a puppy. I wove around the pleather couches that faced the hallway, which opened to the mudroom. Both the mudroom and the garage were additions to the original house.

I stepped over the threshold—and the temperature dropped immediately.

The lights were off, casting the stick-on linoleum floor in gray shadow. The washer and dryer sat patched with rust, both stale from unuse these past three months. Four laundry baskets, all plastic, one broken, were stacked by a wayward, also plastic, shoe rack.

Nothing looked out of place. Then again, I hadn't had enough time to go through anything. And the last time I'd graced Harthwait I might have been seventeen? Eighteen?

Years ago.

I collected my breath and opened the door to the garage. The smell of musk and warm dirt swamped my nostrils.

"Good Lord," I whispered. My face scrunched. "When was the last time you opened this door, Denny?"

As if the walls could hear me. Relay the question back to her.

The garage sat empty, save for the VW Beetle covered in a blanket of dust. Its once bright, cheery yellow now resembled a sun-bleached sticky note.

I waited. Listened, or tried, around the subtle pounding of my heart.

It could have been a mouse. Or a nail had wiggled loose from the tool board on the wall and something had dropped from it? Had a bird found its way through the washer vent somehow and ended up in the garage? Maybe one of the windows in the garage door had broken?

I combed through soil bags, a line of preservatives in unopened boxes, and a cluster of gardening tools. I circled the Beetle.

The door to outside hung ajar. Not a lot—but enough.

I paused. Was *that* the noise?

Three slumped feed and fertilizer bags were piled a few feet behind the door against the wall, beside a tin trashcan and a rake hanger. If the door *had* been opened hard enough, it would have hit the feed bags—not the wall, so that couldn't have been what we'd heard.

Still, I shut the door. Locked it, as if that would prevent anything that might have come in from reentering. There were no animal prints in the thick layer of dust and dirt. No smudges. No flat tires, either. I moved on, skimmed a stack of paint cans on a work bench in front of the car.

The Beetle wasn't the only thing layered in dust—there was no telling how long it had been since Aunt Cadence had been in the garage. She only bought the gardening things because of me. The arthritis had eaten her hands so much over the last ten years, and I'd been traveling for work so much, things just . . . fell away. I could practically feel the grime sifting over my tongue with each inhale—

"*Lanny*," Sayer snapped, throwing open the door to the garage.

I flinched. My hands flew up to cover my throat out of reflex—and slammed into the paint shelf and the trunk of the Beetle at the exact same moment Sayer flipped the light on with his elbow.

"Are you asking for an insurance claim? Walking around in the dark?" His eyes skated the walls, the opened bags of bird seed. Plastic pots piled in corners and rows. "Did you find anything?"

I hissed, rubbing my knuckles. "Someone has to conserve the electric bill."

Especially when I was *only* working with life insurance money. Aunt Cadence had a decent policy, but it wasn't a lot, and I needed as much of it as possible for renovations. Plus, I'd postponed jobs to get Harthwait ready.

Sayer took a tentative first step into the garage. "It's cold in here."

"It's a garage."

"It's June—everything sweats this time of year. I bet the AC unit swims in perspiration."

My eyebrows arched. "Is that fear I smell on you, Sayer? You're supposed to be the fearless best friend."

Sayer's nose crinkled. He picked up a box of mason jars. They clinked together. "Fearless was not in the job description when I signed up to—"

A bang ripped the air behind me.

I jumped. Sayer screamed as I clambered away from the Beetle. More scrambling—but not from Sayer or me. A nail on metal sound—coming from the other side of the car.

Sayer slipped on the step. He toppled forward with a shriek—I grasped for anything, a shirt, an arm, a belt loop, and ended up with a fistful of Sayer's shirt hem. His knee hit a shelf, which sent him into a sprawl, and I with him.

We crashed with the box of mason jars in a heap. Sayer took the brunt of the fall and I landed on my side. Glass shattered. Four or five jars escaped, rolling in different directions, all over the glittering shards on the floor.

The banging continued. Rattling. Furious, uncontrollable rattling.

"You're on my hand," I grunted, struggling to sit upright. At least my head hadn't hit the floor.

"Well, your hand is in my kidney." Sayer pushed at my back.

I rolled away like a wet tangle of laundry.

He straightened his glasses then planted both hands on the garage floor. Dust coated his shirt. "That trashcan is moving—"

I glanced back just in time to see the feed bags beside the door wiggle. They bumped against the tin trashcan—making the same knocking sound from earlier. Something was under the feed bags this whole time and—

A raccoon wriggled from behind one of the bags. It plopped onto the garage floor, all rounded body and tiny, clawed feet. And froze.

There was a raccoon in the house.

"Let it out!" I reared upright with panic. They could carry diseases, right? When was the last time I'd seen a raccoon in broad daylight? The thought sent adrenaline rocketing through my body. *Rabies.* Rabies made animals do things out of character—like crawl out in broad daylight and hide in someone's garage, maybe?

"*You* let it out!" Sayer tried to retreat. He slipped on the slick floor, glass tinkling.

"You're closer!" I tried to get up. Heat stung my shin and my fingernails, but I didn't dare look down. Blood made me queasy, especially fresh blood.

Sayer glanced from the door, closest to the raccoon, to the garage door opener, nearest to us. With a grumble and flushed cheeks, he hurried to the button and smacked it with his palm.

The overhead garage light popped on.

The door jerked two inches up—and stopped.

"It's stuck," Sayer blurted. At the noise, the raccoon scurried under the Beetle in an attempt to find cover.

A distant voice called, "Is everything okay?"

Evanescence-Evangelina was about to find me with a brand across my forehead that read: *Dunce. I am, in fact, not a responsible adult. Please do* not *help me sell this house.*

"Obviously not," I mumbled. I limped over and squatted next to Sayer, who was now attempting to push the door up by hand. We pulled at the same time—enough for the hinges to *click-click-snap* and the door to release.

Sunlight swept into the garage and took the chilled air with it. The sound of heels echoed closer and closer, just as the raccoon scurried out from under the car and into the driveway. It waddled through the landscaping, the tired and wilted peonies, before whispering its way across the lawn and toward the trees.

Sweat trickled down my back. I looked at Sayer, eyebrows raised. "See. I told you it wasn't a ghost."

Evangeline-Evanescence-Elevana found us with labored breaths not seconds later.

"Is everyone—what is going *on*?" she hissed.

I settled my hands on my hips. A twinge of pain shot up my lower back, reminiscent of a needle inserting itself into my pelvis. Just a subtle reminder that I wasn't as young as I once was.

Sayer ran a hand down his hip. "I think I pulled something." Then he paused. Looked over his shoulder. "I ripped my pants."

"What is that on the floor?" she snarled.

I pushed hair from my face and turned to the woman. Not an ounce of concern filled her eyes; only chipped irritation. When she met my gaze, a strange burn started at the back of my throat. The moment felt almost expectant—like I was the adult that should have things under control. The responsible party.

Because I was.

I shouldn't have been, but I was.

My mother hadn't come to her own sister's funeral. My father wasn't here to help me. I had no siblings by blood on my mother's side. No more aunts. No uncles. No grandparents.

Just me and my friend, who I'd almost told not to come, that things weren't that serious. That I could handle the funeral and the food and the wake, just like any adult should.

And now here I stood, in a dirty garage and with a realtor I didn't know, not really, in a pile of broken glass.

"Raccoon," Sayer breathed. "But don't worry. It's gone."

"Well. That is certainly . . . something." She said it with a wrinkled nose and pinched cheeks. *Eleanora*—that was her name.

I brushed myself off, my neck slowly heating.

"So." I swallowed. "How do you like the house so far?"

Sayer had the decency to shift in place.

Her upper lip, which no longer had a cupid's bow from an excess amount of filler, puckered. "I was ready to discuss, ah, things with you. But if you're busy, then I can schedule something another day."

My body went rigid. Calm. Serene thoughts. Deep breaths. I licked my chapped lips, pushed down the condescending hint in her words. I may have given Sayer a hard time about his mother recommending Eleanora, but I'd glanced at her company's website, albeit however briefly. She'd taken many historic homes to large buyers—buyers with the capital and time to put into places like this—selling for well above list price.

I needed this woman far more than she needed me.

"Yes, of course we can discuss things," I said. Casual. Simple. As if there weren't broken jars on the floor and pinpricks behind my eyes.

"Good," Eleanora said. She motioned toward me. "It will only take a few moments. I'll, wait for you in the formal dining room." Her mouth quirked.

She turned and strode through the mudroom with a high chin. As if she had a better grasp upon the house than I did.

As if she knew I was scrambling. Out of place and utterly alone.

Chapter Two

"That is . . . a long list," I said. The paper's corners trembled in my hands, so I steadied my elbows on the dining room table.

Aunt Cadence had always been proud of this dining room set—carved cherry wood, with swirls around its thickened legs and matching chairs. There were still marks in the finish from where I'd dragged my colored pencils through construction paper.

My mom had scolded me.

Aunt Cadence said it gave the table character.

Eleanora leaned back at the head of the table to my right. The sun reflected in grids through the Palladian window that faced the backyard. My eyes skimmed the wilted garden just past the porch, at the edge of the trees. A beautiful day. A shame to be inside for it. Eleanora's voice drew me back in.

"It may be rather long, but it's an effective—and necessary—collection of changes." A miniature tea set glinted in the sun behind Eleanora's head, aligned in a neat row on the floating shelf.

"Of course."

I hated the lilt to her words. Her tongue wasn't lazy with syllables, the muscles in her jaw weren't lax. No drawl, no semblance of home. *Northern*, it told me. But something more. *Rich people money*, it told me.

My aunt would've liked her. She'd have asked where she was from, if she liked to fly or drive when she traveled. Where she'd visited, the houses she'd sold. Rooted herself right there under Eleanora's skin like a burrowing mouse, ready to hear the full story.

Why couldn't I bring myself to do that?

The pounding in my chest hadn't calmed, like my heart knew I'd jumped a precipice. No turning back now. If I breathed in deep enough, I caught the mix of casseroles from the kitchen. Now, instead of just slightly anxious, I was also slightly anxious and nauseous.

"They wouldn't take much time with the right help. I understand you do small project renovations for a living?"

My eyes snapped up. Help?

"I didn't think I'd need to hire help," I said. "Or remove walls." A hint of bitterness on my tongue. Walls and doors meant permits.

"Oh, you don't *have* to. These are merely suggestions."

Which told me they weren't.

"However, if you want to sell it, and sell it quick, we need to make it stand out. People want modern with old bones—vintage chic. Any realtor will tell you this. I know you're on a deadline, which is why I suggested outside help." She flitted her fingers to her copy of the suggestions. "Trust me. The bones of this house are wonderful. But let's face facts. It's old. The market doesn't favor builds from the eighteen hundreds. Sure, Cadence took care of it, but there are worn boards, creaking steps, and it feels—congested."

Her nose wrinkled at the word. I couldn't help but note the way her eyes flitted about the room. As if the ample space was closing in on her.

I swallowed hard. Play nice. Keep an open mind. "I'll need to check with the historic registry."

A wave of a manicured hand. "Oh, of course. Absolutely."

"How much would all this cost?" My eyes returned to the page. *Have central air checked for Nest installation? *everyone prefers smart units these days.*

She rattled off a number.

Sayer, knowing my budget, balked at the back of her head. Then, he met my gaze and mouthed one word:

Insane.

"We've clocked, what, almost four thousand square feet? It pays to play," Eleanora finished. "I can get you in touch with a few contractors. Quick and easy. Painless, actually. And we would be on pace for the proposed listing date."

"I planned on—"

"You can't do work like this, dear," she said with a sad cringe.

I bristled but didn't argue.

"Think about it, okay?" She patted my hand. Her palms were soft. It took everything in my power to not pull away. "Let me know. But I think it would be great if we could get this place on the market by end of summer. Plenty of time, yes?"

I sat, mouth open.

The funeral was just this morning. I didn't even have Aunt Cadence's ashes yet.

This felt wrong—too soon. But I couldn't back out. I couldn't pay to keep Harthwait when I already had other jobs waiting on me. My wallet screamed at the thought. I didn't have a year to get this house in shape. It *had* to be sold by end of summer so I could move on to my other clients.

"Well, Miss Landry, it was a pleasure meeting you. Thank you for allowing me to poke about." She pushed to stand. The chair scratched the floor.

"The pleasure was mine. I appreciate you coming out." The words tasted fake.

With a nod to me and a sharp smile, Eleanora pivoted on a heel and stalked from the room. Sayer and I waited as she showed herself out. I could picture the stained-glass covers trembling like my fingers. There it was again, that fluttering at the base of my throat.

Sayer took Eleanora's seat and snatched the paper from my hand.

"This is typed," he said.

I sighed, brow scrunched. "I noticed that."

"How did she bring this on first meeting, *typed*?" he pressed. "What happened to just taking a look?"

I shrugged. Covered my face with my hands. "I don't know, Say. Maybe she made an assumption from selling homes like this before?" All it emphasized, to me, was the urgency.

That thought burrowed against my spine. Urgency wasn't always a good thing, though—I'd seen it, felt it on my own skin. It could mean impatience or lack of thought for others, a selfishness that could be driven by an undisclosed, rabid desire that I knew nothing about.

Or I could just be letting doubt creep in. I shifted in my chair.

"You don't have to give her the listing," he said, low. "You can wait. Pick someone else. Give it time. Today's already been—enough."

"I don't have a choice." My skin erupted in goosebumps. The projected sell price of Harthwait glared at me from the bottom of the reno list. Underlined in red.

That money could do so many things. Provide cushion. Pay a credit card, or better yet, remove the last couple thousand I owed on my car. Yet somehow, those zeros did nothing to cushion how the house had come into my possession.

I ran a finger over an eye in the wood of the table. It was dull in this spot, where the finish had worn away. How many elbows had sat in this tiny, square inch of space? How many years had it taken to wear it down to the grain?

Had it been my younger elbows, during day visits? My mother's? Aunt Cadence's?

Maybe even my father, the few times before he left Mom.

"This would bother me, too, if I were you." Sayer looked at me over his glasses' frames. Instead of librarian, all I saw was subdued pity.

I settled against the wooden back of the chair. My mouth watered while my stomach churned and churned. Like a cauldron eddying over a rolling flame. It didn't really matter what I thought or what I felt. I was one person—one single, unattached individual that had no partner, no child, no roommates, and no reason to root myself in Stetson. The only logical route *was* selling.

Unbidden, a memory needled me.

Will it get better when I'm old like you, Aunt Denny? I'd asked. Her name was a lilt of highs and lows on my tongue. *Live in a house alone like you? Away from people like Mommy?*

She'd looked at me with glassy eyes. A hard swallow. *Don't know if you'd want a house like this, Lanny. Lot of empty rooms can be lonesome.*

But I wanna be alone.

Well, that's fine.

Is this what better felt like?

"I need to go back to the funeral home," I said, changing the subject.

"What for?"

"I need to pick up the floral arrangements that were left behind. The lady said she'd keep them in the front office for after I met with Eleanora."

"I have a car," Sayer said. "Let me go."

"Didn't you have some work to finish up?" He'd uprooted himself to help me. I couldn't expect him to throw away all responsibility.

"Lan, it's Saturday."

I sighed. "Good point. But I'd rather go myself."

He set the paper down. A long pause. Then, "I'm sorry that you didn't get to see her first."

I chewed the inside of my lip, bit down until the skin pulled away and I tasted blood. That burn brewed again, this time so deep in the back of my skull that I was scared if I blinked that the tears would fall immediately.

I managed a slight nod. I wished I'd been able to see her one last time, too. But I hadn't. And there was nothing I could do about it.

Guilt—that's what the burning was. Guilt that I'd wiped my hands of my family in an effort to keep the hurt at bay, if only a little while longer. What I hadn't banked on was Cadence being taken so soon without any preliminary health problems—that were known, anyway.

A heart attack, the doctor said. Someone had requested a welfare check when a phone call hadn't been returned, is what the officer said. She'd been found that following Monday, on the rug in the office.

The timing had been almost eerie. I'd just finished a job close to Charleston when I'd gotten the call that she'd passed.

Now, with free housing for the summer, all my belongings were stuffed in a storage unit an hour away. I'd given up my apartment, my work schedule, everything to take care of this.

To come back here.

"Do you think you'll see him?" Sayer whispered, as if he could hear my thoughts.

"You're asking all the hard questions." I picked at a hangnail instead of looking at him.

"I ask because I care."

Another tight-lipped nod. "Maybe." Maybe not. I tried to stifle the tiny flutter at the thought. But it might not happen—a lot of our graduating class had moved, like myself, after school. For college or jobs or family.

I tried to keep my browser history empty of his name, either way.

"Hopefully not," I said. Then I stood. "It's only a few months, anyway. If I do, I don't care. What's done is done."

"Lan—"

"I don't have a choice," I bit. The words were painful in my throat.

"We can still—"

The doorbell rang like a gong through the house.

Thank God. I never thought I'd be so thankful for another casserole in my entire life. I pushed back from the table, leaving the list behind for Sayer to examine. "I'll get it."

I sensed his eyes following me as I walked out.

My sandals whispered over the ornate runners before I reached the front door. Only a faded figure was visible through the frosted glass. Probably another casserole dish—or even a pie—that I didn't have room for.

I patted my hot cheeks in an effort to calm down, then opened the door.

"Hello—"

"Landry!" a voice shrieked.

A body slammed into mine. Saturated vanilla and peony drenched my nostrils. My joints locked. I knew this smell—this touch. The blond hair that poked my eyes and stuck to my mouth.

"Emma?" I pulled back.

"Surprise!" My half sister's gold bracelets shook with jazz hands, those familiar, rich eyes sparkling like seltzer water.

Emma, here, in the foyer. With a rolling suitcase behind her, and a single bag strap thrown over her shoulder. Her jeans hung on her lean hips, and a pastel blue, baby doll T-shirt contrasted perfectly against her vitiligo. Happy, helpful, sunshine-breathing Emma.

"You're here," I whispered. Blossoms of light shriveled to worry.

Emma was here.

"You're not happy." Her smile faltered.

"No!" I exclaimed a bit too loudly. Could she feel the lie in the air?

I grabbed for her suitcase, spine tense, and shooed away her offer of help. "Just surprised. I didn't—you said you were going to Florida for a bit?" That was why she couldn't make the funeral.

"I lied," she tittered. She squeezed my shoulder before closing the front door. From my peripheral, Sayer emerged at the end of the foyer.

They both squealed with excitement.

I hauled her suitcase into the corner beside the grandfather clock and waited for Emma and Sayer to finish bouncing in place. A dark, roiling feeling started in my stomach. Emma, here. Emma, in this house. The thought of her *pressing*, if only a little, made my hands shake. I held onto her luggage handle to steady them, then turned.

"You didn't tell me Emma was coming by," Sayer said. A shade of hurt flickered in his expression. The two of them, almost identical in height, looked to me.

"I didn't tell anyone," she clarified. "I didn't want Lanny to refuse me."

"I wouldn't have," I countered. And it was the truth. Having another familiar face at the funeral would have been nice. But I shoved the thought down.

Her chocolate eyes narrowed. "I called you twice."

"We've been busy with things," I said. We stood in a triangle, examining one another, and all I could picture was us as children. At Sayer's house or here in the backyard, in town at the library with Aunt Denny bent over a child-sized table, reading from a notebook page.

Be wary the beds and the space beneath, Aunt Cadence's voice whispered. *The cracks in the floors and the furnace teeth.*

The grandfather clock chimed twice.

"Of course," she said, a bit solemn.

Keep your eyes from the shadows and tongue so still.

"That's why I came anyway. To stay for a bit."

Because once Harthwait grows dark, the monsters become real.

I wish I had that same power now: to tell Emma such a trivial nursery rhyme to scare her away for the night. Or maybe my aunt had secretly wanted to be alone, and that's why she'd read us those scary stories.

Maybe she hadn't really wanted us around after all.

"Well, I'm sure." Emma gave a look, something mixed with empathy and frustration.

"Are you staying?" I asked. That was not the consolation I needed. Even Sayer wasn't staying in the house with me.

The thought made my guts bottom out. I wouldn't have been surprised if I'd looked down and they lay in the middle of the floor.

Emma nodded. Her teeth were white and straight, minus one incisor. It stood a bit higher than the rest, crowded around its neighbors.

Her next words were gentle but honest. Like the grit of sand beneath your fingernails after a long day on the beach. "Vince told me I should come visit for a bit. He said he tried to call but you never answered." A shrug. Unsaid words settled between the three of us. "I cashed in my vacation and everything! I mean, I'm remote, so I guess it didn't make much of a difference. But no more flying to meetings!" She said it like I should be jumping in place.

How could I, when my father sent her in his stead as emissary? He'd never wanted anything to do with me himself.

I shouldn't have been surprised that it hadn't changed now.

* * *

Emma would tell you that she was the product of an affair. Sort of.

My father was the man you might read about in unhinged online articles. The one leading two lives: one where he decided to marry my mother, the second where he had a girlfriend, and neither knew the other existed.

Emma's mother, Penny, got pregnant by my father nine months before he decided to marry my mother. Not only did he move in with his new bride, but he moved in with Penny, too, in an effort to "be a supportive father." For years, he kept both lives separate, banking on work trips and late hours to keep his wife and girlfriend in different corners of his life.

The diligence to keep both secrets amazed me—and not in a good way.

My mother found out about Emma and her mother just after my fifth birthday. Emma was six at the time. There were only so many business trips, missed softball games, and midnight phone calls one could have before someone grew suspicious.

What haunted me the most was not *how* everyone found out, but what occurred afterward.

I remembered the moment my mother stood crying at our back door, watching as the headlights to his truck flickered on and disappeared down the driveway. Because he chose Penny and Emma over my mother and me.

Everything else from my childhood had been a blur. The only buoy of happiness was our family dog, Belvedere. A cane corso, if I remembered right. I used to sit on his haunches while Vince, when I still called him Dad, and I walked to the mailbox in the morning. The driveway snaked this way and that. Belvedere walked tall and sturdy. I'd used him as a pillow, a horse, a prince, and dress-up mannequin more often than not.

Belvedere was put down the day my mother found out about the affair.

Happy birthday, indeed.

After my parents had officially separated, Penny and my mom met one time at the park. Emma and I had gotten along well enough, and my hesitance toward her softened when she called our father a jerk.

"Mommy chose him over Mike," Emma said. Her brow wrinkled, eyes nearly black as she squeezed the soccer ball she'd brought. "I hate him."

"You do?" I hovered by the goal post. In the distance, my mother waved her hands as she spoke to Penny, who remained seated on a bench.

"Well, duh. Mommy says he's my daddy, but *Mike* has always been my daddy." She squeezed the soccer ball so hard that it shot out of her hands and rocketed down the field. She stomped after it, ponytail swinging.

Only when I was older did I realize Emma had admitted her mother had been in a long-term relationship, too. She'd always assumed *Mike* had been her dad—and it seemed Mike had thought the same, until my father came into the picture.

Her fiery attitude made me follow her down the soccer field that day. She kicked the ball farther and farther before turning and kicking it to me.

One word led to another. I asked her about her mom, if she cried a lot at night, too, or if she didn't cry since Dad was there. At one point, she asked me if I ever got angry, and I said sometimes, when the kids at school were mean. Emma told me she'd been bullied because of her vitiligo. I told her I was bullied because of how little I was.

Things shifted, like broken china pieces, bloodied, jagged edges touching one another's until they found a place to fit. Over the years, Emma and I kept in touch. Emma's oldest half brother, Mason, was twenty-two at the time. Emma managed to persuade Mason into driving her over for playdates until cell phones were allowed. Through high school, we kept tabs on my father's extramarital affairs via social media (on my behalf) and physical stalking (on Emma's behalf). By the time we were accepted at USC, we had a six-year-long text thread dedicated to our father's adventures.

"We need to keep tabs in case we run into these people in the wild," she said one night over a bucket of Neapolitan ice cream. "You never know when the opportunity to embarrass him might strike."

I'd pushed my ice cream around in my bowl. "I don't think we'll ever be so lucky."

The TV flickered blues and grays and whites from the other side of the room. Her eyeliner was smudged in deep crescents under her eyelashes. "To pin a cheater? Like him? Never. But it's worth a shot."

"Your mom won't leave him, though," I said. Penny chose to act oblivious. *Vince would never, ever step outside of our marriage*, she said. When she really should have said, *His money is too, too important for me to get rid of him*.

"Nah," Emma grunted. "She won't."

* * *

"Where you heading? I could come." Emma trailed after me, off the front porch and down the cobblestone path. I carried a small box of knickknacks on my hip toward my SUV. A few ceramic chickens rattled inside—Aunt Cadence had a penchant for them. I'd never gotten a chance to ask why. Meredith, a shop owner in Stetson, took donations no matter the day, and she'd never once turned one down. I figured donating what I could to Meredith would be easier than reselling them myself.

"Out," I said, pointed. I tried to keep my expression soft. "Don't worry about it."

"Are you sure?"

"Yes, I'm positive."

I needed a breather. To visit the funeral home without a shadow, to do anything besides sit in that house. With her. Fermenting in my thoughts. Emma's mouth pursed. I hadn't *meant* it as a jab.

I tried to remind myself that Emma was a part of my life, that she loved me, that she cared. That we'd been through worse than a missed funeral and an absent phone call.

Even still, the frustration simmered below the skin of my bone.

"Are you upset I didn't make it this morning?"

The grass kissed my feet as I crossed into the lawn. My SUV sat under an oak tree on the other side of the driveway, mostly hidden from the sun. The last late-spring tree blossoms skittered across the hood and into the woods.

Yes. "No, I know you're busy with work and stuff," I said. "It's just been a long day, and I'd rather go alone." Before I had to find a place for the funeral flowers that smelled too much like Aunt Cadence, *before, before, before.*

He loves her, a torturous little voice whispered to me. *Not you. Why else would he send her?*

I'd heard that little voice before. Predominant when I was young; slithery and distant as I got older. It mirrored my insecurities, enhanced them in all the wrong places, and trailed after me just as I'd followed Emma that day on the soccer field. Except when I grew up, so did it.

With a sigh, Emma took a scrunchie from her wrist and tied her hair into a knot. "I can start going through the food, if you want. Do you want dinner later? I can heat something up. There are so many casseroles that—"

"I don't know yet."

She hurried in front of me and popped open the trunk. Straw lay strewn like confetti on the Hefty Liner. Of course I hadn't cleaned it out. A client had needed straw a few weeks ago, and I'd forgotten after . . . everything.

I sat the box on the trunk lip. Emma retrieved a rooster before I had a chance to push it back.

"Chickens?" She examined his ceramic tail, touched a chip in his plumed feathers.

"They've crowded the casseroles in the kitchen. I figured I'd take a few to Meredith before she closes. Say hi." The chicken collection had gotten worse since I'd last been here. Like a small army, multiplying in secret. But counter space was more important at the moment.

"Oh, I love Meredith," Emma crooned. Her expression softened when she met my gaze. "I love you, too, you know. I'm sorry if . . . my timing was bad."

"I love you, too." I flicked the pieces of straw away and turned to her. "You know I'm always happy to see you."

Her head tilted. "You're sure?"

I nodded. "Positive."

"How are you doing? You know." She shrugged. Looked at the tree branches looming above, then toward the backyard, before landing back on me. "All things considered."

My brow furrowed. "I'm fine." Shouldn't that be obvious? I was here. That was all that mattered. I reached for the trunk handle. "Just busy. Could be worse."

"Lanny." Her eyes said enough: from the way they quickly skimmed my frame, examined how my clothes dangled on my body instead of hugged it. Once, she asked why I didn't wear my hair down more, and I'd avoided the answer—in reality, if I did, strands of hair fell out left and right like a trail of confetti behind me.

"Emma." I straightened.

She crossed her arms. I always marveled at her elbows. How they could be so slender without looking boney. How her collarbone shined just right in any lighting. My eyes burned at the thought. If only I could look like her.

"I'm fine." I made sure to meet her gaze. "I am."

We stared at each other for what felt like an hour until she rubbed the bridge of her nose and nodded. "Okay. Well, I'll pick a room. Unpack my things. Maybe we can clean out one of the smaller rooms tonight, since you're . . ." She eyed the box. "Already manic cleaning."

"That would actually be great," I said with a smile.

"Anything I should know about?" She grinned this time, raised her eyebrows and tilted her chin down, like she was waiting for a spilled secret. "Any stories? Have you heard anything in the house yet?"

I stifled a laugh. "Not you, too."

"Me, too? There are more people?" Hope lit her face. "So, something happened?" She grabbed my upper arm and shook it. "You have to tell me."

I nudged her out of the way and made for the driver's door. "It's not haunted."

"Come on! We watched scary movies all the time when we were young. The nursery rhyme! Just think of the *experience*, Landry. Did you see something, or was it Sayer?" She lowered her voice to a sultry whisper. "Did *he* see an unexplainable entity?"

"We thought we heard something and went to check, but it was nothing. Just a raccoon in the garage," I said. I popped the door and hopped inside.

Emma gasped and covered her mouth with both hands. "No, you didn't."

The interior still smelled of faint mint and—lilies. I glanced down. Sure enough, a quadruplet of seedlings and one single potted plant stood at attention in the floorboard. Someone had given them to me in the church parking lot that morning. Another consolation prize for having to organize a funeral. I didn't feel like getting back out of the car to move them, so the smell would remain.

"You know, raccoons make amazing pets! Haven't you seen the videos online? They eat marshmallows."

"I don't think that's a good idea," I said with a wince. All I pictured were its claws, its black eyes. The way it scurried and slunk instead of ambling like a dog.

Again, the possible disease.

Emma glared. "Don't be such a pessimist. Anything can be tamed if you love it enough. And you can't judge a book by its cover."

I stifled a cringe. "I'll pass."

"Ooooor," she sang, leaning into the driver's window, "if you're so scared, we could get a guard dog."

My expression flattened. "I'm not *that* scared."

She smirked. "Not yet."

Chapter Three

A lone stoplight guarded Stetson's single intersection. Meredith's Gift Shop, Lottie's Diner, and Dosi-Do's Ice Cream lined the street across from the post office and library. On an unlucky day, one might wander a few blocks down to Rosco's Mechanics (a bit dodgy, but beggars couldn't be choosers) or the hardware store, which sat parallel to the railroad tracks behind Main Street. From there, a line of four homes squatted across the railway like afterthoughts. My favorite of the four was daffodil yellow, tucked closest to the swinging bridge over the creek.

Stetson was no different from any other old town. Every building had paneling or brick bleached by the sun, and the sidewalks dipped in the center from hundreds of thousands of feet that walked them for decades. The lampposts—tall, bulbous, with a horse and wagon atop the lantern—leaned a bit.

I eyed the small two-story apartment building from my parking spot. If you went upstairs, you'd find a single studio flat with cigarette smoke-stained walls and shag carpet. Every evening after school once Mom and Dad split, I'd sit at a windowsill on the other side of the building. It faced that little yellow house. I'd wait and watch the family who lived there at the time. The two boys would run in the house, then straight back out while their mother's shadow moved against the curtains. Then the car was loaded with bags and snacks and water bottles.

Once the family left, the boys grown and long gone, an older lady took over. The flower beds darkened with new mulch and fresh flowers and a young man showed up every weekend—a grandson or nephew, maybe. In the summer, they piddled outside. In the winter, the kitchen light remained warm and yellow.

I sunk deeper into my seat. I was stalling—and I knew it. Pushing away the inevitable because of the slight chance someone would see me.

Because if they did, they would speak to me. They would say they were sorry. They would praise Aunt Cadence's life, even if they hadn't spoken to her in over a decade. *Oh, but I always ran into her at the post office when she was a kid. You know she worked there as a clerk before she could even drive, right?*

They would offer sharp shells of memories, thinking it would make me feel comforted, when all it really did was remind me of all of the minutes I'd *not* had with her.

They'd pluck with good intention, taking away the last little bits of myself that protected my composure from my decomposition.

I'm so sorry for your loss turned into *Can I have a little piece of your sternum, dear? Just a bit. It won't hurt.*

Call me if you need anything slithered into *You have plenty of teeth, dear, just give me one and I'll be on my way. You'll be fine.*

Then I'd be left shivering in their aftermath, wondering why they were able to walk away from the pain and I wasn't.

I stared at the crooked sidewalks. The chipped brick sidings worn with age. The paint-peeled window frames, the stout concrete steps, the bike rack outside the library.

I bit my cheek and climbed out of the car. If I didn't do it now, I wouldn't do it at all.

The thickened longleaf pines and river birch trees swayed absently in the soggy breeze, but the gravel was crisp with heat. I hauled the box of ceramic chickens out of my trunk, then locked the car. The SUV beeped in farewell, then I started off down Main Street.

Meredith first—maybe coffee afterward, as a reward. For making it this far.

I moseyed from storefront to storefront, box cradled to my chest. Meredith's sign dangled from an iron pole like a beacon. When I walked in, her door chimed. Air, warm and spiced, greeted me.

The front displays were covered in homeware, dish sets, trinkets like napkin holders and placemats and salt and pepper shakers. The tension immediately fell from my neck and shoulders with the first inhale.

"Well, if I ain't ever!" a husky voice called, as if she hadn't been at the funeral this morning. "You're supposed to be home, sweet pea."

I gave a tentative smile. I meant for it to lighten the mood. She only sighed.

Meredith rounded the checkout counter, her warm skin, wide smile, and throaty hum of happiness like a magnet. It was staggering, really, to see how similar someone could look to a memory, but so different, too. Like time had brushed against a person, but I couldn't quite put my finger on how.

Maybe it was the funeral that made these thoughts surface. Would I look in the mirror one day and notice a change? How old would I be when I noticed the fine lines weren't so fine anymore?

"I brought you chickens, if that's okay?" I held the box up a bit. The contents rattled.

She shuffled up beside me, glanced inside, then squished me in a tight embrace. Her long, tight curls brushed my cheek. "My girl! How dare you. You didn't need to do that already. You should be *resting*," she emphasized.

My inhale shook. "I know."

"Well." Her black eyes were earnest, if a bit teary. She cupped my face in her hands and swiped her thumbs over my cheeks. "You, my girl, are a sight for sore eyes anyway. Now. Why are you bringing me chickens?"

A hairline fissure started in my throat. I couldn't cry. Not already. Not in front of Meredith.

"I have enough casseroles to sink a battleship and the chickens were taking up too much room," I said, and I meant it. Short, tall, round, square, all colors and makes. It made me question Aunt Cadence's intentions—were the chickens merely collector's, or an effort to re-create her own childhood kitchen? Bowing to a fad, maybe? Either way, I couldn't keep them all. "I figured you could use a few?"

"A few. A few means less than eight, surely. But, I won't lie, they sell well enough. Can's see why not." At this, she pulled back. Both hands perched on her hips; her floral blouse managed to look intimidating. She squinted. "You ain't eaten today?"

"Earlier." The word tasted sour.

"Well. You're here. And I did tell you to bring things by when you were ready." She gave me a look. "Follow me to the dungeon, I guess. Just don't judge me. I ain't got but one part- timer and it takes a good day and a half to price every other box your Cadence brought us a couple weeks ago."

Your Cadence.

"I didn't know she . . . brought so much stuff?" I trailed after Meredith, sidestepping a tea towel display, an intricate shelf of kitchen decor, all the way back to a short hallway that coughed us out into a crowded back room. Meredith was right. It did look like a hoarder's dungeon.

"Oh, all the time." Meredith stepped over a set of flat plastic storage containers. "Matter of fact, she brought in a whole load of stuff the week before—" she stopped. Pointed to an empty space, as if neither of us would notice the pivot. She whipped a sticky note pad out of her pocket, along with a pen. "Right here's a good spot, Landry."

I picked my way through, deposited the box, then watched as Meredith scribbled on a sticky note and stuck it on the top of the box.

"You don't mind that I bring her things?" I asked. She stickered a few more. "It's not overwhelming?"

"Oh, no, no. Might take me a while to get through it, but I'll manage. Just keep bringing them," she said. Another stick. Another smack. Then, "Your momma gonna take any of her things and help out?"

"You know Carla. If there's not money involved, she doesn't want it."

Meredith stilled. Turned slowly to face me. I realized then that she'd never turned an overhead light on. Only the opened door illuminated her features.

"She still taking?" she asked. An edge there, but not for me.

"Maybe. Maybe not." I shrugged. I couldn't remember the last time Mom had been clean longer than a week—especially since Meredith met her years ago. "There are more roosters at the house, if you want them. I can bring them by early on Monday?"

I watched the gears shift. Steam built in her ears. But Meredith wouldn't ask for more details if I didn't offer, no matter what questions grew legs in her mind. As if she was luring me out like a dumped animal, gaining my trust, little by little.

My chest constricted at the thought. I glanced away.

She might not ever get that trust. Not completely.

I wasn't sure anyone would. Why would they want it, anyway?

"That ought not to be a problem," she concluded. She stickered the last of the roosters and straightened with a groan. "If you want, I'll pay you extra to help me sort through some of it."

I started to back out of the room. "No—I can help—don't pay me—"

"I mean *all* of it." She swept an arm out and chuckled. "Not just chickens. All this didn't just fall from the sky."

My eyes widened. I held my elbows in a hug as I scanned the scuffed dressers, the antique record stand, the coat rack that looked suspiciously like something that had stood next to the front door at Harthwait when I was younger.

"She brought you all this?"

"Shoot yeah." Sounded more like *shootchyeah.* She led the way back into the hall. "Why do you think I'm still in business? Your aunt gave me so much stuff, my profit margin's through the roof." She wagged her pointer finger to the ceiling. "Saved me by a *hair* sometimes. Stetson ain't what it used to be."

We were at the mouth of the hallway by now. "I don't remember it being much better when I was little."

"'Fore the Kenneths decided to take their money from town, it did."

My spine locked at the last name. I started for the front of the store. Sunlight broke through the spotless panes, creating a dry heat.

"They left?" I asked, gentle. I hovered by the tea towel stand.

"About five years ago now? Back right after you left for USC."

Every fiber in my body begged me to press for more. To squeeze the last ounce of gossip, of possibility from Meredith's chest. But I couldn't—not when I couldn't offer the same vulnerability, no matter her quiet knowledge of my mother.

Because of course they left.

Right after everything. Because why would they stay when rumors floated? Why would they subject their son to defamation of the most *minuscule*, purposeless kind?

Because of you, my thoughts snarled.

Meredith slipped behind the register. When her back faced me, I took a paperclip from the cup on the checkout counter, twisted it, and clutched it in my palm. Waiting. Hoping for it to break skin. For my thundering heart to drip down, down, down.

"I have a question."

Meredith licked a pen and wrote something down on a receipt paper. "Mm?"

"Harthwait. What do you think of it?"

She chuckled. "Don't tell me you scared of that place, Landry. Can't focus on fixing it if you're worried about every shadow."

I rolled my eyes. "Tell Sayer that."

"Poor boy. His knees knocked if lightning hit too close. He helping you?"

"For a few weeks." The guilt for both him *and* Emma taking off work to help me lurked over my shoulder. How much money were they losing because of me? Would their bosses look poorly on them because of it?

"Good. Always liked that boy, you know. Sweet kid." She patted a hand over her heart.

That shred of guilt ballooned.

I gave a weak sigh. "I don't know, it's just—don't you think it's weird how Aunt Cadence never let me stay the night? And you know how people talk about the old places in town."

Her eyebrows rose, indignant. "Just because it's on the registry doesn't mean it's haunted. Besides, who do you take me for? I'd tell you all those plants Cadence had would surely start talking before any ghosts popped out of the closet."

I thought of the now shriveled garden patch at the back of the property. She had a point.

I leaned my elbows on the counter. "Why do you think Mom wouldn't let me stay the night, then?" I lifted my chin like an audacious teenager, eyes squinted.

Meredith leveled me with a steady gaze. So steady that it shook something within my resolve. "Honey, I'm gonna be honest with you once, real good, okay?"

My lungs stilled.

"Your momma didn't want you with Cadence, period. And that's all there is to it," Meredith said. "She wants somethin' just to keep it from other people. Greed, coveting specifically, can make people ugly."

I unfolded the paperclip from my palm and twisted it back to its original form. It didn't look quite right. A little crooked around the top, a smidge bent at the end.

"Did Aunt Cadence tell you that?" I pinched the paperclip.

"She didn't have to."

What I didn't understand was if Mom hated parenting so much, why wouldn't she have let me stay here? Or had Aunt Cadence not really wanted me, either, and I'd built it into something it never was in the first place?

* * *

The Blue Corduroy was the only coffee shop for nearly twenty-five miles.

It butted against the library under a green awning, long since sun-bleached and worn. Burnt coffee beans, a hum of a grinder, and the hiss of a steamer greeted me as I stepped over the threshold.

A man rocked on his heels at the register, eyeing the menu. Round two-seater tables dotted the small space, every other one filled by a laptop or set of elbows. I took the spot in line behind the man, knees bouncing.

If only I had something to hold—like the box I'd dropped off with Meredith—to act as a buffer. At least that would give me the feeling of being guarded. A barrier between the outside world and me.

Halfway through my menu examination, my phone buzzed. I dug it from the depths of my purse, then stopped at the sight of CARLA on the screen.

I locked it. Tossed it back in my purse.

It buzzed again. And again.

Just as the man handed his money to the woman at the counter, I pulled my phone out. I swiped to decline the call, but the phone slipped. A minute counter appeared under Mom's name.

"Landry?" my mother's muffled voice came.

I squeezed my eyes shut. Then pressed the phone to my ear. "Mom."

"You haven't answered my texts."

"I'm kind of busy." I swallowed. When I opened my eyes, the entire menu melded together. "Can I call you back?"

"You won't," she snipped. "You never do."

"I will, I promise."

"You make promises just like your father. You know he called me, right?"

A needle slipped through a rib and punctured a lung. The woman at the counter—a blur of white, long hair and a diamond, wrinkled face—tapped an empty cup as a signal. "You're next, Missy."

I wiped a hand over my face. My body grew flushed. "Mom, I need to go."

"You know, Landry—"

I hung up. Blinked, snappy, rapid successions to disperse the burn behind my eyes. I held the power button as I approached the counter, the barista glaring at me. "Sorry about that."

The woman's head cocked, the fluffed, white hair twisted atop her head shifting with the movement. Her skin was heavily creased from years of sun, the lines around her mouth deep. Her nametag read BERNICE, but the R had faded, leaving BE NICE. Her eyes suggested anything but. "What you want? Ain't got no vanilla today. Didn't come in on time."

I ordered a large black coffee, extra strong, just because I felt like I'd need it. And inconveniencing Bernice was likely a sin.

I stood off to the side for four minutes. She squawked, "CODY!" followed by, "LARRY!"

Close enough.

Given the presumed Cody was already halfway out the door, I figured I must have been Larry and took the boiling, thin paper mug outside. I tightened my cardigan around me, holding the coffee in the other hand, and found an empty bench down the sidewalk in the direction of my car.

Mom was right.

I wasn't going to call her back.

I popped off the lid and watched the steam. How could I hold this and still feel a chill? When was the last time I hadn't felt one? When I didn't have fine, white hairs lining my arms?

While I sipped, I swiped open my notes app and scanned my list of reno ideas for the house. It was cathartic, pulling together inspiration pictures and a list of items to order.

I used to do the same thing with my doll's clothes when she finally got a new outfit. I'd line them up by color, maybe by style. A quiet satisfaction came with being able to do the same thing for my adult job, just on a larger scale with furniture, paint colors, accents.

The golds would accent the sage green. The sage green would tie together Harthwait's first floor. The upstairs bedrooms would be individualized. I could probably watch one of those home renovation shows for a few ideas on tie-in pieces—like doorknobs, or maybe dresser and cabinet handles.

I made it halfway through my coffee, ankles crossed, when I heard it.

". . . couldn't appreciate you taking the time more than I already do," a woman's voice whispered.

"Don't worry. We strive to make the customer experience as individualized as possible, and—*Landry*?"

I stared at the wingback chair on my phone screen.

Every nerve in my body ignited like a live wire. Immediately, my heart strung itself up in the back of my throat. My palms grew clammy. If I stared hard enough, I could just make out the fluttering of my blue pulse in the inside of my wrist.

Footsteps. Closer. I couldn't *not* look.

"Landry?" he asked again.

I glanced up, as if dazed and thoroughly distracted, from my phone. Locked it, and sat it face down on my lap so he couldn't see it. Both hands wrapped around my coffee. His name rolled off my bottom lip before I locked eyes with him.

"Ivan?"

He leaned closer, as if to make sure. The russet undertones of his hair looked too uniform, the blond highlights too intricate. His jaw was square and his cheeks were high and his eyes were deep, deep blue.

Pretty.

I wanted to walk out in the middle of the street and lay down. No. That didn't give me a high enough chance of being killed. A car would straddle me, rubber would graze my arms, and I'd be unharmed. I needed a bridge to jump off of.

"That's crazy," he said, more to himself. He used his teeth to close a pair of sunglasses before tucking them in his shirt collar, his other hand reaching out for my shoulder. How did he get so close all of the sudden?

He was going to touch me. Palm and all.

I smothered a recoil.

"I didn't think you still lived local?" he said. The top two buttons of his shirt remained open, as did his sport coat. The slacks he wore held a tight crease in the front. His hand landed with a light squeeze.

"I don't," I said.

His eyes shuttered, brow furrowed. "Visiting, then?"

"Something like that." Lie. *Lie.*

A woman hovered, half-forgotten, just behind him. He turned back to the her—early fifties, with the aura of importance around her perfectly distressed jeans. Only rich people could look so casual while still give off an air of prestige.

His fingers clenched my shoulder as he motioned to me. "Excuse me, Rene. This is Landry Frederick. We went to school together."

She offered a nod, lips flat, eyes crinkled at the corners. "Landry. It's a pleasure."

"You, too." My cheeks burned with a forced smile as they spoke in low, hurried tones. With a pat on Ivan's shoulder, Rene offered another strained look to me before turning to leave.

Then it was Ivan and I. Two cars hissed by in those eight silent seconds. My reflection wavered, ghostly, across the street in the windows of a law office. Why weren't my legs working? Why wasn't I standing? I should have already left. Made an excuse, an appointment, something, for me to walk away.

"It was nice running into you, but I have to get back," I said, standing. I gave a smile while looking at the ground. Why did he have to stand so close to me? Why did he still smell the same—fresh cologne and dryer sheets?

He stepped in front of me. "Hey, hey. Don't leave yet."

An ugly, dark thing stirred in the back recesses of my ribs. "Tell your parents hello for me," I said.

"For real, Landry. Why are you here?"

I looked up. Squinted against the sun. "I heard from a bird you all moved away."

Unspoken words hovered between us. *I wasn't supposed to see you again.*

"My parents did, to Charleston. I commute back and forth when work brings me here." He unbuttoned his cufflinks and stuck them in his pocket, then rolled up his sleeves an inch. His forehead didn't hold a single bead of sweat. "Last I heard, you were doing interior design, correct?"

I shifted in place. I knew he still followed me on social media—because I'd made a point to unfollow *him*. I should have blocked him to avoid *this*.

A tiny, faint flutter hit my stomach. But if I'd blocked him, he wouldn't be able to see that I'd moved on. That I could live without him.

"I do," I said.

"Your work is wonderful." He cleared his throat. "If I'd realized, I would have hit you up. Maybe brought you onto a project or two?"

"I don't think our clientele is the same—"

"I'm serious," he said.

Ivan stood a head taller than me. I used to think that was so attractive. A football player, interested in little old me. The size of him, the athleticism, the screaming on the field when a down was completed or a touchdown scored.

The hand in mine while he taught me to drive a stick.

His fingers in my hair when he pulled me in for a kiss.

The blood in his neck when he flushed with frustration, only to console the moment with words and promises.

Both of us stood, staring at the other.

Finally, I said, "Well, I appreciate it, but I'm actually supposed to be back soon. I'll see you around, Ivan." His name on my tongue burned. I kept a wide berth as I stepped around the bench, and him, my eyes already set on my car.

I waited for his steps to follow—but they didn't.

"I'm sorry about Cadence, Landry," he called after me.

Just like with my mother, I didn't respond. I just kept walking.

* * *

He knew. He knew about me being in town for Aunt Cadence, and yet he'd acted like he hadn't.

I flipped through radio stations, eyes glued to the road. One good song before I got home. That was all I needed.

I didn't have feelings for Ivan. Quite the opposite. I had feelings, but they weren't the kind of feelings someone might have expected.

I used to have those: the butterflies, the hot palms, the unending smiles. I used to dream about ways to talk to him, pray that he would turn around in history class and ask for help, offer to study together, or look at my answers.

When those moments came, I built them up to mean something. I built them into a safe house, until I realized the house was burning, and the house had never been safe at all.

Stolen moments turned into moments stolen from me. "I love you," turned into, "if you did, why are you looking at him?" when I hadn't been looking at all. Compliments turned into insinuations. I was either *asking for it* from him, or I was *looking for it* from someone else.

"Come in today for forty percent off"—it broke to static. *Click.*

I tried again. "In Hannowville, by t . . . he"—*click.*

My breathing grew ragged. Infomercial after infomercial. Each one settled on my nerves. I needed something else. They weren't working—weren't filling the emptiness correctly—

"Have—or a—ved one—"

A cloud of dust plumed like a kite as I pulled off to the roadside.

Hands shaking, I turned station after station. Click after click, nothing but static or a grating voice, then—a country station crooned through the speakers. I sighed and fell back in my seat, elbow propped on the door lip. I settled my temple into my palm as a harmonica started to whine. Better.

This was better.

The roaring between my ears calmed the longer I sat. I counted the beats through the seat upholstery—the volume loud enough to hit deep, deep in my chest. In the cup holder by my elbow, my phone pinged.

I turned it off. Mom could wait—all of it, for a few moments, could be forgotten.

Everyone dealt with death, memories, and old pain at some point, and it was my turn on the merry-go-round, but I wanted off. I didn't remember standing in the line for this ride.

I didn't want to admit it, but Ivan was tangled to Cadence and Harthwait simply by being a piece of my memories. The thought sent my skin crawling: Ivan had the pleasure of crawling into my mind because he was a section of that puzzle, no matter how ugly.

Saliva pooled in my mouth. Hatred. Shame. I wanted to rip the pieces up, cut them to shreds, and burn them. But I couldn't. The best I could do was ignore it.

I thought of Emma, waiting at home, and how Sayer would be back to help. How they both would look at me with careful eyes, and that only reminded me how I *needed* to be okay.

So I breathed in deep, and I pulled back onto the road.

* * *

Back home, I deposited the seedlings on the front porch—a project for another day—and unlocked the front door. By the time I stepped inside, I realized the foyer was dark. And that I'd unlocked the door.

Which I shouldn't have had to do.

"Emma!" I called. "Are you hungry?"

Silence met me.

I poked my head into the living room. The sink light still spilled yellow over the sink; the refrigerator hummed in tandem with the AC unit. The TV, on mute, flickered over the walls, the ceiling, the ornate rugs. The grandfather clock *tick-tick-tick*ed as I turned the foyer light on.

"Em?" I stepped back and shut the front door.

The house just felt so—big. I was used to an apartment. Not two floors of empty rooms. With furniture that I'd never use. I circled, glancing at the stairwell.

When no answer came, I took a peek in the office, left of the front door. A tiny book nook light glowed amber. That particular book nook resembled an alleyway in Italy: cobblestone streets, sand-colored buildings with moss latched to their clay-tiled roofs. It stood no taller than a dictionary. A dime-sized motion sensor blinked at the bottom—if I were to walk in front of it, it'd flicker the alleyway to life, before falling dark after a few moments.

Had it turned on when Aunt Cadence fell from her heart attack? Had it been during the day, or sometime at night?

Why was it on now, though?

A buzz caught my attention. Back at the foyer table, I dug through my purse. Hadn't I turned my phone off?

Sure enough, three text messages, all within the last eight minutes.

EMMA: Dinner? I can get pizza. None of those casseroles looked appetizing.

EMMA: Or pasta.

EMMA: Carbs are good, just let me know before I leave the grocery store. You had no ravioli which is blasphemy so I'm at the store.

I leaned back against the handrail. It bit in between my shoulder blades, along all the knobs of my spine, as I typed back, *Can you get some greens so I can make my smoothies.*

Tick

I paused. Glanced up.

Then, it came again.

Tick

My heart started to flutter. My mouth watered with adrenaline. I stared at the very spot I'd stood in the foyer earlier today, except Sayer had been leaning where I was right now. I stared at the grandfather clock, waiting, just as the sound came again.

Tick

But the grandfather clock sang *tick-tick-tick*. Even, expected ticks. This sounded like a bug hitting a window, or—

Then I noticed it. Through the open office door, a warm, almost burnt color light clicked on. Two seconds passed, then it turned off.

Then it turned back on.

My breaths turned to shallow, reedy strands. I took a single step forward. The motion light had turned on, sure, but I was too far from the doorway for it to catch me. Even my reflection couldn't be seen in any of the windows—the curtain in the office was pulled tight.

Tick. On.

Tick. Off again.

My heart thundered, the foyer tightening, my nerves firing to run, to leave, to back away. Because something was triggering the light.

And it wasn't me.

Chapter Four

"You're lying."

"I am not," I hissed.

Emma fisted two paper shopping bags. "Where was it?"

I'd been standing on the front porch for fifteen minutes. I didn't care if someone drove by and questioned my intentions. Because why would someone who owned a home stand on a front porch, in the dark? But I was not about to stand in that house without Emma home. The idea made my skin prickle.

I could hear the chaotic laughter from Sayer already. *I told you! I told you it was haunted!*

There could be a logical explanation for the light to turn on and off by itself. Maybe the bulbs were finally biting the dust. Maybe it caught headlights as they swept by, but that wouldn't make much sense with the curtains closed. Or the distance from the road to the house.

I pointed in the direction of the room. "In Aunt Cadence's office."

The two of us stared at each other on the porch, nothing but the crinkling of paper bags and the call of tree frogs to break the monotony.

"And it was just—" She shimmied her shoulders. "You know."

"Turning on and off," I finished. "It's probably the batteries."

A delicate excitement flickered in Emma's eyes. "Did you check them yet?"

"No."

"Then let's," she said with a grin, and immediately bounced passed me. She dumped the groceries onto the foyer table, right next to my purse, which I eyed suspiciously.

I *knew* I'd turned my phone off.

Maybe I hadn't. I wasn't sure. At the moment, I wasn't sure I cared.

Emma backpedaled to the office, flipped the light on, and I trailed after her.

Aunt Denny never married. Instead, she'd made a spouse out of collecting—for a season it might have been artwork, then knitting, then first edition copies of her favorite childhood stories. There was a brief love affair with golf, but she'd tried smoking a cigarette while swinging a club in the backyard and ended up with a broken window and a patch of burned grass. Golfing hadn't been as appealing after that.

Before the heart attack, it had been books. Specifically on travel.

Now, the irony was weighted. She'd never left Harthwait—I never asked why, though if I'd been a good niece, a thoughtful niece, I might have asked. She'd been a human with a life, and maybe she'd had plans to leave. But that thought was even more disheartening than if she hadn't.

Emma zeroed in on the book nook. She waved her hand in front of it. The miniature alleyway remained dark.

"Hm. Maybe it is the batteries." Disappointment.

My chest lightened. "I'm sure there are some AAs around here."

We shuffled through a few drawers. Sticky notes, pens, and printer paper tumbled and sifted about. By the time I made it to a cluster of cabinets behind Aunt Cadence's desk, my eyes wandered.

Photographs perched in welcome on almost every shelf. But there—a lone black frame at eye level. My high school graduation. The only picture with everyone together after the divorce. Vince stood on my right, my mother on my left, Aunt Cadence at Mom's left. Mom looked like she'd swallowed a persimmon. Aunt Cadence, all smiles and curls. Emma hovered beside my dad, with her brothers Mason and Dawson in the background, both with arms extended upward in a wave.

With Mom and I standing side by side, it was hard to overlook the similarities: both of us auburns that neared burnt browns and freckled cheeks. But my structure came from my father. Everyone mentioned it—even my mother.

His hair was a rich chocolate, near black. His blue eyes were mine. His roman nose and full lips also mine, just like the cheekbones. Even his chin, which looked masculine on him, reigned feminine on me. If I held weight, I'd imagine I might have looked more like his mother than I would my own.

"Did you spill something?"

I blinked from the photo. "What?"

She bent and touched the floor. One of the boards was stained a different color, like it'd been replaced at some point. She pulled a splintered corner up and twisted it off. "Never mind. Thought it was sticky. It's just a splinter."

"I say we call it a night and go watch SNL reruns," Emma said. She pushed herself up from a crouch behind Aunt Cadence's desk with a wince. "I'm too old to be crawling on the floor this late without purpose."

At least I knew I'd need to add batteries to the store list. "What else would crawling entail?"

An eye roll was her response. "You know what I mean. I just want to eat pizza in peace."

"A simple creature," I teased. "Pizza or a slew of casseroles. You can take your pick."

"Hate to break it to you, but unless it has four different types of cheese, I don't want it."

Soon enough, the two of us sat settled on the couch, windows shut, curtains drawn, and an SNL rerun flitting across the TV.

By the time I'd picked the majority of the peppers off, leaving the bacon bits and the sausage, a looming pressure took a seat on my chest. I'd agreed to dinner. I could have said no. I could have refused. But then that would bring attention to me, to the issue, and I'd rather act like I was normal than explain the sense of dread surrounding me every time I looked at food.

Control. I wanted control.

To numb all the things I didn't want to feel.

A mixture of heat and condensation had left the bottom of the plate soggy. I alternated hands before feigning a bite.

"I need some napkins," I said. I pushed to stand, taking my pizza with me. "Be right back."

Emma peeled off a section of crust and dipped it in melted cheese sauce. "Can I have a Coke?"

"Cup or bottle?"

"Bottle's good."

I kept my back to Emma as I fumbled in the pantry for her drink. Then, when she wasn't looking, I tossed the slice in the trash.

The tension released from my neck first. Then down, down to my empty stomach, and the hollow bones of my shins.

There. The pressure released. For another night, I looked normal. I controlled the situation. I removed the source of anxiety.

At least—*at least*, I could still control this.

Problem solved.

* * *

Drip, drip, drip.

That night, I sat bent over my notepad, renovation ideas scribbled inside. My bedside lamp washed the room in soft light, somehow amplifying the neon green of my digital clock as it crept closer to midnight. Years ago, the vanity across from me had been a beauty desk for a little girl. Stained and chipped from dress-up games and makeup testing, it was now sanded and refinished, the memories erased. Forgotten. The dolls still dangled over the top of the bookshelf to my left, waiting for me to remove one and start a game of dress-up all over again.

And now you, Miss Patty, I told the little redhead with freckles, because she'd looked the most like me, *I can tie your hair up to keep it away from your eyes while I put eye shadow on them.*

The bread tie was still in her hair, which wasn't more than a single tuft that pointed straight to the ceiling, just like a unicorn.

I rested my chin in my palm. Would I erase all my memories from this house by the time the reno was done? Or only a few of them?

But I wasn't. I wasn't *erasing*. I was updating, while keeping character. The little bits of Aunt Cadence and the little fragments of history—like the family crest molded to the ceiling in the office, or the blocked-off servant staircase in the corner of the kitchen—would still be here.

I took a deep inhale. Blinked away my blurry vision.

"You're doing your job," I told myself, because no one else would. I arranged the heavy notebook in my lap. The quilt felt alive, like it skittered over my bare legs.

I pressed my index finger and thumb to the bridge of my nose. Then I counted the knobs on the front drawers. Two for each drawer. Eight total.

That's what I'd forgotten—I needed to order the knobs for the kitchen drawers. If I went with the sage color I had in mind for the walls, gold accents would match better than the existing brass fixtures. Some things I could spray paint, but I'd seen a vintage-inspired set online that would look much better. Instead of the dull, smooth, minimalist ones I usually found in stores, these were twirls of leaves as handles.

"For only two payments of twenty-nine ninety-nine, you can get . . ." the TV hummed.

I'd heard of people needing a fan to sleep—white noise, something to calm the mind. I needed voices, mindless chatter that resembled incoherent, meaningless thoughts. Most nights, I left the local infomercials on since they ran through the night. If not, lulls of nothingness jerked me out of sleep.

The digital clock flickered to a quarter after midnight.

My room, nicknamed the Blue Room, faced the back of the property. Emma was down the hall, in the opposite wing, in the Austen Room, because she said the aesthetic reminded her of *Pride and Prejudice*. Which was good for her, because the frills and lace of dresser runners and nightstand doilies made my skin crawl.

I started a new column, wrote *price?* before jotting out a few ballpark numbers beside each prospective item. I'd start my renovations with the kitchen, which would be easy. A new light fixture. Remove the rest of the roosters to show that the appliances were, in fact, new, and I could move on to the—

"No, Momma, *no*, please don't let him."

My pen froze, hovering over the paper. Gooseflesh pimpled up my arms.

For a heartbeat, I thought I'd imagined it. Glanced at the TV, which danced to my left on the dresser by a window, angled toward the bed. A new commercial, maybe? But the channel hadn't changed and neither had the murmuring ad for a new vacuum.

All right, maybe it hadn't been my TV. Maybe Emma was still awake and watching something down the hall. Or this was my signal to go to bed.

I shook it off and bent back over my list. The living room would be next—

"Please don't, Momma. I don't like it when he—"

My head jerked up.

"Free shipping if you order in the next fifteen minutes!" the husky voiced, mountain of a man on TV told me. I stared at the TV, watched the ad all the way through. There was no way it had been that guy—his voice was too deep. Too adult.

It sounded like a child. Distant. Maybe outside.

My thoughts buckled. Had we left the doors unlocked? Had a kid gotten lost and somehow ended up on the property? Or was it a dare—kids always made up stories about old homes and tricked the meek into stepping on the haunted grounds. Ding dong ditch, then run for the hills. *I* would have knocked on a haunted house door for approval.

"I dare you to step on the porch, Fanny-Lanny," Sarah would have snarled with her buck teeth and slicked-back pigtails. "Or you're a *baby*."

"Momma," the voice cried—faint. Either breathless or far away or both. "Momma, please."

I detangled myself from the quilt and stepped onto the cold floor. I didn't bother to grab a sweatshirt—I braved the hallway in shorts, a T-shirt, and no bra. That's how much confidence I had that I was just tired and hearing things.

I poked my head out into the hall. Listened. Emma's door was shut, the lights off beneath the door crack. The longer I stood in the doorway, the more the shadows seemed to settle. Like they wouldn't move until I turned away. Still, no voice came.

I counted the ticks of the grandfather clock. Three minutes. The refrigerator whirred downstairs, twice, before I stepped back in the room. My hand grazed the doorknob and I slowly pulled it closed.

An inch from clicking shut, I heard it.

"*Please*," the voice whimpered.

I opened the door again. The hallway was still empty.

A cold sweat dewed along my neck. Hundreds of possibilities trampled through me. A kid, like I suspected. But to plead like that? Why?

Then, that other option, the one I'd convinced Sayer wasn't true: The house was haunted.

Could this—could this be what Aunt Cadence was talking about? That teasing nursery rhyme she'd made up, that warned us not to stay at night. Was it real?

I wiped the sweat at the back of my neck and edged down the hallway. The air hugged, tight and cold, against my bare legs, sending shivers over every open inch of skin. Blood pulled from my extremities, making my hands and neck clammy.

"Momma, *no*," the voice cried.

I hurried to the stair landing. It sounded far away, but not too far, like the voice came from the first floor.

Through the darkened entryway downstairs, a shadow hovered on the other side of the front door. The hazy silhouette shifted from side to side. Short. Like a child.

I was right.

I needed to call the police, I needed help—I needed to wake up Emma. I kept my eyes on the door, hands gripped white-knuckled on the banister rail, and started, "Hey, Em—"

"*Momma, no.*"

The voice was everywhere and nowhere, so close I could almost breathe it in.

This child needed me. Right now.

A sick, twisted feeling exploded in my gut. There it bubbled: fear. Fear of what might happen if I didn't open the front door, or worse, if I did—what I might find on the other side.

My feet moved on their own accord. There was no time to wake Emma.

In a possessed hurry, I tripped down the stairs, gripping the railing the entire flight. There was a child on the front porch, and he needed help. Someone could be hurting him. He needed me *right now*—

I yanked the front door open.

That child needed help—they needed—

The door opened so fast it hit the wall behind it.

Nothing but empty porch and cool night air stretched in front of me.

The rocking chairs sat as still as sentinels. Not a breeze could be felt; not a cricket chirped. The vicious urgency within me vanished like a gasp, there one moment, gone the next.

No one stood on the porch. It was quiet, like I'd imagined it all.

Chapter Five

I didn't sleep well for days.

The call from the funeral home iced the cake. I shouldn't have forgotten—I knew the ashes would be ready at any point, but I'd gripped the reminder as well as an oiled hand caught water.

I'd forgotten to get Aunt Cadence's ashes.

To make matters worse, Mom called. Nine times in the span of two minutes.

On the final ring, my resolve broke.

"How could you forget to *pick her up*?" she snarked over the phone. "They called me *while I'm at work*. Do you know how *embarrassed* that made me feel?" Every other word seemed emphasized, like they carried their own personal exclamation point. A teeny, tiny knife, just large enough to poke at a sliver of my exposed guilt.

I huffed a strand of hair out of my face as I slammed my car door shut. Phone pinned between my shoulder and ear, I retrieved Aunt Cadence from the back seat. I bumped the door shut with my hip.

I hadn't realized urns could be so big.

The urn fit her personality. Larger than normal, a standout of green and white marble with a little dragonfly atop the lid. David, the funeral home director, had told me prior to her service that she'd purchased the urn nearly ten years ago, just in case. "Didn't expect to fulfill it in my lifetime, but people have a way of surprising you," he told me.

It felt like a sign that I'd picked that same green for the kitchen.

"I've been busy," I told Mom. My steps were sharp up the porch. I didn't bother looking at any of the windows—scared of what I would find looking back at me, even in daylight. I told myself I was watching my step so I didn't drop Aunt Cadence.

"Maybe if you organized your schedule like I've told you to do, we wouldn't run into problems like this."

My nostrils flared. Yes, because my mother was the queen of planning.

I used my elbow to wedge the screen door open, careful to hold Aunt Cadence close and firm. Once inside, I gingerly set her down on the foyer table, which was already crowded with a few sample paint cans and Sayer's satchel. I shifted the phone from my shoulder into my hand.

"You know, if you were down here helping go through Aunt Cadence's things, maybe I wouldn't be so forgetful," I snapped. "You didn't even come to the funeral."

"The tone isn't necessary," she quipped. "And that's mighty high coming from someone who stole all my sister's things out from under me."

I stood ramrod straight. My jaw buzzed with adrenaline.

She hated this place. She hated the wide-planked floors, the memories embedded in the wallpapered bathrooms, the empty rooms that begged for guests. She wouldn't have wanted any of it if she had been willed it.

"I didn't steal anything from you, Mom." Defeat edged my words. Then, the longer the silence stretched between us, guilt rubbed around my legs like a forgotten cat, ready for dinner.

Mom hadn't had a choice in getting the house. Aunt Cadence had willed it all to me—not her. If I were in her shoes, wouldn't that make me mad, too?

I pinched the bridge of my nose, thinking. But the money.

What would she do with it? There was no telling.

Upstairs, the hum of the portable speaker lowered to a murmur. Sayer's long strides followed, then he peeked around the corner, paint and dust all over his jeans. The skylight, far above on the third floor, made his thinning hair look even thinner.

His brow quirked, mouth pinched. A silent question.

I only gave a tight head shake, then I turned my back to him so he couldn't read my lips.

"You should be here," I said, voice narrow. "You know that."

"I will not step foot in that place," she retorted. "Do you know what I went through in that house?

I pinched the bridge of my nose again. I didn't want to diminish what my father had done, because we all knew he didn't make the best decisions, but neither had she. But this had never been her house. I knew she only badgered me about the house because she didn't get it, but the thought of arguing with her over what was and wasn't true drained my energy just thinking about it.

"Do you not remember what I told you about that man?" she said. "He gaslit me, he abused me—"

"Mom—"

I could practically feel the fire blowing from her lips when she said, "You, little girl, will not tell me what to do. Do you know all I sacrificed for you? All I made sure you had? You had a roof over your head and food in your stomach and you had a *great mother*. I know you like to idolize Cadence because she was the *fun one* to be around, but that house won't be a home any more than the one I gave you was."

My chest blossomed into flames. Every joint in my body locked.

I never expected Harthwait to be a home. That's why I was selling it. I didn't need a home, I didn't *need* anyone, including her. It all needed to go.

All of it.

I opened my mouth. Stopped. Closed it.

I wanted to say it. But I couldn't bring myself to remind her of the years I'd waited for her to come home after work, only to have to eat boxed, stale cereal with water and get myself ready for school the next day because she'd gotten strung out in someone's living room. Couldn't bring myself to remind her of the times Mrs. Tomes had taken me aside and asked if everything was okay at home because I'd worn the same clothes to school for three days that week.

I couldn't repeat her hissed threat when I'd found her in the bathroom the night before the divorce anniversary: *If you tell anyone where I've been, I'll tell them you're a liar, Landry May. Do you want to know where liars go?*

I shook my head. But could I blame her? Truly?

I knew how she'd treated me was wrong. But she was my mother.

Mom and Vince had met in college. From what little I'd been able to piece together—through her inflated, ever-changing stories and the tidbits of information I'd gathered from Aunt Cadence or other adults in my mother's life over the past few years—they had been the toxic couple that should have broken up long before I had been born. They'd bonded over drugs, then were on-again, off-again until one had convinced the other that getting married would change things.

Then The Affair happened.

I didn't blame her for spiraling. She'd sunk into depression, refused help, and turned to substances, which she'd racked up a probation for after I was born. She'd taken his child support money and blown it without a second thought, then cried herself to sleep every night while I curled on my bed, knees to my chest.

There was no custody battle. No arguments over vehicles. Only child support and the removal of both my mother and me from his life.

Vince didn't take me on weekends. He didn't come visit on my birthday. He sent one Christmas card when I was ten, only for Mom to shred it like it held the plague. I reached out once a year on his birthday.

The last time he'd called was my college graduation. Asked me to come over for lunch. I'd let myself gain a teeny, tiny bit of hope as I'd driven four hours to his coastal home. Maybe seeing me as an adult would make him realize how much he'd missed. Maybe he regretted his lack of involvement.

That evening he'd offered to pay off my tuition loans. He was a lawyer. Had plenty of money, he said.

"I don't need it," I said.

One, because the money would only be a consolation for all his missed time. And two, because I couldn't guarantee that Mom wouldn't find a way to take it before I managed to move out.

And if I took it, I would be indebted. I couldn't pay back something I didn't possess, let alone from someone who wouldn't deign to see me half the time.

"We already agreed to pay Emma's, Lan," he'd gone on, in his marble kitchen with his stainless-steel appliances, while his phone vibrated on the counter every couple of seconds.

I wondered if it was a mistress calling him. If Emma was there, she'd have written it down in her notes and dissected it later.

"No," I'd said. "I can pay for it myself."

"Student debt is no easy feat to pay off," he urged, distracted. He unwound himself from his perch on the barstool when his phone started to vibrate again. "Just promise me you'll think about it."

He didn't look up when he retrieved the phone, pressed it to his ear, and walked away. I was left sitting on the recliner arm, purse cradled in my lap, eyes stuck to the spot he'd just vacated.

He opened the sliding door to the back patio.

"Hey, no, I'm not busy." It closed.

Was it bad that I wanted him to argue with me? To *make* me take the money? To tell me I was being ridiculous, to take the handout, to just let him be a father for once?

But he didn't say anything about being a father. Only that he'd paid for Emma's, therefore he must pay for mine.

An emptiness settled in my bones.

Emma hadn't *told me*. It shouldn't have hurt. But for some reason, it did. Maybe she figured if she was to suffer a continuous broken home, why not take what he offered?

Did that mean I was spiteful because I hadn't taken it?

I pulled myself back to the present. The phone whispered in my ear—not a deadline, just the sound of my mom waiting. Simmering.

"Do you want me to send you part of her ashes?" I asked, voice small.

One, three, five fiery heartbeats.

Mom's single-word answer twisted the knife further. "No."

The line went dead.

* * *

Birds chattered as my box cutter ripped through the packaging tape.

The kitchen smelled of primer, newspaper, and hot Lowcountry air. A final, neatly arranged assortment of decorative roosters stood at attention in the breakfast nook to my right. Somewhere upstairs, a faint procession of thuds vibrated through the walls. Sayer was taking action on one of the guest bathrooms, trying to remove the shelving unit from above the toilet so we could stain it with the cabinets tomorrow.

I'd spent the better part of my day base-painting the kitchen, which had been a bloody russet red and had taken *three* coats of white to correct. I waited for the paint to dry while sorting through knickknacks, then starting on the first layer of sage-green paint. The cabinets would be next. I'd take the doors off, sand, and stain them to a bright driftwood brown before reattaching the doors and touching up the trim. Then I'd get the handles screwed on.

I peeled the shipping lid back, stared at the handles inside, and frowned.

They weren't what I ordered.

I pulled out a barstool, collapsing into it and covering my face with my hands. "I should have just gotten the ones from Home Depot," I groaned. I suppose this was my punishment for trying to save a few dollars.

The front door burst open.

I jumped.

Emma strode in, white tank and shorts plastered to her body. Sweat dewed her collarbone. Her knees were patched with porcelain, as were her hands and areas around her mouth, but it only emphasized the honey in her hair and the deepness in her eyes.

"I come bearing gifts." She dropped two reusable shopping bags on the counter, both covered in palm trees and toucans. "I'm ready to strip some wallpaper, boss." She withdrew a bottle of fabric softener and a handle of vinegar. When mixed with portions of hot water, it usually stripped wallpaper like a champ.

I sighed. "Hopefully."

Her nose wrinkled. "What's wrong with you?"

I shrugged. Mom. The primer taking so long to dry. The cabinet handles. Everything.

When she continued to stare at me, I said, "That wallpaper's been up so long, I don't know if it'll come off in one go."

Emma's hands dropped, but her shoulders tightened. "I got it. Don't worry."

A muffled, "No!" came from upstairs. Then a heavy thud, like a box filled with donation clothes, dropping to the floor. "Lanny!"

I stifled a groan. My head dropped back, eyes closed. "What?"

"I think I chipped the sink." A pause. "Or not."

I sighed, then said, loud enough for Sayer to hear me over his music, "I'm replacing it anyway."

More banging. Emma slipped out of the pantry with an old deli meat container and a pack of toothpicks. She peeled the plastic lid off, set it aside, and got to work opening the vinegar bottle.

With all these fumes, we'd be as high as a kite before sundown.

Sayer's footsteps grew louder. I pictured him leaning over the banister, glasses askew. "I'll go ahead and tear up this transition strip. I splintered it when I tripped and—"

"That's fine."

He shuffled away.

I slipped from the stool and opened one of the three windows in the breakfast nook, then flipped the living room fan on. A separate, short fan hummed in the corner of the kitchen floor, facing the last section of wall that hadn't dried yet.

"See? Who needs expensive contractors when you have us to help you," Emma said, pert. She poured a cup of vinegar in the container, then unscrewed the fabric softener. "Cheap labor and great community."

I nodded, biting my lip. She was right. Not necessarily about the cheap labor, but the great company—and a reason for the house to be filled with explainable noises. Not children crying, which I'd failed to mention to either of them yet.

The idea of explaining what I'd heard—or what I *hadn't* heard, since the crying hadn't woken up Emma—made all four corners of my heart twist into knots.

"I saw Ivan in town," she said. She measured out the softener, careful to not look up.

"Mm."

"He asked about you. I didn't know he still lived here."

I continued arranging the roosters.

"He seemed—interested."

"You know I'm not the dating type," I told her. Heat started in the middle of my back. Tingles through my fingers, but not from butterflies.

"He's a nice guy, Lan." She started stirring the stripping concoction with a couple of toothpicks, then unpacked the rest of her finds. A packet of switchblades, a new set of screwdrivers, and a box of 120-grit sanding pads. "If nothing really happened back at graduation, why don't you just talk to him? He doesn't have hard feelings. Otherwise he wouldn't have asked about you."

I left the roosters to grab the shipping tape. I ripped three long strips off and plastered the rooster box shut. "I told you. We went different ways. It would be awkward."

"But people reconnect all the time—and he said he'd already run into you." She paused. "You didn't tell me."

I prickled. "There was nothing to tell. He said hi. I said hi. I left."

The air grew charged. Metallic shards, jittering between us.

"Lan—"

A crash from the second floor broke Emma's sentence. The dingy kitchen light fixture, dangling and centered above the island, rattled.

Both of us stood frozen. I turned, ready to storm the steps and see what had happened, when there was a rustle. Not as loud, but similar to shoes scuffing over hardwood. A low grunt followed. Almost meek, Sayer called down, "Uh . . . guys."

The music Sayer had been playing quieted. Then clicked off.

"Can you, uh, come up here for a second?"

* * *

"What . . . is that?"

The three of us stared at the hole in a lengthy, detached silence. Walls were easy to patch. I'd done it before. Still, my lips parted, then shut. Over and over, until I swept my hair off the back of my neck and sighed in defeat.

"I don't know," Emma whispered. Her fingers drummed against her cheek.

"There's something behind the wall?" My stomach pulled into itself like I might throw up. The hole gaped large enough to see through, but dark enough that I couldn't exactly tell what it was.

"I'm so sorry," Sayer said, hands in his hair. He started to pace. I shook my head, eyes shuttering. "I can fix it."

"I don't care about the strip," I said. "Are *you* okay?"

"So I was pulling, right." He bent down and grabbed the broken transition strip in both hands to re-create the image. "The strip broke and I fell backward into the hall and my head hit the wall and—" He splayed both hands open and shook them in emphasis. "This happened. I swear I didn't mean to. It was really hard to pull up." He held out the transition strip, as if proof were needed.

"Sometimes they can be." I winced.

Emma stepped between us, arms out, then took Sayer's cheek in one hand and grabbed the back of his nape with the other. "Are you dizzy? Can you tell me what day it is?"

"What are you doing?" He tried to pull away. "Stop. It. I'm fine."

"There's plaster in your hair."

"It's sheet rock, not plaster," he corrected. He brushed himself off, then batted Emma's hands away when she tried to grab his head again.

"Recite the date and time." She took him by the shoulders instead and looked him dead in the eye. Sayer barely stood an inch taller than Emma. "I mean it. Pronto."

He blinked. "June, uh, twelfth? Maybe four o'clock—"

"Wrong. It's four thirty."

"You know what I mean."

I knelt while they bickered to get a better look. Sure enough, there was something on the other side.

She shook him a bit. "Sayer." Held up her index finger. "Follow it."

"What are you—"

I pressed at a dangling piece of sheet rock, then pulled it off in a puff of dust, as Emma exclaimed, "Just do it! It's for your safety!"

"Okay, okay!"

I leaned closer and flicked the dust away. Whatever it was, it was solid wood. Not a support beam or a stud. Had it been covered on purpose?

A tightness started in my throat. I scratched the inside of my wrist. Dug a fingernail in. A slight, barely there hint of pain to ground myself. Focus.

I'd seen people cover plenty of things before—fireplaces they didn't want to take out, linen closets, sometimes crawl spaces (which I wouldn't recommend). But this looked different.

With a sharp breath, I stuck my arm through the hole. Brushed my fingertips over the bevel—sure enough, it felt like a door.

Emma crouched next to me. "Oh! What is that?"

"Is that a door?" Sayer leaned over my shoulder, his head inches from mine. I leaned away.

"I think so?" I said. I swallowed once, twice, a trickle of excitement bleeding into my veins. Sayer grumbled something that sounded like, "Should be, it hurt well enough."

"Should we try and open it?" Emma whispered, so quiet I almost missed it.

"I don't know," I said.

The molding was bumpy in a few places, which usually meant it was handcrafted, not mass-produced. I stretched my arm completely through, fingertips searching for an end. There it was.

By feel, I couldn't reach far enough to tell if it were bedroom door—where would the room have been? Or overly large window shutters. But where this was placed, right beside the stairs that led to the third-floor attic and my bedroom, meant this wasn't a window, but perhaps an old linen closet.

But I didn't remember Aunt Cadence mentioning a renovation. As far as I knew, she hadn't so much as changed furniture since she'd moved in.

I reached up, searching.

"Do you feel anything?" Emma whispered. Her breath tickled my temple. Sayer, unable to see anything, straightened.

I winced. "I can't—"

My fingers wrapped around a knobby doorhandle. Then something shifted in the air, like a wet blanket draping over a shivering body in a cold wind. Goosebumps crawled all over me. My peripheral grew shadowed, spotty, until the speckles bled into splotches and everything vanished.

The hallway went dark.

I blinked but saw nothing but darkness, as if someone had turned out the lights in a windowless room. Only muffled voices—maybe Sayer and Emma—mumbled far, far away. I squinted, squeezed my eyes, focused on the thrum of my heart in my ears.

Tell me I am no man, a voice growled. Unfamiliar, gritty. *Tell me!*

I blinked again, hard. Then, ever so faintly, shapes appeared in a gray haze around me. I wasn't in the hallway anymore, but a . . . room.

Specifically, a library. Or an office. Like dust gathering, the haze formed a desk and shelves and cracked windows. Black grease slithered from the shelves and crevices, like someone had turned an ink pot over and not wiped it up in time.

My body jerked to stand. My joints were oiled and strong, my frame . . . different.

Something told me I was no longer *me*, but someone else. When I stood, I was eye level with the top shelf beside me. The tingle under my skin screamed the desire to move, to walk, to pace, to leave, but yet this body kept still.

The eyes that were not mine shuttered. A cherrywood desk with bulbous legs, one broken, teetered at an angle to my left.

A garbled voice, not *this* body's, said, *You are a coward before you are a man.*

Then, distant, separate, over and over the same string of words: *Nor I, you. Never you.*

When I blinked again, the room disappeared. The desk, the voices. Everything—gone, like a daydream.

Now, I sat crouched by the hole in the wall, my fingers still wrapped around the doorknob. Emma still hunched beside me, waiting for my response.

Every hair on my body stood on end.

"What?" I choked.

Her eyes bounced from my brow to my chin and back. "Are you okay?"

I gave a jerky nod. "Yeah, yeah, I'm fine. Why?"

She shook her head. "Nothing. You looked sick for a second."

"It's just cold up here," I said.

Wrong thing to say. Emma's eyes narrowed this time, just enough for little alarm bells to ring. "Okay."

I withdrew my hand from the doorknob and stood to brush off my shoulder. My sweatshirt was littered with little flecks of broken sheetrock. They peppered the floor, scattering.

"I'll get a broom," I said. I had already turned to head back down the stairs, my heart racing, face emptied of blood.

A door. A door that led to something.

Rationally, it could have been a closet. There wasn't enough room for a bedroom to be there. Which was a completely logical explanation. Maybe it'd been covered before Aunt Cadence bought it, or maybe she'd covered it. Why would she waste perfectly good storage space, though?

Still, the little hairs on my arms stood at attention. A hidden room didn't settle well in my stomach. First the light turning on by itself, and then the crying?

And what I'd heard—no, what I'd seen. Because I had *seen* something on the porch.

A hairline fissure cracked through the certainty I'd built up. What if there had been truth to Aunt Cadence's words?

What if she hadn't been lying?

I'd watched enough true crime and horror movies to make assumptions. A ghost haunted a place where they were tethered. Tethered to a place where they were murdered. Bodies could be hidden in walls, backyards, and attics.

Or boarded-up closets.

I needed to tell Emma. Sayer would faint from fear, and I'd be lying if I said the thought of him leaving didn't make me anxious. There was something comforting about having them both here, so if I told either of them, it would need to be Emma, but even then, the thought of telling her about the boy made acid eat the back of my throat. She'd get excited. Do research. Tell someone. Someone would tell someone else, and then before I knew it, the house would be nearly confirmed haunted and it wouldn't sell. It would sit on the market, collecting dust, and burning a hole in my already thin pocket.

By the time I found the broom and made it back up the stairs, Emma had Sayer's head firmly grasped in her hands.

"You have a knot on the back of your head," she said. Sayer made a grab for the broom, so I stepped out of reach.

"I'll do it," I said. "Just go get an ice pack and sit down."

"Fine." His nostrils flared as he slipped out of Emma's grip.

"Wait, don't walk too fast." She trailed after him, one careful step at a time. I waited until their voices faded down into the living room before turning back to the hole.

The broom handle grew slick in my hand. What would happen if I touched the doorknob again? Could I open it without knocking out the rest of the wall?

Would I see something again?

I set the broom down, wiped my hands on my leg. And reached back through the hole. I fumbled for the doorknob until I finally found it.

A cold sense of disappointment filled my stomach. I turned it and tugged, but the sheetrock was too close for me to get a glimpse inside. I'd need to knock the rest of it out if I wanted a better look.

That fissure of doubt grew larger, morphed into a crack in my chest.

Once Harthwait grows dark, Aunt Cadence's voice had whispered.

The sun started to slide up the walls, closer to the ceiling. The foyer would be dark within the hour. By seven thirty, the trees would have the house blocked from most direct sunlight. We'd be in a cocoon while the sky started to streak with pinks and reds. The house itself already shrouded in night.

I shivered and started to sweep the dust and sheetrock from the floor.

She couldn't have been telling the truth.

Hauntings didn't happen. They were stories, make believe, a figment of the imagination, and all I had to do was box it up and toss it away.

Once I'd gotten most of the pieces, I used the hammer Sayer left behind and removed the nails from where the transition strip had broken, and gathered everything into the dustpan. I ignored the tug behind my belly button when I turned to leave. Almost like a nudge—or a tether.

I started down the steps.

Don't leave, the door seemed to whisper. *Please come back.*

Chapter Six

I fell asleep on the couch sometime after ten o'clock to the sound of a cooking show. Emma had disappeared upstairs hours before, and I should have followed, but my body ached too much, and the thought of mustering anymore energy to crawl into my own bed felt almost sinister.

Down here, the dishwasher hummed with the murmur of the TV. I hadn't bothered to shut the windows in the living room, so the symphony of frog chirps and owl hoots accompanied the far, far distant sound of cars whispering over paved roads. Every once in a while, the honk of a tractor trailer sidled in.

With the company of noise, the loneliness avoided me.

"Call now and receive a free gift . . ." a woman on the TV said.

I shifted under my blanket. The cushions didn't feel all that lumpy or cramped. I never understood why anyone would complain about sleeping on the couch when it felt like this.

I wiggled my toes. Stretched a bit. If I focused, I could almost convince myself that I was young again, and after years of needling, Aunt Denny finally relented and let me sleep over.

"But only down here," she might have said. "We can watch a movie."

Sleep nudged me. Then it swallowed me.

Not just sleep—but a dream.

Stars peppered the sky, the air blanketed my shoulders heavily, the feel of a truck bed against the sharpness of my tailbone. A driveway?

No, the sunroom off the library. Not a truck bed. A wooden bench.

That familiar scent—musk, sand, and shampoo that I would recognize anywhere.

Not this—anything but this, I thought.

Dreams, I'd come to find out, weren't always a happy figment of the imagination. Sometimes they were the ugliest moments, long shoved in a box and tucked away, brought back out for show and tell. A reminder of what could have happened. Of what didn't happen.

Or, of what did.

A hand slipped up my shirt, the other in the waist of my shorts.

"Ivan, wait," I whispered.

Ivan's russet head looked almost golden in the moonlight. The glass ceiling to an open sky the only source of luminescence, the door to the main house shut tight. Just us. He curled over me in a partial crouch, his mouth against my neck.

"Ivan," I urged. I pushed at his shoulders.

"What, Lan?" he whispered. He pulled back. My neck remained damp. I wanted to wipe it off. All of it, away, dirty, *filthy*—

"Someone might see—" I started.

"You always say that," he said. He looked seventeen again, all prematurely broad shoulders that hadn't filled in yet. I glanced to the ceiling.

Yes, there I was. My face looked angular, my collarbone gaunt, my legs awkwardly open to steady myself. And him, right there, everywhere in front of me.

"Just real quick," he said. "Is it wrong to kiss you?"

I looked back down. Wrapped a hand around his wrist. "It's not that." Tugged.

With a sigh, he pulled his hand from my shirt, the other still hovering at the waist of my shorts. He knelt, close enough for me to smell the peppermint on his shirt and the faint hint of sweat from the humidity.

"What is it?" he pressed.

"My aunt is here," I said. This wasn't what I'd wanted to do. I wanted to talk to him, *really* talk to him, because we never had time alone. This was supposed to be that moment.

"No, she's not," he said. "She left with your mom. Do you really care what they think? They don't have to know." His eyes were blue. So, so blue, I wanted to drown in them, and I didn't want anyone to save me. "Only I will. It's okay. We don't have much time, anyway."

He scooted closer, on his knees in front of me, and we sat eye level. Both his arms blocked me in, so the only way out was if I fell backward on the bench. And even then, there was a wall.

Suddenly the sunroom felt small, secluded, the plants too far-reaching and the ceiling too high.

"I know," I whispered. He was right. Wouldn't any girl want this opportunity?

"Then what's stopping you?"

A slow creeping feeling started up the base of my spine. "I just . . . wanted to talk to you a bit. About some things."

His expression remained neutral, his eyes on my mouth. "Like what?"

Distracted. I was distracting him by talking because he wasn't listening, only watching. But maybe if I told him—maybe he would listen. Maybe it would hit his emotions, and he'd help me.

"I've been having thoughts," I whispered. Pressure started at the back of my neck and trickled down my spine.

He leaned in. Our noses nearly touching. The tendons in his neck strained. Football and track and wrestling. He would know what to do, he would know how to help me. I helped him in school, he could help me with this. "About?"

My heart stuttered, near to bursting. My pulse felt so far up my throat, it could have hopped out of my mouth.

He would know what to do. He cared. He cared about me.

"About . . . things."

"Be more specific, Lan. Is this about that project? I told you I wouldn't tell Monovan I used your notes. You're good." His words whispered against my lips. Seconds, before I lost him.

"I've been feeling out of control with things." Mom and her using. Dad being gone.

Better not let that boy get to you, Mom snarled a few days before. *You'll end up pregnant and alone, just like* me. *Keep your legs closed, Lan, or I swear on my dead momma—*

That's not nice, had been my weak retort.

Would it kill you *to be* nice *once in a while?* she'd shot back.

I bit my tongue. Tears seared my eyes, my nose, blurring my vision until the colors muted.

Ivan stopped. His jaw clicked. "Huh?" The word fell just soft enough, like he might be worried about me, that I pushed forward.

"So I've been—compensating." My fingers trailed to my forearm. I picked at a spot, that same spot, which had just scabbed over. Exhaled at the small bite of pain. Everyone always said to talk to people. That you would be brave in telling someone those thoughts. To get help.

Ivan was the only one left that could help me.

"With . . . food," I whispered. "And other things." I couldn't say it. Couldn't give it that power. If I said it, it was real. This was as close as I could get.

Ivan's jaw worked, throat bobbed. "You mean, like, because you're a rail?"

My mouth went dry. The thundering in my ears morphed to a roar. "What?"

His hands started back at my waist, down to the edge of my shorts, this time from behind. He hauled me closer. "You're too small. Skinny. That's what you're saying?"

"Maybe—I guess—" Was it? No. That's not what I meant. *Skinny.* The word stung. No, it burned. The way he looked at me—with eyes on my chest, then lower, the faster he bent in, and his mouth landed back on my neck. He reeled me closer.

"Ivan, wait, stop—"

"Just eat something, Landry," he bit into my skin. I was going to throw up. That tone didn't feel gentle at all, any hint of reassurance I'd told myself was there, vanished. I slipped closer to the end of the bench. "Is this about what I said? About Wren? I didn't mean it, not really."

I tangled my hands in his hair and pulled him back. My stomach was all knots and a cold sweat started over my skin, mixed with trembles.

"You said you got off from her Instagram pictures, Ivan." My voice hardened a bit.

He looked incredulous. "So? She's not you. It was just a spur of the moment thing, okay? I told you because I want a clear conscience. I could have *not* told you about it, and that would have been worse, right?" His expression turned almost incredulous. "And you didn't care before. Why care now?"

Make this stop. I wanted to shake myself awake. Guilt, shame, muddled with anger, flooded my veins. How had I ever let this happen? Why didn't I walk away?

Why had I let him talk to me like this?

Ivan's hand started back up my shirt, cupped my breast, and I reared back, but he kept me close. Closer, until our bodies were flush, and I suddenly felt sick. The emotions from that moment roiled around me, pressing in farther and farther until each inhale turned into a choke, while the dream continued.

He was right. He told me. He could have *not* told me.

"Because—I didn't bring it up," I said.

He pulled back completely, the distance jarring. "Maybe if you gained some weight, I wouldn't have to beat it to someone else's pictures, Lan. How many times have I told you to eat something? Yes, you're beautiful—I've told you so many times, you should know this by now—and I still don't get further than putting a hand up your shirt. How am I supposed to feel like you love me if you keep me at a distance?" His voice grew gritty, frustrated, splotches of color creeping over the collar of his black shirt.

I struggled to stand. He stood, too, shoulders heaving. "I do love you, I'm just trying to tell you the things I'm feeling. It's supposed to be good to talk about feelings, right? And I didn't bring up Wren, *you* did."

"I wouldn't have to if you just listened to me!" he shouted, veins thickening in his neck. He ran his hands over his face, laughing. "I swear, it's like talking to a wall when I'm with you sometimes."

"I do listen," I whispered. I reached out. "Ivan, please."

"Stop, Lan." He reared back when my fingers brushed his forearm. "Don't touch me."

I wiped my cheek with the back of my hand and pulled away. I'd asked him so many times to not touch me, and he'd made advances anyway. What made my requests different from his? Was it my tone? Did I not say it forcefully enough? Or was I too mean?

Would it kill you to be nice once in a while? my mother's voice echoed, so sharp that it was like she leaned against my shoulder when she'd said it. *Always so hateful.* Then her voice morphed into my own, bristled and angry. *How far will it go? Does it make you angry that he thinks so little of you?*

Does it make you hate him, just a bit more? You hate *him, don't you? I know you do.*

You hate them all.

I turned my back to Ivan. The sharp angles of moonlight cast the sunroom, the wicker furniture, and the shelf of seedlings into a gray shroud.

I froze.

Ivan continued talking, as if I'd never looked away. I watched his reflection in the door to the house, his hands moving as he spoke, neck red and jaw set. He went on as if I were facing him, not facing away.

But there, just three feet from me. A shadow hovered in the door window, watching us. Not a person, and not Aunt Cadence or my mother. A silhouette, tall and solid, yet misted at its edges.

My blood ran to ice.

The face wasn't human. Sunken bits of jaw and dangling teeth from the roots, shredded clothing around its torso and stringy white hair from its scalp. The only lively part of its person was the eyes: as if untouched by decay. Yellow, with black slits no thicker than a pen stroke.

Its smile ripped far past its jawbone.

Then, it jerked behind the doorframe, and the dream broke apart.

* * *

I sat up with a gasp to the grandfather clock ringing.

I pressed the heel of my hand to my forehead. Nausea rolled in the roots of my belly. I started to lean over the side of the couch, then thought better of it, and took measured breaths instead. A low throb echoed behind my eyes. Not enough water during the day; that's exactly what was wrong with me. I was dehydrated, and now I was paying for it.

The dream wasn't real. Yes, it had happened. But not here. It had been in Cole Poston's driveway after a football game on the tailgate of Ivan's truck.

My skin grew clammy, my body curling into itself. I felt dirty—and—and *disgusting.*

How long would I feel that way? How long would these images, these choices, *his choices* haunt me?

I untangled myself from the blanket, threw it over the back of the couch, and swung my legs over the side. I needed to go to bed. To forget. Sleep would take it away, and then this would all be a fevered afterthought in the morning.

Pressure crawled over my skin, like someone walking two fingers up my spine.

I glanced around the living room. The TV flickered over the walls. The foyer light was still on, just as I'd left it.

I stretched for the remote on the coffee table. Muted the TV. I don't know how long I stood there, waiting for the pressure to release—the thunderous roar in my ears from the dream crept in.

Then, I felt it. A thread of floss that wound through my intestines and cinched around my spine. A tug, ever so slight, to go upstairs. The same tug I'd felt from the door earlier.

I couldn't help it; I started for the steps. I didn't realize until I entered the foyer, but the tree frogs no longer chirped. No distant, muffled highway.

The windows, I noted, had been shut.

I took the steps two at a time. Emma's door, along with all the others besides mine, were closed. I rounded the landing, ready to find the hole in the wall, but stopped.

My lungs hitched.

The hole in the wall didn't exist. Instead, a five-panel door stood, as if it had never been covered in the first place. Not a speckle of debris to be found on the floorboards.

The door glistened like oiled skin when I approached. My reflection warbled in the finish. I kept my steps light, leading with my toes, when I stopped in front of it. The tugging in my stomach eased.

Downstairs, the ticking of the grandfather clock grew louder, closer.

My eyes burned. Only once. I could open it one time, just to see what was on the other side. Then the paranoia would be put to rest and I wouldn't have to think about this anymore.

I reached for the knob. All sound dulled in that moment—I didn't hear anything but the rattle in my lungs. I forgot about the house, I forgot about the funeral, my mom, Vince, I forgot about everything.

The knob was warm to the touch. As if someone had held it for a long while before I came up here.

I twisted. The latch released with ease. I pulled the door open, ready to find blackness or empty shelves or dust bunnies or bones.

But I didn't.

Chapter Seven

Cobwebs and musty particles floated through air on the other side of the doorway. Wide-planked floors—Harthwait's floors—sat layered in dust, warped from years of abandonment. A few of the floorboards poked up at odd angles. Moth-eaten rugs lay bunched and flipped up at the corners, as if discarded in either a hurry or from a search. An old rocker sat in the corner, its back rail splintered in half.

I felt that tug again.

Something was *off* about the place. It looked like Harthwait, sprawled like Harthwait. But instead of opening to the hallway I currently stood in, as if by an inverted mirror, it opened to what I assumed was the living room downstairs.

Or what had been.

A rug stood, rolled and propped, against the far corner of the room. A chandelier, swaddled in a thick layer of cobwebs, dangled in the center of a ceiling lined with crown molding. All of it much too elegant for a modern living room. Even the window latches were different: rounded, with a single latch in the center, instead of one on each side. Wallpaper unspooled from the walls, drifting in a breeze from the cracked windows. Leaves scattered across the furniture—wingback chairs, a sloped sofa that looked too hard to sit on comfortably, and a broken side table with the most delicate, bubbled legs I'd ever seen.

This was a hazy mirror of the living room I'd grown to know.

Every instinct in my body screamed to close the door, but my curiosity strengthened the longer I stared. My fingers inched closer to the doorframe. Just a peek wouldn't hurt anyone. Then I'd close the door and be on my way to bed.

I took two steps inside. My hand fell away as I crossed the threshold. The air hung humid; much heavier than the other side of the door I'd just come from. It stuck to my skin, strangled my lungs.

"Hello?" I called. I coughed.

The door slammed shut behind me.

I whirled.

Oh no.

The tug that brought me here snapped, replaced by an eruption of panic. I grabbed the doorknob. It was cold now, not warm like it had been a moment before. I pulled—it didn't so much as jiggle. This couldn't be happening right now.

I shoved my shoulder into the door. The hinges didn't even rattle, and no matter how hard I twisted, the lock didn't release, as if it were cemented in place.

I was locked in.

I beat against the door, frantic. "Emma! Emma, let me out! The knob won't turn!" I pressed my mouth against the door crack. Labored breaths grated my throat. "Please!"

Still, the door didn't rattle. My words bounced back against the humid air, each one falling to the floor in defeat. I strained to listen, for footsteps, for movement, but nothing came.

This side of the door wasn't polished like the other side was. It wasn't beautiful and enticing; just dull and brittle, like the floors beneath my bare feet.

Pretty on the outside, broken on the inside.

It had lured me in. And I'd taken the bait like a naive child and waltzed right through.

I needed to think—logically. I was still in the house, that much was obvious. Aunt Cadence had lived in Harthwait for years, as had other people before her. Not once had I heard her talk about someone going missing that lived there, which was a good thing. It wouldn't swallow me alive. Maybe if I waited, the door would open on its own. No need to jump off the deep end just yet.

A faint, distant trickle of laughter sent chills over my skin.

I wasn't alone in here.

"Hello?" I tried again.

No response.

I gathered myself, hands fisted in the hem of my sweatshirt, and examined the room for possible signs of life. The dust on the floor remained undisturbed of footprints, which meant the laughter had to have come from outside.

I crept closer to the closest window.

Everything was so *green*. The type of green that bloomed just after all the petals floated away in the last spring breeze. The kind of green that promised the start of early thunderstorms and newborn animals. That explained the heat, if summer was coming, but there were . . . snowflakes. Flecks of white drifted from the sky.

With a quiet exhale, I pressed my face to the warped glass. The longer I watched, I realized they weren't white at all, but gray—because they were ashes.

I blinked furiously against the sharp, cloudless, blue sky. No sun, no rain, just ashes. It was so pretty, so unnervingly unnatural, that I wanted to walk outside to get a closer look.

Immediately, the muscles in my neck tensed, the little hairs on my arms stood at attention. I'd heard laughter. I was supposed to be looking for its source.

With quiet steps, I made my way through the parlor and into the foyer, only to stop again. A chandelier lay in shattered bits at the room's center. Unlike the crystal one in the living room, this one's iron-coated handles pointed at odd angles, candlesticks split and smashed around it.

"Momma?" A voice.

I looked up from the chandelier.

There, in what should have been Aunt Cadence's office doorway, stood a boy. His hair, so blond it bordered white, stuck up and out in all directions. Dirt and grime clung to the creases of his neck. He couldn't have been more than five or six years old, his feet bare, his pants soiled.

Ice swept through my blood. His voice, his stature—it matched. *Momma.*

"It's you," I whispered. He was the one I'd heard at night. And he'd been here, in this room, this entire time?

Blood dribbled from the boy's mouth, onto his buttoned shirt. Three of those buttons were missing.

"Oh my—what happened?" I breathed. I dropped to my knees a few feet from him. If I got too close, would he run? "Where did you—y-your mouth."

The blood trickled so bright, like little rivers, down his chin. Tears threatened to spill over. He placed one hand on his flushed cheek, glancing around, ignoring me. "Momma?"

"I'm not your momma, honey," I whispered. "But I can help you find her. Is she outside?" What kind of place was this, where a child would be lost, bloodied, and alone?

Was the door covered to keep him in?

Then, a sickening thought that I hadn't considered, *Was this even real?*

"Momma?" he asked, louder this time.

I gave a soft smile in an attempt to placate. "I'm not—"

"Momma!" The word morphed into a cry. This time his chest heaved with the word, like a release, a cry building up behind those little ribs. "Momma, I want Momma, where's Momma!" he screamed.

I glanced around, searching for anything, anyone to help. "It's okay, everything is going to be—"

His chest lurched with hiccups. Then he looked *through* me, searching while tears spilled down his round cheeks and muddied the blood on his chin to a watery pink.

I scooted closer, shoving away my growing sense of helplessness. I couldn't leave him here, not like this. It made me wonder how long he'd been here, crying and waiting, alone.

He needed me.

"Hey, maybe I can go look?" I started to reach for him. The whisper of slippers stopped me. The boy's moans, which had started to build to a wail, turned into hiccups.

A young woman rushed down the hallway by the stairwell. I couldn't see the kitchen beyond, only shadowed walls that stretched for miles. A worn frock billowed around her ankles; a stained apron covered her lower half. She wrung a threadbare rag between her hands as if she'd been caught in the middle of something.

She tutted when she spotted the boy.

"Oh, Haddy," she breathed. Her skin dewed with sweat, her dark hair tucked behind her ears. She wiped her hands on the rag and stuffed it into the waist of her apron band. The ties were frayed, stained, but edged with a faded plaid pattern. The beige in the plaid matched Haddy's waistcoat, which hung crooked with one missing button at the top.

A knot formed in my throat. I knew exactly where I'd seen a waistcoat like that before: a history project Ivan had copied from me. I remembered it specifically because it was the first time he'd touched my elbow. I'd researched interior design for different eras throughout history, and that waistcoat looked almost identical to one I'd seen another child wearing in a textbook photo.

"Momma," he said. His tears were almost dried now.

I sat back on my haunches. The woman didn't appear to be his mother, but the way he gaped at her, how his arms reached up, up, the desperation in his curling fingers, sent a bolt through my chest.

I watched as she bent for the boy. She reached, just as needy as he did. As soon as her hands scooped under his arms to hoist him to her hip—her silhouette broke away. Little by little, she dissolved, like smoke dissipating in a gust of wind. She floated away like ash.

Just . . . gone.

I stared, mouth open.

The little boy's eyes widened.

Then he *wailed.*

"Momma!" he screamed. His neck turned purple, face twisted in anger. Blood teemed like an open spigot from his mouth now; the louder he screamed, the faster it poured.

I looked around, frantic, trying to ignore the itching under my skin, the realization that I'd just watched a woman vanish into thin air.

"Wait, wait. Haddy." I tried to inch forward in case he tried to bolt down the hall. "I can help you, Haddy. Just please, talk to me. Actually, I think you can help me. I need to get home, and you know this place, right?" Only a foot separated us now. If I touched him, what would happen? I couldn't vanish. *I* was real.

Still, he screamed.

"Haddy," I choked. I reached for his shoulder.

Just as my fingers brushed—actually *brushed*—the child's shirt sleeve, all sound vacuumed out of the foyer. My ears popped as if I were in a car, barreling up a mountainside, the silence beyond it humming like a rattlesnake.

Haddy yanked away in a flurry of splayed arms. He scrambled backward, toward the same room he'd come from, and vanished, as if he'd never existed. Then *something* came forward from the shadows the boy entered.

I froze.

A creature slunk into the doorway. Taloned, reedy fingers hooked into the floorboards. Filth shuffled around its claws.

I fell back with a gasp, so quickly that my hand slipped beneath me. My teeth snapped down, sending a hot wash of metal through my mouth.

"Get away from me," I blurted, eyes wide.

The thing crawled forward on all fours, a red, forked tongue flitting against the air. An unhinged, gaping set of fangs dripped spittle onto the wood floors. A couple teeth were missing in its lower jaw, the holes visible, as if the roots had been pulled, too.

Its head tilted. A growl rumbled from its throat.

"Get back," I choked. Saliva fell from the corner of my mouth.

Citrine yellow eyes tracked me. It tilted its head to the other side, muscle coiling. Its skull wasn't sunken, but it wasn't healthily fattened, either. Protruding cheekbones, browbones, and a chin poked violently against its grayed, slick flesh. Two curved horns, longer than my forearms, jutted from its head.

"You," the creature said. Its voice gravelly, otherworldly.

I clutched every pearl of self-control to keep from bolting. Predators tracked prey like this thing was tracking me. If I ran, it would likely give chase.

As if to taunt me, the same dainty laughter from before bounced distantly in the house followed by Haddy's soft cries. This thing—was it keeping this child here?

A snarl, like a crocodile's growl before it hissed, rippled from its maw. "Are you deaf?" it sneered.

"N-no."

Those slitted yellow eyes didn't blink. It slunk forward. If upright, it might have very well resembled something human-like, but the angle it crawled—

"Why are you here," it snapped.

"The door," I blurted. I pointed, as if that would help me. "The door won't open."

Those slits flitted to the parlor behind me. Its nose wrinkled. "Liar."

"I'm not," I urged. I tried to scoot back, but the fabric of my shorts picked along the floor. My elbows shook as I tried to keep myself from falling flat on my back. "I had to come, I heard him crying."

A slick, saccharine smile pulled at the creature's lips.

"You find it alluring, to save a child?" it purred. "How did you find this place, dearest?"

I swallowed. My tongue felt fat, and so, so dry. "I-It was covered. We found it renovating and—"

It feigned a lunge at my feet. "You opened it."

I scrambled upright—and the thing *chuckled*. I stepped back, chest heaving, body near a constant tremble, without letting my eyes leave the creature.

"I did," I admitted. There was no point in lying. I couldn't have gotten here if I hadn't.

Blood leeched from my face as it stopped in the middle of the foyer beside the broken chandelier. The creature's shoulders rolled as it pushed to stand. A waft of heat, of dried ash and earth—not quite metallic, but almost—followed, as if it had emerged from a cavern in search of sunlight after years of hiding.

"Something brought you," the creature grunted. "Did you feel it? Hear it? Tell me, what have you seen? *What did you do?*"

It wasn't the words that alarmed me, but the way its body moved. The angle of its head. Every inhale, its eyes dropped to my chest, then flickered to my feet, my hands. It was calculating my next move.

Without a second thought, I bolted through the parlor, the child forgotten.

I couldn't believe I'd done this—I needed to leave, right now. Fight or flight took hold of my body with the terrifying realization that a creature standing nearly seven feet tall would rip me to shreds. What if it wanted to keep me, too, like the boy? What if this was a mistake? What if Aunt Cadence had been right, and now I'd ruined it, and that door was covered for a reason—

My hair whipped like a snapping flag, my lungs heaved, and I slammed into the door in a flurry of limbs. Pounding, heavy, scraping feet gave chase.

Don't leave the boy, my conscience urged. *Would you have wanted to be forgotten so easily?*

I needed to choose me. I needed home. Right now.

I twisted the knob and yanked. I cried out in relief when it popped open. Freedom—home—right there—a familiar hallway beckoning me forward.

I stepped over.

As soon as my foot stepped over the lip of the door, a seed of guilt made me hesitate.

What did that say about me, if I left the child here?

A clawed hand grabbed my shoulder, sliced clean through my sweatshirt. I whirled, elbow first. It didn't knock away its grip, only pulled my shirt, and in a panic, I bared my teeth at the creature.

"Let go," I growled, jerking back. It's clawed hand cut farther down my sleeve and captured my wrist. I teetered—then stilled.

My lips parted. The smell of acrid burnt flesh, curdled blood, hit me next, so strong it made my eyes water. Acid rose at the back of my throat. I was going to throw up, right here, right now. The smell didn't come from the house, but the creature's chest.

The way the creature had angled its body before had covered the wound, but now everything was on full display. Its sternum was cracked down the center, ribs broken and brittle over the expanse of its heart. The organ fluttered helplessly beneath. I could have reached out and touched each ventricle, both atriums, even the cushion of its lungs. So many delicate pieces of a body, right there in the open.

"You're hurt." My voice sounded strangled.

Whatever flitted across my face set the beast's mouth into a twisted snarl. "Do not take pity on me," it growled.

My ears made a loud *pop*—I couldn't tell if the creature released me, if I tripped, or if the tug that had brought me to the door tore me back into Harthwait. One moment, the hot feel of the beast's grip was on my arm, and then it wasn't.

I landed on my side, in a heap on the floor. My ears roared for a split second before the rushing quieted, replaced with the familiar whisper of AC through the vents. The dainty laughter was gone, the smell of summer air and daylight and burnt flesh with it. An ache bloomed between my eyes.

I rolled over with a pained hiss, half expecting to find the creature in the doorway, watching me, but it wasn't. I sat upright, brow furrowed.

There was no door. No hole where Sayer had fallen and broken the sheetrock with his head. I pressed my palm against the smooth finish.

It looked just as it had this morning when I'd gotten up: an unblemished stretch of wall.

The door, and the creature, were gone.

Chapter Eight

I caught Sayer rubbing the back of his head as we worked to remove the shelf in the bathroom. If I mentioned him falling into the wall, would he remember? What if he didn't?

He hadn't mentioned it. Neither had Emma.

I chewed the inside of my cheek. "You okay?" I asked.

He sighed. "Just a headache. I'll take something for it after lunch."

My eyes darted to the crown of his head. I tracked his swallow, the way he squinted against the low light. How his jaw worked left and right.

Now was my chance. I needed to bring it up in a way that didn't sound accusatory—in case he didn't remember. But if he did, I didn't want to look stupid.

I shuffled a bit. "It looks like you have a knot on the back of your head."

He scoffed, then looked at me. "What do you mean?" His left hand searched. "I don't feel anyth—oh. I must have bumped my head."

I tried to suppress any recognition—or sudden flush of anticipation—that crept up my neck in pink splotches. If he didn't remember, why did I? The thought boxed me in, pressed close, causing a shred of worry to claw its way into my neck. "Are you all right?"

He sighed, then wiped the back of his hand over his forehead. "It doesn't help that it's hotter than the Devil's basement in this place." He wedged the flathead farther between the shelf and the wall, used both hands to push in, then angle it away. Like a lever, it separated the two. Finishing nails released, one by one.

I stole a glance over my shoulder. An inkling started in my fingers—a tingle, as if they wanted to touch the wall, to run down the section that had been missing yesterday.

"Should I go turn the AC on? Close a few of the windows?" My eyes flitted over Sayer's shoulder where he stood in the doorway. "I'm a little warm, I think." I fanned my shirt open to be rid of the imaginary sweat.

"I'll be . . . fine?" He said it like a question.

"Good, that's good." I rubbed the side of my neck, then pivoted to the steps. "I'll get you a water and Advil, just in case."

And so it went—Sayer and Emma and I chipping away at my task lists. Emma would work remotely early in the morning, log off at two, and start helping with odds and ends. Sometimes she would get coffee or lunch from town or run to the hardware store for something I'd forgotten to pick up myself.

Every night, I checked the hallway. The wall didn't change, and neither Sayer or Emma mentioned it.

One late afternoon, in a desperate attempt to feel like I hadn't imagined the whole ordeal, I snuck into the sunroom while Sayer and Emma set up our takeout in the dining area.

The air still pressed on my lungs when I stepped in. The wicker furniture sat in the same place it had for the last decade or two. Nothing had changed—not even the bench I'd dreamed about.

I took a seat, strangling the bench lip, trying to steady my breathing. My heart skittered as I lifted my attention from the floor to a potted fern across the room, then to my right—to the door I'd seen that *thing* in.

But nothing was there.

That night, at exactly 12:15 AM, the cries started again like clockwork.

They lasted for days.

Momma, no.

Momma, please don't let him.

Momma, take me with you. Please don't leave.

I tossed every night. The pleas, so similar to mine when I asked Aunt Cadence to let me stay, ripped layers from my lungs like a peeling onion, until one night I stumbled out of the bedroom, grabbed my keys, and locked myself in my car. I slept in the reclined passenger seat until sunrise kissed the trees, and got rewarded with a stiff neck.

To compound my rigidity, text messages filtered through sporadically from my mother. It only exacerbated the fact that I left that little boy on the other side of that door, alone. How many times had I cried like he had, wishing my own mother to come back in the middle of the night?

MOM: You need to send me pictures of things before you take them to donation.

MOM: Some of those items are mine.

MOM: I will drive down there and get them myself if you don't mail them.

MOM: Speaking of mailing. Why haven't the ashes shown up yet?

A poorly veiled threat.

I'd just finished removing the painter's tape from the kitchen baseboards one Thursday when my phone vibrated on the island. I didn't need to check to know it was Mom. I balled the tape up with more force than necessary, stood, ripped the retractable trash can out of its hiding place, and chucked the tape ball inside.

I could block her. Act like I broke my phone and didn't remember her number. But if I did, what would I do if she actually drove down?

At least when I'd invited her to the funeral, I hadn't expected her to actually show up. At a funeral, with witnesses, there was nothing she could ask me for.

I should have known that would change as soon as I was alone.

Ping.

I stared, blank, out the breakfast nook window. I could go outside. Take a break. Plant those seedlings before they died.

Or, I could break down the wall. See if the door was there. Prove I wasn't crazy.

Ping.

Slowly, I turned to where my phone lay face up on the island.

Eleanora Peluska blinked over the screen, the realtor. A second later, it lit up again, but with a different name. *Carla Matterson.*

I shouldn't have been surprised Eleanora was reaching back out. I'd kept my interactions at arm's length, because that uncertain part of myself couldn't fully commit to giving her the listing. Not yet. Tack on Mom's incessant calling, and my blood pressure was ready to bubble through the roof.

I couldn't do this. I turned the phone off, stalked to the garage and grabbed a pair of gloves, and headed around the back of the house toward the shed. The seedlings stood tall against the shed side, a few leaves slightly curled. They were probably rootbound at this point.

I carried them down to the edge of the lawn, where I remembered Aunt Cadence's garden used to be. I kept my head down and trudged back to the shed to dig around for a two-pronged hoe. Ten minutes later, I had a rectangular outline in the dirt, and I started to swing.

I didn't look back at Harthwait once.

* * *

My body was on fire.

I slithered from my bed late the next morning. A cold sweat clammed my skin, plastering the thin sheet beneath the quilt to my legs and arms. I never understood how that happened: I could go to sleep, semi-comfortable in a huddle of blankets after a shower, then wake up sticky as a marathon runner by daylight.

I shut my windows, one by one. I thought I'd closed them before I fell asleep to an infomercial. Eyed the dolls on the shelf by my old desk, as if they had anything to do with it.

I retrieved a (maybe) clean shirt from a pile I'd let collect in the rocking chair. Laundry was a priority like hot tea ran in my bloodstream: seldom. Then again, the thought of doing anything that didn't revolve around renovations made me nauseous. I averted my gaze; if I didn't look at it, maybe the mound would disappear.

I forewent the jeans I'd left in the hamper and opted for shorts. Instead of brushing my hair, I finger-combed it, then tied it a knot at my crown. I didn't make it far down the hall before Emma's voice echoed up the steps.

"Of course! Let me go and see if she's up yet and we can give you the full tour."

"A bit late to be sleeping in, yeah?" This voice was deeper, familiar.

I rounded the corner, met by three sets of eyes. Two I knew, one I didn't. Ringing started in my right ear.

Emma spotted me first.

"The woman I was going to get! Look who stopped by." Emma's expression brightened. I could have counted every single one of her teeth, top and bottom row, she smiled so wide.

Ivan stood in the doorway in casual clothes, Wranglers and a pair of boots. Not a lick of dirt coated the hems. A man I didn't recognize, similar in age to the three of us, with long braids that fell past his shoulders, lingered just behind Ivan.

I floated, disconnected, until I reached the first floor. I wanted to curl into myself, so small I could disappear, from the way they watched me.

"Is something wrong?" I didn't like how breathy my words sounded.

Emma leaned against the doorframe. "I asked Ivan and Trevor to come by and take a look at the house. You know, for a second opinion."

Fire ate through the pit of my stomach, working upward out of my esophagus. Why would anyone else need to look at the house? It'd been inspected—twice—which I'd made a priority. "I didn't know," I said, pointed.

"We haven't decided if we're letting Eleanora have the listing," she told both of them, as if I already knew this. "You know, it's an old house. I'm sure you guys have seen plenty of relevant comps to tell us if the suggested renos are worth the hassle."

Ivan's smile was slick when he leaned in, his shoulder pressing against the doorframe. "Of course. I'm glad I ran into you. Landry hadn't mentioned doing the renos *here*."

Emma shot me a look that said, *Why not?*

My cheeks heated with embarrassment. Of course I hadn't told him. I didn't want him to know *anything* about my work or why I was here. But Emma had opened the front door wide for them.

I took a step back, closer to the stairs. "I'm sorry—but it seems I've been left out of this conversation," I said. I didn't look at Emma. "Why exactly are you here at my house?"

If only Sayer was here today instead of taking time to be with Wade. Don't get me wrong, I was all for quality time with a significant other. But I now drifted in the middle of the Pacific with no life raft, and I needed a buoy. Sayer was that buoy. My self-control was slipping like granules through dry fingers.

"I have my real estate license," Ivan said. "Trevor's a trusted contractor."

"We've done homes up and down the coast," Trevor added. His smile remained honeyed, gentle, as if he smelled my unease. "Historic homes are a soft spot for me. We can take a look, draw up an idea of what any changes might look like, and—"

"I don't know," I cut in with a tight smile. "No offense."

"No pressure," Ivan said, hand raising like he might placate a rabid dog. "We just wanted to give you the option."

No pressure.

A gnarled, sore part of me reared.

No pressure, he'd promised, before backing me into a corner days later and whispering, *Haven't I waited long enough, Lan?*

Ivan's eyes met mine, and for a split second, I could have sworn I saw the memory there, too. Then that casual smile slipped back into place, and any indication of the frustration he might have felt toward my snippiness disappeared.

Emma gave a light clap. "How about you two go take a look around and Landry and I will talk options, yeah?" She leaned out the front door, closer to Trevor. "You can go through an inspection, too, if you'd like."

I saw red.

I watched, stiff, as Ivan and Trevor nodded, then moseyed their way through the front yard, speaking in low voices, before rounding the side of the house.

I jerked to face Emma, my hands clenched. "What was *that*?" I snapped.

"What?" Emma's expression faltered, only to turn incredulous.

"Why are they here?" I whispered. My voice shook.

"I had an appointment for today. Here. I made it with Ivan back when I ran into him."

"Well, *I* didn't make an appointment. For today. Here. When I ran into him," I echoed, stark. Suddenly, I was at the base of a waterfall, mouth opened wide, and suffocating.

Her eyebrows touched her hairline, tongue poking at her bottom lip. "You didn't have to be so crass, you know. It's an inspection, so what? Besides, the contractor is cute." She raked over my hair, then my outfit, as if it only just now hit her what I looked like. "Why didn't you fix your hair before you came down?"

My eyes widened. "Excuse me?"

"I'm trying to make a good impression?"

My arms fell to my sides. Was this really happening? I snorted. "Oh, please."

"What?" Her voice rose. "Seriously. What's wrong?"

"Did I *tell you* I needed an inspection?" I shot out. "Did you *tell me* about them coming by? Did *you think* I hadn't covered this already?"

"Well, no, but it needs to be done anyway, right? I looked it up—"

"I had two inspections done before the funeral," I snapped. I shook my head and crossed my arms over my chest like a barricade. "This is my house. I know what it needs."

"I was just trying to help!" Emma shut the front door, as if they wouldn't have heard us already. "You've been caught up in this huge to-do list of yours, tearing out stuff, and I thought we should get a move on."

I balked. "It's not your house," I said, exasperated. "I don't need you calling people in here for the fun of it when I'm trying to get things done. Have you seen that bathroom upstairs? It's a wreck. Any of the bedrooms? Not even started. The study? Don't even get me started on going through all those books. And the *attic*?" I gave a pinched, hysterical laugh. This was the last thing I needed. Another thing to stick on my plate. "I don't have time to entertain Trevor and—and—"

She blinked, flushed. "Who pissed in your cereal?"

I pressed the heel of my palm between my eyes. *You did*, I wanted to say.

"Ivan's the best around," she defended. She jerked a thumb over her shoulder. "Have you looked at the reviews online? Have you seen his portfolio? He was featured in *Lowcountry Living*, for God's sake."

"I don't give a *flying*—"

Emma's hairline turned red. "You're upset over a high school relationship that didn't work out, Landry. Get a grip," she barked back. "You can't be bitter your whole life over a guy you lost that ended up being more successful than you."

The entire room was sucked of oxygen. My teeth vibrated in my skull. Tears burned the backs of my eyes. More successful than me? Really?

Bits and pieces of that memory, the grimy feel of his hands, the pull to his mouth, ran like black-and-white film in front of my eyes.

I stalked off to the kitchen, vision splotchy. I found my purse and a discarded sweatshirt on the back of the couch and stalked right back to the front door. I flung it open. "I don't need this," I grumbled.

Emma's entire face was red. Her shoulders were nearly at her ears. "*Landry.*"

I wrangled my keys out of my bag. "I'll be back in an hour." The front door ricocheted off the wall, I'd opened it so hard.

"Stop!"

I whirled halfway down the steps. "What?"

"I just—I can pay for the inspection."

"That's not the point, Emma!" I snapped. I might have been shouting. I didn't care.

Why did she have to do this? This wasn't her house, her project, her responsibility. I hadn't asked her to come. It was one thing to visit because of a funeral, but she hadn't come to the funeral. Instead, she'd rolled up two weeks after I'd told her about Aunt Cadence's death while Sayer had been drifting around me like a hovering parent, making sure I didn't run into a lamppost while my marbles rolled away.

"Then tell me the point!" she shouted back. Her hands were splayed like she was waiting for gold to fall from the sky. "What happened? Why are you—so—snappy. I feel like I need to walk on eggshells to keep you happy, just like your mom."

The shards in my stomach crashed to the floor.

Just like Mom.

I stood there, taut with unsaid words, before I took a single, traitorous inhale. It rattled in my chest.

Then I said, "Don't sign any papers. You don't own this place."

I stalked down the driveway, the sound of Ivan and Trevor's distant voices nothing but a tangled suggestion in my wake. Emma stood on the porch, her body strung tight.

I didn't know where I was going. But anywhere was better than here.

* * *

There was a serenity that came with a hardware store's atmosphere. Professional-grade rubber, mulch and cement floors, and metal shelving all melded into a smell so distinct, so reverent, that I almost fell to my knees and wept when the double doors whooshed open.

The hardware store was a turning point—it was the bookend to a project or the start of something new.

I wandered for a few minutes through the gardening section before I beelined for the tools. My list was four items deep, but there was one thing I needed in particular.

A sledgehammer.

My eyes skipped over yellow tags and display signs. I found myself hovering over items I knew I didn't need—like a new rake—before I eased toward the far end of the aisle where the sledgehammers were. I traced a handle, debating. I could use a hammer and body weight to pull the sheetrock off and away from the hidden door. I didn't *need* this purchase.

You don't need new clothes, Landry, Mom said.

I just bought you new notebooks last year for school. Why do you need more?

The anger from earlier and the hiss of memories fueled me into a sudden haze of justification. I needed it just *because*.

Without a second thought, I grabbed the sledgehammer, then went in search for spackling.

I scanned my email—mostly caught up, save for two tentative new client requests, ushered in from my renovation website—while I stood in line. Then paused when a thought occurred to me.

I'd never looked through Ivan's social media. Maybe there was truth to Emma's words. I was a little angry he was doing well, when for years I hadn't. When I'd struggled to stand on my own two feet emotionally. To be dependent of my mother, my father. Even now . . . I didn't feel like I could.

Had Ivan been with anyone after me? Had I been the only one? Were all these feelings warranted, or was Emma right, was it simple jealousy?

My curiosity got the best of me. I typed in his name and started scrolling.

By the time a self-serve register opened, I'd found two separate accounts, all recently updated. A lot of the posts were about work, which I'd expected. A few notes on his personal life (something about golf and a trip with his family out of the country), and then further down, dating three years ago, a relationship. All his posts with her remained up. I scrolled down further, and sure enough—two pictures of us together. One at the famed football game where we'd had an argument on the tailgate, and the second two months after, his arms around me from behind while we stood outside of Dosi-Do's.

My heart bounced into my throat when I scrolled back up. To the relationship he'd had after me.

I zeroed in on her pictures, paying little attention to her handle. She was local to Charleston. I scanned her profile, noting the dates of each post. For a couple weeks, she'd posted daily. Then, during the same time frame they had been pictured together on Ivan's timeline, there were absences. A few updates here and there, otherwise—radio silence. As if she'd deleted things.

She also wasn't friends with him online. Whereas he still followed her.

Just like he followed me.

"Thank you for shopping at Welsworth Hardware," the register greeted me.

My thoughts whirled as I scanned my items and stuffed what I could into the bag.

I carried my finds out to my car in a daze.

I could message her. Just to see. But what if I was wrong? She might think I was creepy for even reaching out.

A sinking feeling enveloped me as I crawled into the driver's seat. I didn't even start the car, just cooked against the upholstery while staring at the steering wheel.

By messaging her, I would be putting myself out there. Unless I made a burner account.

But I needed to know—had it been *just* me? Was I really chalking everything that had happened up to nothing? Who was I really angry at? Was I mad at Ivan for what he'd done, for how he'd treated me, or was I mad at myself?

I knew Ivan hadn't loved me. I knew what I'd felt hadn't been love, either, but a desperation for something he couldn't give me. And all he'd offered me in return was abuse.

That was what it was: abuse. Because if it wasn't—all these years, wouldn't I have healed a bit by now? Wouldn't I have been able to reconcile with my choices instead of harboring this hatred for what had happened?

No, I couldn't do it. If I messaged her, too many things could go wrong. What if she told him about me? What if I only ended up embarrassing myself and their relationship had simply ended, not festered like ours had?

I buckled my seatbelt with one broken realization. I was alone in this.

I was the tree that got felled by an ax. The ax might not remember the tree it cut down, but the tree did. And like that haggard stump, I would just keep bleeding from the same place, if only a trickle.

Chapter Nine

Curtains hung open despite the night encroaching up the back lawn. The lower the sun dipped, the sharper Sayer and I's reflections became in the dining room windows. Shadows from the trees reached over the grass, closer and closer to the light pooling from Harthwait's lit windows.

Mom never let me open the curtains as a child. "You never know who's watching," she'd said.

There was something exciting, almost tantalizing, about doing something she'd told me not to do, even over a decade later.

". . . didn't know what she was thinking with that dress, but—" Sayer leaned back and eyed my food. "You good?"

I broke from my daze with a startle, fork hovering halfway to my mouth. I nodded. "Yeah, just a long day."

He cleared his throat. Lowered his voice. "You know what I mean."

And I did.

I ignored the way his eyes danced from my fork to my untouched chicken salad. I took a sip of my water, set my fork down, and wiped my mouth.

"I'm serious," he said, gentle.

Sayer knew. He'd always known. But still, there lay a painful exposure in the smallest of confessions like this. Especially when it was easier to push them under a rug and act like they weren't crawling back every few seconds.

If I didn't answer, he would wait.

"It's been worse," I offered. An olive branch—a smidge of acknowledgment without blowing anything out of the water. When Sayer didn't say anything, I blurted, "I think I'm going to take out that wall upstairs. See if there's anything behind it."

He half choked on his water and his eyebrows inched to his hairline. "Which wall?" Aversion successful.

"The one down the hall from my bedroom. I think I could move it back a bit. Maybe build an open closet or shelf space."

"Remove it, like, a load bearing kind of thing?"

I sat forward with a smile. "Nope."

"And you know this how?"

"I, my dear friend, just have a suspicion." On a normal job, I wouldn't dare touch something that required a permit. But I wasn't technically removing it. Just uncovering.

Sayer wiped a speckle of dipping sauce from the table. "I'll take your word for it. Need me to help? Like, tonight?"

I started to gather our paper plates, then squished them into the to-go bag that still sat tall in the center of the table. "I should be fine, but I might change my mind. Haven't decided yet. Don't know if you've earned a gold star yet." Sayer had made a competition in grade school about who could collect the most gold stars in a school year. The ambition wasn't yet lost to him when it became a running joke.

He clutched his chest. "So demanding." He took another swig from his bottle. "Where's Emma?"

"No clue. Out, I think." The forced indifference in my words leaned more chilled.

"For the night?"

I shrugged. "Maybe." She'd texted me one word, "out." My only response had been a thumbs-up.

Sayer nodded and stood from the table. "And you two didn't fight about Ivan magically showing up today?"

"She told you?" I cradled the takeout bag.

"Didn't have to. I read minds, remember?"

"Maybe you earned your gold star after all."

We moved to the kitchen, but I felt his gaze following me, waiting for elaboration. So I gave him the CliffsNotes version, where I admitted I may have flown off the handle, and that was why Emma had vanished for the night.

Which left me alone for a few more hours. Likely until late in the night.

"I can see why you'd be upset." He leaned on the island. "But I think jumping down her throat might not have been the best approach."

I bristled. "I know. I said that. But I just—don't like her acting like it's her house. It's mine. I make the decisions. Aunt Cadence left it to me." *It's all I've got right now*, my heart whispered.

"So . . ." his tone shifted, tentative, like I might bite. "Ivan Kenneth. Taking *this* listing. The same guy who said you'd only dated him for clout and you were a stage-five clinger after you broke up? Really?" Sayer reared back like he smelled something putrid. His glasses flashed with reflected light. "Everyone's gonna just"—he swiped a hand over his head—"act like that never happened?"

I chewed the inside of my cheek, leaned against the counter, and crossed my arms over my chest. Tightened my sweatshirt against me.

"He's the best realtor in town," I whispered. "Emma said they have great reviews. What am I supposed to do? Turn him away because of something that happened eight years ago and make Emma look bad for even bringing them here? Or, even better, give the listing to Eleanora?" I covered my face with my hands. "If she takes it, I'm going to *have* to hire a contractor. The load-bearing wall will have to go, not to mention there's an outlet there, so I'd have to get an electrician, too."

He took a measured inhale. "Lan, you can tell her you won't do the changes."

"And I can guarantee you, she wouldn't take it. Then I'd have to find a new realtor anyway. Did you look at the houses she'd sold? They'd all been gutted on the inside and updated. Antiquely modern, and I just . . ." My hands slid down my face until I cupped my neck. The visions of this house, stripped of all the character, its originality, and replaced with a grayed color scheme and open floor plan, no door arches, refinished floors, made my stomach sink. Maybe it was my own inhibitions that made it even harder to accept, because if I changed this house completely, that meant the last shreds of Aunt Denny would be gone, too. "Not to mention the money it would take to do it."

Sayer shivered. "I guess you're right."

"I wish I wasn't."

He sighed. "But—does Emma know about what he said?"

"Everyone knows, Sayer. Everyone knows he said I was trying to sleep with him because Mom needed a job at his parents' firm." Among other things that I refused to revisit. "And you wanna know what I've been told by everyone when I've brought it up? That we were 'emotional young people who let emotions run too high.' That I was probably on my period and made some pass at him and got my feelings hurt, or hoped that by letting him use my homework that he'd stick around a bit longer. So yeah, people think I was a clinger. Despite the pictures of us, they still don't think we dated."

"But you weren't a clinger," he urged. He rubbed both palms against his temples. "*He* wasn't nice."

I straightened. "He was plenty nice." All I could picture was Emma's exasperation earlier, the way she stared at me as if I were delusional.

"Don't defend him." Sayer stiffened with a glare.

"I'm not." I don't know what made me say it. But sometimes, when Sayer attacked Ivan, if felt like an attack on me. Because I'd picked him willingly, I'd pined, I'd rolled over like a dog, and by saying Ivan was a bad person, Sayer was inadvertently telling me I had poor judgment. It only emphasized the quiet, underhanded comments Ivan had whispered while I still foolishly defended him to Sayer.

Why'd you look at him? You expect him to come over and talk to you?

Come on, Lan. Just once. No one has to know.

Are you being serious right now? How do you think that makes me feel? How am I supposed to love you when you won't listen to my *needs?*

I shook them away. "I just want the house to sell, okay? Maybe Em's right. Maybe he's the best one for it."

"What do you want, Lan?" he pressed. "*You*. Not Em. You."

"To get this over with so I can drive two states away and everyone gets to leave me alone again," I groused. And that was the most honest thing I'd said in weeks.

* * *

Sweat slicked my back, sticking my tank top to my skin like window tint. The house practically exhaled every time I inhaled, smothering me in humidity and grime.

Three swings and the sledgehammer broke through the wall. I probably could have gotten away with a regular hammer, but it would have taken too long.

Particles of sheetrock and chipped paint littered the tarp I'd placed over the floor. The TV murmured from my bedroom, a new requirement because I refused to have nothing but silence and risk hearing something I didn't want to hear. The TV, at the very least, acted as a stand-in during Emma's absence.

I coughed and fanned the floating debris with my hand. Stepped closer, sledgehammer still in hand, I bent to get a better look through the hole I'd made.

There it was.

I straightened, took a breath, and swung. With a grunt, I heaved the sledgehammer upright and brought it down on the bottom section of drywall. Bits connected to the doorframe splintered away with the sheetrock—enough for me to grab and pull open.

I propped the sledgehammer against the wall, weighted end down. My hands moved with urgency, pulling and yanking and snapping as I tore away piece after piece of wall and piled them to the side. The longer it took for me to pull parts away, the sloppier my hands felt.

I'd really left that little boy behind.

The weight of it festered anger, not for the boy, but myself. Why hadn't I tried to usher him out?

And maybe, just maybe, it was the conversation with Sayer today that spurred the urgency. What if I went back in and I couldn't find him?

"Come—*on*," I grunted.

Once I removed the majority of the sheetrock, I wedged the heel of my shoe against the base of the doorframe. If I could get all this out of the way, I'd have a bigger opening in case that creature came after me again. The last thing I needed was a child in tow and the both of us getting tripped by something I could have cleared out.

Grip tight, but not tight enough to entice splinters, I leaned back with all my weight—and the splintered frame snapped free, taking another chunk of drywall with it. I coughed away floating debris and examined the piece—indents, like wood burn marks, ran along the wood. Maybe I needed to have the house tested for termites, just in case.

Gooseflesh pimpled my skin. A tangy excitement, anticipation, started to seep through my body. And maybe, just maybe, if I found the boy and brought him out, the crying would stop at night.

I ran my thumb over the divots in the polished door. For my sanity and the child's safety, I needed to get him out of there.

And if things went south—I didn't know what I would do. Maybe it was the fact that the creature hadn't followed me through the door last time that hardened my resolve. If I made it to the door, we could make it through, but not the creature.

I pulled my phone from my pocket, just to check. No notifications, no missed calls. If Emma did decide to come back for the night,

I didn't expect it to be before midnight. It was still early—only ten o'clock. I had time.

My eyes drifted back to the sledgehammer. Then the door. Then back to the sledgehammer.

I grabbed the handle. At least I had this. A weapon was better than no weapon. Sledgehammer in hand, I made to open the door.

At first, the door hitched, like it was stuck, so I used my body weight to pull. The latch popped open an inch.

My breathing trembled, adrenaline already coursing through my extremities.

The icy air hit me first. Like an exhale against my cheeks, it pushed my hair away from my face, making me squint. My hands tightened around the sledgehammer. Slowly, I opened my eyes, part of me expecting the creature to be sitting by the door where I'd left him nearly two weeks ago. I paused, my pulse throbbing hot in my jaw.

Harthwait had changed.

The framework of the house stood tall, crooked in the majority of places. Holes in the brick wall gave glimpses to a withered lawn, windowsills gaped empty, vacant of their glass panes, and the ceiling—didn't exist. Nothing but charred framework dangled above me. It looked like the house had caught fire and only the resilient bits remained.

Plink, plink, plink.

I craned my neck back. Thunderheads crowded the sun. Raindrops careened from above, peppered the open floors, my face, the tattered and eaten gauzy curtains. A single wingback chair sat in the corner, completely untouched, even of dust.

I held my breath when movement caught my peripheral. The door drifted shut with the quietest of clicks.

Now I was alone. I was doing this. No turning back now.

I held the sledgehammer like a sword as I stepped through the parlor. Strained to listen. No child's cries, no hurried footsteps. No claws on the floor.

I ventured into the foyer—and almost dropped the sledgehammer. Not just the parlor had changed—everything had. Like the house switched shirts while I was gone. The first time, it looked abandoned, untouched for years. But the ash made sense now: Instead of drifting from the sky, the house was eaten by it. Somewhere along the way, the exposure to rain had soddened the boards, the floors, what little remained of the roof.

Outside, where there had been a perfectly manicured lawn, a maze of shrubbery now grew. From the house, winding pathways snaked from one end of the patch to the next. It extended farther than the eye could see, so far that it touched the horizon.

Dread crawled into my mouth, my nose, my eyes. A maze made good hiding for a boy of Haddy's size.

This house—was it sentient? Did it pick and choose the people it let in? Was that why only I remembered the door? And why did it change inside? If I went back into the hall and stepped back in, would it show me something else again?

I stepped up to the front door. The door itself was gone, leaving only hinges.

"Haddy?" I called.

My voice echoed, echoed, echoed until it faded into nothing. Overhead, thunder rumbled.

Faint, so quick I almost missed it, the bramble in the maze rustled. Was that Haddy?

I glanced over my shoulder, left then right, just in case. No creature. It might have been the beast in the maze, not the boy. But did I want to take the chance?

"Haddy?" I called again, this time louder, more from the chest. Angry clouds shifted above me. I nearly turned back to search the rest of the house when I heard the voice.

"Landry!"

That wasn't Haddy.

It sounded like Emma.

I hissed to myself. The innards of the maze rustled, frantic, like someone searching for a way out. How had Emma found her way in here? How'd she seen the door? Had she come home and I hadn't noticed, or had she found it after me?

Was it really her, or did I want to take the chance that it wasn't?

"Emma?" I called. I scrambled off the porch steps, almost rolling my ankle at the bottom. I tried to keep the sledgehammer readied, secretly damning myself for bringing it along.

I ran left, right, winding through the maze of bushes, taking turns blindly. I held my breath every few seconds, listening over the sound of my heart. "Emma!"

"Landry!"

I followed it like a kite tethered to a child's fist.

Minutes felt like hours. Rain threatened, only to back off and sprinkle again.

I stopped, winded, sweat trickling down my arms, my middle back. By that point, the rain decided to come down in hard sheets, dripping into my eyes and down my throat. The cloud cover made it difficult to see, so I used the sledgehammer to swing down brush.

"Emma!"

"Landry?" Closer.

I rounded a corner, sledgehammer dragging, and froze.

In the middle of the path, in a pool of black rainwater, sat a little girl. Tangled, knotted red hair in a fuzzy ponytail. She wore a yellow sundress with white daisies, stained with mud and rusted red splotches. Her face too thin, her chin too sharp.

Six-year-old me.

"Landry?" she asked. Her voice changed, matured. I gasped, stumbled back, as she morphed in age. Older, older, thinner, thinner, until she stood at my height, with my same build, wearing my very clothes. They hung on her, and her eyes—they were almost sunken.

It was one thing to look in a mirror because mirrors lied. They warped things I didn't *really* see, parts of myself that I didn't like, emphasized areas that made me nauseated. But seeing myself within reaching distance was different.

I swallowed, hard. I strangled the sledgehammer, unsure if I should wield it or drop it.

"You found me," she whispered. "How did you find me?"

If I ran, would she catch me?

"I-I—" My brain short circuited.

"You let him hurt me," she wheezed, teeth bared. Dirt coated her neckline, the dangling bits of fabric around her shoulders. *My* shoulders. Her knees bled with hairpin scrapes. Bruises, all over her chest, glowered through the shredded material. I looked college age, nineteen, twenty? Years ago. I sounded like me, moved like me, but I didn't realize I'd looked so . . . tired.

I knew without asking who she was talking about.

Ivan.

Still, I tried to keep my expression dumbfounded, and took another step back. A sick, roiling sensation started in my gut. Like a wave, it traveled up, up. "Who?"

"I hate you," she whispered. She trudged closer, only feet from me now, and gestured to herself. "Look what you did to me." Even her nails bled, ripped from the quick. "*You* did this."

I shook my head, eyes wide. "No, I didn't."

Her expression turned rabid. "*You did!*"

A surge of anger hit me. "I didn't do anything to you!" I shouted back. Brambles and thorns poked at my back when I hit the maze wall. My feet were leaden, eyes locked on her.

"Yes, you did. You liar. All you do is lie."

"I never lied about what he did," I spat. Because I didn't. Not really.

"You never told anyone!" she roared, spittle flying.

Then she lunged for me. I dropped the sledgehammer out of instinct to catch her hands—I grabbed one wrist, but she grabbed my other—the two of us, a mirror, struggling against the other's hold. One pushed, the other gave, only to shuffle. Her nose came a breath from my own. Her voice warbled, broken. "You hurt me. Why did you hurt me?"

Tears welled behind my eyes. I shook my head. "I didn't mean to."

"Momma?"

Both of us looked to the voice.

Haddy streaked through the bramble path, only to vanish a moment later. Fast enough for me to see his tiny untucked button-up shirt and his bare feet, but nothing more.

Without warning, my doppelgänger's hold vanished. Just like the woman had when Haddy had touched her. Nothing but a cold kiss of air was left in her wake.

It took two seconds to gather myself, one gasping breath after another, the breaths so large that they hurt to swallow.

"Haddy!" I coughed. Rain bled into my eyes, down my cheeks, dribbled off my chin. But Haddy didn't turn around and come back—and by the time I realized all sounds had ceased, it was too late. From the corner of my eye, something moved.

Shivering, I slowly looked to the movement. And there, through the bramble thicket, a face hovered.

A beautiful face.

Like cornered prey, I froze. Even the earth stopped turning.

"It hurts to see it, does it not?" the voice said. Not just a voice, but a man. He stepped from the thorns, slightly curled over, as if he'd been hunching. Listening. Waiting.

Gray eyes, sharp as steel. White-blond hair disheveled, short at the sides. He was sodden from the pouring rain, all the way from his unbuttoned cotton shirt to beige trousers. He wore no shoes. A beautiful grin stretched over his pink lips—before turning feline.

"Hurts, does it not, dearest? To see your sorest memories come to life?" he hummed.

Dearest. That word.

And what did he mean by memories? This was nothing close to a memory. Not once had I gotten lost in a maze as a child.

"I believe you have the wrong place, though." The man's jaw flexed, tightened. It was almost as sharp as his eyes. He eased closer, careful not to touch the thorns. He didn't so much as look in the direction Haddy had gone or where my double had just evaporated.

"Who are you?" I scooted to my left, back the way I'd come. I ground my teeth to keep them from chattering.

"You need not know who I am," he said. "Not until you tell me who you are."

I tried to gather myself. "I was only here for the boy. He's stuck here."

His eyes narrowed, uncertain. Maybe he didn't understand. Or maybe I'd chosen the wrong person to ask.

I tried again. "Maybe five or six, with blond hair and . . ."

His hands were stuffed casually in his pockets, but the tilt of his head told me differently. He was calculating. His eyes caught mine, stealing every ounce of oxygen from my body.

His pupils were slits. And though a moment ago they were gray, now they shifted—like an animal in the middle of a forest. Yellow, like a snake's.

Yellow, like citrine.

This time when he smiled, it was cruel and alluring all at once. I wanted to run, but my legs didn't obey, my feet didn't pull from the earth.

His voice slithered into a deep timbre—the *creature's* voice.

"You came back," he crooned. A rumble, like a growl, vibrated from his throat.

I struggled to step back. "I came for the boy," I choked. I blinked away a sudden wash of fear, of angry, terrified tears. What had I done?

As if he heard my thoughts, he chuckled. Squared his shoulders with intention.

"Oh, dearest," he breathed. "You shouldn't have."

Chapter Ten

"You," I breathed. The word slammed down like a gavel between us. "You're . . . it."

"Ah, yes. Me. Much easier on the eyes when the horns have not grown in for the night, yes?" He removed one hand from his pocket and rubbed the length of his jaw with his thumb. As if this were a common conversation.

"The boy," I said as I tried to control my breathing. "I'm here to help him. That's all. I don't need you to—to—" To what? Chase me? Corner me? Keep the boy from me? How was I supposed to reason with this—*this*—

"Ah, sympathies. I'm afraid you could not remove the child, even if you tried."

A hysterical sound, mixed between a laugh and a bray, bubbled from my lips. "No, no, no. He's coming with me. I touched his sleeve—he was crying and—a-and—"

His head tilted again. Waiting. Listening.

Stark embarrassment ate my skin alive. "You're holding him here, aren't you?" I took another step back. The man followed. One for one, until the edge of the bramble wall stuck the backs of my arms. I jerked away, dots of blood already welling.

"I do not hold the child here," he said.

"Prove it," I blurted. I retreated sideways and he continued lazily after me. "How long have you had him here? What kind of—monster—"

"Fitting," he cut in.

"Do you have to be, to keep a child? Is he here for some sick—obsession?" Fury twisted my face, the thought springing forward so violently that I had the all-consuming urge to swing my sledgehammer at him. If he was keeping this child here for something like *that*—

His words went razor thin. "I *do not keep the boy*. If you suggest something of such a nature again, I'm afraid we will have much more interesting things to discuss than *intention*, don't you think?"

The threat rang clear.

I should have bolted already. I should have been fighting my way back to Harthwait, back to the door; instead, I stole every feather of courage and squared my body to his.

"I don't stand for child abuse," I growled, pushing as much hate into the words as possible.

"And neither do I," he said, so quiet, so calm, a shiver bolted down my spine. If he lunged in that moment, I wouldn't have had time to flinch.

My knees wobbled. If I ran, I might make it. I'd made it once before.

He strode closer, almost to arm's length. "The child is not real. Just as much of this place as a figment, so to speak." The profile of his nose was strong, his mouth full, his chin harsh. "I find it awfully bold of you to sweep back here, unannounced, after I welcomed you so warmly upon your last visit."

"You almost killed me." The clouds rumbled overhead; a fine mist of rain began again, tickling my lashes.

"Kill you, was it?" His eyebrows lowered. "Hm. I am intrigued to hear your definition of attempted murder. I seem to remember grabbing your shoulder, but you were pulled through the door anyway."

I shifted my body so I continued to face him, but kept the house in sight. Harthwait lurked just above the bramble thorns.

"Why are you here?" If I could stall—or distract—I might be able to make a break for it.

"I could ask you the same."

"I told you the first time."

His nostrils flared, eyes narrowed. "And you never answered my question."

Not a simple statement, but a threat.

"How long? Since I moved in?" Somehow, he knew my name—there was no telling what else he knew or why. "Longer?" *Did you know my aunt?*

He sniffed. "A while."

"That's not an answer. You want me to believe you about the boy? Tell me. How long have you been here."

"You failed to answer *my* question the first time, I recall. Tit for tat."

Something told me if I wasn't careful, this man would walk me like a dog.

And he was right, no matter how much I didn't want to admit it: *This* area was his. Not mine. He wasn't denying that he'd been here a while. He probably knew it like the back of his hand, whereas I was (clearly) unable to beat my way out of a wet briar patch. So I tried another angle.

"If the boy doesn't really exist, how do I know that you do?" I spoke through my teeth, struggling to keep the sledgehammer slightly at the ready.

A grin was his response. "You are nervous."

"Answer one question, and I'll answer one of yours."

He huffed. "If I weren't real, I would not be speaking with you. Go on. Use your little weapon. Hit me." When I made no move, he slunk forward. Even his shoulders rolled when he walked. "But yes . . . Landry. I am real."

I shook my head. "Stay where you're at."

He stopped. Then his demeanor shifted, just a bit. He cocked his head as the creature had, eyes assessing, narrowing, like his patience might be withering. "And if I do, you will answer my question. Honestly."

I nodded. For a moment, we looked at one another.

"What do you want with the boy?" The question was no more than a whisper. Almost pained.

I struggled for words. Instead of throwing a front, I showed my cards. "I felt bad for him. I wanted to put him to rest, somehow, and thought maybe if I brought him out of the room that maybe . . ." I cleared my throat and blinked. "He cries, every night, down to the minute. I want it to stop."

He nodded. Hummed a bit, but his jaw remained tight.

"Why can the boy not leave?" I asked.

Not even a hesitation. "He is tied here. He is not real." Before I had a chance to process that information, he asked, "Pray tell, how did *you* get in here?"

The grass had wilted while we were in the maze—as if it hadn't rained for months. I didn't realize how close we'd managed to inch toward the front of the maze, or how I'd been able to navigate while walking backward. But the way he walked, one step at a time, reminded me of a dog herding cattle. Like he was guiding, and I was blindly following.

"I . . . am not sure," I said, candid. "A friend accidently knocked a hole in the wall and we found a door. I felt a tug to it. But then it vanished that night, and I was curious, so I took the wall down. Then I found Haddy. And you." The sledgehammer drooped an inch. My hands ached from holding it up for so long.

"Interesting."

A thought occurred to me. "When I disappeared through the door, what did you see on the other side? When you said it sucked me back in?"

"I saw nothing but blackness." He tucked his chin and looked up from beneath his lashes.

A shiver skittered down my spine. So he hadn't seen Harthwait on the other side. "Why?"

"If I knew, I would not be asking you," he said, lip curled. "I do not have access—"

In the distance, a gong sounded. No, not a gong—but an echo of a clock striking midnight.

Everything went still. The birds in the far trees quieted. Even the clouds hesitated.

"What was that?" I perked, scanning the yard. It rang again. So muffled, I wouldn't have heard it if I didn't pay attention. It reminded me of the grandfather clock in the foyer. "I thought I heard—"

A crack split the air to my right. At the edge of my vision, I saw the man's head snap to the side—like someone took his skull between their hands and broke his neck. I choked on a strangled shriek. Blood should have trickled from his nostrils, but he only blinked back at me.

I whispered under my breath—a prayer, a plea, something—and dropped the sledgehammer. His skin grew gray, from the broken area of his neck outward. His shoulders snapped and rolled, reformed, his legs cracked then—spiderwebs of black veins grew from the base of his jaw. His body reforming, healing, his skin turning gray, his stature expanding.

I covered my scream. Everything blurred, tinged black. The man—the creature's—jaw unhinged. He tried to speak.

"Show me the—" But he didn't finish.

From the house, a strangled cry. A child's cry. I didn't need a clock to know it was a quarter after midnight.

He bent over; the bones in his shoulders rippled.

The man or the boy? Which did I choose? I pictured myself making it to the child, trying to wrangle him into the house before the crying started and not being able to get him over the threshold. The boy kicking and wailing, blood pouring out of his mouth, and me, clueless about what to do next.

And then I would be leaving this man behind, with a broken neck. Was he right? Would it not work?

What did he know that I didn't? This was his place. And if anyone knew what might be going on, it would be him.

The crying turned to screaming.

Panicked—I chose the boy.

"No!" he choked. A garbled moan chased me, but he didn't stand. Didn't give chase.

"No, no, no," I muttered. I raced up the front steps. Gnarled ripping sounds came behind me.

I careened into the foyer. Haddy's cries were quieter, but somehow near at the same time. The grandfather clock echoed a final ring, and I started up the stairs out of instinct. The railing groaned at my ascent. I had just passed halfway to the second floor when the front door burst open.

"Leave him!" the creature roared.

"Papa, hurts," the boy cried. Yes—he was upstairs. Papa, not Momma this time.

I couldn't move fast enough. If it wasn't the creature that was hurting the child, who was?

I reached the attic door as soon as Haddy's words turned to a low groan. The latch to the attic room was open, giving an inch of light.

I shoved the door. It swung wide.

"Sit still, brat," a gritty voice said.

A man stood over Haddy, who crouched in the far corner beneath a window, his knees to his chest. Shelves lined the walls, drooped from double-stacked tattered leather books and trinkets. A globe lay on its side, forgotten, in the farthest corner of the room. A desk sat centered on the wall to my right, crowded by three chairs.

The skin of Haddy's bare back tinged pink and red in streaks, but no blood trickled from the marks. He looked older than he had when he'd run through the maze; his face less rounded, his neck a bit thinner, his hair combed into submission.

The man above Haddy had long, white hair swept into a low ponytail. I knew without a doubt that this was Haddy's father. Still, he looked familiar—similar to the man from the maze, the creature. Whereas the creature had looked to be in his midthirties, this man was a bit older. Deeper caverns to his cheeks and creases around his eyes, but he held himself the same. Even his sleeves were rolled up, as if in annoyance, like the other man's had been.

My trance broke when a riding crop swung high. Heading straight for Haddy's bare back.

A strangled noise emitted from my throat. "Stop it!" I exclaimed, but no one turned.

I lurched forward. I needed to tackle him or—but a clawed hand yanked at the back of my shirt.

"Enough," the beast bit.

I shoved against his grisly arm. "But he's—let me go—"

"You can't stop it," the monster hissed. He bent at an odd angle as to not hit his horns on the ceiling as he struggled to hold me.

The first *crack* made me recoil. I stopped fighting. I covered my ears and turned away like a coward when the cries started. I ground my teeth, forbidding the sounds from burrowing into my chest and rooting there.

Had I sounded similar, begging my mother to listen? Asking Dad to stay?

I shook my head. I didn't. I couldn't.

Another whack.

I stared at the wall, at a knot in the wood. An arm, then a shoulder, shifting in front of me, blocking the doorway. Still, it didn't muffle everything, didn't remove what was happening in the other room.

A hand circled my wrist, light as a feather. I started to move away, but the monster's grip flinched, drawing my attention up. His features twisted, lips peeled back in a noiseless snarl. His shoulders bunched closer to his pointed ears, almost as if this—pained him. He stared at a point over my shoulder in the opposite direction.

I read his lips when he said, "It will end."

A delicate part of my heart cracked right then.

I watched him, entranced, as a veil slipped over his face. The points of his cheeks tightened, his yellow, slitted eyes hardened and turned vacant. Like he existed but chose not to acknowledge it.

I'd seen that look before. Well, not so much as seen it, but felt it.

"Mommy, can you stay? Please?" But it hadn't been Haddy asking, it had been me.

"Let go, Landry. Stop touching me." Momma jerked her sleeve away and motioned to the kitchen. "You got food. I'll be back after a while."

I wanted to ask. The words crouched, right there on the tip of my tongue, but I couldn't do it.

We sat there, the monster and I, my body just as taut as the dig of his clawed feet into the wooden floor. Not soon enough, the rhythm of leather on soft skin fell away. It wasn't until I felt the vibration of footsteps over the floors that I looked back to the room.

"Maybe that will show you," the father said, low.

Wet, pliable, the sound of a hammering heart next to my ear.

Thump-thump, thump-thump. The monster's heart, nearly careening out of his chest.

The beast's body stiffened as the older man started toward the doorway. I attempted to step aside, but he held me fast. Just as Momma had when she'd touched Haddy, the father vaporized in the doorway the moment he brushed against my shoulder. The mist lingered for only a moment, a chill with it. Haddy still sat in the corner, hunched over his knees, facing the circular window. Silent hiccups shook his shoulders.

I tried to pull away.

The monster held tight. "Leave the child."

My hair fell in my face when I turned to glare. Creases marred the space between his brows. His attention flitted from my mouth to my throat, then back.

"He needs help," I said with another tug. I glanced to his opened chest. A single drip of black ran the expanse of his torso, thick as molasses.

"How many times do I need to tell you that the child does not really exist? "

"I touched him last time." I had to try—I had to see it for myself. He could be lying—

He merely growled at me. "Trust that I know more of this than you. He is a memory. He will not be the same tonight, tomorrow, or the day after. He will change, he will not remember you, and he will not be solid—you saw your own self and you do not believe me? You watched yourself disappear before your own eyes, and you lean into ignorance? For *what*?" Our faces only inches apart, so close that the waft of his breath made me recoil.

The gears in my mind began churning. He was right—whatever happened in the maze, he was more experienced in. If I touched Haddy or even lured him out . . . what if it only made his existence worse? What if he'd only end up back here, stuck?

What if he really was a memory? I'd heard of spiritual echoes before. Their energy stayed after a traumatic event, and it took more than breaking the cycle for them to be put to rest.

But this—he wasn't a spirit, was he? This creature—this man—called him a memory, like what I'd seen of myself.

"And if I leave without him . . . what will happen to him?" The thought was nauseating. I wouldn't want to be left to relive an abusive father for years on end.

What I didn't like to consider was that Aunt Cadence might have known about the boy and done nothing to help him.

"Why the desperation to help someone that cannot be helped?" he whispered. He released my wrist.

"He's a child." *He's like me.*

"That child is dead."

I shook my head. "Then I need to find a way to let his spirit pass."

A bitter laugh. Something passed over the creature's expression. I couldn't pin it—a mix of frustration and pity, maybe. "A memory cannot be released by someone who does not hold it, dearest."

I searched his eyes. He stepped back, the shadow of his body arching menacingly over the wall, the ceiling. The distance between us felt cavernous.

"You know things about this place," I said, flat. "About him."

His lip pulled back, his words thick with sarcasm. "Observant, are we?"

"I mean—how long have you been here?"

His shoulder brushed the wall as he turned. Coils of lean muscle ran down his spine, the back of his neck, gnarled like the roots of an ancient tree. "Decades."

How could this man listen to this child for so long and not want to stop the cycle? How could—

A memory.

He is a memory. You saw yourself, and you do not believe me?

Like an echo chamber for memories—or people.

Wayward puzzle pieces clicked together, one by one. The hair coloring. The sloped shape of the creature's shoulders like Haddy's father. How he spoke about the boy. How I'd seen myself, younger, real but not real.

I stared at the monster, mouth slightly agape. How had I missed it?

Over the creature's shoulder, Haddy continued to rock in place on the floor. His bare toes splayed to keep himself steady, oblivious to our conversation. As if he *existed* in the same space, but not at the same time or on the same plane, not truly. Just as my memory had.

I thought back to the dreams I'd had. How eerie the memories had manifested, realistic but not quite right.

I looked to the monster. The man.

"You're Haddy," I breathed. I thought of every night I'd heard the boy crying. Like it was on loop. Was it because he was stuck here?

Or was he trapped on purpose?

My skin grew clammy.

He paused in the middle of the landing before dropping into a crouch, like a gargoyle guarding a home. The wound in his chest—what if it was on loop, too, unable to heal?

"*Hadrian* Belfaunte," he corrected. "No one calls me Haddy anymore."

Chapter Eleven

Hadrian.

Haddy.

My mind reeled. As soon as I touched the child's sleeve when I'd first found the door, the monster had come forward. He'd protected the child, stepping between him and myself.

I struggled for words, swimming in something far heavier than surprise. Guilt? Sorrow? Pity? For myself, or for Hadrian?

No: kinship. Ever so small, no larger than a flutter against the back of my ribcage. I knew nothing of his story, how he came to live in this place, who he was. But I'd seen the rawest part of his life—as he'd said, a memory—just as he'd seen part of mine.

I pressed my finger to my temple, blinking against the onslaught of thoughts. If he was here, just like I was, did that mean he'd existed somewhere else before? Did that make him a real person? What if Aunt Cadence *had* known about him? What did that make her?

Hadrian's lips twitched, as if he could sense the shift in tides. "Ah, ah, none of that, now."

"He—that man—was your father?" I was still reeling.

"No father to me," he snipped. His teeth glinted in the low light. My instincts urged me to step back. "Now, if you don't mind, I have matters to attend to that require little company."

I watched him, paying attention to the tension in his shoulders, the slight curl to his clawed fingers into the floorboards. He slunk to the steps like a cat hunting a canary.

What was so important for him to do in the house alone? Either he was lying about needing to be alone, or he was lying to get rid of me. My money was on the latter.

My hands wrung. "Wait. Don't go yet. I just—I'm—Are you trapped here?"

A chuff, but he did pause. "No business of yours. I'm afraid you are only a waste of my time, dearest."

"My name is Landry, not dearest." I chewed the inside of my cheek. Then, under my breath, added, "But you seem to know that already."

He tapped a claw to his chin. "Ah, yes. *Landry*," he murmured. He started down the steps without a backward glance. "Names grow more and more adventurous these days. I heard that one through the walls and thought I'd lost my hearing for a moment."

I couldn't tell if that was a compliment or a snide remark. I started after him.

"And *Hadrian* isn't?" I fired back, just as spicy. What he'd said finally sunk in. "Are you saying you can hear everything that goes on in the house, outside of here?"

I could only imagine how we would look to a bystander: me, a woman, trailing after a demon-like beast as he crawled down the steps on all fours. Still, all I could picture was human Hadrian hovering over me, with a throat that swallowed and heart covered by skin and bone.

A man, not a beast. Only a beast when his inner child began to cry, on the hour, every night.

"Sometimes the house is kind to me," was all Hadrian said.

My hand trailed along the railing as I followed. "What does that mean?"

He grunted, his only answer. We passed the second floor. I stole a peek into what should have been my bedroom. The door hung slightly ajar, the room filled with a charred canopy bed, shredded black curtains from the lick of flame, and a heaping layer of dust to match.

A breeze met us back at the entrance to Harthwait. The door still hung crooked. Stars winked in the distance, clouds long forgotten.

"Where are you going?"

A glare over his shoulder. "You intrude into my home and expect me to answer all your questions?"

Fire sparked in my veins. "On the other side of that door, this is also my house. I don't know what you expect from me, but finding *this*"—I motioned around us—"is a little jarring, and I'd really appreciate it if you'd answer my questions like a polite human being." My fingers tightened on the railing.

His nostrils flared. "Do I look human to you?"

"Half-human."

Eyes narrowed. "If I answer, will you leave?"

I mimicked his stare. "If I can. Maybe."

A grumble under his breath. I took that as a yes.

"Did you live here at one point?" I asked.

"It was my home." He stopped just inside the parlor, crouched by the rocking chair. His ears twitched, at a noise only he could hear. Tendrils of black hair, so stark compared to the white-blond it had been earlier, hung around his shoulders. "It is home. For the foreseeable future."

"Lovely choice of decor."

He stuck a claw through the corner of a rug and yanked. It split to the trim. "I agreed to speak, not to listen to you smart mouth my decorating skills. And if you must know," he said, snide, "what you see changes based upon the memory of the day. Come back tomorrow, and you might find something a bit more becoming of your tastes." He let his hand drop. "Unless, of course, you're too frightened." He gave a wide, gaudy smile.

I hovered at the banister. "Meaning you can or *cannot* leave if you want to?"

"I assure you, if leaving were an option, I would be long gone." His expression turned haughty. "Need I spell it out for you in the dust on the floor, or can you not read, either?"

I crossed my arms in front of me. What a one-eighty from the first time I'd come through that door. I would have had to wipe tears from laughing too hard had I told myself I'd come back and start bickering with this creature.

"I can read just fine, thank you. Excuse me for making conversation—or would you rather me leave you to your dust and termites? I'm sure they'll make extraordinary company—or did you bore them to death already?"

He snickered. "Ah, so there is a bit of fire on that tongue after all."

I shifted my weight. I didn't know why I was standing there. What exactly I was waiting for. But if he was here, alone—and stuck—I'd have been lying if I said the thought didn't make me a bit sad.

"I never had a mind for other people," he said, flinty. He slunk across the parlor and found a spot by the closest window. He crouched there, half the height of the window, even relaxed.

"I think that's obvious."

He shot me a look.

"If you left, where would you go?"

He stretched his neck. Stared at the ceiling. It was such a human, impassive thing to do, I almost smiled. But I didn't.

"I have little clue."

"Where's home, exactly?" I leaned against the opposite wall. An idea started to bloom.

If he left, surely that meant Haddy would stop crying every night? It could be a win for both of us. But he didn't even know the logistics—or where he would go—would there be a point?

"Here, as I said." He flicked invisible dirt from underneath his inky, stiletto nails. They were as thick as a bear's. "I do not understand why you need to know, dearest. Leaving might never be an option. Besides, perhaps I prefer it here, and I doubt you have the resources to help me." He gave a wistful sigh.

My arms fell to my sides. "You suck at lying."

"Says the human that tells me she knows nothing about entering that door," he groused.

I couldn't help it—I stepped forward, pointing a finger at him. "I could walk out right now, board up that stupid door, and leave you here. I'm trying to be nice to you."

"Nice to me? What did I say about pity, dearest?" he said, glaring at me.

"So you don't want help?"

He flipped the script. "And I should believe you would follow through on a promise, why, exactly?" He leaned against the wall, temple in his palm. As if I was trying to drag him away from a day spa, but a shadow lurked in his eyes while he watched me. Followed me across the entryway and against the wall where I leaned. A cruel sort of entertainment. "Ah, but alas, me coming with you would help no one. Two can be stubborn, but only one is smart about it. I would be very, very careful about what you offer me."

"I didn't say to make a deal."

"I did not agree to make one."

My fingertips started to tingle. I knew I teetered on the edge of a precipice, something unknown, and the longer I stared at it, the more likely I would be to take a step. To take the leap, just out of curiosity. And maybe he was right—out of pity, too.

"Tell me why you're here in the first place and how to get you out. If it will help Haddy, or your memories or whatever, stop . . . Then that's enough for me."

His pupils contracted, then dilated. A slow grin peeled his lips.

"I'm afraid it's not so much why, as how. I have tried to open the door before, but it will not change from the darkness I see on the other side, so I know little of what she . . . I'm stuck here, in this alternate place, until it changes."

She.

So someone had locked him here. In that moment, I thought of a rabid animal being trapped right before euthanasia. Was I offering to help something, someone, that was locked up for a purpose? Was I being blinded by a child's echo into helping someone that didn't deserve it?

The thought made me hesitate. Could my own aunt have put him here?

I shifted tendrils of hair away from my face, making sure the door was within eyesight. As if he wouldn't be able to catch me if I tried a second time to bolt.

"What do you promise me in return? I need collateral," I said. *Stupid, stupid, stupid.*

Still, if I changed my mind, I could leave and lock the door. I could never come back. That was my leverage. And he couldn't leave without me. I just needed to be prepared—do a little research, if I could find anything—before I figured out a way to release him. Because if I released him and he didn't leave, and I was supposed to get this house ready to sell—

"Oh, Landry, I am certain I can offer something in return."

My name on his lips sent a hummingbird through my chest. I gave my blandest expression, because if he saw it, how that affected me, he could use it. They always used it. "Okay. I'll see if I can find a way to help you—but only if it means the crying stops. And whatever else is going on in the house stops, too."

His attention snagged as I said it. The faintest, barest flicker in his jaw, but it vanished as quick as it came. "Oh, not this place, dearest. I mean this curse upon me."

I blinked in confusion. "Letting you out wouldn't break this . . . trap?"

"If you believe I turn into a beast upon my own volition, you would be sorely mistaken. I have . . . inklings that it would not cease, no." He pushed to stand, his horns surpassing the height of the window. If I hadn't been paying attention, he would have blended in with the wall, they were so close in color.

Casual, languid, I walked to the door. "I'll see what I can do."

Hadrian trailed after me like a shadow. I kept my pace even, unhurried. I didn't need to look guilty or scared.

Slip out, leave him here for a while longer, then maybe come back.

"Pray tell . . . What do you mean, whatever else is going on within the house?"

I stopped in front of the door. It sounded ludicrous out loud; I didn't look at him when I said, "There are things happening in Harthwait that I can't explain. Besides hearing your crying at night."

"Go on." His expression remained placid.

"I was worried it my aunt may be haunting the place." I didn't realize how much that worried me until I said it. "She passed not long ago. She'd always said I couldn't stay overnight in Harthwait as a child." I nodded to him. "Maybe it had to do with you . . . or maybe it was something else." After all, Hadrian seemed to be confined to this one space, though his memory wasn't. I didn't feel comfortable assuming everything was connected, not yet. But it made sense: something like him, trapped inside, slowly seeping out from its confinement.

"I fear you place a great deal of your faith in me," he said, teasing. He stopped a few feet short, just enough for his body heat to be palpable.

I shrugged. "Even if I let you out of this room, it sounds like you can't leave Harthwait, right?"

His cheek feathered. "I am unsure."

I shifted my weight from one side to the other. My hand searched for the doorknob behind me.

"You grow nervous. You do not want me to be anchored here." Another head tilt. "Do you? You fear me. Or do you fear what this room does?"

I fumbled until I finally felt the cool metal of the doorknob. "I want to help—"

"You will not return," he said, his voice unnervingly calm. "Not for a while. Will you? Your heartbeat is loud."

"I will," I assured. I twisted the knob, and thankfully, the lock released.

He chewed on those two words. Outside, bugs started to hum, and the crisp sound of lapping water echoed from somewhere far away. A light breeze drifted through an open window.

"I will *help* you remove me, if you desire," he offered, creeping closer. Closer. "And if you leave me out to dry? I could make things hellish for you, you know."

I knotted my hands together so tightly that my nail nearly broke the skin of my palm. That was fair enough. I had threatened him. He threatened me. Now we were even.

"I thought you weren't in the nature of making deals?" I breathed.

His teeth snapped together twice. "Tread carefu—" Hadrian's sentence broke. His attention trailed behind me, down the gap in the wall, over the floor, which was still littered with my tarp and pile of sheetrock. I had the strongest urge to back away.

My nerves started to quiver. "What?"

That flicker in his jaw appeared again. It reminded me of a cat watching birds through a window and that sharp, mechanical clicking that ensued, the way their eyes didn't leave their prey. Like he could see the other side.

"The . . ." He sidled himself against the wall to my right and inched forward, the floorboards protesting against his weight.

One clawed hand grabbed the doorframe. The wood groaned. Hadrian's eyes drifted to the floor and stopped. Right at the broken section I had pulled off earlier. Slowly, thoughtfully, he bent down and picked up the broken piece, then ran a claw over the hole it had left. Then he flipped the piece of wood over. The underside revealed carved markings, which I wouldn't have seen unless I had been looking for them. As soon as his claw touched them, they shimmered silver—like liquid metal, catching in the light—before fading away.

He'd just put his hand through the door.

He'd said before that he'd tried to open it but couldn't get through, couldn't see anything on the other side, and now he was—

He grinned up at me, all sharp points glimmering in the dull light.

"See you on the other side," he murmured. Then he stepped over the threshold—and vanished into the hallway.

Nothing more than a shadow in an already haunted house.

Chapter Twelve

Hadrian had crossed the threshold and he was inside the house.

Red flags popped up like gophers. The same image replayed in rapid succession: his toothy, vicious grin, the glint of hallway light on the curves of his horns, and his body dissipating into the woodwork. This couldn't be happening—he couldn't be in the house yet. That wasn't part of the plan. It ruined my leverage.

Emma wasn't even home yet.

"Hadrian." I hurried after him and tripped through the door juncture. Bits of sheetrock scattered, the tarp crackling underfoot. The hall was empty.

If I found him, what would I do? Stuff him back in the closet like a snow jacket? Half our deal, gone, just like that. Clearly, whatever had been keeping him inside that closet was broken.

I ran to my bedroom first, turning lights on as I went. Dolls loomed from the corner of the room, every set of beady eyes following me as I bent to check under the bed. I threw open the closet. I looked behind the door. No Hadrian.

How did such a large creature vanish into thin air?

"Hadrian." In a frenzy, I went room by room, opening doors, closets, wardrobes, and bathrooms. I checked both guest rooms that

Emma wasn't using, the other hallway closet, under every bed, behind every dresser, and in every wardrobe. By the time I made it to Aunt Cadence's bedroom, my face was nearly purple, my shirt stuck to my body, and I struggled to grab the doorknob.

"This isn't funny!" I shouted into the empty house.

As soon as I managed to open the door, I hit my knees to check under the bed. Nothing but dust bunnies. Something told me not to look in the mirror when I searched her ensuite bathroom. I kept my breathing shallow and my eyes quick—tried to ignore the smell of lavender and citrus or how a set of clothes was still folded on top of her dresser.

The only room left was Emma's.

I shut Aunt Cadence's room tight behind me. Just a quick peek. I wasn't going through Emma's things—I wasn't invading her privacy. Not really. I was protecting her from this—this—decision I'd made.

Hesitant, I opened the door, just a crack. A wayward T-shirt hung off the desk, barely visible.

Careful, I leaned in, using my shoulders to edge the door open farther.

A shadow jerked under the bed.

My jaw clenched. "Hadrian?"

A steady, lazy drip of water echoed from her bathroom. I wavered. Eyed her desk, which sat to my left. I reached for the chair back and used it to lean on when the door swung open. As if I might hit Hadrian with it if he came out from under the bed.

Or, by some chance, if it *wasn't* Hadrian.

"You're acting like a child. What am I supposed to do if Emma comes home and sees me with every light on in the house?" I muttered.

"I do not know this Emma you speak of."

"My sister."

A long pause.

"Maybe if you turned the lights back *off*, I would not have to hide under this monstrosity," came the grizzled snarl.

I pictured a vampire, evaporating in the sun. "Does it hurt?"

A growl. "No, it feels like . . . resistance."

To humor him, I flipped the bedroom switch. The room plunged into darkness. Emma's gauzy, cobweb-like curtains hung open, drifting with a breeze. I had the sudden urge to shut each one, but that would involve walking closer to the bed. Knowing my luck, he'd grab my ankle for the fun of it.

"Are you happy now?"

A grunt. "Quite." With care, an arm snaked out first. Hadrian's body moved unnaturally, awkward bent joints, his chest pressed close to the floor. I watched two droplets of blood land on the floor, but as soon as his foot passed over them, they vanished, as if they never were.

He was bleeding again?

"What do you think you're doing? You're supposed to be in—that." I took a step back and pointed down the hall.

"Perusing my house. So kind of you to allow me inside so soon," he chuffed. "Why? Does it unsettle you, thinking I'm meddling in your things? I have to admit, much time has passed. It looks nothing as I left it." His forked tongue slid over his teeth.

I tried to stifle the surge of panic those words induced. I *broke a seal.* As if there were things he still wasn't telling me.

"My house, not yours. You're here because I let you in," I corrected. I widened my stance, as if that would make me more intimidating.

"A mere technicality." He drew himself upright, both of his knees popped, and he rolled his head as if to loosen his shoulders.

The only way to keep him in check was to keep him under my thumb. He spoke with confidence—an air of certainty that came from high social standing or rank. Just like Ivan; though Ivan's social standing was propelled by his parents', and Hadrian's felt sturdier. Older.

If I wanted to play his game, I would need to keep up.

"You're hiding in a woman's bedroom." I kept my words breezy. "Last I checked, creatures with horns didn't hide under beds if they had the leg up, Hadrian. You need me. And if you decide to blow it, like you're doing right now, I won't help you. At all."

He smirked. "You mean to tell me this isn't your bedroom? Where you tremble in fear every night of what might be hiding in your closet?"

My jaw worked. "This is Emma's bedroom."

"Ah, the sister. Yes, I heard you. Are you jealous? Would you rather me hide in yours?" For the first time, he grinned, and it was almost . . . playful.

"I would rather you go back to your *closet*." I motioned down the hall again. "I don't have time to worry about you floating around like a wraith. It's late, and if I'm being honest, I have other things to worry about"—like how I was going to pull everything out of the library to start renovating this week since the kitchen was nearly finished—"while I think about this little issue I have on my hands now."

"I am a small issue to you." A dark, delicate chuckle.

He leaned in. So close that I caught a whiff of ash and a hint of earth. A flash of hot summer days and sweat-slicked skin and tunic fabric stuck to a chest came to mind.

My breath shuddered.

"Do I *look* to be a small issue to you?"

"I'm tired, and if Emma sees you—if anyone sees you—I swear on my life—" I stopped myself before I said something irrational. Threatening him would only go so far and make me sound immature.

I cupped my face in my hands and took a deep breath. "So, please. Go back to your closet."

A rumble came from his chest. "You cannot make me go back there, dearest. You have two options. You turn a blind eye to me wandering my own home, or this little agreement—which you already said yes to—is over. Unless your word is nothing to stand by? You promised to help me. Otherwise . . ." He flicked his wrist, gesturing to the hall behind me. "What's yours is mine, yes?"

I rolled my lips together. "A promise is a promise. On both ends," I emphasized.

I wasn't going to win this fight. Still, the thought of him around the house made my skin prickle. What would he see or hear or do? Would the activity in the house get worse?

Or, would it be like having a cat? I would only see him when he needed something? What would he do now that he had freedom to roam? Did that mean now that he was out here, Haddy would follow? Would his memories trail after him, or would whatever was inside that room trickle in, too, like a disease?

I pushed the thoughts away. I couldn't stuff him back inside if I tried. But that slipping control, that *need* for a plan, made my hands clench.

Finally, I managed, "Just make sure you stay out of the way when Sayer and Emma are here. If they can even see you." Emma would probably break out an EMF reader and a Ouija board if she spotted him. She'd already tried to persuade me into letting her use the board when the book nook turned on and off by itself. If she saw so much as a curtain move the wrong way, there would be no stopping her.

He snorted. "I do not think that will be an issue. I already have difficulty keeping my human face during the day. I doubt you'll see much of me until the night."

My head fell against Emma's doorjamb. I let my eyes close. Shoved the ball building in my throat farther and farther down. "What am I even looking for? To break this—what did you call it? A seal?"

I opened my eyes when he didn't answer. He slouched a bit, close to the darkest corner of the room—his torso curved as if in protection of his open chest. "You know as much as I."

I balked. "You don't know? You said—"

"I never *said* I knew." A smug head tilt. "You assumed. So, if you want to move things along, I suggest you start digging."

This made me stiffen. "Are you threatening me?" Because it sounded like he wanted to make Harthwait *unwelcoming*.

"Not a threat. A polite nudge."

A thought, barely a seed, sprouted into a seedling. I wanted to reach out and strangle him, demand he spill every ounce of detail he knew, every single seemingly unimportant fact about himself—where he was born, where he came from, when he lived, when he died, what he'd done—but I stopped myself. There were other ways of gathering information. Other places I hadn't even dared sort through yet.

If Aunt Cadence had gone to such lengths to keep me away from the house, she must have known. I thought of the attic: Her boxes upon boxes of collectibles and antiques would be a good place to start. But what would I be looking for?

I couldn't imagine her leaving me the house knowing there was a creature like him within it. But then, a slight, razor-sharp shred of doubt crept in. What if she hadn't known? Or what if she had, and she had only been trying to cover something up before anyone found out?

I didn't realize I had been staring at him, silently brewing, until he stood just inside the doorway. He leaned forward, as if to tell me a secret. "So, now do I have a deal?"

"Will you tell me what you know?"

This close, flecks of ambered gold broke up the sharp yellow of his irises. His pupils, though slim, were of the darkest skies. My reflection, warped and short, looked pale in comparison to the color. The light of the hallway cut edges over my cheekbones, my neck, my shoulders. Is that what he saw when he looked at me? An easy deal? An opportunity? A frail, badgered young woman with no other option?

Or worse: a doormat.

His cheek twitched. Barely. "Perhaps." A non-answer.

"Okay," I said. Because what choice did I have?

"Then we have a deal."

Just then, footsteps thumped up the steps—and I watched, wide eyed, as Hadrian stepped back into the darkest corner of the room, and vanished.

I swung around. Emma, red faced, stared at me from the top of the steps.

"What are you doing?" she breathed.

I hadn't heard the front door unlock or the grandfather clock starting to chime two in the morning.

"I was just—I heard something," I stammered. My face grew hot as I gestured to the lit hallway. That old anger from our argument, now stifled, shimmied back to the surface like a bloated, dead body.

"So you turned on every light in the house and go in my room?" she pressed. Emma's hair was tied in a loose bun, her shirt partially untucked, her face bare.

Because, yes, Landry, after giving yourself a pep talk about keeping Hadrian from Emma, the first logical thing to do was to mention hearing something that could make her bust out the EMF reader.

When I didn't answer, Emma shook her head, forehead creased. She brushed past me, tossed her purse onto the end of the bed, and switched on her bedside lamp. "Don't tell me that when I'm supposed to sleep in here tonight."

I scooted closer to the door. Emma untied her hair, cheekbones still tight, and started pulling her shirt over her head. I searched for words as she retrieved a sweatshirt and a pair of old, worn shorts from the floor.

Here we were, in our late twenties, giving the silent treatment.

She kept her back to me as she pulled her sweatshirt on. I settled into my frustration as I stood there. It hadn't been completely my fault—she'd stepped over a line, too. Still, I could almost picture Sayer, glaring at me, while eyeing Emma as if to say, *Apologize.*

I hardened myself. Apologizing meant I was wrong, though. And I wasn't.

"I thought you were going to be out tonight?" I tried instead.

She eyed me. A chill to her words when she said, "Stetson isn't that big." Then, "What happened to the hallway?"

I couldn't tell if her words were an olive branch. Not that I'd offered much else, so I gave my half-truth about expanding the hallway.

"Hm," was all she said. Like she didn't care.

I turned to leave but stopped at the last second. It was the thought of Hadrian eavesdropping from a recessive place that hooked me.

Pressure built at the back of my neck. I glanced back, hand clutching the doorframe.

"I'm sorry for before," I said. "I kept Ivan's packet. Just in case." I swallowed around the words, like a thousand bees had stung my lips. "I might have him come take another look in a few weeks."

Emma collected a trio of bobby pins off her nightstand and started spoking them around her hair. The fly-aways slowly disappeared.

"Emma." Her name withered on my lips.

She stopped and turned toward me, her hands propped on her hips. "Why don't you tell me things?"

My chin dropped. "I do tell you things."

"No, you tell me what you think I want to hear. What happened to how we were in middle and high school?"

I didn't meet her gaze. The floor became oddly interesting.

"You don't tell me anything anymore. Secrets. Jokes. How you're feeling. What you're doing. All I get are directions on what to do, what to tear up, what to throw out or box away."

"I don't have secrets because I don't do anything exciting, I don't go out and drink or party or have this huge group of friends," I said, exasperated. "I'm an amateur interior designer that reno's. I don't know what kind of exciting things—"

"No, Landry. You. Not your work. Even . . . even the funeral. You don't talk about her. You don't talk about your mom. You don't talk about Dad."

Her. Not Aunt Cadence. *Her.*

"Talk about her? What is there to say, Em? You weren't even here for the funeral, so why should I think you'd *want me* to bring up Aunt Cadence?" I pressed, an ember catching hold in my chest. "And what if I don't *want* to talk about Mom and Dad? I can't change the past. I don't want to reminisce on a childhood that wasn't great. I don't want to talk about feelings and emotions and feel-good energies like you do."

She huffed. "I don't talk about feel-good energies."

"I was trying to apologize," I said. "Not be told everything that's wrong with me." A broken, hysterical laugh bubbled out of me. She wanted honesty? I could unload honesty. "I get it. Everything is wrong with me. I don't do anything right. I don't talk enough, I don't show enough emotion, I don't do enough things, I don't have any hobbies besides scouring mood boards, Reddit threads, and job leads, and I have *one* friend that isn't family. I get it, Emma. I *know* I'm nothing."

"That's not what I'm saying—you're not nothing." She knotted her sweatshirt in her fist. "You know that."

"But isn't it?" I whispered. I shook my head. "I don't need an intervention for things I know I do wrong. I get it. Boxes checked, signed, sealed, delivered." I grabbed her door handle. "Goodnight."

I shut the door behind me. She didn't follow me. And I was glad.

I floated through the house like a husk, turning off every light, every lamp, closing every door and window. One by one, the rooms blinked into shadow. For all I knew, Hadrian followed me from room to room, mouth split wide in a smile.

Maybe Emma was right. If a problem followed someone continuously, it was the product not the user, right? That's what a counselor in middle school had said. "If you can't keep a relationship because everyone's "too toxic," maybe it isn't the other person. Maybe it's you."

Maybe it *was* me.

What reason did I have to believe it wasn't?

* * *

The door didn't disappear again, but Sayer made a comment while I was cleaning that stopped me in my tracks.

"I cleaned out that hallway closet, by the way. At least I didn't dent it."

I stilled, dust rag in hand, standing atop a chair in the breakfast nook. The chandelier swung back and forth from where I'd wiped off a bulb. "What?"

He waved his hand from the pantry. "Where I hit my head. I'm glad I didn't bust it."

Then he walked out.

I didn't have the courage to bring it up again.

Sayer left after dinner the following evening, leaving me alone in the kitchen with every cabinet thrown wide open. It had started simply enough: While he stood by the island and talked, I looked through each drawer for a can opener. I never did find it. I did, however, fish out a set of mushroom-shaped birthday candles, a stack of worn BoxTops from when I'd been in elementary school, and a yearbook photo from fifth grade.

"They still make these?" He'd examined the baggie, nose wrinkled.

Something about the BoxTops still being in the drawer, long forgotten, opened a hole from my heart that tracked straight down to my toes. What else had Aunt Denny saved that I'd never seen? And why did going through her things make the back of my neck warm? I felt like I needed to ask for permission, but when I looked up to find someone, anyone, the one person I wanted to talk to wasn't there.

Each breath grew thick after that. I fought tears until they were nothing but a fat wad of cotton in the back of my throat.

Now, the sun had vanished, Emma was holed away upstairs, and the kitchen looked like it had exploded. And I couldn't even remember why I was looking for the can opener in the first place.

"So much junk, Denny," I complained, more to myself. Maybe she could hear me. "Why seventeen kinds of birthday candles?"

With a huff, I turned to the fridge. I wanted dinner, but didn't want to make anything, so I opted for my go-to jar of pickles in the fridge door. I didn't bother to close it, instead using the refrigerator light to see what I was doing. My knuckles purpled, then turned white, when I twisted the lid.

"Open," I snarled. I ground my teeth, planted my feet, and tried again. My hand slipped.

"Stupid sweet-and-spicy," I grumbled. Whatever sweetener they'd used had probably sealed the lid shut.

I shut the fridge and moved the jar over the sink, grabbed the dishrag, and used it to get a better hold on the lid. My grip-strength was better, but just as I thought the jar would give, my hand slipped again.

I sat the jar down beside the sink. The last thing I wanted to do was ask Emma to open it.

There was one more trick I could try. I turned the hot water on and grabbed a knife out of the cutlery drawer. Four quick taps, all the way around the lid, then I stuck the jar under the water when steam started to rise. Then I used the edge of the knife and tapped around the lid again.

"All right. Play nice." I grabbed the dishrag—one last time. Gripped hard, planted my feet, and twisted.

I turned with the jar, twisting harder, *harder,* and pressed my left side into the sink to get better leverage with my arm. Then—with a sweet little *pop*, the lid released.

"Thank God," I breathed. I started to straighten. Then I glanced up. My heart somersaulted straight up my throat.

A razor-sharp silhouette reflected in the breakfast nook window in front of me. I wasn't alone in the kitchen.

I jumped with a yelp—and dropped the pickle jar. It shattered all over the kitchen floor in a wet, sticky spray, over the bottom of the opened cabinets, my feet, and the dishwasher. The lid rolled the opposite way, toward the living room.

At least I'd left all of Aunt Denny's items on the island top instead of the floor as I'd found them.

I clutched my chest with both hands, frozen, as the silhouette stepped *out* of the wall behind me, almost as if from the pantry.

"The jar never stood a chance," Hadrian said, low and slow, like he'd only just woken from a deep sleep. My first instinct was to look at the clock—it wasn't even ten o'clock yet—but my attention latched onto our reflections in the window. He moved with languid grace, and before I realized it, he was behind me. I started to face him, but without hesitation, he dropped to a crouch and splayed a large hand against the tile. I'd have been lying if I said a part of me wasn't relieved to see him.

"Don't touch the glass," I blurted.

"Never you mind. Your feet would get cut. Step here." His voice remained matter-of-fact, gritty, and almost too placid. I didn't notice I was staring until he looked up from under his brows. "Do I need to enunciate? Step on the back of my hand."

My forehead creased. "Step on your hand?"

His jaw worked. "So you do not cut your feet."

I searched the sharp points of his cheeks, the tendons of his neck, the way he hunched as if it weren't just out of habit, but to keep a bit of distance between the two of us.

Did he find me repulsive in some way? Or was he scared to touch me?

A dead, shriveled part of my heart unraveled. Stretched a bit, and I didn't know why.

I obliged, careful to move quickly and not put too much pressure on the ball of my foot, but teetered at the last second. I grabbed his horn without thinking, near the base of his skull. An unnatural stillness came over his shoulders. I tried to ignore the ridges of the horn, how cold it was to the touch, or how his head was *right there.*

I stepped over. Hadrian's hand felt no different from stepping on a garden stone. There was no give. A catch of breath—but not from me.

I moved closer to the refrigerator corner. He stood without a word, his eyes not leaving the floor, slowly traveling up to the breakfast nook, then over the cabinets I'd left open.

"Quite an organizational process you have here."

"Where have you been?" I asked, ignoring his comment. I crossed my arms over my chest and gathered a bit of snark. Really, it wasn't to start something, but more to cover the fumbling heartbeat in my ears. If he'd heard it before, could he hear it now?

"You miss me already? I'm flattered." He tore his attention away from the window with a pointed grin, then drifted between me and the island and into the hallway. Like his reflection bothered him.

"I don't like having a guest in the house I can't see."

"You see me now."

"After you vanished into thin air." I inched forward. "How do I know you aren't off doing something weird, like counting the dust bunnies under my bed or snooping in my closet?"

"So you *do* want me to hide in your room instead. I will do my best to keep that in mind."

"I didn't say—"

Upstairs, a door opened. I paused.

Emma—she would have heard me drop the jar.

Sure enough, there was a long, soft pause with the shuffle of sock feet, and then, "Are you okay? I heard something."

"I'm fine, just dropped a jar. I've got it."

Hadrian tilted his head to keep his horns from hitting the ceiling. Even in the nearly pitch-black hall, his chest glimmered where his sternum opened. I watched his heart flutter as blood oozed from the inside out then evaporated when it fell down his midsection.

Emma's only departure was the shuffling of her feet and the gentle click of her bedroom door.

"I interrupted your . . ." He sniffed the air. Delicate wrinkles appeared along the bridge of his nose. "Meal. A sad meal at that."

"I didn't expect company so abruptly." His eyes fell, heavy, on me then. In a huff, I hurried to gather a pair of shoes, towels, a broom, and the wet-mop. I was scared he'd go up in smoke as soon as I walked away, just like the blood from his chest.

I whirled back down the hall, arms full. Thankfully, his figure still hovered at the end, closest to the living room.

"I can assist."

"I've got it."

A clawed hand shot out and blocked my path just as I made to brush by. That earthy scent, the feel of unnaturally warm skin so close to my own, engulfed me.

I stopped in place.

"Allow me." He reached for the towel, and this time, I didn't object.

I put on my shoes and swept in silence while Hadrian kept to the corner of the room, careful to not touch the light that pooled from the lamp in the living room. By the time most of the glass was in the dustpan and the cabinets had been wiped down, I asked, low, "It still hurts?"

He stopped by the pantry door, the wet towel dangling between two pinched claws. He draped it over the sink. I didn't think he'd answer, until he said, "Not the skin. Within the room you found me, I felt no different, like this or as a human. Within the house, if I stand in it too long, it burns here."

He tapped his chest. Right beside his heart.

I dumped the glass in the trashcan by the island, careful to wipe out any glittering remnants.

"Imagine trying not to blink." His voice turned smokey, gritty. I could have sworn his silhouette feathered at the edges. "It burns, begins to hurt, and as soon as you blink, the need comes on tenfold. You have to blink so many times your eyes water. It's simply an urge I cannot control."

"So you don't decide when you change?" I'd gathered as much from when I'd found him.

His jaw ticked. "I could not in that room, no. I am unsure, but it feels similar out here. But there is—" he stopped himself. "There is much that has changed. In this house. It feels different from before."

The strained, borderline hostile way he said this piqued my curiosity, but a flicker of tension radiated over his shoulders, like he might bolt at the first chance. I decided to treat him like a cat: Give a little, but don't push. Eventually, he'd tell me.

"What do you do, then? During the day."

That stillness came back. The air thickened, like he was debating whether or not he wanted to tell me.

"I am here but not. I can see you all, but am still along the shadows. The slightest of places," he muttered. Those yellow eyes latched to me. "I can hear some conversations, some movement, but not all."

I waded through the surprisingly heavy moment and propped the broom against the wall. I forced a slight smile.

"So you really could hide in a closet if you wanted to?"

"Wherever darkness touches, I am there."

My smile fell. "That's so sad."

"I've had worse things to do with my time." He slunk back into the pantry, angled just so to where I couldn't make out his expression. "That lamp is horrid, just so you know. The bulb makes my eyes ache."

"Remove LED bulbs." I feigned a checklist. "Got it."

The door groaned as he slipped inside. His horns scraped along the frame. Then, it was just me and two floating eyes and an ugly lamp shining from the living room.

I tried to search for the right words. Did he want me to remove the bulbs and find warm ones? The idea of being cooped up in the house all day, unable to do anything, sounded as appealing as making me take up public speaking.

I reeled the idea back. Making him comfortable might not be the best idea. He could be lying to me. There was no telling what he actually *was* doing, if he could only move along the shadowed areas like he said. Maybe I'd wait a little while and see how things went with him here before giving an inch. Knowing my luck, he'd take a mile if I let my heart soften.

After a moment, I reached for the towel over the sink.

"Did you hear anything last night? Like crying?" *While he had complete free rein of the house,* I thought. So many shadows, so much to slip through. "I didn't hear anything, but I fell asleep pretty early." And Emma hadn't mentioned anything. Not that she'd tell me.

A long pause.

"Hadrian?"

I draped the towel back over the sink and opened the pantry door. Nothing but shelves full of nonperishables, stacks of reusable storage containers, and an unnecessarily large bag of flour on the floor.

Hadrian was gone.

Chapter Thirteen

The house seemed to settle for a few days.

It made me anxious, now that I knew he was there. Existing. Listening.

"Keep or throw away?" Sayer held up a box labeled ATTIC. A welcome breeze sent the tree branches rustling overhead. I stopped, hand on my trunk liner, lips parted.

Immediately, Haddy—Hadrian's—curled body materialized in my mind. It was difficult to walk up those steps, to clean out that room little by little, and not think of him—the way his voice echoed off the attic ceiling, the muted floors and dusty coat hangers. I shook my head, willing them all away.

"What's in it?" I croaked. I wiped my brow with the back of my hand.

Behind us, Emma stood on the porch, separating bags of clothes that were good enough to give to the women's shelter and then others that were too moth eaten or holey to reuse. We'd decided to take a break from working on the actual house today—mostly because sorting through items was easier than peeling more wallpaper. With my tentative September deadline inching closer, I didn't want to end up panic-dumping anything to the landfill when things could be reused.

And it gave me time while Sayer and Emma sorted through boxes to go through paperwork—not only to submit death certificates to the bank, Social Security office, and insurance company, but to look for journals. Notes. Envelopes. Anything personal that might have been left, besides the official power of attorney and the will. But I came up empty.

My promise with Hadrian loomed the more I searched and the less I found. I could only flip through so many folders, desk drawers, and cabinets before doubt crept in. Fear of what I might find—or what I wouldn't.

Sayer jiggled the box. "Don't know. Old toys, I think?" Squinting, he rubbed his chin on his shoulder to wipe away a drop of sweat.

I stood on my toes to get a look inside. An old threadbare toy harp sat at the top. The strings were frayed to the point of snapping, and if I focused, I could just make out tiny teeth marks on the plastic bottom. Donald The Chihuahua, most likely.

"If they're all like that harp, they should probably be thrown out," I said.

"I'll put them in the garbage pile," he concluded. Just as he turned, I couldn't help it. I reached out and grabbed the harp. I needed to touch it. One last time.

It was the palest of lavenders, with worn edges and light creases in the frame. The memories sat on the edge of my mind, as if to say, *Wait, come back, just one more time.*

I'd sat for days on the back porch, singing to the birds with the dream of being in an opera one day. The dream hadn't lasted long, because I remember the harp had disappeared not long after that, and my newfound fixation had been dolls. I think I'd decided fashion design was a more enticing route at that point.

I suppose part of *that* dream had come to fruition. Except dressing people wasn't my forte—now I knew I didn't have the emotional capacity to deal with people all day. Dressing a home, so to speak, was a lot more fun. Houses always seemed to speak to me when I picked out palettes and inspiration ideas. Unlike people, who spoke *at* me most of the time.

I plucked a string on the harp. It made a sad, loose twang.

Sayer shivered.

"Do you ever look at old toys and get sick thinking about how time moved so fast?" I said, voice thick. Not just where the time pranced off to, but how life could pivot just as quickly. It needled you in the side some days; others, it grabbed you by the throat and spat in your face.

Each inhale burned in that moment. Especially lately—it squeezed my throat so tight I could hardly see straight.

I'd been so lost in the little things—paint colors and paperwork and item orders—that I'd not stopped to breathe. Four weeks had already passed since the funeral.

How would I feel in the next four? Six weeks? Eight?

"That's why I made my mom go through everything after I left school. I couldn't look at it." Sayer sighed. He examined the rest of the box's innards. "It's too depressing for me. Kudos to you for at least getting rid of some stuff."

I gave a watery smile. "Really?"

He scoffed, nodding, then rummaged through the box. "Absolutely. Me, going through old toys? A recipe for a midlife crisis. I'll pass."

I gave the harp one final sorrowful *plunk* before setting it back on top.

"This looked cool, though. I found it under a pile of clothes. I tried to open it but almost lost a fingernail." He held out a wooden carved box, no larger than his palm. A rusted metal latch sealed it shut. Something rattled inside when I shook it. I tried to use my thumbnail to pry it open, but as Sayer said, the latch held true.

"Careful," he warned. "If you damage a nail, it might not grow back the same. All thick and curved and—what?"

My nose wrinkled. "Thank you, Doctor, for that lovely mental image."

"My grandfather could show you his feet if you need proof. The number of times a horse stepped on his big toe. You should see how ugly it grew back—"

"I think I'll pass." I shook it again. "The box is neat, though. Reminds me of a trinket tray. It could go on one of the mantels, maybe the library. It might match the feel of the room when it's finished." Most of the rooms had a hearth, even if they weren't functional.

"What about this bag?" Emma called. She held up a white trash bag and shielded her eyes from the sun. "Do you want me to put it in the hallway closet for now?"

I hesitated a moment too long. Did she want me to answer? I couldn't tell if she was looking at me or Sayer.

"Donate," Sayer said. He swiveled back to me. "And shame on you."

I stalled, eyes going wide in silent question.

"For not letting me help you clean up that wall after I hit my head through it."

A chill—similar to how I felt when a fork scraped across the bottom of a bowl wrong—raced over my spine.

Sayer remembered the first wall incident, but didn't go on to mention the night when I told him I'd break the wall down anyway. As if his memories had been flipped completely.

"Mind telling me why you two are acting like the other hasn't showered in a week?" he asked, changing the subject.

"I showered this morning." I gathered my composure. Maybe the memory issue was nothing to worry about.

"I mean the wide birth you're giving each other."

I tried to keep my shrug nonchalant. "We've agreed to disagree." And left it at that.

Still, I knew that Sayer knew. But I'd rather stick my hand in a flooded toilet than bring up the words Emma and I had exchanged—especially when she was bound to hear from the porch.

By lunchtime, Sayer agreed to help Emma go through the rest of the boxes we'd collected from the garage that wouldn't fit in my car to donate. I would either take the rest to the shelter, which was a forty-minute drive outside of town, or to Meredith's. By late afternoon, I'd already unloaded a few boxes at the shelter and made it back to Meredith's before closing.

I wiped my palm over the back of my knees as I pulled the trunk lid down. "Can I ask you something?

She sat the last box in front of the store's door as a momentary doorstop. Her T-shirt was damp around the neck. I'm sure I didn't look much better.

She fanned herself. "Sure, sure. What's on your mind, honey?"

"Did Aunt Cadence ever talk about the house's history?" My words were breathy. What I would have done—the amount of money I might have paid—just to go lay in that puddle off the sidewalk, no matter how inappropriate.

Meredith pulled a tissue out of her pocket and blotted her face. I propped both hands on my hips. "Oh, this and that. I know she went to the deed's office once or twice. She usually just brought me my junk, talked gossip a bit, then left. Why?"

"Just curious."

"You check the info on the historical registry?" She folded her tissue. "On the house, I mean?"

A wilted nod. "Yeah, I saw when it was built. The first owner. Not much else." The first owner, who wasn't a Belfaunte. It wasn't that I didn't believe Hadrian was telling me the truth about it being his house at one point. I just wanted proof. Something solid to point me in a direction.

Or something not-so-solid, like speculation, that would give me an idea as to what exactly I would be looking for.

"Well, if it ain't on the registry or in the historical records, I don't know what to tell you, dear." She huffed, then eyed me. "Somethin' wrong with it?"

"Oh, no. Right as rain."

She made a noncommittal noise. "You're a bad liar, honey."

My mouth fell open. Maybe the comment stung since Hadrian had said something similar. "I'm not lying." The half-truth fell out before I had a chance to think. "I just have nights where I think I hear things."

She scoffed. "Well, *that* doesn't surprise me."

I shot her a look, only slightly offended. "I thought you said it wasn't haunted?"

Meredith's cheeks tightened. "Haunted? Oh, heavens no. I never said it was haunted. You poor thing—is Emma not keeping you company enough?" I must have given her a look that asked, *How do you know that?* When she added, "Oh, Ivan told me she was staying with you. Said you might be giving him the listing when the time comes to sell."

Because of course he had.

"But no, I'm not saying Cadence is haunting you, dear, or that Harthwait is haunted by anyone." She shuffled over and patted my shoulder. Gave it a squeeze. "I'm saying, it's normal to hear things after someone passes. I know Cadence talked nonstop about hearing that dog after she had to put him down. Heard his nails on the hardwood all the time. Heck, I had the same thing happen when Annie died. You know that droopy rescue I had when you were little?"

I nodded. A smile threatened my lips. "The basset hound?"

"God bless that thing. Lived to be sixteen, can you believe it? I heard her ears swishing all over the floors, the couch." Meredith's mouth turned firm. "What I mean to say is, there isn't anyone haunting that place, Landry. It's just grief. And that's normal."

Just grief. Those two words clanged down from my nape, all the way to my knees.

My eye twitched. Well, I might not have had a dead chihuahua scratching at my bathroom door, wanting to shred the shower curtain, but I had a *something* that slithered from the linen closet that wasn't really a linen closet.

But if I said that, I'd be the next candidate for an inpatient program.

"Who did Aunt Cadence use for researching the place? Was it the town records, or—"

"Please don't use those people. Go to the Hemlock if you do." She gave me a hard head shake for emphasis, then started back toward the store entrance. "Those clerks are absolute"—a wide-eyed, raised-brow glare that told me the workers were anything but—"peaches. Don't even waste your breath."

Well, it wasn't much, but it was something.

There wasn't much reason not to. So before four o'clock, I drove out of town.

Hemlock was the same to Stetson as twins were to each other—the same word, just a slightly different font. The thought occurred to me that I could have done a search through the library, but starting with something solid—like a name on a deed—felt more enticing.

Much like Stetson, Hemlock had one stoplight that blinked every thirty minutes and three antique shops per street corner. Where Stetson nestled against a railroad track, Hemlock teetered on the edge of the Wasleck River, which eventually bottomed out into the marshes before reaching the Atlantic. Roads were crowded with heavy live oaks blanketed with Spanish moss and the promise of acorns. In the near distance, sea oats danced in the river breeze. Side to side, like a woman's skirt—almost tempting enough to wade through. If you did, you'd get a few feet out. Before you'd know it, you'd be drowning.

I parked across the street where the shops had already gone dark for the day. My reflection followed through the windows as I crossed, then beelined for the clerk's office. Like everything else, closing time was in six minutes.

Hopefully it took six minutes to get a deed.

There was a burst of cold along with the scent of dingy brown carpet when I opened the courthouse double doors. The only sound was the air conditioning humming overhead.

I headed to a sliding-glass window halfway down the hall. A seating area waited, empty, with one magazine resting on a tapioca-colored coffee table. Likely a year-old copy of *People*.

A woman glared at me as I approached. Slender glasses perched on the end of her nose; the chain around her neck swayed as if I'd caught her mid-task.

"Hello," I breathed. As if she couldn't see me already.

She didn't speak. She also didn't open the glass window. Only, pointedly, moved a stapled stack of papers from one side of her desk to the other.

I waited. Pushed a smile.

Seeing I wasn't going to leave, she sighed and slid the window open. "Can I help you?" The mole under her eye moved with each chew of her gum.

"I need a deed record," I said. "For my property."

Her nostrils flared. Penciled in eyebrows, arched like two rainbows, inched to her permed hairline. She turned to her computer and started typing, fingertips first. Her wrists didn't rest on the desk. "County?"

"Colleton."

A grunt. A fat butterfly pin glinted against her purple turtleneck.

Minutes, maybe eternities, passed.

Then, to my relief, she spun in her chair. With a huff, she pushed to stand, vanished around the corner, then returned with a sheet.

She pushed it through the window. "Fill this out. Ten dollars."

Once I'd signed, stamped, and promised my firstborn child, she disappeared again and then returned with a folder.

"What dates?" Her seat sighed when she sat down.

I stared, mouth slightly open. I didn't know what today's date was, let alone when Hadrian was alive. I probably should have asked, but I could almost hear his excuse while I came up with a guess: *My age? Oh, dearest, that was a long time ago.*

How long is a long time?

Long enough, he'd have said.

"I'm not sure of a date, but is there a Hadrian listed on any of the deeds?"

She shot me a look over the rim of her glasses. Okay, then.

"Last name is Belf—"

Before I finished, she made a noncommittal noise and licked her thumb and flipped through the pages without looking down, only watched me while flicking the sheets. Because having her glower at me wasn't unnerving enough as it was. More importantly—how was she reading the names if she was staring at me?

I took an awkward step to the side. As if that would somehow redirect her attention. She looked like one of those women that sniffed fear.

"Last name."

My mouth pursed. "Belfaunte."

With an indistinguishable mumble, she exhaled through her nostrils again—this time it whistled—before slamming a page down into the copy machine, punching a green button, and posting on her armrest.

We stood there in silence as the copy machine whirred. Strained. Then spat out a paper.

She rolled back over to me and shoved it through the window.

"Hadrian Belfaunte. You and that Irene Blankenship, I swear," she spat. "Is that all? It's four o'clock and we're closed."

"Yeah, I think that's—"

She pushed the window shut and yanked a beaded metal string. A set of blinds fluttered down between us. My reflection gaped back at me.

What a lovely, lovely woman.

I could only imagine how *peachy* the Stetson office workers were if Meredith had recommended this one.

I took my ten-dollar deed and exited the double doors. I didn't look at the paper until I climbed back in my SUV and rolled my windows down to let the heat escape. I wiped my forehead with the back of my hand, cursing the ninety-four-degree weather, and stole a glance at the page in the passenger seat.

I stilled.

Fearing the paper might fly away, I lifted it. It crinkled between my fingers. The date—the numbers were so close to each other.

I read over it once, then twice, my breath growing shallow.

By All Men Verify

Colleton County hereby grants Hadrian Belfaunte the property of Harthwait House / parcel 12 of 1252 acres by * death of Father, Howie Belfaunte ~~dollars~~ in the month, day, and year of our Lord: June of the 15th of one thousand eight hundred and seventy-eight; designated by the number of . . .

The copied deed's edges were worn with rounded edges, tiny creases and tears throughout. The document's decorative boarder was faded in places. What hadn't faded was the penmanship. The delicate curves and swoops of pen lines held strong.

At the bottom, a star.

Right below it, it read:

*Father—deceased

Recipient of passage, no assets, building good condition
Granted by Stetson Treasurer Office, witness Sherriff Jonathan Kimbal and Judge Marshal Yearly

Water filled my lungs. Slowly, it filled my throat, my ears, and pressed deep against my brows. My palms began to itch. Deed still in hand, I cranked the ignition. Hadrian had existed. He was real. And I, inadvertently, was not hallucinating. This was the validity I'd wanted, right?

But it wasn't enough.

I wanted more. I needed dates, pictures, and words on paper. Because a deed only proved that Hadrian had at one point been a real person. Solidified the man I'd seen in the maze of briars as he'd smiled at me.

What about his life? What did he do? How long had he lived? Did he have a job, did he live in the house until he died, or was he stuck there for other reasons?

A thought occurred to me. The other name the clerk had mentioned.

In my phone, I searched: Irene Blankenship. A job profile appeared, one for the Wasleck library on a recruiting website, the other for one of the university's research committees. Then, something further down—a Reddit thread by a user named *IreneBlanketMonster178* that started with, "So I've worked at the library for a while and . . . never heard of something like this before. . . . thoughts? . . ."

I did a U-turn in the middle of the street and started for the Wasleck library.

* * *

I opened the Reddit post in the library parking lot out of sheer nosiness. It might not have been the same person. I might have been jumping to conclusions or getting ahead of myself. Preconceived notions never did anyone any good, and that's exactly what I was falling victim to.

I guess I didn't care.

I opened the thread.

I don't believe in ghosts but I've got a problem?
u/IreneBlanketMonster178: [MOD] 2.5 y ago

So I've never believed in ghosts, right? As a child, my parents were always very up front with my sisters and me. (No Santa, Tooth Fairy, Boogeyman. Our childhoods were fairy dust-less and Magic of Christmas No More.) So ghosts were piled into that category. We didn't play with Ouija boards because, in our minds, lame. We only did Halloween for the candy and to time how fast each of us could run through a haunted house.

Life moved on. I graduated college. Parents moved out for a one-level home because knees started to hurt. I kept the family house. Got a job at the library while doing research, because money. Then this one lady came in—she came in religiously, always checked out four fiction books and one nonfiction book.

She owned an older home somewhere near the marshes. We started talking about ghosts somehow one afternoon. Then she let everything spill. She said she'd been hearing a child crying at night, and a woman would hover near her bed at least once a week. Said she'd seen the apparition of a dog in the backyard, all that fun stuff. And scratching on the walls? Said she couldn't have family over because it happened at night all the time.

We got to talking about it, and she asked if I could come check out something she'd found at the house to see if I could tell where it might have come from. (No, I didn't ask for pictures, but I should have at the time, I see the err in my ways, because she could have been a serial killer and lured me in so easily.)

I knew of the house from a few of the land directories. But when I stepped inside, the vibe changed. I'm talking I could feel the little hairs on my arms go up. Then she took me upstairs.

Not going to lie. I thought I was gonna get murdered (by her, not a ghost). Anyway—upstairs on the second floor, some wall was torn down. The place was probably built in the late 1700s? Idk. Think creaky. The house moans on its own, kind of thing. Then she showed me what she'd found on the inside of the wall she'd pulled down. Said she was taking off the "ugly beadboard" and spooked herself.

[attached image]

An electric current lurched through me. I knew, without opening the attachment, what it would be. My eyes jumped to the end of the thread:

I've never seen those symbols before? From any religion? And from where the house is, I went through all of the local info and couldn't find anything about any cults in the area out of the ordinary? Does anyone know what it could be? Any leads helpful.
(13) Comments

Chapter Fourteen

With a sharp hiss, I locked my phone and climbed out of my car. I could read the comments later. The clock on my dashboard already threatened the library's closing in a mere thirty-two minutes, so I needed to hurry if I wanted to find Irene—if she still worked here, anyway. My esophagus felt like it was peeling, my hands shaking a bit, as I hurried into the library. Its door jingled in welcome, and the first thing I saw was army-green carpet, heathered with red and navy spots.

I scanned the shelves to my right—mystery and romance and nonfiction—until I landed on a beige L-shaped counter at its center, separating the YA and middle grade from the rest of the sections. Standing behind the counter was a woman around my age, with high cheekbones, waist-length braids, and coal-black eyes, perked up from a monitor. Her mushroom-colored slacks matched her blouse; gold accents tinkled on her wrist and ears.

I gave a tiny gasp. I *knew* that face.

That face was the same face I'd stalked online: Ivan's ex. The girl I'd thought about messaging. And she was right there.

"Hello," she greeted, her expression faltering when I didn't move. Casual, holding my breath, I approached the counter. "Can I help you find anything?"

A wet fish floundered in my throat. Think, Landry. *Speak.*

"Yes, actually," I choked. I eased up to the desk but stopped a healthy distance away. Like a barrier. "I'm looking for anything you have on the name Belfaunte?"

Irene's nametag shimmered in the fluorescents. A line formed in the middle of her chin. "I recognize that name."

Because Aunt Cadence brought it up to you, maybe. Because you know something? A few moments passed, and all I could think of was how close she stood. She'd dated Ivan. She'd talked to Aunt Cadence, if the thread was hers. It had to be.

If it wasn't—and if it was? It matched. All of it made sense.

But none of it made sense.

"Belfaunte, you say?" Eyes danced to me.

"Yes, ma'am." I held up the copy of the deed, in case she needed the spelling.

I suddenly felt underdressed in my worn shorts and T-shirt. Plaster speckles dotted my forearms. If she eyed them one more time, I'd launch into a detailed explanation as to why I had paint all over myself, how I didn't usually look like this (though I usually did), and how I wasn't inept at showering.

"Articles, obituaries . . . ?" The monitor reflected in her glasses as she searched. "Belfaunte is an old name." The mouse clicked; her tongue poked at the bottom of her lip.

"Hadrian," I said. Then, thinking of the second name I'd seen on the deed, "Or Howie?"

I looked around as Irene continued clicking, typing, then clicking some more. The library teemed with childish chatter. An instructor urged the children to settle around a circular table. Not far off, a college student had their head hung over a mass exodus of textbooks and paperwork from their emptied backpack. Summer classes in full swing, it seemed.

Irene made a *hmm* in the back of her throat.

"Hadrian owned Harthwait when it was well over a thousand acres—" She stopped. Her expression remained even. "I know exactly which house you're talking about."

I bit my cheek, slightly expectant, as the printer started to spit out papers.

"The woman who owns it comes in all the time searching for information on the place."

I swallowed a ball of sand. Of course she used present tense—how would she have known unless she'd seen the paper?

"Cadence Caldwell was my aunt. She passed away a little over a month ago."

Irene's eyes widened. "Oh, I'm—I didn't know. I'm so sorry." Her cheeks tightened as she bent for the papers. She shuffled us farther down the counter, next to a display that screamed in rainbow colors: *Summer Reading Sign Ups Are Here!* A stuffed elephant leaned against the exclamation point. Beside it, a stack of business cards. Irene flipped through the papers, and I leaned in to the card stack.

One of them had Ivan's face on it. *Wasleck Real Estate Group.*

My tongue grew leaden. If she had his cards on display, that meant they were at least cordial to each other.

"This is some of what I got," she said. She tapped a page. I gravitated to the paper.

Sure enough, there he was.

"This is Howie." Upside down, Irene pointed to a man with long, white-blond hair. It looked to be a commissioned portrait of sorts. Without a doubt, he matched the man I had seen in the attic whipping the boy. Whipping Hadrian.

His nose was strong, his chin and jaw cut, and from the side, his throat rose and dove in all the right places. A serene, serious expression donned his features. The date at the bottom looped to read *December 12, 1876.*

Her finger drifted to another. My eyes skimmed. This one was of Harthwait, centered at a distance, sometime in 1894.

"The land was sold off gradually after Hadrian died, it looks like," Irene murmured, picking up one of the other pages, bringing it forward. A map, hand drawn in careful detail. "This shows the plots after 1891. See how they're broken up by dotted lines and have parcel numbers? There's probably a key somewhere. Let's see who did the map . . ." She squinted. "Commissioned by Silas Haste. Probably a friend of the family if Mr. Belfaunte didn't have any kin left."

"Does it say how he died?" I whispered. A child's laughter pealed through the air.

I wondered if Hadrian had ever laughed like that.

Irene's finger traveled again. This page, much like the deed, was a copy of a full-page article with weathered edges and creases and stains. She pointed a peach nail to the center headline.

"Looks like that's what you're looking for," she said, just as gentle.

The Virginian
July 23rd 1890 (v.71)
Belfaunte Death Felt from Stetson, SC

Hadrian Belfaunte died at his home from natural causes on June 2nd of 1890. Belfaunte came to own the Harthwait Estate via his late father, Howie Belfaunte, in 1878. Belfaunte was a business man of oil for his time traveling west; either via business partners or acquaintances or both. He accumulated a net worth of 1 million outside of his father's inheritance. Wakes called Belfaunte, "a riotous man that none would think to double back—a show for the bored." Silas Haste was the only attendee to the ceremony. It was held at Covert Lutheran. There was no burial.

Belfaunte married Cora Pho in 1878. They never had children. Cora preceded Belfaunte in death a year after marriage from natural causes.

The estate affairs are to be dealt with by Haste and their enterprises.

The article was so . . . dry.

My attention circled the man's name—Silas Haste—from Virginia. He'd dealt with Hadrian's affairs post-death. Not a relative, not a cousin, not a wife or child or aunt or uncle. A childhood friend who didn't even live in the same state. Perhaps it was the dealing of wealth? Enterprises could mean a corporation—maybe Hadrian left it to him because he knew he would take care of matters instead of fight over the money.

And a "show for the bored"? It was as if the man thought Hadrian to be spitfire entertainment and nothing more. Like a puppet to watch crash and burn.

I leaned back, a sour taste in my mouth. What would be written about me when I passed? Would my parents still be alive, or would it be Emma? Would they talk about my work and my worth with such crassness, or lack thereof? Or would it be brittle and bareboned?

I blinked against a sudden blur overtaking my vision. I handed the paper back. "Do you have any photographs of him?"

Irene licked her teeth. "I think I do. Oh, look! I forgot this one was colorized."

After a moment of shuffling, she handed over another sheet. This copy took up a fraction of the page—the photograph itself was no larger than a Polaroid square.

And yet.

And yet.

There he was. The date scrawled into the page read 8-8-89. A year or so before he died.

The picture was straight on, squared, and candid.

Hadrian's features sat too strongly for black-and-white portraits. His lines too taut, his mouth too resilient, his shoulders too rigid. And still, there was a languid aura to the picture. As if the photographer might not have the good enough graces to even be in Hadrian's presence.

As if anyone else were less than he. But not out of arrogance.

Hadrian's hair was white, his skin tinged with color, cheeks hollowed with maturity. Not a hint of baby fat remained. And his eyes—all gray. Not an ounce of yellow.

A shiver skittered along my spine.

He looked like the man I had seen and somehow not. Like identical twins: the coloring, the lines, the features on paper matched, but once they were put into motion there was something missing that I couldn't put my finger on.

In real life, he was different, but I couldn't place why.

"Can I keep this?" I breathed. I sounded like a frog. "I think I might"—the lie came easily, and I should have been ashamed—"I think I've seen pictures of him at the house."

"Of course," Irene said. She gathered the copies into a haphazard stack and held them out. "Take them all. All yours."

"Thanks." I gave a tight smile. "I appreciate it."

Her eyes softened. "Of course."

I straightened. The business card started to burn in my peripheral, as if whispering, *IvanIvanIvan*. She was right here, available, I could ask her right now—even if it was just about the Reddit thread—

The silence hit me, then, and I realized the children had been ushered out of the building. The college student was gone. One older gentleman held a book in his arms behind me, ready to check out.

My time was up.

"Come back if you need to look for anything else?" she asked. The corner of her mouth turned up. "And . . . I'm sorry to hear about your aunt. She was very sweet."

"Thank you." I hesitated, the words right there. I wanted to take that leap, but her eyes held pity, and it threw up a barrier.

She moved back to her monitor.

And I turned and left.

* * *

My bedroom glowed a pale blue from my TV, but it was muted. I saved the document I was working on and exited out of it. My hoodie was tucked over my mouth, my hood up and knees propped for my laptop to sit upright. The wind whistled outside, tree branches skittering over the glass panes in preparation for a thunderstorm.

I really needed to get a mock-up ready for a client. But I couldn't bring myself to open her file. Instead, I'd spent the better part of my afternoon scouring the internet for anything related to the property. Library archives, my old university source compilations, research papers, *anything*. But instead of finding leads on what I should be worried about—Hadrian being stuck in this house—I'd searched articles that detailed his time period. What he might have seen in the newspapers. What he might have done in a day's time. Historic events around the years that would have mattered to him. What kind of lightbulbs they had before he'd . . . passed.

Then I'd searched burial records. I'd stopped myself before I'd gotten too far.

I set my laptop aside and reached for my nightstand drawer. The papers were folded together, one over another, so at first glance they didn't look like anything important. Prying eyes wouldn't notice.

I took Hadrian's photograph off the top. Was it the eyes that were throwing me off? Or the way he held his jaw, clenched and rigid?

Then—a faint *click click click*.

My fingers tightened on the page. The TV's mute sign still held strong in the screen's corner. To focus, I patted the bedsheets for the remote, and turned it off.

Immediately the house *sounded* vast. The whir of the refrigerator could be heard from downstairs. Gently, I placed the papers back in my nightstand. It was probably the tree branches on the window, if I thought about it. And even then—

A shadow swept under my closet door. The room was dark, but the shadow was so deep it looked like a hole that swallowed the floorboards.

My fingers tightened around the nightstand drawer handle.

For a split second, I thought it might be Hadrian taking me up on the closet hiding. But then I thought about the light issue I'd had when I'd stayed that first night. How things had happened *before* Hadrian had been out of that room.

"Hadrian," I whispered. My throat tightened when the *click click click* came again.

Maybe it wasn't him after all.

I started to pull my sheets back—sleeping on the couch would be better than this—when the door unlatched and drifted open, tender, before stopping a few inches later.

One clawed hand curled around the closet door's edge.

Both relief and anger flooded me.

"You"—I lowered my voice to a hiss, grabbed a pillow behind me, and chucked it at the closet—"you *jerk*. You scared me."

That chattering came again. A glint of ivory on the other side—jagged and sharp—made me realize it was his teeth that were making that noise. He was chuckling.

At me.

"I wanted to give my gratitude."

"I don't want gratitude, I want my blood pressure to come back down."

"Either way, Landry, I would appreciate it if you at least took my thanks." A long pause. He ushered the pillow aside. "The lightbulbs you chose are much better."

The sudden seriousness in his tone felt like a weighted blanket on my chest. Any hint of irritation seeped straight out of me. If there were any moment to be thankful that the lights were all out, it was then, because the heat crawling up my neck felt like a collar ready to strangle me.

I tucked myself back under the covers and set my laptop on my nightstand, next to my water bottle. I glanced at the closet door crack, but his figure wasn't defined enough for me to see exactly where he stood—or crouched.

"You're welcome," I said softly.

Rain began to patter against the glass. A rumble of thunder rattled the walls before falling silent.

"You spend much of your time renovating this place," he said.

I inhaled through my nose. "I do."

"You do this for work."

"Well, not this house, I suppose. It just kind of happened."

"Because of the woman before who passed."

A nod. My cheek rustled against my pillow. I tucked my hands under my chin for warmth. He was here, talking to me. At night. And that realization made my skin feel too tight, the air too sharp.

"Tell me about it."

No one besides Sayer and Emma ever really asked me about my work. So why was Hadrian asking any different?

"My work or my aunt?"

His inhale caught. "Anything."

I pulled the sheet farther over my nose. "Why?" The single word was supposed to come out a bit stronger, sturdier, than it did. Instead it sounded wilted and a little pitiful.

"Maybe—" He stopped. Cleared his throat. "I have a lot of free time to roam, Landry. Perhaps you intrigue me."

I scoffed. "I don't do much besides wait for an order to show up, strip wallpaper, and paint things." But even I knew that was a lie.

What I really wanted to ask was if he knew where I'd gone today. If it was wrong that he kind of intrigued me, too.

I wanted to ask him about his life. What it had been like before cell phones and cars being the main mode of transportation. I wanted to know what it was like waiting for updates in the newspaper instead of social media. Or what had changed the most from his time to now—what he missed, what he didn't miss. What he used to like to do, what he hated.

"You brought a trunk with you. I want to know where you come from. What you do." Another pause, this one baited, heady. "Whatever you wish to tell me."

"A trunk," I echoed. I scooted closer to the edge of the bed. Still, I couldn't see him. "You mean a suitcase?"

"Yes, a traveling case."

"Well, my mom and I lived in Stetson, in an apartment, after my parents got a divorce. I went to school here, through high school, before I went to college for design and business. And now I'm back here."

His laugh darkened, the clicks turned sharp. "So that is all? Your life in a few short sentences and nothing more?"

I curled further into myself. What more would anyone want to know?

"Why interior work?" He opened the closet a few more inches. Lightening flashed, briefly illuminating the jagged edges of his shoulders, the dips and valleys of his , his hand. "I know little about jobs nowadays. Enlighten me."

"I don't know. I was good at it. I liked creating mood boards. Organizing ideas and stuff, how textures would play off each other. Coming up with ways to make a house a home, I guess." I didn't know why it was so hard to look him in the eye when I spoke. I stared at an eye in the wood floors, instead.

"Mm. A house a home."

When he repeated it like that, anger bubbled inside me out of nowhere. And I *knew* why. All I'd ever wanted as a child was a *home*. So I'd found myself in giving that to other people.

And here I was, with the very home I'd always wanted, and I didn't even want it anymore because it was too painful. I'd diminished it to a set of zeros behind a dollar sign on paper. I'd told myself that it was a thing to fix, to remove, to give away to someone else who would love it and care for it.

Because what was a home worth, if it only held memories that hurt? What was a home if it just reminded me how much I hated how my life had turned out?

"What about you?" I said, a bit reedy. "Mr. Business Man."

His hand, which idly dragged along the closet edge, stilled. "Pardon?"

Oops. I floundered for another reason—besides my going to the library—to explain myself. "Your clothes. I figured if you cleaned up nice enough, you might have been a semi-important guy back in the day."

His slitted eyes narrowed. "Do I hear a jest from your mouth, or do my ears deceive me?"

"I doubt it, they're kind of big. You could probably pick up radio signals with those things." Not so much large as pointed, but he reacted, which made my heart flutter.

This made him sit forward. Before I knew it, he crawled out of the closet like a creature from a horror movie, but the riled irritation in his eyes wasn't mean—but playful.

"Now you stoop as low as to make jokes of my appearance in relation to items that I know nothing about. A rather cowardly way to make fun of a person, don't you believe?" His nails dragged along the floor. I held my ground—well, I held my side of the bed. I didn't back up, only narrowed my eyes back with a suppressed smile.

"Says the creature crawling along a woman's floor in the middle of the night. I'd say your peeping Tom act could use some work."

"Now you're being cruel. You know regal businessmen like myself have little social skills outside of ledgers. *And* I am out of practice. How else do you expect me to speak to women?"

I couldn't help it—I laughed. I covered my mouth to muffle it and sat up. He'd stopped in the middle of my floor, his figure flickering in and out of sight with every dash of lightening.

"I'm sorry, Hadrian, if I hurt your feelings." I stifled a chuckle. "I was teasing."

He relaxed a little. "Your voice. The hum."

My eyes dropped. "What do you mean?"

"Just now, when you spoke, you smiled and hummed. It sounds like the wings of those tiny birds . . . What are they called . . ." He scratched the side of his neck. His heart, I noticed, oozed freely, but as it always did, the blood disappeared as soon as it ran down his hardened midsection. "They come to the window every now and then. Small little things, needle beaks. I saw them all the time as a child around my mother's—ah—flower beds." He made a pinching motion with his fingers.

I wrapped my arms around my knees. The rain grew louder against the roof, a steady hum, around us.

"You mean hummingbirds?"

"Is that what they are called?"

My brow furrowed. Hummingbirds had been around long before Hadrian's time. At my worried expression, he cleared his throat. His horns waved as he glanced around.

"I apologize. Some memories are not always clear. I can recall my favorite breakfast as a child but some parts . . . are gone. And, as you saw, there was no one else to speak to in that room, so I have no one to ask."

A hole in my chest yawned wider. Sadness. Was he admitting that he was lonely?

I chewed on my lip. "That's okay. I didn't mean to . . . I really am sorry, if I hurt your feelings. The joking, I mean. I just—sometimes things come out, and I don't know if it's always received how I hear it in my head."

"You did nothing to hurt my feelings, Landry."

A nod. "Okay. I trust you."

"And when you say my name, your voice lowers. Just a hair." He paused. It was ironic, seeing *him* trying to articulate how he was feeling so eloquently. A blush rushed under my skin.

"I'll make sure to say it with gusto next time," I said with a smile.

His expression remained serious. "No."

"No?"

He shook his head. "I like how you say it much better."

I wiped my hand over my face. Prickles of heat started up my neck. "Well, I'm flattered."

"Now, Landry," he said, but this time, my name turned into a growl. "Tell me about this inspection that went so poorly."

"You heard that?" Because of course he had.

"Well, I may have followed." He cocked his head. "But conversations would waver in and out before if I was not near. This one, however, I heard from upstairs."

"Before, as in before you got out of the room?"

His jaw worked side to side. "Yes, I suppose so."

My thoughts churned. Hadrian made it sound casual, but even in his creature form, there were two lines between his eyebrows. Concern.

"Does that worry you?" I whispered. Did it worry me? I couldn't tell. Not yet.

"I suppose not. It keeps me aware."

I don't know what it was. Maybe it was the expectant, sharp attention that he held on me. The way he crawled over to the dresser and sat down, leaned back, and watched me in the shadows. Back to the two floating eyes that illuminated like a cat's with every lightening flash and thunder rumble. Or maybe it was that I knew he, of all people, might understand about this house. Because it had been his once, too.

I sighed. Licked my lips, and whispered, "The house means a lot to me. And the person that Emma brought in, I'm not fond of. I just—want it to be in good hands."

He nodded. "All right. Tell me more, if you would like."

And for the first time, I did.

Chapter Fifteen

With the papers tucked away neatly in my room, I spent the next few days touching up the bathroom paint and the kitchen. The heat climbed like a lethargic spider over the walls, the slick edges of my lungs, and skin of my lower back. I managed to sift through the other half of the office, but came up empty handed, just as I had in the attic and Aunt Denny's bedroom.

Then, like a roach I couldn't be rid of, Eleanora appeared in the middle of the front porch one late afternoon.

My clothes were speckled with paint. My legs and arms were flecked with dried greens and deep teals—feathery strands of auburn hair hung in my eyes, plastered to my temples, my forehead. I needed to take the garden hose and shove it down the front of my shirt.

Emma didn't look any better. Our uncomfortable silence gradually teetered into small talk—I think there was an unspoken agreement to let it lie for the time being. When Eleanora had knocked on the door, we'd been in the midst of said small talk, me on the ladder, painting the accent wall in the library, with Emma as a base. It scared me so badly, my toe slipped, the paint roller slipped, my other hand slipped—everything slipped, including Emma's grasp on the ladder legs. My leg went through the step rungs, the roller clattered against the wall before bouncing into my face, then fell and hit Emma in the eyes. I ended up dangling from the last ladder rung, both hands on the floor. Emma shrieked and tried to wipe the backs of her hands over her eyes.

"Oh my God," she hissed. "It burns! Why does it burn so bad!"

I tried to pull myself up. Paint dribbled into my mouth. "Wait, wait, I'll get a towel."

Emma leaned against the wall closest to the hallway, cursing.

Then the doorbell rang again.

Now, we both stood, hands folded in front of us, feigning professionalism. Eleanora shuffled through her papers, making preening noises every few moments as she looked at the library. At least she hadn't commented on the dried green paint on either of our faces.

"Yes, yes," she cooed, like we'd done something magnificent. "Love how it's coming along. The place looks wonderful. I see you took my suggestions to heart?"

I scratched at the corner of my mouth. It pulled, likely from the paint. "I did," I lied.

Emma's eyes snapped to me. Widened a bit, as if to say, *Don't placate her.*

My shoulders relaxed. *I'm trying to make her leave,* I said with a tiny chin jerk. My eyes flitted to the door for emphasis.

I was almost 95 percent positive that the wall she'd wanted taken out was the one I had just painted, but the fact that she hadn't mentioned it yet remained. Then again, if I were desperate for a listing, I probably wouldn't have mentioned the wall yet, either.

Eleanora leaned through the doorway, straining to peek down the hall, as if to make sure the kitchen hadn't evaporated in the last ten minutes. "Mm, yes, I suppose. The kitchen is amicable. A bit—cabin-esque, but it will do for now." She tutted. "That wall, though."

Ah. There it was.

My jaw tightened. The kitchen looked a lot better than when it had been infested with roosters, and her thoughts were *cabin-esque*?

Emma caught the sleeve of my shirt and gave it a tug. Gave me a look.

Then, with the sweetest, thickest smile she could conjure, she turned to Eleanora.

"Eleanora. Yes, hi."

Eleanora's eyes slid to Emma like she was gum on the bottom of her shoe.

Emma lifted herself, as if oblivious. "Listen. The timeline is a bit tight for the list you gave us, yes? We're—*Landry* is moving as fast as she can. And there hasn't been a chance to inform you that there is another realtor we've had come out to the property to take a look as well. Everything we're doing right now is based on the betterment of the house—not what you think will sell."

I stifled a cough. Emma's eyes darted to me, but I turned briefly, covering my mouth. She really just said that.

Like an owl, Eleanora's head swiveled. The room grew tight.

I fanned my neck, then stepped in front of Emma. "Emma is right. We're still shooting for end of summer, but I'm afraid I'm still considering my options and what will be best for Harthwait."

Eleanora licked her teeth. A drawn pause.

"Well, either way, I'd love to see the rest of the house," she breathed. A false sense of optimism. She gentled the sharp corners of her mouth, but I still saw the shark lurking below the surface. "I do apologize, I was under the assumption that we had a, how would you say, gentleman's agreement about the listing going under my name?"

My eye twitched. "I never signed any paperwork, and I never agreed that the listing was yours. You came recommended by a friend, which I'll take into consideration, but as you know, this house is a special piece of architecture. It deserves a good fit."

For the first time, wrinkles appeared around Eleanora's plumped mouth. "I see." She brushed by me, the smell of her saturated perfume following her. "I suppose I should hurry along with the rest of the house, then. I have other listings to go to, and though I'd love to stay and negotiate, I think it would be a good idea to let you sit on it for a while."

I motioned for Emma to stay put as I followed Eleanora, who had already crossed the hall into Aunt Cadence's office.

Dust particles—the lived-in kind, not the forgotten kind—floated through the air, hovered over the ornate rug and pooled sunshine. The front lawn glowed with afternoon light, the curtains peeled back enough to hint at the treetops canvassing the property. Eleanora stepped through the opposite door, chin high, spine tight.

I paused in the middle of the office, shut my eyes, and took a breath. Just to exist. It would be fine—things would work out. At least this gave me a bit of leverage with her and—

The office door slammed.

The momentary warmth in my blood vanished. Little hairs along my nape stood up.

The house fell eerily quiet.

I opened one eye at a time. Eleanora wouldn't have been as petty as to slam the door on me. Sure enough, when I opened it to the sound of squeaking hinges, Eleanora stood with her hand on the banister, staring at me. Her face was white.

I jerked a thumb over my shoulder. Chuckled. "I opened the other door. A draft."

Eleanora's eyes didn't leave a point behind me. As if she was looking at me, but not really. For the first time, she looked unnerved.

"The upstairs," she said. She took the first few steps on her toes. "I understand the bedrooms will need painting and stripping, and the bathrooms are being redone as well? Have we thought anymore about opening up one of the rooms to be a den of sorts?"

Each inhale tasted sour, like my body rejected her words as soon as they were spit out. "I'm not sure a den would bring much more value, when the extra room could still—"

I saw him before she did.

The upstairs was shadowed because of the position of the sun. Not quite evening, not yet past afternoon. The hallway door, which Hadrian had come from, was cracked. Utter darkness shifted inside. Which was odd—because I hadn't opened it.

Two yellow slitted eyes appeared, standing nearly six and a half feet tall. He angled his head sideways so his horns didn't hit the walls.

I froze. Then my eyes widened. Why was he visible during the day?

Hadrian blinked slow, languid, as he waited. I prattled on as I followed Eleanora, rolled my lips together, and tried to keep myself from looking in his direction. Because the last thing I needed was to find out if Eleanora could see him, too.

Eleanora watched her steps until she hit the landing, likely not even listening to what I was saying. Hadrian's eyes tracked her movement. She walked by, so close to him he could have reached out and touched her shoulder, before beelining to the closest guest room.

"—be used as a den, wall intact," I finished. I stopped a foot from the door. The sound of her heels on the hardwood rang twice as loud, twice as heavy.

Eleanora considered this with her back to me. Her fingers drummed her chin as she moseyed, then disappeared down the left wing. A spare bedroom door clicked open.

I took my chances. I spun to Hadrian, a finger already pointed.

"What do you think you're doing?" I whispered. "It's broad daylight."

"Here I was, under the assumption that you would enjoy my company." He was nothing but two eyes and a sharp smile. I wanted to shut the door in his face. Still, I'd found myself waiting at night, hoping my closet door would open and he would come talk. But he'd only flitted in briefly, once, before the house had gone silent.

"This woman. Who is she?" he asked.

"A realtor," I snipped. "Is something wrong? Why are you *here*?" Even now, when I looked at those yellow irises, all I saw were the colorized gray ones, that perfectly coifed head of white hair, and his blank stare at the camera.

"I was lurking, as you put it, in the library. Figured I would come to see. And I saw you looking for me in the night. I am rather flattered that you scoured even the shadowed, dusty parts of the house for me."

I swallowed against the rising heat. "Maybe I was looking for you so you could help me figure out what's keeping you here."

"You think I will not help you?"

I wiped my palms over my hips. I was worried I would get distracted. That I'd be more interested in talking to him in the middle of the now-silent midnights than searching for answers.

My expression grew incredulous. "I still have a house to sell."

"So impatient."

"It lists in September." I crossed my arms. "I have clients waiting on me to finish this place, Hadrian. The world does not stop turning so I can look for clues. And I can't wait around for you to show up, either, to help me."

His mouth twitched. Shadows lurked beneath those yellow eyes. My words, it seemed, were not the ones he'd wanted to hear. "It seems there has been a misunderstanding. You did not give a date as to when the house would not be yours, dearest. And from what I overheard"—he inclined his head in the direction Eleanora had disappeared—"you are in no rush, yes?" His tongue flitted behind his teeth. Crescent moons lined his under eyes.

I settled back on my heels. Waited until I heard Eleanora's steps move farther away. "Why do you think I was looking for you? Of course I'm in a rush."

A rumble came from his throat. "I'm afraid you can't rush these things, Landry." I could have sworn his form flickered—grayed skin to sun-kissed. "I do not have the ability to *show up* at every beck and call. I come forward when I am able, so I'm so terribly sorry that I cannot *appear* like a genie."

"And this room?" Eleanora called.

I ignored her and grabbed the closet door handle. I opened it an inch farther. That ash and earthy scent filled my nostrils, that familiar *thump-thump* of his opened chest echoing in the closet. "Hadrian. I'm serious. Go away. We need to talk about this later."

A strangled chuckle. "Pot to kettle."

I knew he was needling me. I knew it like I knew the sun would rise in the morning and that my father had an infidelity problem. But still, my tongue started moving before I had a chance to reign it in.

"What happens if she sees you?"

"Ah, by the time she realizes I am here, I will be gone." His horn scraped the door. Inches separated us. "And she will think you are a loon, talking to an empty closet."

"I thought you couldn't control it."

"It has been easier, the last few days, but I didn't want to raise your hopes."

I shot him a glare and exhaled through my nostrils. "Why don't you stick to—"

"The bathroom could be worse." Eleanora's steps started toward me.

I leaned on the door. It didn't shut.

"Hadrian," I snapped.

Another laugh. This time when I pushed, the closet door closed. I turned, back pressed to the door, just as Eleanora entered the hall, her finger pressed to the corner of her mouth as if to rub away excess lipstick.

She stared at me. Glanced to the closet. My face flamed.

"That's great!" I blurted. Too enthusiastic. I snapped a finger. "I actually want your opinion on a few things over here before you go—"

"And upstairs?" Her red nail pointed up the spiral staircase just as I turned to one of the empty bedrooms. It was so much smaller than the main stairwell, spindly and old, like an old man's spine.

My throat started burning. Hundreds of needles pricking my skin at once. "You mean the attic?"

"What are the plans for it?" She brushed by me so she faced away from the closet. "If there is a closet in it, technically you could call it another bedroom." Her eyebrows arched and her forehead didn't crease.

The closet door clicked open behind her. There Hadrian hovered, right over Eleanora's shoulder.

Dread flooded me. The tiny baby hairs at the crown of her head danced when his mouth curved into a grin.

"I didn't plan on it. It's great for storage." Even to my own ears, my words wobbled a bit.

"Can I take a loo—"

Hadrian's claws slipped from the shadows. Curled around the edge of the door.

I grabbed her arm. She froze. Stared at my hand. Immediately, I jerked it back. "There are a lot of things up there of my aunt's. If you don't mind leaving it, for now."

She huffed. "All right."

His claws slipped away, and the door drifted shut. The message was clear: *The attic is left alone.*

I couldn't say I blamed him.

* * *

If I was a smoking kind of woman, I would have lit up right then.

The air brushed cool against my skin, but not cool enough to warrant the warm coffee mug in my hand. Tendrils of steam curled up, over, and around the lip. The only sounds were the hoot owls somewhere from above, the whisper of rustling leaves, and the rocking chair's legs on the porch concrete. Every time I rocked forward, I thought of the moment I catapulted over the edge as a kid, right into the bushes. No railing, no soft landing.

Maybe that's why I wanted to down a mug of stout coffee well after dark. I needed a reminder that I was alive. That the world didn't revolve around projects and getting through the day to only repeat it the next. That Hadrian hadn't almost blown his cover today, on purpose, or whatever it was he'd planned on doing, if only putting my feet to the fire.

The front door squeaked open.

Emma's head poked out. A moth flapped around the porch light, its powdered wings whispering low.

"I left you fettuccini alfredo in the fridge if you want it," she said. Her mouth puckered, half in thought, half-expectant.

"Thanks." I gave an in-between smile and stopped rocking. "I might get some in a bit."

Her expression turned thoughtful. We sat in silence for a moment. I couldn't tell if she caught my lie or not.

"I'm sorry," she said. "For what I said. All of it."

I nodded. "Me, too."

She stepped barefoot out onto the porch and crossed her arms in front of her. Her T-shirt swallowed her to midthigh, bleach splattered and oversized. "I might have to go back home for a bit to finish a few work things. I didn't want to, you know, vanish. Because we weren't talking much."

I shrugged. It was like she stood on one side of the property, and I on the other, while trying to communicate via hand signals. I didn't like it.

But I didn't feel like I could help it, either.

"I didn't help things," I murmured. I looked back out over the front lawn. Moonlight stitched through blades of grass.

She traced that same patch of skin on top of her hand, brow furrowed. "Can I tell you something? You don't have to say anything, if you don't want to. I promise."

My spine fused. The grip on my mug turned to the point of scalding, I held it so tight. "Sure."

"I used a lot of laxatives in high school. It happened the summer after junior year. You'd started talking to Ivan about that time, I think?" Her gaze grew distant. The moth fluttered from the porch light, around the crown of her head, then back again. "I didn't have the . . . restraint, I guess you could say, to not eat. The laxatives were the easiest thing." A measured breath. "And the throwing up."

Crickets.

I didn't realize I'd stopped rocking. I kept my eyes to my sandals, how my toes brushed the lip of the sole, how the wind had even quieted.

A sudden familiarity overwhelmed me. Anger, at what Emma was admitting to. Not anger for her actions, but anger that her brain had convinced her it was necessary.

"In the spring, one of the guys went around asking the girls how much they weighed because they wanted to stick one of us in that giant tire they used for track. You know the one?"

I nodded absently. "The one the football team used to flip during practice."

Her throat bobbed. "I remember I said how much I weighed. You wanna know what he told me? He said, 'That's not too bad.'"

A hot, brittle thing stretched awake inside my gut. It clawed, inch by inch, up my ribs, until it curled against my heart and hissed, vicious. *That's not too bad*, as if Emma could have done better. As if she wasn't enough, just as she was.

"And then you started . . . changing, too," she whispered.

The coffee swayed in my mug. I started rocking again. Tipped my head against the wooden rungs as her words washed over me.

"No one noticed," she murmured. "But I did."

I shook my head. I wasn't sure at what—maybe because she hadn't said anything. Hadn't told me sooner. Or it was in disgust and frustration with me—for not wanting people to notice, but feeling almost *valuable* when they did. As if they cared enough about me to only say something when I was slowly dying, inside and out.

"But I—I didn't want you to think you're alone," she whispered. Still, eyes forward. When she finally looked to me, I made a point to look away.

The knot next to my heart burned.

Maybe you started it, that little voice said. *You made her that way. Look what you did.*

"I'm sorry, Emma," I whispered.

"Why are you sorry?"

I shrugged. "For everything." Everything, the last few days, for our life. For my choices. For the ones I kept making. Sorry that I'd wanted her to see me as perfect, so I'd never told her. Sorry that, even now, I couldn't bring myself to be brave like her and talk about it yet.

Her mouth pursed. "I just hope . . . you know I'm here. If you ever need someone to listen. And not judge you. Because I don't blame you for your struggles, Lan. I want you to know that."

Emma slipped back inside. Then it was just me and the crickets.

* * *

Well past a quarter after midnight, I walked by the paneled door in the hall, a tugging sensation holding me near. I walked by once. Then again. I sat on my bed. Rustled around in the sheets. Then I got back up, walked to the bathroom and hovered there, unsure.

Open me, the door whispered.

Still, my heart raced at the thought. What would I find if I opened it now? Would another version of Hadrian be in there? Another memory he'd had? Something that would help me? The thought made me consider it. I hung on that precipice, holding the doorknob, so close to letting go. Would it swallow me whole and get rid of these emotions twirling in my chest? Would it momentarily take away Emma's words and quiet my mind?

That gritty, heavy feeling had been festering since she'd left me on the front porch.

How had I been so narrow-minded? For years, all I'd seen were my issues.

She had noticed my struggles, but I'd never once noticed hers. I'd assumed she was perfect. All smooth edges and polished finishes, while I'd crumbled in a corner, but I was *wrong*.

My sister had been hurting.

And I'd turned a blind eye without meaning to.

That gritty lump in the back of my mind turned into a burning ember. Then, slowly, a fire—crackling and spitting and *hurt*.

I padded back to my bed and curled on my side. Tonight, the trees were still while the TV murmured.

A squeak spiked my attention. I squinted in the low light, at first thinking Emma had opened my bedroom door—when I saw the closet. The door was ajar, only a crack. No more than what Hadrian had peeked out of before.

I rubbed my eyes. "Hadrian?"

I waited for two yellow eyes to appear, maybe his rows of serrated teeth and stretched lips, but nothing did.

I couldn't help it. Maybe it was the silence that lured me in, spurred the worry in my mind like stoking a flame. Maybe it was because I couldn't see him, if he was there, that encouraged me a little.

I needed *him*.

"Hadrian, I messed up," I whispered. It was easier, in the dark with my eyes to the wall, to talk as if he were listening. The pressure of his attention, the shifting of expressions, no longer applied. It was just me and the shadows and my trembling words. "I didn't know. All this time, I didn't know Emma was struggling. I ignored it because I was only worried about *me*. Why was I so selfish?"

Words began to tumble out. I told him about how my mother found out my father was cheating, and walking home in tears because I'd been bullied off the bus. I told him about the ants in the kitchen cabinets and the fear of food because eating the food meant it was gone, and once it was gone I couldn't control it—and somehow, even now with a job and money, I couldn't find a way to jump the hurdle. I told him about the nights I used to sit in my apartment and watch the cars drive by until the early morning hours while I picked at scabs along my arms.

I told him about the struggle of keeping friends because everyone wanted to *know* each other, but the last time I let someone *know* me, he used my own bones as picks and slowly, slowly removed the thick skin I'd carefully crafted. Until I was nothing but a raw, sensitive woman who had to figure out how to put herself back together, because people hurt people. I'd hurt people.

"And I ignored her. My own sister, I ignored her, Hadrian." I cried into my pillow, eyes squeezed shut. "And I have this . . . this ugly thing in my chest that I can't get rid of."

So ugly, it was only a matter of time before Emma saw it, too. Before she left me, just like everyone else had.

Chapter Sixteen

Thwack, thwack, thwack.

The root split in two beneath my hand trowel. Sweat trickled down my neck, between my breasts, and settled in the band of my sports bra like an anxious memory. My knees were the only cool part of my body, and only because of the damp, fluffed dirt I kneeled in.

I despised tilling dirt, especially by hand. I really did. There was something about the idea of little beings—bugs and worms, specifically—crawling through the dirt just beneath my fingertips, slowly decreasing the distance between my body and theirs, that made my hair lift at my nape. It was one thing to rip open a bag of potting soil; another beast entirely to dig my fingers into the ground where maggots and beetles lived.

You'll be here one day, it whispered.

The tornado of whispers wouldn't shut up.

Images continued to flit before me. My mom, tossing another liquor bottle into a heap in the corner of the apartment. My father, asking why I smelled the way I did. Ivan, his nose an inch from mine, his brows slammed over his eyes as he asked, "How embarrassing can you be, Lan. Don't embarrass *me* like that again."

Three words had circled like vultures when I'd found that closet. Touched the door. A sick feeling coiled in at the base of my throat. I wasn't sure why I hadn't thought of it before—but if memories replayed in that room, they'd come from somewhere. I'd seen the attic, then, as what I assumed it used to be. What if those words were from him?

Don't embarrass me, Lan.

Over and over they tumbled, morphing into a slew of snide remarks, ranging from Ivan's voice to my mother's, then to everything my father *didn't* say.

What will other people think?

I don't need you.

This is why everyone leaves you.

Mom's voice hissed in my ear. *Your father left me because of you, Landry.*

If you didn't exist he might still be here, Landry.

Tears clouded my vision. My hacks into the soil became restless, desperate, urgent. Last night, I felt it: the slow unraveling of my resolve. A realization that I didn't want to accept.

Even now, the fettuccini noodles sat like curdled milk in my gut. Dirt flew like tiny needles, peppering my skin.

I grunted. The roots were chopped at the ends, but the stupid weed still stood tall, and suddenly I hated it, I *hated* that weed. So I grabbed it by the neck and I ripped it from the earth. Part of the roots held strong. I threw it into the bushes beside the shed, then pushed my hands into the flower bed, grasped for every last tendril of root, and ripped it some more. I threw that away, too.

What was wrong with me?

I curled over the earth. I dug my gloved hands into it, squeezed it until the dirt pushed out around my fingers.

The first sob hurt. Worse than last night. For the briefest of moments, I wondered if Mom was right. Would things have been different if I wasn't here? Better? Easier?

I thought of Hadrian. They were sick, my thoughts. How terrible was I, to consider someone else's lack of living family a form of luck? Because he *was* lucky.

No, not quite a sickness. But a rancid, evil form of jealousy. I was jealous of Hadrian. The way he had stood there while his memory played before him, how he'd been able to tell me to leave the boy behind—to leave *him*. I never would have asked that.

Wasn't that what I'd been doing all this time? Even in middle school and high school, as I'd attempted to beat my way into adulthood, hadn't I begged the universe for help? I would have asked him to stay. Had I been him, I would have *begged* him to save myself as a child.

Worse than that, I was jealous of everything he'd gained from his father. A home. A life alone. At one point, he had no family, no children, no spouse. No one. Everything I'd ever wanted.

It must have been easier to be Hadrian—even to be a creature, locked away in that closet. Even forced to live memories over and over again. At least he knew they weren't real. And yet I awoke every day and there was always a little splinter in the back of my mind, reminding me of everything I hadn't done. That I couldn't do, couldn't say. My memories followed me. And reality never escaped me.

Shouldn't yesterday have been example enough? I couldn't even talk to Emma, and she and Sayer were the closest people in my life, and I couldn't handle a simple conversation.

Pathetic.

I grabbed the trowel, fisted it like a knife, and stabbed the fluffed dirt bed.

"I hate you," I choked. I stabbed over and over and over. "I hate you I hate you I hate you."

That was it—that was the problem. It wasn't that I hated people, so much that I hated myself. I hated what I'd done to myself.

I hated what I'd let happen to me. I hated that I'd never said anything. That I physically couldn't bring myself to do it.

I chucked the trowel against the shed with wet cheeks. It bounced off with a *clang* and plunked right into the grass.

* * *

Days began to bleed together. A Tuesday held no specialty to a Friday. The only way I kept track was by the TV shows I watched at night before midnight came.

Sometimes the closet opened, and other times it didn't. Thankfully, the next time it did, the yellow eyes came with it. Paint prices were my topic of choice that night.

Each night he visited, I realized I liked talking to him more than I did keeping my thoughts to myself.

"He asked me if my husband was looking for something," I complained, eyes closed, talking with one hand. The other hung limp over the side of the bed. The TV whispered, lower than it ever had, because I was worried Hadrian wouldn't be able to hear me talking over it. "Couldn't he see that I was alone? Not every woman has to be married to be in a freaking hardware store."

Another evening, when Hadrian hadn't shown yet, I pulled Irene's copies out of the nightstand.

Maybe there was something I was missing. I started searching key words again, until I landed on the library's contact page. I chewed on the inside of my cheek, then glanced to the closet.

Would he mind if I asked Irene if she knew anything? Surely he wouldn't.

But what if she said no? What if she'd not wanted to help Aunt Cadence any more than she had? What if the idea of the house being haunted had scared her away?

I highlighted her email, copied it, and opened a draft before I had the chance to think twice. This wasn't about pride or fear of being rejected anymore. This needed to be logical, and the only logical thing to do was at least ask Irene if she knew something.

I kept the email concise, out of fear that I'd scare her away:

Hi Irene,

I hope this email finds you well. I came in a while ago asking about my aunt's house, Harthwait, and there have been a few developments while I've been here. Do these look familiar to you, by any chance? I happened to find a Reddit post that sounded similar to the issue I'm having, that I believe you wrote. Please let me know if you'd like to talk—if not, I understand.

I double-checked that I'd typed my phone number correctly and attached the photos of the doorframe before hitting send.

After that, I flopped back on my bed and glared at the ceiling.

"Hadrian."

A scratching sound came from under the bed. It should have been concerning that I didn't jump, only held completely still, until a familiar voice said, "Yes, dearest?"

I rolled over onto my side. One clawed hand edged out from under the frame. "Did you ever go to college?"

A dark laugh. "To be frank, I didn't need to."

The conversation started with my interest in history during college, then somehow snowballed into my lack of dating since then.

"I just never felt the need for it," I told the nightstand. It felt good to get it off my chest.

He chuckled.

"Maybe at first I thought it was me," I muttered. I ran a finger along the edge of the nightstand. Then the corner of the paper. I turned Hadrian's picture to me. "Then, as I got older, the idea of dating felt so tiresome. Why put that much effort into something that would only fail?"

"Not all relationships fail."

"I mean, like—when you're changing so much as a person. Your twenties are so pivotal."

I didn't realize that he'd crawled from under the bed and perched against the dresser, as he'd done before. The TV continued its murmur. Maybe it was the low light, but I could have sworn his skin wasn't as gray as before. The tips of his ears seemed rounder, shorter, but those eyes—they were still as bright as they'd always been.

Almost as if he were a bit more human tonight.

". . . . buy within the next thirty minutes and receive a free . . ."

For the first time, I reached for the remote and turned the TV off. But he felt too far away.

I slipped from under the sheets, situated my sweatshirt, and took a seat on the floor at the foot of the bed directly across from him.

"There is truth in finding people for a season in life. Sometimes they are building blocks. Others, they're a foundation for you."

"You speak like you've had that before," I said, content.

"Not particularly. I have seen it, myself, but never experienced it."

I tucked my chin into my palm, thoughtful. "What do you mean?"

"I was never in a place to give someone all of myself, Landry. I took. I did a lot of—taking, before."

The air grew charged then. Unsaid questions formed on my tongue, but the churning of his eyes made me think twice. *Taking* could mean a number of things. My brow furrowed.

I said, "I wish I'd done that. Taken instead of given so much."

"No, you don't. Not truly."

I ran my hands over my knees, down my shins, and onto the rug. I shrugged.

"I don't know. You ever just—want to start over? Go to a new place, become a completely different person? Date a ton of people, go out of your element, push yourself a bit?" I asked. My eyes shuttered. Little by little, my brain quieted. I could almost see it. A new town, states away. Doing exactly as he'd said not to do.

"I did. For a while. Leave, I mean."

My eyebrows rose.

"Sometimes dreams are better as dreams. Because once you have them, you realize you were running from something. Not chasing the dream itself."

My eyes met his. Measured the inhales and exhales when I felt it again: that flutter in the recesses of my chest cavity, like an awakening.

Sometimes dreams are better as dreams.

Which was a shame. Because sometimes, when I went to sleep at night, I'd hoped that I'd dream of him.

* * *

One morning, the universe decided to break up my monotony, if only for a little while. I'd hoped for an email from Irene.

I was sorely disappointed. I received a text from someone else instead.

IVAN: I understand picking someone to represent you as a seller is important. Remember that I can always give you the contractual agreement to look at without actually signing.

I chewed on it. Weighed my options while I stripped more wallpaper in the dining room and bubble wrapped the tea set for safekeeping before I decided to respond, fingers trembling—but only a little.

LANDRY: We aren't taking down any walls
IVAN: Understood
LANDRY: Send me the contract to look at please. I'd like to list sometime in the next couple months
IVAN: Sounds good. I really appreciate you taking the time to think about it.

I'd be lying if I said I didn't think about that first dream while I waited for those three little bubbles to appear, telling me that he was either typing or sending the file. How that thing, which I still wasn't so sure had been Hadrian or just a figment of my imagination, had hovered inside the sunroom door while Ivan inched closer, closer. Instead, I counted to ten, flipped my phone over, and went about my day.

* * *

The day Ivan was scheduled to show, Hadrian found me in the library before dawn. I'd just started hand sanding a piece of baseboard trim, right next to the built-in bookshelves, to see how it lifted. Emma wouldn't stir for another few hours, and the idea of uninterrupted silence was too enticing to pass up. Then again, I'd have plenty of silence when she left today. She said she'd be gone again for a week this time, maybe a bit more, she wasn't sure. I never had asked specifics on the vacation time she'd taken; there were days I'd caught her sitting at her laptop with spreadsheets pulled up. Others, she'd help organize Aunt Cadence's paperwork like a madwoman.

Now, the more I thought about it, the more guilty I felt. I knew her position allowed flexibility, but I'd not appreciated that she'd taken her free time—where she could have gone anywhere but here—and come and helped me instead.

I hadn't invested any *real* time with Emma. I'd callused myself, expected little, but given little, too.

"You woke early," Hadrian said.

I sighed. Most of the books had been removed from the shelves, stacked in the hallway, and labeled by genre and shelf position, leaving me with nothing but a wall of emptied built-in bookcases.

I caught the flash of his buttoned shirt, those same rolled sleeves. My mouth went dry. As if my midnight ramblings somehow amplified how very *human* he looked in the morning light.

Completely human, just as he'd been in that room the first time I saw him. The picture from the library come to life, save for that one thing I couldn't put my finger on.

I paused my hand sanding. "How come you don't look like Krampus right now?"

He glared at me.

"Do you know what Krampus is?" A grin slithered over my mouth.

"No. And I'm afraid I do not wish to." He took a seat on the floor next to me. His knee almost touched mine. If I bent to the left, they'd probably touch. "Here I was, thinking you might have been happy to speak to a beautiful face instead of a monster."

I faced the bookcase. He didn't know how right he was. Still, it worried me, the changing. First it had been what he'd been able to hear—and now this?

"Why is that, do you think?" I flipped the sandpaper over and started on the corner of the bookcase. The paint dusted away easily enough. If only the baseboards were the same.

"I do not know all the answers, unfortunately."

"Do you think it's being out of the room?" Whatever had locked him in, maybe?

"Perhaps. Here." He reached over and slipped the sandpaper out of my hand. I don't know why I let him, but I did. He leaned in with all his weight and gave the sandpaper two solid swipes. The baseboard came away stripped.

I glowered. My little patch looked pitiful in comparison.

"And here I was, thinking you were just a creature of night. You missed your calling, Hadrian. Should've been a handyman."

His eyes—mismatched in color, one gray and one yellow—met mine. "Is that so?"

"You're meant for fine, hard labor with muscle like that." I took my sandpaper back. And that wasn't because the flex of his triceps branded itself into my memory. Teasing, I gave a wry look. "You know, when you're not stalking around the house, brooding like a creepy boogeyman, I could use the extra set of hands."

His jaw clenched. "I would have you know, brooding is a full-time job."

"Is that so?"

"Someone has to count the cobwebs at night. Hang from the rafters and stare longingly at the moon. Follow an unsuspecting woman down the hallway in case danger should arise."

I pictured Hadrian wearing a cape, like Dracula. "Very vampiric of you," I goaded. "Do you flinch at garlic, too?"

He huffed. "I abhor garlic." Then, "I pay no mind to physical labor, if you must know. I'd much rather make money from something that stations itself and doesn't require my constant attention."

A businessman to his core, I thought, the obituary coming to mind. When I said as much, his nose wrinkled. "And you know this how?"

"Believe it or not, women read in this day and age."

His eyes rolled. "I meant *from where* did you read it."

I almost preened at his attempted insult. Instead, my expression softened. I thought of his photograph. Everything that I *hadn't* found yet in order to hold up our deal.

I situated myself to face him. "I may have snooped through the Colleton library. Found a few articles and pictures of you, for proof you weren't lying to me. That you did exist at one point."

An evil grin curled over his mouth. He looked almost like a hyena. My stomach dropped—not out of fear, but anticipation. "Ah. And what did you find? Portrait wise?"

"Nothing outstanding." I felt like this was a test. I couldn't stifle the tingle that started at the base of my spine.

"Is this why you have a printed picture of me at thirty-three hidden inside your nightstand?"

My breath caught. "You didn't!" I winced, then lowered my voice and bent forward. "You went through *my things*?"

"It was not just you, dearest. I may have gone through much of your aunt's things, too." He shrugged and looked at me from under his lashes, which were the richest of honeyed browns. "But I suppose everything is yours now."

The sandpaper crinkled in my hand. My face immediately lit on fire. All I could think of was my nightstand. Dumbly, I said, "What."

"I told you, I roam." His voice took on a rough quality, smug to the point of a rumble.

Looking at Hadrian felt—too susceptible. Because I didn't know what to feel quite yet. Or if what I was feeling was even okay.

I shoved at the mental image of Hadrian, either in his creature form or as himself, snooping. In his defense, I should have thought about how he could go through anything in the house. Heat curled in my chest at the thought of him rifling through the closets, drawers, my bags. *All* of my things.

He must have seen the tortured look I tried to hide, because he said, "I'd be wary of looking at my portrait too much before you fall asleep. You might dream of things you wouldn't wish to."

His expression suggested anything *but* unpleasant dreams.

I was going to light on fire. Right here. Nothing but charred rug would be left in my wake.

"Do not look so near to death, Landry. I find it quite enthralling. It's flattering that you find me so attractive, even with the lovely set of horns I possess from time to time." He bumped his knee against mine. "Who knows, next time I think I should fulfill this character you've painted me as and grab your wrist from beneath the bed instead of just crawl out from under it."

The thought of him—grabbing my wrist—pulling me down—I shouldn't have blushed at the thought, shouldn't have started to picture him with slightly parted lips and—

"I'll hit you with a lamp," I said, but it was too wispy to be a threat, "if you try to do that."

He laughed. Actually laughed, deep from his chest—the sound was beautifully intoxicating. Like he knew what I was picturing. It only electrified the air, the space he took up, emphasized the looseness to his shoulders and the dip of his arms, the swoop of his thighs.

I tried to straighten, to puff up a bit. Anything to quell the burn now crawling up my spine. "All right, since you're so keen on snooping through people's things, did my aunt have anything to do with you being trapped here? Did you find anything?" My words cracked. I cleared my throat and scooted back until the crushed velvet of the armchair pressed between my shoulder blades. That should be enough distance.

His expression solidified a bit. "No, it was not her. I heard her once or twice in more recent years—your aunt, I presume—while I was confined, but not much else."

"Who, then? Trapped you?"

He sighed. He drew his knees to his chest and captured each wrist in the opposite hand. My eyes started to travel over his fingers, the veins that laced up his shirtsleeves and over his forearms. It made my throat dry.

"It might help us pinpoint what we're looking for," I suggested. I looked away. I needed to think—not let my mind wander. "Actually, you don't have to tell me if you're not comfortable yet."

His eyes, slitted, traced the edge of the bookcase before turning to me. "How about this. I tell you something about my past, you offer something in return."

My usual defensive shield started to pull into place. Instead, I held it fast. Just for a moment. A grain of honesty for honesty. He'd already listened to me talk at night. The only difference now was that I could see his reactions.

"Deal." Outside, the sky had already started to melt into a faint pink. Within the hour, the colors would stretch far over the treetops, anchored by the sun.

"I know who put me here. The, ah, circumstances may be best shown instead of described, though." His head tipped back until he stared at the ceiling. The curve of his neck, the tilt of his chin, made my cheeks heat. "It was Beulah, my nursemaid. I called her Bunny. She cared for me since I was a babe. It was not common for a mother to take care of her own, especially in high society, so the child was given to a wetnurse and was socialized with the parents once or twice a day." His Adam's apple bobbed. He stretched his legs and leaned back on both hands. His shirt pulled. "I remember I called her 'Momma' once, on accident, and that memory was the most replayed in that space. I just . . ."

I didn't so much as breathe while he considered his next words.

"However young, she was my mother in every way. She was there when no one else was and it . . . all—hurts, how things ended."

"You miss her," I whispered, a tinted note of longing in my voice. I wanted that, too, this pain he had, of knowing someone was there to love you, to build you in ways only a parent could. I wanted a Momma to love me, despite my mistakes. I wanted to miss her like he missed Bunny. But I didn't miss my mother—not like that.

It made me think of what he'd mentioned before, about not all relationships failing. Because he was right. I did want that, the connection, the ability to work on things with someone, the privilege of baring the ugliest parts of myself to another and having them not shy away.

I wanted to look another person in the eye and see the love in their irises, shimmering like broken lake water on a gentle breeze. Steady and soft. Persistent.

Hadrian's eyes turned glassy. Once he blinked, they cleared, and his words came out rough. "I miss her greatly. Because there is no love like the guidance of a parent—by blood or no blood. She was that for me."

Outside, the sad cry of a mourning dove split us.

"I have had a long while to come to terms with what happened, Landry," he said, sincere. "She did what needed to be done."

"What did she do?"

"Her concerns . . ." He scratched at the corner of his yellow eye, as if he could feel the difference. "I know little of what she did, since I was so young. I do know she always concerned herself with matters of the house." He sighed, then grumbled, more to himself, "She made a comment once or twice about the atmosphere within it. That she needed to sustain it. Protect the place from my father in any way possible."

"I don't understand," I whispered.

"I remember . . . so little," was all he said. I didn't want to push. Just like those moments at night when I felt a tug from down the hallway, I was suddenly holding myself over the side of a bridge, watching the water rush below. If I let go, I'd fall. If I held on, I could wait for the water to calm.

Hadrian was the rushing high tide. His jaw ground too hard. His finger tapped atop the back of his hand.

"Hadrian?" I asked.

A shift. Whatever thoughts he'd been close to saying, evaporating. Sunlight started to peek farther over the treetops, magentas and peaches and warmth. "Yes, Landry?"

"Do you think—do you ever—" I tried another angle. "You never told me how long you were alone."

Another pause. "Hmm. I do believe it is your turn to tell me something honest, yes?"

My tongue stuck to the roof of my mouth like a wet rag on sandpaper. "I'm getting to that."

"Okay." The word was ponderous.

"From your years," I tried, and this time I tried to meet his gaze, "do you think that it's possible for someone to not feel alone?"

"Are you asking if I was lonely in that place, or are you asking as a generality?"

I shrugged. "Either. You've experienced more life than I have. That holds more value to me." I wanted to know if this feeling would ever go away. The emptiness. That no one would quite understand the guilt I felt for how my family fell apart. How I'd handled it. How sometimes it felt like no matter how many people I was around, familiar or not, I was always a little alone.

"I should hardly consider my life experience more valuable than yours."

"That's a bit presumptuous."

"If you mean, is it possible to not feel alone because of a lack of family, then no. I do not think it is possible for someone to not feel alone, if only a little bit." He pressed the toes of his shoes to the bookcase. His eyes hardened. "However, families come in many forms. If you are asking how long it was before I did not feel lonely within that place, I would say never. The memories berated me on a constant rotation. It was hard to remember what *normal* felt like, or what life was beyond my child-self crying, my father appearing, and Bunny searching for me."

I soaked in the words. The images his voice conjured.

"It was painful. At first, I always seemed to be the creature. I could never will myself to be *me*. But over time, I accepted some things. Like my father's choices. And Bunny's. I gained more liberties with my form, and as time passed, I only relived select memories at night. But the house always changed with them. It was like a pressure—right on my chest."

I sat the piece of trim down and wrapped my arms around my knees. I held my wrists in a desperation grip, the skin on the underside of my arms softer than fresh marshmallow. My jeans were stained with paint and something like oily ink I couldn't identify.

"I think I'm having a hard time understanding how you're not still angry," I whispered. "At your father. What he did to you, and reliving it so much."

Hadrian leaned forward, mimicking my position. Our shoes—my open-toed sandals versus his shined, tied black loafers—sat an inch apart. Like two children hiding in a closet, readying to tell each other secrets.

"I think you misunderstand." His eyes grew heavy, knowing. "I was angry. For many, many years. You wouldn't believe the things I did while I was in there."

"Over one hundred?"

A nod. "And at least sixty were spent in hatred." His mouth closed. Lips pursed. "I still am angry with him. Anger means I care. But left too long, that anger will rot. Here." He tapped a spot over his chest. "Who was it that said, 'I sat with my anger long enough until she told me her real name was grief'?"

I searched his cheeks, his neck, the collar of his shirt, but not his eyes. "C.S. Lewis, I believe." The quote had been one of Aunt Cadence's favorites.

His voice wavered, barely there. But when he caught my eyes, they were earnest. Tender. "Anger is a prerequisite to a lot of things. Think of it like a train station. You can head north, west, east—wherever you wish. All you need to remember is that there is another stop after that first one. And each will be different. You decide where you go." His fingers found the back of my hand—the only sounds the catch of my breath and the rustle of his shirt. "You can ride it until the ends of the earth. But then you will have to live with the consequences of never leaving that train. And every opportunity you could have had will already be gone."

The words spread like balm over me.

"What if I don't want to leave the anger behind?" I murmured.

His jaw feathered. His fingers tapped on the top of my hand. "But what if you did?"

Hadrian was right: The anger meant I cared. I cared what people thought of me, I cared how they saw me. I cared that my younger self saw justice.

But how long could I hold onto it before it hurt me?

Could I really forgive myself for staying in situations that killed me from the inside out?

The sunroom bloomed in morning light by now. Long, welcoming shadows stretched over the walls, the floors, through the door to the sunroom.

"You'll find your own way, Landry," he said. A hint of the creature laced his voice. When my gaze met his, both eyes were yellow. The sun dripped over his cheeks like honey. "And we will figure things out together."

I nodded. Without asking, I knew I was losing time with him right now. I explained the scouring of the office, the attic, the library, to no avail. "So what do you think I should start looking for?"

"You, ah . . ." Two creases appeared between his brows. "Your aunt kept old things, did she not? I saw boxes in the attic but did not—" He stopped himself. *Did not go up there*, was what he didn't say.

"She did."

"Where did she get them from?"

"Meredith said antique shows, I think. Why?"

"All the items were from shows?" he pressed.

I stared and my hand slipped from his. "Hadrian, don't play with me."

Hadrian gave a dry chuckle. "You have a knack for donating things. How much did you remove before I came into the house?"

My eyes grew round. "Are you saying there might have been something in those boxes I took to Meredith? Why didn't you say anything sooner! You've been here long enough!" I smacked his shoulder. "I've been taking junk to her for months!"

He snatched my hand. "Breathe. It was a thought, nothing more."

The back of my head started to tingle. I feigned shaking him. He only snatched my other wrist.

"You said you don't even know what we're looking for!" I said, blustery.

"I don't," he countered. "I am simply making a suggestion. Think—ritualistic things."

"Like candles and salt rings and . . . dark magic."

"Like curses."

I could strangle him. If only I could wrap my hands around his thick neck, shake some sense into him. My hands balled into fists instead. He drew my wrists in, pulling me closer, close enough that I caught the smell of open water and something distinctly masculine. Flutters erupted in my stomach when his words brushed my cheeks.

"I'm sorry I'm of such little help. We know, at least, the room recycles memories. Maybe start there. And I will attempt to come forward more." The words almost sounded pained.

"Then when you can, find me at night," I breathed. I didn't realize how it sounded until I said it.

Something in his eyes glittered. "Is that a request? Am I being invited?"

"Maybe." We stared at each other, both breathing a little heavy, like the air between us was more nutritious if the other inhaled the other's exhale. Like he might give me patience, and I might give him a dash of anger. Just enough to spur things along. Then his expression tangled, his pupils turned to razor-thin slits.

"What else aren't you saying, Hadrian?" I whispered.

"I'm saying," he said, "I hope you're the praying type. Because I have little idea what I am tangled in, and I do not know what will happen when we find it."

"The confidence you have in us finding anything is quite refreshing."

A smirk kissed the corners of his lips. "You said you went to the library looking for pictures of me?"

"Not just pictures of you, you twit—"

"Any religions you know of that you could research?" he pressed. I couldn't focus when he watched my mouth like that. With reverence.

That's when it hit me. Religions. Cults. Aunt Cadence had asked about it before.

My stomach dipped. That meant Irene very well might know, and that she hadn't emailed yet wasn't promising.

Maybe I had scared her away.

"I trust you, Lan." His words grew labored, feathered at the ends. The sun had slid down his chest, his shoulders, right to his elbow. Enough that it warmed my back. "And if I am honest, you are all I have."

His mouth wavered inches from mine. I didn't realize my head had tilted until it started.

Like whisps of smoke, Hadrian vanished in the morning sun. I was left with warm wrists and flutters far, far down in the center of my heart.

Chapter Seventeen

I heard the truck before it pulled into the driveway. A fine layer of dust coated its sides. Across the road, the open field of waist-high grass swayed in unison.

Something about the conversation with Hadrian spurred me. Meeting with Ivan didn't have to mean I was forgiving him. It was just a packet. A review, really, if I thought about it. This was a toe to the line. An *attempt* to move in a direction. That's what adults did. They set aside their differences, tugged up their bootstraps, and tried to work with the person they hated.

I set the last half of my protein shake on the foyer table and made to unlock the front door. Ivan had already thrown the truck in park and climbed out of the cab. The very sight of his smile made the farthest corners of my heart curl up, curl *away*.

His attention immediately snagged on me as I opened the front door. His laptop, stacked against a manila folder, was pinched under his arm. I suddenly wished Emma hadn't left yet. Or, even better, that dark had fallen and I had the assurance of Hadrian lurking in some odd corner.

"Landry," he greeted, hand shielding his eyes.

I braced myself. No, I couldn't rely on other people to handle my issues. This was for me to work with.

I gave a strained smile. "Ivan."

"You look lovely."

I put on my brave face. "Thank you for stopping by." Maybe something had changed in the last near decade—maybe Emma was right. Maybe I was being too hard on him.

Ivan started to climb the steps when my pocket vibrated. Emma and Sayer both knew Ivan was stopping by today, which left one person: Mom.

"I never got a chance to tell you what a beautiful place this is," Ivan said. I offered my hand, elbow locked, but he reached for a side hug.

Holes emerged in my intestines, pushed bile up my throat. He didn't seem to notice the stiffness to my body when he squeezed my shoulders.

Heat—everywhere. And not the good kind. Not the heat I felt when I was watching Hadrian watch me, when I felt the brush of his fingers on my hand, when I noted the glitter in his eye. A sickly kind of heat.

A dry, deadly heat.

I cleared my throat. "Thank you. Aunt Cadence kept up with it well."

He licked his bottom lip. "That she did."

Even the skin around his jaw shined. He'd probably oiled his face before he'd gotten out of the truck.

"I read through the packet, but I wanted to go over it in person." I slipped through the door first, careful to not keep my back turned to him for long. He ambled in, eyes fondling the archways, the hall, the wide floorboards. He touched the office doorframe, mouth slightly parted.

"Cherry?"

I nodded. I hated to admit it, but Eleanora hadn't noted such a small detail.

I let my wall inch down. If only a little. It almost felt normal, talking to him like this. It reminded me of the times—the good times, though few—we'd had together. The times he'd visited me at Meredith's when I was hiding from Mom. How he'd taken me to a haunted house, religiously, each Halloween. How he had always tapped me on the shoulder three times before whispering over the desk in class, "Have you finished yet?"

I stared at his hands. The strong but slender fingers, the lack of blemishes on his palms. I remembered how they felt, covering my own hand, as he showed me how to shift a manual in the middle of a backroad. How he'd said we couldn't go home until I drove us to my mom's apartment. How I hadn't wanted to disappoint him.

A tendril of that same feeling—expectancy, almost—fluttered inside my chest when he met my gaze.

"I have my notes from before," he said while removing a pen from his shirt pocket. He tucked it behind his ear and nodded down the hallway. "The dining room is fine."

Cautious, I nodded. Maybe this would be quicker than I thought.

My phone buzzed again. A third time. Ivan led the way and I followed, but about halfway there I slipped my phone out of my pocket, just to make sure it wasn't important.

Three texts from my mother.

MOM: Why didn't you tell me?

MOM: Emma knew. You two have been conspiring. That's why you won't talk to me.

The last one stopped me in my tracks.

MOM: Care to explain why Penny left your father?

Thinking bubbles appeared. I watched the new message blink onto the screen:

MOM: Are you home now? Where are you?

I stopped in my tracks. The world tilted on its axis. This couldn't be true. Emma and I had joked about it growing up, sure—but neither of us had expected Penny to leave Vince. She'd always denied the affairs, no matter how obvious they were. Had she finally gotten sick of the cheating, or was it something else?

The tiniest of thoughts came in that moment. Is that why Emma was gone? Was it *really* because of work, or was that a lie? I hadn't been honest with her about everything. The thought that she'd known, or at least had a feeling, and hadn't told me stung.

But if she had—when had I done any better about being open? If Penny left Dad, would Emma have to help her mom move out?

Either way, it would need to wait. I reeled in my thoughts, silenced my phone, and floated into the dining room.

Ivan already had the paperwork sorted at the head of the table by the time I pulled a chair out. The front page explained the usual—a promise for how long the house would be listed with his group, the commission rate, a marketing plan, a portfolio of the similar homes they'd sold before, and a company information section.

Before he flipped to the following page, he scooted his chair closer to mine.

"I understand you've already got the financials settled? The deed is in your name?" One eyebrow arched. He licked his lips while watching me.

"The house was in a trust. A new deed was issued already." My mouth turned sour. Aunt Cadence had a trust made years ago, which she'd documented with a lawyer, while also planting me as her estate executor. Every last ounce: in my lap.

"Good, good," he said under his breath. I eyed the distance from his elbow to mine. How his leg inclined toward me. I edged the other way.

"Everything on the financial side is settled," I said simply. "Don't worry about it."

"Awesome." His voice turned husky. "So, marketing wise. With the comps I pulled, what do you think?" Ivan leaned back, his pen playing between his fingers.

I bit my lip. "What do you mean? I think the comps are in the same range, if that's what you mean."

"Are you okay with the marketing plan?"

I glanced down at the sheet. They'd list it on the MLS, per standard, have a few open houses and work with other agencies, which all seemed normal for any larger listing.

Slowly, the wall I'd pulled down started to inch back up. "Ivan—it all looks fine. I don't think I understand what you're getting at." Shouldn't this have been where I was asking him questions? The commission was a standard commission, which changed depending on the sale price. Unless I was missing something.

He gave a breathy chuckle. Then, he looked at me like he had before, his eyebrows slightly arched and a smile teasing his lips.

Like he might be testing me.

"Do you mind me asking who the other company is you're debating listing with?"

My eyes narrowed. "I don't see why that matters."

"I mean—come on, Lan. You know me. I'll do what needs to be done to get this thing sold in a good time frame for the best possible price." His mouth tilted up at the corner. He raked his fingers through his artfully messy hair, which I suddenly had a strong urge to hold a lighter against. I bet it'd burst into flames from the amount of hairspray he'd used. "I just want to make sure you're taken care of. I know—I understand everything that happened may have dampened our relationship a bit, but I want to set things aside. Everything."

I blinked fast at his words. May have dampened—not it did. As if dampening a relationship didn't hover in the same realm as *ending* the relationship that he then claimed we'd never had. Not to mention that he not only diminished what had happened before, but he cushioned the statement with a good deed.

I just want to make sure you're taken care of.

As if it were a service to me. An honor.

I stared at him, blank. Was the bar really, truly so low that the bare minimum was supposed to knock my socks off?

I felt a snide, younger part of myself settle back in the corner of my mind with a twisted glare. *It worked before, didn't it?*

I guess it had. Still, I paced myself. This was transactional. A business meeting, and nothing more, which didn't need to involve personal feelings.

Yet.

Upstairs, a floorboard creaked. Ivan didn't notice.

I sat up straighter. Redirect—that's all I could do, wanted to do. "When do you think would be a good time to list?"

He took a breath and I readied myself. Normally, spring opened strong for new listings. There was another jump before the holidays, since people loved to move and decorate before Christmas. It didn't mean that September was a bad idea, but I knew it might sit for a few months, especially with its size and the fact that it was older.

"Landry, please." Ivan's voice wasn't as guttural as Hadrian's, but it held a weight to it. An authority, finality that made you feel as if his mind was settled, whether you stepped into his circle of agreement or not.

"I really think we should talk about the problem at hand, right now," I said. "Which is the house." That was what he was here for. But I was getting the feeling that he was stalling.

"This *is* pertinent to right now. I want to work with you. I think we'd make a great team," he conceded. "I just want to discuss things first. How everything ended."

I knotted my hands together, anticipation vibrating through me, followed by a sticky, bubbly feeling in my gut.

"What are you talking about." I didn't let it sound like a question.

His chest lifted, mouth settled into a sure line. "You understand that things—how they ended, did a number on my parents' reputation, don't you? They moved their office because of it. It's why I commute."

I sat, dumbfounded. *His parents'* reputation was injured?

All regard for keeping personal feelings out of this discussion flew out the window.

There was no way he was actually opening this conversation right now. Even the idea made me sit forward, my eyes turning to moons as I tried to keep myself from floating out of my chair.

"You weren't affected after you left for school, but the things people were speculating in town were absolutely absurd and—"

"Excuse me?" I blurted. I pressed a hand to my throat. "I wasn't affected? Really?"

Images, like scenes on a movie roll, clicked in rapid fire before me. Still shots of moments between us, the silent tears in my bedroom, the moment on the back of the truck, his hands in my pants, his nails digging into my skin, his teeth on my shoulder, pressure, so much pressure as he pushed me into the place he wanted, the feel of his knee splitting mine apart and his weight trapping me. Everything. All of them, all at once, so stout and bitter that my lungs caught fire.

He made a withering sound. "Let me finish."

I turned mute with shock.

Like so many times before, he took my silence as a go ahead, and went on. "I wanted to say that I forgive you for what you said. Or, well, didn't say. I didn't take it to heart—I know you were hurt by our breaking up, and in the end, I truly think it was for the best. I'm sure you've had some amazing relationships since, as have I, and I think we can both agree that the tension is still there but what people said afterward is more important. I didn't appreciate the bullshit you managed to catch fire to, and to be frank, I had to work pretty hard to convince my coach that I wasn't bullying women in my free time."

It was like someone had sucked all of the air out of the room.

I saw red.

"You *bullying* women?" I snapped.

He gave a look as if he agreed. "That's what I said."

"And how were you just bullying women, Ivan?"

Either he was plain stupid, or he was really terrible at reading people, because he waved a hand, almost nonchalant as if we were talking about the weather, and said, "Someone overheard you speaking with that friend of yours. Sayer, I believe? And there was some suspicious connotation to it, about how you didn't seem comfortable with me and then it run rampant and people started to speculate that I was, how would you say"—he rolled his hands together, in a *get-on-with-it* motion—"pushed myself upon you. We both know it was consensual, and teenagers will be teenagers—"

My heart was too fast, my limbs too buoyant, my brain too clouded.

I exploded.

"You think I ruined your life? You think I hurt *your* reputation?" I ground out.

His posture didn't so much as tense. It was languid. Easy. Lazy, as he watched me. "All I'm saying is that I didn't appreciate the speculation, especially when it affected my family, is all."

I couldn't breathe. I couldn't do this.

Did I want to list with Ivan? Is this *really* what I wanted? This house, this money from the sale, to go to him?

Was this a sign? Was I pushing things too quickly? Did I really, *really* want to give Aunt Cadence's home to someone—someone like *this*?

It took every fiber of my being to clench the arms of the chair instead of his papers and rip them to shreds. Images of the house selling, of me being unsuccessful in the search for Hadrian, someone who didn't love the house for its character, flooded my mind. My chest clenched so hard that I felt it in my spine.

This could go well—but it could also go very poorly. I wanted this place to be loved.

It was supposed to be a home. I wasn't sure Ivan could provide that—history or not. I didn't *need* to do this. I was done—absolutely, completely done.

Maybe Hadrian was right. I gave the project such a tight timeline, all for the sake of getting it gone, replenishing the monetary hit I was taking, and running so, so far away, just so I didn't have to sit in *this* any longer than I needed to.

"You know what," I said gently. But the words were strangled. Choking. Just like my heart was. "I don't think Harthwait needs to sell. I think I'm going to pull back on listing."

"What?" He sat forward, expression shuttering.

Weight rolled off my shoulders, away from my ribs. The slightest of pressures released from my heart. "I'm not selling. I'm sorry. I've changed my mind."

Ivan's laugh was scratchy. I stared at the floating shelf on the wall behind his head, now empty of the tea set. "You've got to be kidding me."

"No. I'm not."

He shook his head and pushed up from the table. "This is out of spite, isn't it? You thought you'd dangle something in front of me now, just like before? Is this to get back at me?" He placed both hands on the table and leaned over me while I held my seat. I could smell the cologne—rich and intoxicatingly sweet, so much of it that I wanted to vomit. "A tease?"

I schooled my features. My phone vibrated—again. This was starting to get ridiculous. I should have turned it off.

"I think you should go, Ivan." I stood, already pushing my chair under.

He held his place. "You're not even going to give me the courtesy of discussing this?"

"No. I have somewhere I need to be. So if you could move along—"

"You're upset I dumped you. You strung me here, dangled the chance to sell this place in front of me, and now you're cutting me off just to prove a point, aren't you?"

I stilled. Turned, robotic, to Ivan.

For the first time, I didn't feel intimidated looking up at him. I should have. But the dormant frustration morphed into a rabid creature, sprouting claws and spikes and razor-sharp teeth. I leveled him with my most poisonous glare.

"Why did you come here, Ivan? Be honest."

"The listing—"

Before he even got the words out, a hot flash of hate flooded every crevice of my body.

"*You used me*," I snarled. "I didn't ruin your family. I did nothing—I gave you everything while we were together. I showed you every ugly thing about *my* family, about *my* life, and all you wanted was a nice, solid lay. You held me under your thumb, you kept me at your beck and call"—my voice rose, to the point I felt the veins in my neck bulge—"and you enjoyed it, you narcissistic *prick*. I gave you a chance to prove you'd changed because Emma brought you here." I started to walk around my chair, then stopped.

I pointed my finger at him, and this time, I was the one that leaned in, teeth bared. "You want to know something? I didn't tell anyone about the things you said to me. You assaulted me. You tried to *rape me* and *no* I *did not* enjoy *any* of it!"

His cheekbones purpled. "What *I* did to you, Lan? Really. Get a grip. We were teenagers. Do you know what a tease you were? Making me beg like a dog? Hormones—"

I threw my hands down and roared, "You told me I'd end up pregnant, alone, with no friends, and that I'd never be loved by a man!" My voice broke, garbled—and that's when I felt it. A chill washed through the room.

Still, I pushed on. I grabbed that last mangled thread inside my chest cavity and yanked it free.

"I said I loved you, and you said I was too ruined by my own daddy issues to ever know how to love you like you needed. You said that the women in my family didn't know anything about pleasing men and *that* was why my dad had to cheat on my mother all the time."

Silence.

Wide and expansive, vast and acidic, it stretched between us. The room overflowed with it. Ivan went from staring at me, to staring over my shoulder. His pallor leeched of color.

The sound of three sharp clicks.

I knew those clicks.

"This is absolutely insane. You are insane," he muttered. He turned to leave. I wanted to give chase. I wanted to shout, I wanted to slam the door in his wake, to be the one to cut him out, but I didn't. I listened to the whisper of his shoes over carpet, until the front door banged shut. The stained glass rattled before falling silent.

Then, I glanced behind me to see where the clicks had come from.

It was the darkest corner of the room—the opposite side from where the sun usually hit. A corner cabinet, filled with antique crystal, sat behind a stack of taped boxes I hadn't gotten to yet. There, in the glass door, I saw my reflection—and beside it, Hadrian's, just as I had the night he'd appeared in the kitchen, but this time it was daylight.

He smiled. It was not a kind smile.

A war of emotions twisted inside me: confusion, relief, and the sharp, tangy taste of fear. Relief, because I'd need to figure out what to do about selling, but—I'd said it. After all these years, I'd said *something.* I'd stood up for myself.

For once.

I released a shaky breath; gasped to catch it again.

Okay. This was happening. I wasn't selling the house. At least for right now. That was probably best. It would give me time to finish things up—and find someone I trusted. That loved the house and would help find the right buyer.

But the fear lingered. I clasped my hands on the closest chair back and dropped my head, eyes closed.

"Hadrian?" I whispered. The dining room echoed with his name.

"Yes, dearest?"

My tongue weighed heavy on my next words. "He saw you, didn't he?"

A long, pained pause. "Yes, Lan. I believe he did."

Neither of us needed to say any more. He was progressing. And we still didn't know why.

* * *

I sat in the breakfast nook, laptop open, when my phone vibrated. The sun had already started to set, sending a chill through the open windows despite the humidity that lingered from earlier in the day.

Hadrian lurked in the living room since I'd turned the lights off while there was still daylight left.

He jerked when my phone buzzed across the table. Even from where I sat, I saw his pupils contract, then dilate in what I knew was irritation.

"Why does it make such a noise?"

I checked the caller ID. An unknown number, but it wasn't listed as spam. "It means someone is calling me."

"Such tedious things." He turned away. His shoulders bunched closer to his neck, his top lip curled.

Emma or Sayer were the only ones that would call after five—clients usually emailed, but not always. I swiped to answer, just in case.

"Hello?"

"Landry?"

"This is she." I closed my laptop and straightened. Hadrian's head tilted just so, enough to tell me he could probably hear the person on the other end.

"It's Irene. I'm sorry I didn't contact you sooner—I just—there were a lot of things I wanted to get together for you. Do you have a minute?"

My eyes widened. I waved Hadrian closer, mouthing, *Come here.* She'd gotten my email—she hadn't ghosted me. I wiggled closer to the edge of my seat and pulled a second chair up against my own, then pointed for him to sit down.

He eyed the chair. Wrinkled his nose.

"Sit!" I whispered. Then, to the phone, "Yes, of course I've got time. I'm so glad you called, I was worried it would seem too—forward." *Or creepy*, I thought.

A rumble, close to a growl, came from his chest as he glared at the phone, similar to the disgust I'd seen when he mentioned the lightbulbs in the living room.

All right. Maybe he hated technology completely.

Still, I put the phone on speaker so he could listen, laid it flat on the table, and grabbed a notepad and pen from my purse. Writing by hand always felt faster than typing, and the last thing I needed to do was forget anything.

"If anyone has to apologize, it's me," she started. Her voice crackled, sharp, on the line, making it echo through the first floor. Hadrian's lips curled back, so I turned the volume down. "I didn't mean to leave you that note. I thought Cadence wasn't good with texting, so I left her a note one morning when I was couriering books from the Stetson library to the Hemlock branch. I didn't mean to scare you. I'm assuming you saw it?"

My mind whirred, trying to catch up, as I sat back down. Hadrian's arm brushed mine. We sat close, his thigh to my knee, my elbow near his. "What note?"

A nervous sigh. "I actually found something three months ago. On those symbols she'd asked me about."

My eyes brightened. Then—a sinking in my stomach. She'd found something. I should be happy. This was what Hadrian wanted, what I'd agreed to.

"You did?"

I replayed my memories—over and over. A note.

It hit me like a far, distant wave breaking before shore. One of the women dropping off a casserole had found it on the porch and gave it to me the morning of the funeral. I hadn't even stayed a night in Harthwait yet. The house had been empty from Aunt Cadence's death until Sayer helped me move in after the funeral. Of course no one would have seen the note—and there was no telling how long Irene waited for my aunt to respond, only to later find out she'd died.

"I did," Irene assured me. "I'd been digging in my free time after Cadence asked me about it, but she hadn't responded to my calls, so I left a note one morning, and—anyway, I think I found something, but it might not mean much." A hesitant sigh. "Or be what you're looking for. I just texted you the file."

Right on cue, my phone vibrated. Hadrian leaned away, unsure.

My finger shook as I tapped the file.

"A woman brought a boxes of journals she'd found from her adopted grandmother. These were in there. They almost match what you sent me."

I zoomed in.

A scanned copy of a thickened journal page stared back at me. The symbols weren't exactly the same as the ones on the doorframe, but they were close.

I shot Hadrian a look. The chair creaked as he leaned in.

"Do you think the woman that brought these in would know anything?"

"I doubt it. Her grandmother long since passed and she was the only surviving grandchild," she said, with a sad huff. "I asked, but she didn't know much else. Anyway, I thought I'd seen them before, so I started searching through some old folklore forums. Someone had that top symbol, there on the scanned sheet? As their banner."

"Really?"

I could almost hear her nod. "Yep, so I messaged the guy. He said his family was from Appalachia. *Old* Appalachia. And his grandparents used to talk about this old man up the street that was tried for blasphemy when they were children, but something happened when they went to retrieve him for Court Day."

Without thinking, I grabbed Hadrian's wrist with a gasp. "This must have been—" The dates raced through my mind.

"Mid to late 1800s," Irene said.

My other hand covered my mouth. I shook Hadrian's arm. I didn't realize how close he sat, how near he was, until I heard the flutter of his heart and looked up to those yellow eyes locked on me. That was when Hadrian was born. It had to be related somehow.

"Right," I said, breathy. I remembered Court Days from researching aesthetic inspirations. I'd somehow landed on a homestead in North Carolina, and my research had told me that Court Days would take place once or twice a month in older towns. Most were open to the public, and citizens could line up to give grievances to the judge—or cases were open for public observation.

"Anyway, the man had vanished. But he had these symbols all over his cabin."

My mouth formed an O. My palm, I noticed, burned with anticipation against Hadrian's skin. Hadrian had supposedly vanished—just like the man. Had his obituary listed him as having died from natural causes, too?

"The guy who ran the forum was looking up the symbols for a separate disappearance, but he'd found a few translations over the years." Irene's words turned a little breathless with excitement. Another buzz. Screenshots of text messages filled my screen. "This is what he said."

The phone went quiet as she let me read.

ZACH: Hey, sorry it took so long. I think I figured out some of it. Some of the symbols aren't in the artifacts recovered from the cabin but I got enough for you to maybe fill in the blanks. Looks like a sort of loop lmk if that sounds right to you

I got:

1. The first symbol is for attach, or bound/tied (maybe something similar)
2. The next two look like the phrase "to be meaningful" the best I could come up with
3. Don't know the next three, they look scratchy tbh they look like drawings, not symbols
4. Last one means "circle"

An echoing sort of disappointment filled me. It wasn't specific enough to tell us *what* it did, and with the missing symbols, there was no telling what it really meant. How were we supposed to untie a knot when we didn't know how it'd been tied in the first place?

Then, the next text:

ZACH: Don't know if that helps much but if it's on a door I would think it's keeping something in or out. As long as the door is closed you should be good.

I snorted at that last part. Too late for that.

IRENE: What about the seven symbols on the floor in front of the door?

ZACH: Let me check.

ZACH: Not sure, sorry. Looks like "latch." I know this sounds like a classic haunting, but sentimental items can hold stuff. Or are you sure there aren't any remains in the house? They could be holding anything to it until it's destroyed. I've only seen these symbols used as a way of channeling things, not creating them. So whatever is in the house already existed, it wasn't created from them, if that makes sense. Basically it was either put there on purpose or accidently brought in.

I gave Hadrian a look. Well, at least I could confidently say that there was, in fact, an entity in the house. And it was a full-grown man with horns.

"He's saying the symbols are there to contain whatever was inside," I said. I couldn't keep the defeat from leaking into my words. It might help explain the echoes of memories in the room, but it didn't explain the things happening outside of Hadrian's presence. Or why he was changing, and not at will.

"I'm sorry. I know it's not much help, but—was there anything that might have been left in the house from before?"

From the 1800s? I doubted it. Still, I thought of the few boxes left in the attic.

"Maybe." I released Hadrian's wrist and pinched the bridge of my nose. "I'll think on it for a bit and see if I can find anything."

"It's just—if it's haunted, there have been reports of energy festering. You know? Like something is left behind with a heavy pull and then other malicious things follow. Maybe that's what's in the room."

My thumb pressed flat between my brows. "Did she ever mention cleansing the house?"

"All the time, but it never did much. *But*, if there's something in the house, the cleansing wouldn't work."

It made sense. I'd heard stories like that before, too, but it didn't tell us what we were looking for.

The phone was silent for a few seconds. "I'm sorry, I know it's not much."

"It's okay—I appreciate your help."

Hadrian stood, quiet as a whisper, from the chair and padded to the open window in the living room. The sun had ducked completely out of sight, taking the oranges and reds with it, leaving us in almost complete darkness.

As Irene and I said our goodbyes, the slightest urge to ask her about Ivan emerged. But I clutched it, squeezed it until it vanished, and ended the call.

"Well," I sighed, "that wasn't as helpful as I'd hoped."

Hadrian kept his profile to me. The lonesome call of a mourning dove answered for him. I couldn't tell if it was because my hopes had risen too high, which had me at a loss for words, or if it was a soft sense of hurt.

Hurt that we didn't get any closer, but also because the air was strained, Hadrian's posture remained rigid, and I had an overwhelming fear that he was disappointed he was here a while longer with me.

"Are you upset?" I whispered.

"No, dearest." But his words were so, so tight.

My lips flattened. "Promise?"

He rubbed a clawed hand over his jaw. Then he shook his head. Not as an answer, but more to himself.

"Do you remember anything that Bunny might have used? Or kept? Something that maybe you had, of importance, back then before anything happened?"

The air grew heavy. His eyes danced between the floor, the table, and back. I could almost see the curtain pulling down over his expression, the hesitancy.

My lips parted, but a distant pounding on the front door stopped me.

I looked toward the foyer. Emma and Sayer wouldn't knock, and the only other person I could think of was Ivan. Surely, he wouldn't be persistent enough to come back and try and persuade me. Then again—

I cursed under my breath. The chair scratched the floor as I stood. I situated my sweatshirt then stalked through the living room.

"I swear on my life, if he came back, I'm going to bury him in the backyard under the shed," I hissed.

Hadrian's answering snarl followed me. "Wait—"

I didn't. I yanked the front door open. "I told you—"

The words shriveled on my lips, floated away on the breeze. The sick press of dread sunk into my shoulders, like teeth cutting through muscle, straight to the bone—I wanted to turn back, to see if Hadrian was still in the living room, to rewind time just thirty seconds and get him to look out the window for me before I'd unlocked the door.

The porch light haloed her hair like she might have been from the heavens.

"Well?" my mother snapped. "Aren't you going to let me in?"

Chapter Eighteen

"Mom?" I didn't step aside. "What are you doing here?"

"Was that Ivan Kenneth here earlier? Are you seeing him again?" How had she known about him?

She pushed me aside, all red hair and leathered skin. She'd sat out in the sun or gone to the tanning bed weekly since I was old enough to remember. She told Aunt Cadence once that the freckles would connect eventually, whether she got skin cancer or not.

I almost stepped in front of her to keep her from coming in, but as soon as I turned to look in the living room, I noticed the spot where Hadrian had stood was empty.

"No, I'm not. Why would you think that?" If I told her he was a realtor, she'd find a way to flag him back down. She'd always liked him. Only for his family, though.

I let her circle the foyer with her sunglasses on. She pushed them atop her head to squint at the skylight. The smell of cigarette smoke, cheap perfume, and peppermint candies trailed after her. "Ran into 'im at that gas station up the street. Got to talking for a bit, and I hope you know, you *should* be. He's got money. You know what men with money do."

"Cheat on you and pick the other woman?"

Her head snapped down, her mouse-colored eyes narrowing. "Is that a snide remark?"

I kept my face placid. "Why are you here, Mom?" I ran through a mental list. Besides my ignoring her—not unusual—and the text about Vince and Penny, there was no need for her to visit.

"What, I can't come visit my daughter?"

She never had before.

"I don't know. There was a funeral a while ago. Maybe you should have come. I was there." I gathered her comment aside and tucked it away for later.

Something was definitely going on.

She was too busy looking around—peeking in the office, the living room, up the stairs, to catch the tone in my voice. Instead, she made her way to the living room, dropped her overfilled purse on the couch. Her wrists, I noticed, were slender. More so than last time.

"Whew. I'm starving. What do you have in here? Why's it so dark? You keep the lights off to save money?" She flipped three on while making a beeline to the fridge.

My feet were rooted to the floor. She rifled through the fridge, the cabinets, then the corner pantry. Finally, she withdrew a box of crackers and sliced cheese from the fridge. She tore the crackers open with ferocity.

My marrow curdled. All that food, and I knew exactly what she'd do with it. She'd leave crackers strewn over the counter, the floor, never clean them. And then, in a day or two, the ants would come in, if I didn't come after her to clean it up.

The pressure from earlier migrated from my shoulders and morphed into an ugly, tangled creature that wrapped around my stomach. My hands clenched at my sides. I wanted to tear everything from her hands, tell her it's mine, she can't *have* it, she can't do this in my *house*—

"Kitchen looks nice." I couldn't help but notice the dark circles under her eyes, which were bloodshot and smartly offset by the dark charcoal lining them. I bet if I tried to run my hands through the back of her hair, there'd be knots, disguised as artful teasing. She'd always said knots like that were normal. As I grew older, I found out that a lot of things came with matted hair. Sometimes it was depression. Neglect.

I'd cried when I'd realized the second one.

Her nose upturned. "Better than the last time I saw it." She must have been talking about the chickens I'd donated.

"Yeah," I said, dead. "No roosters."

It felt almost like an out-of-body experience, watching her eat in Harthwait's kitchen.

She didn't feel like a person. She was the ghost of an idea that returned once in a while to remind me that a void was still there. That I wasn't wanted, that I wasn't good enough for her then, so why would I be now?

Oh, right. *Money.*

She wiped the back of her hand over her mouth, then brushed the crumbs straight onto the floor. "Smells odd. Like sulfur." She motioned to the open breakfast nook windows, which I knew I'd shut this morning. "God, Lanny. You're letting all the AC out." With a handful of crackers and cheese, she shoved them shut and turned each of their latches.

I could feel it: my body dying while I watched her.

I couldn't ask her to leave. I couldn't ask her to stay. I couldn't do—anything.

"You drove here today." I needed information out of her, but digging too obviously only made her defensive. I needed for her to talk about *her* problems. The rest would spill along with it.

"That's right I did," she said. She pointed a cracker at me. "Three hours. Can you believe it? Didn't stop once."

She could make a three-hour drive today, but she couldn't have driven three hours for her sister's funeral?

"I didn't text you because I was with Ivan." My hands fisted.

She nodded, more to herself. "That. That right there. Don't get me wrong—great looking kid, right—but you didn't answer my calls!

Why didn't you tell me, Lanny? Vince! Of all people. Single. Can you believe it? Why didn't you say anything?" She stuffed the crackers back in the box, didn't fold it shut, only stuffed it back on a shelf in a cabinet it didn't come from. Then she reached back in the fridge and pulled out a jar of pickles and Emma's leftover fettuccine. I watched with stifled horror as she opened the container, didn't microwave it, and stuck the pickle in as if the fettuccine were a dipping sauce.

"I didn't know," I said.

"God, more lies. Your father loves you. Of course you knew." She took a large bite. Juice dribbled over her chin, down her T-shirt. Stains already marred the pink cotton. "Lanny, that man knows what he did wrong. Tell him. I need you to tell him that I was right, all those years. A cheater."

"He knows, Mom." Even if he didn't know, Dad didn't care what anyone thought. There was a reason he was able to go about his affairs while Penny turned a blind eye.

"Well, then why isn't he here?" She motioned to the house. "If he knew, he'd be apologizing already. It's been years."

"Why would he need to be *here*?" Besides the fact that he hadn't called me in months.

"Because! I need a place to live." She took another bite of the pickle. "He can't disrupt everyone's lives and then expect to get away with it, right?"

Bingo. It was like I saw the edge of a waterfall and the little life raft I knelt on had no paddle.

"I thought I could stay with you for a bit. Of course, I knew you wouldn't mind. Then I can talk to your father once you get ahold of him and bring him here. So we can have a family discussion. Is that what the kids call it these days?" She took a single piece of fettuccine between two fingers and slurped it up. "We've always had this unrequited love thing going on, your father and I. I figured it was time he came around. I always *knew* he'd finally leave that wench and come back to me."

I balked a little. "You just said *Penny* left—"

"The point is, they're done." She rubbed her sauce covered fingers together. "And now he knows he made a mistake."

Mom thought this was her chance to get Vince back? As if he'd finally, after over twenty years, saw the err in his ways?

I wasn't quite sure she understood the definition of unrequited love.

"Besides." She waved her hands at the ceiling. "You've got all this money now. You can afford to have me for a bit."

A sharp, residual pain started at my middle back. Twisted left, then right.

I swallowed a scream.

"We're still renovating the rooms," I said. "Emma and I are going to be switching—"

"She is here, isn't she? Oh, honey." Mom wiped her purple stiletto nails on her frayed short-shorts and hustled over to me. "See, what did I tell you? Nothing but a mooch. She's just here because she thinks your father loves you more. I told you." She poked me in the shoulder.

I shook my head, bypassing what she said. "I'm paying for you to get a hotel room, okay? That way we can get on with the renovations—"

"What? No!" she exclaimed. Squeezed my shoulders.

I took her wrists, pulled her hands off me, and took a step back.

"Mom. This is work to me. I can't do it with extra people in the house."

"I can help. I've worked before." Her nose crinkled. "It can't be that hard."

I took a breath. "No."

A dash of anger ignited in her eyes. "Lanny, I can't believe you. After all I did for you growing up. When those kids teased you so bad you didn't go to school. I helped you through all of it. Now you won't help me? Your own mother?"

Oh, get up, it can't be that bad, she'd snipped, *just show the boy your tits and go on your way. That's all he wants anyway. His parents have money, Lanny, come on. They can pay for things that I can't.*

I held my breath, thoughts tumbling like I'd stuck my head in the dryer.

She wasn't here to help me. There had to be another reason.

As I held her wrists, she confirmed my suspicion. Her eyes began roving again: surfaces, doors, halls. Searching.

If she needed money and had no place to stay, she'd either gotten evicted again or taken money from someone and promised to pay them back, and hadn't.

I thought of Aunt Cadence's things in the attic. In the spare bedrooms. The portraits on the walls, the crystal on the dresser, the antique carriage trunks at the foot of every bed. Little things, big things, all worth money, that she could sell. That was supposed to be auctioned, only now, I wouldn't be auctioning it if I wasn't selling the house. All things she could get her hands on and steal if she was left alone.

There was no doubt in my mind that she would steal from me.

"How about this," I offered. "I'll give Dad a call and tell him you're here. But I need to get you a room for the night because things are cramped."

"Oh, hell, Lanny—cramped? Five rooms?"

"You hate this place," I said, firm. "Let me get you an Airbnb or something."

"*Landry.*" Her lips started to tremble. Not quivering from an onslaught of tears, but out of anger.

"I'll give you money." My heart sank at my own words. I just couldn't have her here. I needed Emma. I needed something, someone to help me keep her at bay. I just didn't know how.

"You would?" Her breathing heaved. It smelled like vinegar and alfredo sauce. I tried not to curl away.

"Four hundred dollars for your own pocket. And I'll buy your stay for the next three days." That was at least enough time to call Dad, pray for an answer, and maybe—call the police if she kept coming back and get a trespassing notice.

Her mouth puckered. "Oh, see, darling?" She patted my cheek. "I think that would be just fine. I'll do this for you. Give you your space.

I know it's hard, cleaning out after someone dies. But trust me. It gets easier."

* * *

"Just send it, Lan. It can't hurt," Sayer said, his voice lined with static over the phone.

"Okay, okay, I did it. There." I swiped out of the message tab and silenced my phone. My father would probably see the notification come through and clear it without opening it, but it was worth a shot. Irene wouldn't see the one I sent her, either. It was too late at night.

At least I could say that I tried.

Which was exactly why I'd sent it now and not the middle of the day.

I sat on the attic floor. Boxes spread around me like a small army. A floodlight—which I'd been able to find in the shed, after searching all over the garage—pointed up at the ceiling. Even with the door open, not enough light made it from the second floor, and the only other time I'd ventured up here was during the day. With the windows and constant sunshine, the lack of a light switch hadn't occurred to me.

"I can't believe she's there!" The line crinkled. It sounded like Sayer had shoved his hand into a bag of chips. "Who does this woman think she is?"

Just then, Hadrian crawled up the last step on all fours. He stopped, glanced around. His nostrils flared as he huffed the floor, like he was searching for something.

"Because she's delusional," I said. My hands fell in my lap as I watched Hadrian. "And she probably needs money, so she thinks I can just whip out the life insurance policy. She said she needed a place to stay."

"But—you were left with it—not her! None of it is hers!" His words turned staticky. "Don't you dare give in, Lan. She's lurking for a reason. I can feel it in my bones. Is she using again? Did you see any evidence? Did she have an ankle monitor on?"

I sighed. I'd been too surprised to even check.

Sayer went on his tangent. "You know what? It's a full moon. Of course, she'd show up now." A pause. Crunching. "Have you told Emma yet?"

"She's not back from her work thing." I sighed. "I thought about texting her, but it'd just make her upset." Emma loved my mom as much as oil loved water.

"And the divorce thing." More rustling.

"Right, and the divorce thing." Who knew if Mom was only blowing smoke or if it was true? I hoped Emma would have at least texted me if it was.

I paused. Glanced to my phone. Weighed the pros and cons of reaching out to her. But what if she wanted to keep it private? What if there were reasons I wasn't aware of?

Sayer and I said our goodbyes—him promising to come back soon, because he had a sixth sense Wade was going to ask for a break (to which I shared sorrows, but Sayer's only response was, "The chips fall, I eat them. Nothing more to it."). I promised to keep him updated and to keep the doors locked.

I hung up as Hadrian angled himself through the door.

"Don't hit your horns," I said. I scooted over to another storage container—all framed photographs and albums layered in an inch of dust. "I'd hate to see that banister need to be replaced. It's original."

His claws scraped along the boards. Shoulder blades rolled with each step. "Hm. Kind of you to think of my horns. I've grown fond of them." The sarcasm that layered his words was better than the silence from earlier.

"Sure." I hefted a large overspilling binder from the bottom of the box. More dust plumed. I coughed. The binder fell open when I dropped it to the floor. At first, an ember of hope filled my chest—they might be documents, maybe something Aunt Cadence had kept during her time researching? Maybe from when she'd talked to Irene?

I squinted in the low light.

A picture of my grandparents stared back at me. My shoulders sank. I snapped the binder shut and started piling everything back in the bin.

"Care explaining why you are up here at such an hour?" Hadrian came and crouched—similar to a gargoyle on watch—beside me. He used a nail to nudge open another photo album. "What are these?"

"Photo albums. And, if you must know"—I gathered four albums and stood from a squat position—"I'm looking for whatever it is that might help us with your situation." Because my mother's presence had kicked things into overdrive. God forbid she get her greedy hands on something without me knowing. And, just because it was my luck, *she* would find this unknown thing that could free Hadrian before I could and sell it to a pawn shop.

He squinted, yellow eyes aglow. "Sorry to be the bearer of bad news, but I do not think family photos will help—"

"Hadrian."

Tendrils of sooty hair fell in his eyes. The muscles around his neck and shoulders coiled. "Yes?" he murmured.

I thought of what someone might see, looking at him. How I should have fainted from terror. Maybe thrown myself down the stairs to get away. Instead, I turned my back to him, scared he might be able to see the fluttering in my stomach. The warmth pooling there. "You're not helping."

"You wouldn't wish to have my help, anyhow." He huffed.

"Why not?" I closed the bin, scooted it aside, then moved to the next. It was hidden by a coatrack that looked like it'd belonged in a department store. "I've seen you protect a little kid. Surely sorting through old junk is easier."

His mouth tugged at my comment, but he didn't acknowledge it. "Everything from this day and age confuses me. Your vehicles. I likely cannot open one of these"—he pointed to a container—"or I would break it. God, and that terrible contraption in the parlor infuriates me."

"Contraption," I echoed. Surely he meant the living room.

"The flat, black device that shows moving pictures. You have one in your chambers."

"The TV?" I laughed.

He shivered. "I hate it."

I tried to hide a smile. "Really? Why? You don't think it's neat?"

"God, no," he groused. He rubbed a pointed ear and closed one eye. "The sounds it makes are horrid. Not the voices but the high-pitched whine. I find it appalling that anyone would spend their time sitting in front of that disgrace when there are plenty of perfectly fine windows to watch out of."

"I think your ears are a bit better than mine." I chuckled. He'd probably heard static. "I'm assuming birdwatching is a more prestigious pastime, then?"

"Prestigious? More like acceptable." His eyes flitted to me. I could have sworn a flush heated his face.

I sat back on my haunches. "Hadrian Belfaunte. Are you embarrassed?"

His cheeks tightened, jaw ticked. "Do not mock me, human."

I scrunched my face and lowered my voice to mimic his, "*Do not mock me, human.* Sorry to break it to you, Boogeyman, but I'm not scared of you."

I grinned for good measure.

He grunted.

"You were scared a bird had gotten hurt," I said, softer, but not teasing. "You like the birds?"

His chest heaved. Finally, he admitted, "Yes. That's why the windows are open all the time. And for—other reasons."

Every muscle in my face relaxed. He opened the windows when I closed them.

My chest welled with something unfamiliar. Warm and seeping. He pretended to be particularly interested in a box labeled *Halloween decor*.

I muffled my teasing and worked in quiet. While I shuffled, Hadrian sat beside me and watched. Every now and then, he would move something I was finished looking through, or he'd stop and examine the contents—an old rice cooker, another box of children's toys, a rainbow-colored wooden xylophone with a neon pink stick to match. We didn't pause until the clock struck two downstairs—even then, the idea of going to bed seemed revolting. There wasn't enough time—we needed to find *something*, and soon. Anything. A lead, even the slightest.

"You need to rest," Hadrian said, as if reading my mind. His clawed hand grabbed my own as I started stacking rubber-banded folders by function—old bills, important Social Security paperwork, and more, which I surely didn't need to get into tonight. The numbers would only float together.

"There has to be something in here," I grumbled. I reached for another folder.

What I didn't want to admit was that I'd have ask Meredith if I could raid her back room. Hadrian was right. I could have given her something unknowingly.

This time, Hadrian stood from his crouch. "Landry. It is late."

"And I'm not tired."

"Truly?" His eyes searched mine.

"Yes, truly." A tug pulled at the base of my spine.

I could walk downstairs and take a hard right into the closet. I could see what lay behind the door when the creature wasn't in there; maybe it would be empty, and I could just hide there for a while. Or maybe the tug meant something else.

Just as soon as the thought came, Hadrian bent toward me. "Landry."

"Hadrian." I leveled him with my best glare.

His teeth flashed, their delicate points pearlescent, and there at the very bottom—the open spots on his jaw where molars should have been.

Air became scarce.

More puzzle pieces. One after another, falling into place. Our breaths mingled for a moment. He stood closer than I'd thought, but I didn't recoil. My body moved without thought. A tiny step closer.

My fingertips brushed his jaw. His breath hitched. I could have sworn his skin lightened where I touched. Not so much gray, but his normal, sun-kissed color. His head tilted.

There, beneath the surface: *yearning.*

"Landry." This time, not just my name, but a warning.

I froze.

Maybe he didn't feel it, what I felt. Maybe that curl of heat, those hummingbird wings, was only me. Maybe they were real, maybe they weren't. Maybe they were desperation to fill the hole in my heart, the one I still didn't know what to do with or what belonged there. I just knew that he was here.

If anyone could understand me, my situation, it was him.

My thumb touched the corner of his lip. Drug it over the smooth skin, the crease of his mouth, so close to the point of his teeth.

"He took them, didn't he?" I whispered. As if I spoke too loudly, he might bolt. "Your father took your teeth." I didn't know why it hadn't connected before, but it made sense as I said it. It had been right in front of me, all along: Haddy running around, his chin constantly bloodied and dripping.

His nostrils flared. "He did."

Sizzling coals rolled inside me. "How old were you?"

"Fourteen." He closed his mouth to swallow, but his lips parted again. He inched another breath closer. The scent of aftershave and ash between us. This time, I didn't hear the wet sound of his heart beating or smell the acrid scent of dried blood—it was as if it didn't exist. "I don't remember what I did. Just the moment he pulled the teeth. One, I had replaced, but . . ." He shrugged.

"I'm sorry." Because I was.

"It made me stronger," he said. His words ran together. I felt his breath on my cheek, the tip of my nose. Hadrian's silhouette threatened to shift—a flicker of his human self. He lifted a hand. Brushed his claws over the tender spot below my eye; I felt the points retract, vanish, and then his human palm was against my face and his bones were changing. The points of his cheeks, his ears retracting, his body rearranging and then—

"I don't know what I would have done if I were you," I breathed. The double meaning to my words didn't get past me.

I don't know what I would have done had I been alive when you were, I wanted to say.

I don't know what I would have done had I seen you on the street and seen your smile, is what I didn't say.

"I'll tell you what I did," he whispered.

My eyelids shuttered. This was it. He was right there. Every inch of my body ignited in a slow burn of anticipation. His hand raked into my hair, right at the nape of my neck. Knotted into a fist and tipped my head back. He had to feel it, too. I didn't stand on an island alone.

I answered so faint, I hardly caught it. "What did you do?"

His resolve—the shield he sometimes erected between us—cracked.

"I killed him," he whispered.

And then Hadrian kissed me.

Chapter Nineteen

Words burst into ash. Anything he said fell away as soon as his lips met mine. They pressed, lenient at first. Tentative, like I might pull away.

A soft sigh slipped through my lips.

Then—more. More pressure, more urgency as our exhales knotted and his tongue pressed at the seam of my lips. I opened, needy and ready, as a grunt fell from his throat. The way it reverberated into my mouth made my knees week.

What kind of man would he have been had he lived in my time? Would I have frozen when our eyes met?

Would I have let myself fall in love with him?

My hands landed on the opened buttons of his shirt, slipped around his neck. His skin felt cold at first, but then it flamed to life. I reveled in the way his shoulders felt under my hands, how his body curled over mine. How I leaned in, how he leaned over, how he was everywhere. The kiss was life in an inhale, need in an exhale. His free hand cinched my waist, pulled me close. Every hard part of him pressed against the concaves of me.

In that moment, I'd never felt more beautiful and ugly all at once.

Did he feel the divots in my hips? Did he notice the way my shoulders had no cushion, how fullness didn't live in the right places?

Gnarled warnings reared then. All those angry, snide comments.

Too skinny.

You look dead.

Why do you have peach fuzz on your arms?

Why does your face look like that?

Just as I felt myself stiffen, he murmured, "Divine."

My hands stilled. The white-blond tresses tangled in my fingers. He couldn't be telling the truth. He might think he meant it—but it couldn't be true. Suddenly, I thought of the years he'd spent alone, isolated. Breath by breath, I felt my hold loosen. I was the first warmth he'd felt, the first body he'd cradled, and I warred with the idea. Of course, he would latch onto me.

Divine, he'd said. A visceral hunger lived inside that single word.

A single thought: A starving man would eat anything to gain satiety.

Would that same hunger, that rawness, been in his words for anyone else? Or was that admission only meant for me?

Because Hadrian wasn't meant for this world, he wasn't meant for this time, he wouldn't *stay* here. Hadrian *couldn't* stay.

He bit my bottom lip. It took every ounce of willpower to not give into the feeling, the rush of heat, the need. Suddenly, I was keenly aware of how fast my heart thrummed, how fast his matched mine. As if they were trying to tangle through our sternums.

"Hadrian," I whispered against his mouth.

Immediately, he stilled. Our lips barely broke apart. When he opened his eyes, they were yellow.

Then, the single sentence wiggled its way to the forefront of my mind: *I killed him*.

My brain scrambled to gather itself; I was a basket that had been dropped, contents spilling in every direction. His mouth, still wet and pink, seemed too real. It was too much.

Slowly, I pulled away.

Hadrian let me go. His absence was stark.

"What did you say?" I couldn't bring myself to adjust my shirt, my hair. Only stare at him in the nasty florescent lighting.

He looked me dead in the eye this time. Didn't flinch when he repeated himself.

"I killed him." He rubbed his jaw. "On my wedding day."

A punch knocked my breath out of me. "You killed your father on your wedding day?"

"That's what I said, is it not?" he asked, a bit fervent. Brick by brick, the wall came back up between us. He shook his head. "I shouldn't have said anything."

"You mean—what did you think? That you shouldn't have told me? Why?" I motioned at him, not sure what I was trying to convey. Maybe his shift, or emphasize my confusion. I didn't know. "That's kind of important, don't you think?"

His jaw tightened. I'd crossed an invisible line, and I didn't know how to back up.

"And you tell me everything?" he bit.

I startled. "What's that supposed to mean?"

"No secrets in your closet? Nothing you failed to share with me yet, Landry?" For the first time, he bared his teeth lightly at me, as if out of instinct. "If you want to see so badly, go look. I am sure the room will show you. It showed me enough times."

Where was this coming from? I understood being defensive, but this wasn't as simple as making a mistake and lying about it. This was larger. It was a life. It would have been the same if I'd tried to off my mom or . . . But his father had taken his teeth and—no, I couldn't justify it.

I couldn't. And he'd hid it. On purpose.

Was this it? The moment the wool was torn away and I saw that he only used my emotions to further his own gain? I was the only one that could help him.

The thought splintered a part of my heart.

I'd known it was a possibility; but for that broken, heady moment, I'd let myself think that he felt that warmth, that tether, too.

"I'll tell you *anything* you want to know," I said, stern. "I didn't—didn't lie." I straightened my shirt. Brushed my hair over my shoulders, and marched over to the floodlight, turned it off, then whirled to the doorway. But before I left, I caught myself.

I owed it to both of us to tell him. I might not have been hiding murder, but I surely hadn't been completely honest.

Jaw clenched, I looked back. Hadrian stood in the dark, almost shaking.

"I have a whore of a father and an addict for a mother. I have an eating disorder that eats me from the inside out and I don't know how to stop it because *just eating* doesn't *work*. Some nights I pray I won't wake up because I know dying in my sleep would be easier than beating my way out of this godforsaken wet paper bag of a life, okay? I was bullied so much in high school I tried to go live with my dad, but he sent me back to my mother. CPS never got involved when I was a kid because she'd clean up just long enough to get them off our backs, get an okay job, before she'd start using again. Even after she woke up in her own vomit because she'd almost OD'd the night before, no one cared. You want to know what my dad said?" I pressed. My hands balled to fists. "He said, 'She's a waste of life, Landry, what do you expect?' And then he still wouldn't take me!" I shouted. All the blood in my core suddenly rushed up my neck and through my mouth. "Are those enough skeletons, Hadrian? Because I can assure you, the last thing I'm worried about is you killing a man when you're already supposed to be dead."

He flinched.

A gaping, screaming hole opened inside of me. I shouldn't have said that. *Too far. Wrong, wrong, wrong.*

My motor skills worked on their own accord. Before I could think twice, I stalked through the door. I slammed it behind me, leaving Hadrian in the dark.

* * *

I didn't sleep.

Whether voluntary or not, my mind raced.

Around four in the morning, I gave in. I didn't care that Hadrian might see from the shadows. I didn't care that I was alone in the house—that if something happened, no one would notice for days. If my aunt hadn't wanted me to find what was in this house, to meddle in it, she wouldn't have left it to me.

That realization spurred me forward.

I crawled out of bed and headed for the closet. If Hadrian wanted me to see, if that room still held the memories, then I'd go look.

The tug materialized as soon as I opened my bedroom door, like an urge that whispered, *Once Harthwait grows dark, the monsters become real.*

The tug *hummed*, the floorboards warmed against the bottoms of my feet, almost as if in invitation, excitement, as I stepped into the hall. A need—the same need I'd felt when I'd heard Hadrian crying that first night—teased up my throat, around my neck, and into my chest.

A shaky breath fell from my lips. The doorway—had it changed, too?

I paused at the edge, right where the frame had been pulled up. I didn't know what I sensed on the other side, but the air felt alive, writhing and ready, when the latch released.

Without a second thought, I stepped through.

* * *

The room tasted different. Sharp and heavy, like a boot pressing on my esophagus.

Mingled, slurring voices tangled through the open windows of Harthwait House. Furniture christened, what I could only suspect was a parlor now, but in my time was the living room. Wallpaper hugged the ceiling. Wingback chairs faced a writing desk, while a separate seating area curled around a hearth to my right.

Outside, darkness encroached onto the property. Wagons rattled down what sounded to be a gravel drive. I leaned to look out the window—sure enough, hands flapped in farewell.

Out the other window, men and women sifted on the lawn like a school of fish, all bright colors and happy, ruddy faces and lifted glasses. It felt like I was in a bowl, observing the outside world through a twisted lens that made the trees too green, too fluffy, the sky too bright. Even the grass swayed in unison, despite being ankle height.

I had the strongest urge to step back, to press myself into the farthest corner away from the window, to revel in the protection of this room. What was it that Hadrian had said? If I came back next time, maybe the room would be different? More to my liking?

He was wrong. I wasn't so sure I liked this.

A woman with inky hair, beautiful porcelain skin, and a rounded face nodded to a couple near a garden bench, her hands knotted delicately in front of her. She wore a gown, closer to ivory or light beige than white, with ruffles along the bodice and rouching that waterfalled down the front of her skirt, giving it the illusion of layers, like peeling the skin from an apple. It cinched at the waist, likely from a corset, and fanned out above the hips.

She was beautiful.

I knew a wedding gown when I saw one—even from many decades ago.

Hadrian had been right. The room *could* show me. This was what I'd wanted to see, was it not? The reason I couldn't sleep because I was thinking about this truth he'd kept from me?

A jagged twinge of jealousy turned at the back of my lungs. After tonight, did I have the right to feel this way? Gradually, I smothered it.

I pulled my eyes from her and scanned the room, left to right, and I saw him.

Sitting in one of the wingback chairs, though I could have sworn he wasn't there a moment ago, was Hadrian. His face wasn't as sharp, but his frame was just as wide, his elbows firmly planted on the chair arms. A button-up shirt hung open around the neck, his hair was slicked back, a tie loose at his collar. A wayward groom.

He watched the crinoline and voluminous skirts and parasols float about the lawn like leaves down a river.

I tried to touch the back of the couch. My hands slipped right through the wood frame. Nothing but a chill raced up my arms. I was an invisible bystander and nothing more.

"Mr. Hadrian," a voice started, burly and cushioned. I jerked to the voice. An older gentleman stood by the door to the foyer. Sparse hair lay combed over his bald spot, brow sweaty, mouth perpetually flat.

Hadrian straightened his cufflinks. How had no one missed the groom on his wedding day?

"Does it grow tiresome having to wipe the perspiration from around your neck so often, Bertie?" Hadrian asked, giving a cufflink a final tug. Then he stood and plunked a wayward wine glass from the writing desk.

Bertie blinked. Two stout caterpillar brows shot to the middle of his forehead. "I beg your pardon, Mr. Hadrian?"

Hadrian threw back the remnants of his glass. The stark scent of moonshine wafted to me. Sparkled in the air like dust. Everything amplified, as if the house was telling me, *See? See? This is what you wanted, right? Here is all of it. Take everything.*

I didn't miss the tremble in Hadrian's wrist.

"I am sure there are many more important things you could be accomplishing right now than simply gawking at me, yes?" he asked. He straightened to his full height. He dwarfed Bertie. But the set to the old man's shoulders told me it had been reversed for a long while.

Bertie blinked and glanced to the floor. He pulled at his lapels. "My apologies, sir. Your father was merely requesting your attendance for a moment. I had trouble finding you, as I realized you were within the house instead of outside with your guests."

Hadrian stared until the old man met his gaze. "Is that so."

Bertie's jowls wobbled. Face reddened. "Yes, young man. Now, if you will excuse—"

"Can I ask you a question, Bertie?" Hadrian stepped forward. Slow. Methodical.

Bertie exhaled through his nose. Then nodded.

Hadrian's coattails fell delicately over his hips; his sleeves were an inch too short for his wrists. "Do you suspect that I should be away from my betrothed so soon on my wedding day?"

Outside, as if on cue, a howl of laughter split the air.

"I am not sure I follow, Mr. Hadrian." Bertie's jaw tightened.

Hadrian chewed his bottom lip.

"Very well. Have a drink, then. I have more than I could need." Hadrian turned his back to Bertie, quick to retrieve an extra glass from the writing desk. He held his sleeve over the lip—a dusting of powder fell to the bottom. Then he poured from a decanter atop the liquor cabinet, which hung open in welcome. Extended it. "Take a moment with me."

"I assure you, the offer is appreciated, however I truly need to return to duties—"

"My wedding day, Bertie. After all we have been through? You helped guide me so much as a boy." Hadrian's words, now that I'd heard him speak before, sharpened like blades. If Bertie was smart, he would have heard it, too.

Bertie eyed the glass.

"You are worth your weight in gold, are you not? Don't deny me the privilege of having a drink with you, man," Hadrian crooned. His words were thick with Lowcountry, of a fine upbringing. Sultry.

Like a prized jockey, Bertie preened a bit but held his tongue and back stiff. "Never, never. Very much a success. To you and Mrs. Cora, both."

As soon as Bertie took the glass, Hadrian threw his back. He licked his teeth against the burn. When Bertie took a tentative sip, he cawed, "All of it, Bertie! You've snuck enough of my father's liquor before."

Bertie coughed half of it down. "I assure you, Hadrian—"

"Mr. Belfaunte," Hadrian corrected, deadly soft.

Bertie blinked hard. His crow's feet deepened, then spread to his hairline. His brow rose. Sunspots decorated his skin there. "Yes. Of course." Sarcasm lined his words.

Hadrian eased around the chair. Steps echoed like gunshots.

Another step.

Then another.

The grandfather clock pattered like a heartbeat. From the foyer, no doubt. I whisked closer, and sure enough—there it was. The same grandfather clock, shadows circling it like fingers.

A choked gasp made me turn.

Bertie stumbled backward, clutched at the closest shelf. It rattled against the wall. Books shook, shoe soles scuffed. His lapels fell open. Red bubbled around his pressed, white pointed collar, the tailored suit that framed it, and his wobbling chin.

Faint as a whisper—the back door clicked shut.

The sound of a key tumbling into place.

I glanced to Hadrian. He watched Bertie with feigned earnest, his forehead and brow a mess of concern, then turned his attention out the window to the lawn. In the midst of guests, one single man stood still. Carefully placed waves and sharp as sin blue eyes. He might have been an inch shorter than Hadrian, and I knew without a doubt that he was looking into this parlor.

The man brushed a finger under his eye. Stole a glimpse over his shoulder. Nodded to no one in particular.

Then turned away.

This reaction seemed to satisfy Hadrian. He stuffed his hands in his pockets.

"You—you—" Bertie struggled.

"Enlighten me."

"—bastard," he choked.

"You look green, Bertie." Hadrian spoke as if the weather had turned fine.

"You deserved it," Bertie gasped. He started to tremble on the floor. Cold, straggled bits of rage shone through his eyes. "*All of it.*"

Hadrian squatted down beside the butler and set his wine glass on the floor. Watched as foam erupted from between Bertie's lips. My hand fluttered to my throat.

Hadrian's tongue poked where his teeth should have been. "Sometimes good men do evil things," Hadrian said, dry. "I wouldn't say you were one of those good men, Bertie."

The man's neck purpled. "*Pathetic* . . . child."

Hadrian's head tilted, cheeks tightened. "That's a shame. You believe I care what you think. Well, I have news for you." Hadrian took the man's collar, pulled him near, until they were nose to nose. "I wouldn't have killed you if I did."

He shoved Bertie to the floor.

"Burn in hell, old man," he whispered. Then he got up. Brushed off. Straightened his jacket, tie, then suspenders.

He walked from the parlor.

This was the Hadrian that had gotten trapped. This was the man he'd been.

I followed Hadrian's long strides. I took the steps two at a time to keep up. Past the second floor, up to the attic.

He shoved the door open with a firm push of his shoulder.

Shadows clung to the room. Not nightly shadows that came after the sun fell, but alive little tendrils. They caressed the floors, the chair legs, the desk in the middle of the room. I blinked, but nothing changed.

The air hung heavy with cigar smoke. I had just stepped through when Hadrian shut the door.

The man at the desk—Howie, if I remembered his name correctly—sat with a dip pen between his teeth. Reddened whites of his eyes, carefully tied hair. It fell past the chair back.

"Bertie sent for me." Hadrian's chin dipped, mouth parted. The whites under his eyes were visible. Dead eyes.

Howie didn't look up.

The grandfather clock continued to tick.

"I'm busy," Howie muttered to his pages. He gave his son a similar glare. "Or are you blind?"

"No dire negotiations you need to make while mingling? Or have all your important connections left?" Hadrian grunted. He dragged one hand, languid, over the back of a chair. He continued, until he stopped in front of a shelf. Perched atop it was a typewriter. Ran a fingertip over the K, S, R, and F keys, which had faded.

Howie's jaw ticked. Just like Hadrian's. The stiffness he held in himself, the haughty assurance in his movements—they were the same. Where Hadrian's were not as confident, Howie's insinuated assumption. As if everyone should know what he thought.

"A quick tongue has never gotten you anywhere, son," Howie snarled. He set his pen down, then pushed back in his chair. His chin jutted up. "Actually, there was something I intended to discuss with you." He sniffed. "There are . . . shipping containers missing."

Hadrian continued his perusal of his father's shelf. "I am no bookkeeper."

Howie's voice remained chilled. "You know where they went."

"I do not."

Howie's neck blotched with color. He slammed both hands onto his desk, shot from his chair, and shouted, "You ruin me! Every chance you get, you take it. Where are they?"

Hadrian turned, shoulders loose, hips canted to one side.

Gray eyes ate gray. The face, the nose, the chin, all identical.

Hadrian's hand smoothed the front of his jacket, then slipped inside, under his shirt. Howie tracked it.

"Not a clue."

"You have not enough balls to lie to me," Howie muttered.

"Who said I would lie?" Hadrian said. And grinned.

Howie shoved the desk, then flung a drawer open. He yanked out a navy revolver and pointed it at Hadrian. "Do not take me for a *fool*. You dare to think I would not realize what has happened? My own blood, paid my own men off to work for him? To turn their backs on me?"

Hadrian stared down the barrel. "I find it difficult to pay men off that choose to work with me instead."

Howie's nostrils flared, neck nearly purple. "All I have done for you. And this is how you repay me?"

I heard Hadrian's teeth grind. As if I needed to hide, I eased back toward the right corner of the room. The air started to hum, whisper. Little pokes of memory, voices, grew louder and louder until words formed.

Haddy, crying, asking for Momma.

Haddy, screaming, against rusted pliers.

Hadrian, weedy in adolescence, with a purpled eye and swollen jaw.

Hadrian, the creature, with a gaping, bleeding chest.

The hand in Hadrian's jacket withdrew—the men fired at the same time. The faint, broken click of a jammed round. The other, a smoking pop of a filled chamber.

I clamped a hand over my mouth with a gasp. The room—no, I—was shaking.

Howie fell forward against the desk. Blood bloomed against his shirt, his gun clattering to the floor. He grunted before taking a kneel. Then he fell back against his chair. It screeched backward.

He didn't fight. He didn't scramble.

Not an ounce of fear danced in his eyes.

Hadrian's eyes flashed as he stalked forward. Frustration? Disappointment, maybe? His pulse fluttered, crazed, in his neck.

"Coward," Howie hissed. His fingers stumbled to stanch the bleeding. Blood started to bloom through the wound anyway. "You couldn't even do this like a *man*."

Hadrian's expression splintered. The last straw—I knew that feeling. Saw the familiar, brittle fury that snapped into thousands of little pieces. "No man?" he roared. He prowled to his father, grabbed the crown of his hair and pulled his neck open. He looked Howie dead in the eye. "Tell me I am no man," he demanded. Hadrian slammed his head into the shelf behind him. The room shook.

My breath caught in my throat. This was the moment I'd seen in the hallway when we'd first found the door.

He huffed.

"Tell me!" he shouted, spittle flying. "No man? You and Bertie *were men to beat a child?*"

They breathed heavy together. The blueprint and the carbon copy. In that moment, the expression "There is a fine line between love and hate" never looked truer.

"I will always be more of a man than *you*," Hadrian snarled. He gasped, choked on a swallow, teeth bared.

"If that is what you believe," Howie croaked. His lips cracked, beaded with blood.

Tears welled in Hadrian's eyes. Hatred, a burning, gasoline-lit flame.

"I asked not for you to be my father," he spat. "I never chose you."

Blood stained Howie's tongue when he wheezed, "Nor I, you."

Hadrian's expression twisted into hate, hurt, and fury. He pulled the knife from his trousers, and swung down.

Nor I, you.

I squeezed my eyes shut before the knife hit home.

Hadrian killed his father and butler. Hadrian meant to do it.

A war storm tangled through my body. A version of understanding, hurt, confusion, and empathy all in one. A sob ransacked my body, tight and uncontrollable—and all that jealousy that I'd felt for this man, this creature, suddenly slipped away. Because I wasn't jealous of what he'd been through now. Before, I wanted the strength he'd had at handling his family, his life. But now I knew it had been desperation.

I hurt *for* him. We were two halves of the same coin. He'd chosen a different path than I had. Whereas I secluded from my pain, he'd imploded.

The question was: Could I forgive him for doing such a thing? Those words echoed through my mind: *Sometimes good men do evil things*. I bit down hard on my tongue, tasting metal and grime. I cried, in a gut wrenching, visceral way. I'd let this man kiss me. I'd let this man dig his way beneath my skin and burrow there.

What else had his father done to him? And was I okay with forgiving him, for keeping this from me? What kind of person did that make me if I did?

Pot to kettle, he'd told me once.

Parts of my heart warred with each other. How had I let a man that killed his father slip his claws into my heart, when Ivan had been just as vicious in a different way? Could his actions be justified any more than Ivan's could, or even my own?

Hadrian isn't this man anymore, I thought. That was why.

Ivan continued his hurt, he kept his head in the sand, and moved on. I'd seen it—Hadrian wasn't the same man he used to be. He'd *changed*.

And I was ravenous to do the same. Because if someone looked at me, at any of the things I'd done and deemed me unworthy of redemption, how would I handle that? Would I think it was justified, like Hadrian did? Would I hide in my hurt and wait years for someone to come and find me? Is that not what I was attempting to do to myself right now?

Wouldn't I want someone to seek redemption for me, had I been in his shoes?

I swallowed bile.

The room broke apart.

Chapter Twenty

I'd once heard that self-sabotage was a coping mechanism for some people. I couldn't help but think about that when I checked the text thread I'd started with Irene.

A miniature blue check told me Irene had seen my message. I almost wished I'd turned off read-receipts. Either that, or shoved my phone into a bowl of water and frozen it so I couldn't check it every three and a half minutes.

After I'd pulled myself into my bed sometime just before day-break, I'd replayed last night on rewind. Hadrian's urgency, his touch, then those words. An hour of tossing later, I decided the best thing I could do was get up and start my day. Or at least keep myself busy.

"I'm sorry," Sayer groaned through my phone. I shuffled outside to my SUV, chill bumps eating up my legs in the cool, damp morning air. Mourning doves cooed in the bramble. If I paused, the trees could be heard whispering to themselves. "I might be down tomorrow, though. If that's okay?"

"Take the time you need," I assured him. I unlocked my car and took a tentative look back at the house. "No rush. Not at all."

All the windows were shut, doors locked, valuables put away. Mom never had been a morning person, but I wouldn't put it past her to show up unannounced, expecting something since her night away had been completed, as promised.

"Are you sure?" Sayer seemed to home in on my feigned peppiness. "Is your mom there already? I thought you paid her to scoot."

"I did. And she isn't. I just had an idea for something for the house, and I'm going to check if Meredith might have it." I had a feeling if I didn't start looking now, I'd find myself back in the attic, buried under boxes of paperwork and dust, staring into a corner with a wondering imagination. Of all the things that could have happened last night instead of that argument.

I climbed in the driver's side. I was already pulling out of the driveway by the time Sayer said, "Well, let me know if the loon shows up. I'll bring my taser. I've never had the chance to use it."

"I've had too many firsts lately," I teased. "Maybe don't put assault on my list."

"Tasing someone isn't assault," he guffawed. "This is self-defense we're talking about, Lan. Your right to a peaceful house. With no money swipers."

"Okay, fine. I trust your judgment." I flipped my blinker on and turned toward Stetson.

By the time I parked and approached Meredith's, I regretted not making a cup of coffee to go. My eyes felt heavy, my throat hoarse. Without thinking, I hurried across the street to The Blue Corduroy. The door tinkled in welcome.

I didn't want to be here. But I knew I needed to try.

Last night made me realize that.

He'd changed. So could I. I could start small. Tiny, tiny steps. In a different way.

This time, the waiting area was stuffy with laughter and voices. A short line of three people waited, while two hovered by the pick-up counter. An older gentleman with sprigs of white hair scribbled down orders. A heavenly warm scent clouded the air. I took a place in line, and by the time he waved me forward, I'd already decided. A tumble of anticipation in my belly.

He gave me a crinkled smile. "And what can I get you, young lady?" His glasses' lenses were so thick his eyes looked like needle points when he blinked. It was cute.

"Can I get a bagel with cinnamon cream cheese?" I scratched the inside of my arm. "And a vanilla latte?"

"Why, absolutely." He rattled off my total; I told him to keep the change.

My fingers tingled while I waited in the huddle of people at the pick-up end. The same woman from before—Bernice—flung drink after drink out onto the counter. Not one spilled.

"LARRY," she hollered. She smacked a paper-wrapped bagel and plastic sample cup next to it, then my coffee.

I gathered my breakfast. "Thank you."

She glanced up at me. Her wrinkles didn't so much as twitch. "No problem, dear."

My chest warmed.

Just as I turned to leave, my phone vibrated. I pulled it from my pocket, coffee and baggie in one hand, as the door jingled above me. A text.

MEREDITH: Hey honey, can you stop by soon? Got a question about one of the chickens.

I found the same bench I'd sat on the first time I'd come by and took a seat. The humidity hadn't quite set in yet, but a hint of balm hovered at the edges of my face. Within the hour, it'd be sweltering.

I took a sip of the coffee, then unwrapped my bagel. Stared at it.

I couldn't remember the last time I'd had a bagel.

I held it tight with both hands, scared I'd drop it. I didn't have to eat all of it. Just some of it. Just a little. Or I'd feel like trash the rest of the day.

Anger is like a train, my heart whispered with a squeeze. *You don't have to take the first stop, but you can always get off the train whenever you want to.*

I couldn't keep doing—this. I wrangled with my heart, the feelings of empathy toward Hadrian and what he'd been through, chewing on his advice while trying to keep my logic intact.

Was my frustration with him because of what he'd done? Or was I pushing him away as punishment for myself, for still wishing I'd had the courage to act on my feelings as he did? I could acknowledge what he'd done was wrong. I could acknowledge that my own actions were wrong, too—but did I have a right to play God? Did I have any room to shove him into a box, when I'd done the same thing to myself in the vein of protecting my heart, my feelings?

And was I pushing him away so *I* chose for him to leave me behind? To avoid him deciding to leave himself?

Because it was easier to turn my back when I'd been the one to walk away.

My chest tightened at the words I'd hurled at him. The anger behind them I hadn't meant, not really.

I inhaled. Dipped the bagel in the cream cheese, and took a bite.

I didn't step off the train, but I stepped onto the platform. At the very least, it was a start.

* * *

It wasn't.

As soon as I walked into Meredith's, their voices rang clear through the storefront from the backroom. Every thread of composure I'd tied together out on that bench immediately burst into flames.

"Did I say you could?" Meredith snapped. "I can call the police for trespassing."

I stopped at the checkout counter. "Meredith?"

My mother's voice shrieked, "Just tell me where her things are! Where'd she hide them?"

I dropped my wrapper, leftover bagel, and empty coffee cup into the trash can and hurried through the displays. A metal train caught on my hip and fell over—I muttered as I picked up the pieces, hooked them back together, and rushed to the back.

Meredith held one end of a hefty cardboard box, eyes wide. Mom grappled with the other end like she was readying to wrestle an alligator.

"What are you doing here?" I blurted. Both women's attention whipped to me.

Meredith's forehead glistened with sweat. "Landry, tell your mother—"

"She has Cadence's things!" Mom pressed. She tugged at the box like a rabid dog. "She can't just sell them!"

I stalked forward and attempted to wedge my way between my mother and the box. The side ripped. "Mom, let go. I gave them to her."

She released. The box toppled sideways. Meredith grunted. I stepped between the two, but Mom's expression had already crumpled into betrayal.

"Why would you do that?" she sputtered. "Her things—"

"They're mine now."

Mom drew up to her full height. We were eye level with only a taped box between us. "Landry May Frederick, you listen to me, and you listen good. This is selfish of you. You don't even offer me a chance to look through her things before you get rid of them?" she spat.

The slightest niggle of guilt worked its way into the base of my skull. I tamped it down—no, I'd asked. I'd offered. I'd sent ashes, I'd tried to have civil conversation, and she'd trapezed over it each time.

"Mom—"

"Who do you think you are, Landry? Is this the person I raised you to be?" she sputtered, cheeks reddening. Meredith stood still behind me against a storage shelf, eyes bouncing between the two of us. "After all I did for you? How ungrateful can you be. I get it, I'm a horrible mother. I did an awful job with you, I ruined you, I ruined your life, but have you ever thought about how you ruined *mine*?"

The room became uncannily still. Whatever little pieces of hope, sympathy that congregated in my chest a moment ago suddenly whisked away on a cold breeze.

Mom stepped over another box and stopped inches from my face, angry tears puddling in her lower lashes. "You ran him away, you took my sister, and you took everything she would have left me. You're *so much better than me*, aren't you? Ever since you hit high school, it's only ever been about *you*."

The tang of liquor floated off her breath. I didn't dare inhale all the way.

This wasn't my mother talking. I knew it wasn't. But I'd be lying if I said the words didn't hurt all the same.

With a final huff and pat of her hair, which dangled at the nape of her neck in a knotted bun, she stalked from the storage room. Something hit the floor with a thud—likely from a display. Then the door jingled.

Meredith sighed. "Well."

I bit my lip, unsure what to say.

"You okay, Lanny?"

I bit my tongue and willed the lump in my throat down. So many emotions. Too many. What was more exhausting than being reminded of everything that was wrong with your life?

"I'm fine," I murmured.

She set the box down. I didn't turn when she wrapped her arms around me; she gave me a sturdy squeeze.

"It's okay, baby. She's not mad at you. She just hates life a little bit more than most."

I let my head fall on her shoulder. "She's always been like that."

"I know."

I don't know what made the words fall—maybe because it was Meredith, and Meredith felt like a warm place to sleep, like sitting in a chair in the sunshine.

"I was always mad that Aunt Cadence didn't let me stay with her," I said.

I felt her sigh. Then nod. A bit quieter, she echoed, "I know."

"She probably broke a display."

"Ain't nothing a bit of love and patience can't fix. And super glue."

If only that were true.

She patted my shoulder. "Well, now that you're here—I think I found something you might have been looking for."

I perked up a bit. "What?"

Meredith wove back toward a shelf with an opened box labeled CHICKENS.

In my handwriting.

She peeled the flaps back, pulled out a rooster, and twisted his head. When she dumped him upside down, a key jingled into her palm, attached by a leather strap and a rolled-up envelope, no bigger than a greeting card.

My heart flipped. Spots emerged at the edge of my vision. Was that—

Her eyes softened. Turned watery.

"I've done sold everything else you brought me, but this was the last box of stuff I had left. Was going through it late last night. And I heard something rattling in that rooster and found this. Figured you might need it." She held out the key, then the envelope. On the keychain: BOX 148, and on the little teal envelope, one word looped across the front:

LANDRY

Chapter Twenty-One

My throat burned the entire walk to my car. When I sat in the front seat, I locked the doors. Perched the little envelope on my dashboard and dropped the key into the cupholder.

This might not be anything important. It might not be what I hoped for it to be.

It might *just* be a letter. And that was okay.

My eyes welled until everything swam. Short, choppy breaths came from my chest. The car was hot, like a toaster oven, and I knew I'd start sweating soon. But I needed the silence.

With jerky movements, I picked up the letter. Ran a finger over her penmanship. She'd always curled her *y*'s at the end in a little twirl so it looked like a flower sprouted from the bottom. I tore the flap with care and pulled out a single folded sheet of paper.

My lovely Lanny,

I know you may think me crazy, but I promise this has a purpose. I'm leaving the house to you. Then again, if you've got this, you probably already know that.

Don't worry: right now, I'm not sick. I'm not dying, at least on my watch, anytime soon. I just want to be prepared. I think Charlene next door having an aneurysm got me thinking. Who knows, I might tell you I've stored this somewhere so you can find it if the time comes. Maybe I won't want to deal with this place and I'll give it to you and just be done with it. Get me an apartment, something I don't own, and just die there when I'm wrinkled and ornery in twenty years.

But yes, the house. It's yours. I'll set it up in a trust, write a will, all the fun stuff. At least it'll give me something to do.

One, then two tears plopped onto my lap. I wiped my eyes. Propped my elbow on the car door and covered my mouth. Willed myself to keep reading.

The point of this is to tell you something I know nothing about. My Granny used to say never to play with things you don't know. But then Charlene died and I got to thinking about what would happen if I wasn't here no more. How I'd feel about leaving you this place and knowing what I know about it. I can't do that to you, Lanny. I know you loved this place, loved visiting, as a little girl.

But this place isn't right. I know you think it was cute, that little rhyme I used to tell you and Sayer as kids, but I did it because I wanted you to be wary. I wanted to scare you away a bit, and I'm sorry. I've ignored it for a long while, thinking it would just go away. It never did. So it's time to try and figure out what's going on instead of ignoring it more. I'll start at the beginning for you:

You were about four or five when I realized you noticed things. You said you'd seen someone in a window late one afternoon. To be honest, you scared me. I ignored it—you talked about it for months, so I didn't forget it—but I was hoping it'd go away. And it wasn't just that, but you'd bring up the oddest things: hearing knocks and creaks when your momma or daddy didn't. They thought you were playing, but I knew better. Because I'd heard things sometimes too.

It got worse the older you got, so the more I ignored it, the more I worried. By the time you were away at college, I tried to replace the beadboard in the hallway and busted a hole in the wall on accident. That was when I found the door. These were around it.

In the margins of the paper, she'd drawn a few of the same symbols I'd found.

For the longest time, I didn't find much. I always heard that sometimes energies were tied to items, so I figured it might very well be an untimely death that left someone lingering. I tried to find remains in both the front and back yards, in the crawl spaces under the house, in the attic. But I never did.

Until I replaced the floorboards in the office.

My heart rocketed up my throat. I squeezed my eyes shut. The floorboards in the office?

Then it hit me: When Emma and I had been looking for batteries when the light turned on and off, one of the boards had been stained a different color.

I'd heard a little boy crying at night. Every hour, on the dot. It continued for weeks. So imagine my surprise when I get a contractor to replace the floorboards and he finds not one, but two different child's shoes, a toy train, a couple wooden boxes, and a tiny bowler hat.

I thought I'd fixed it—I'd found the little boy's remains. Maybe he was attached to the toys and the shoes since they'd been his, I don't know. I burned them, thinking it'd stop whatever was going on. Salt and burn, incense and cleanse. For a while it worked.

But then it started again. I guess that old lore about shooing spirits away doesn't work after all. I read somewhere else that traumatic events can amplify energies, and sometimes I wonder if the house itself was a beacon for bad things. That something was already there, besides the child, that made it worse.

So I don't know what else to do, Lanny. The crying won't stop. I've read every article online, watched so many videos, pulled my hair out over this, and I'm starting to worry that whatever is going on will always be that way. I even asked the library for records and had a girl come out to take a peek, but I'll be honest, I gave up after that. I don't know if it's worth trying to fix anymore, and to be honest, I'm tired.

I'm sorry, honey. But I couldn't not tell you. I had to at least let you know. Who knows, maybe you can fix up the place and sell it one day.

Now—the safety deposit box key. I've gone ahead and put some of the jewelry I don't wear in there for safe keeping, just in case. I have the papers to the Beetle in there, too, with a couple of bonds that I never cashed. They aren't much, but the ring was your Granny's, and the necklace was one of mine. The earrings were supposed to be a wedding present for you one day, so if you're reading this after you're married, I hope you liked them. I thought they were pretty. If you aren't married, take Emma to Vegas and pawn them or something. Make a memory out of them. Just please don't give them to your momma.

I love you, dear. And I'm sorry for how life's been so far. But you've got this. You've turned a corner, and if not yet, I know you will soon. I can feel it in these old bones like you can smell rain on the wind on a humid summer day.

I love you bunches,
Aunt Denny

I folded the page back up and stared at my steering wheel.

Like you can smell rain on the wind on a humid summer day.

She'd tried. She'd gotten no further than I had, not really, except I knew what some of the symbols meant. And I had the man from inside to prove that what she'd heard wasn't a simple spirit haunting the halls.

There's something about grief that ages a person. One moment, you're alive and breathing, and the world is colorful but quick. The lines are blurred and you're moving, you can feel the air on your skin and hear everything at once. But then the grief slows you down.

Latches you into a single place and makes you watch as everyone else passes you by.

I wanted to think. I wanted to get up and move, I wanted to put pieces together, I wanted to comb through the attic and try and find the things she'd mentioned, but my chest hurt. My chest hurt so bad, and I wanted to sit in my car and cry.

And then all I could think of was the two little shoes she said she found. The bowler hat and the toy train. And I found that I was grieving not just for my aunt, right then, but the little boy that never had a chance to be a child, and how I never would have met that man if none of that horrid abuse hadn't happened.

Whether I was ready to admit it or not, I didn't want him to leave. Not yet. Whatever loop kept him here, whatever was changing with his appearance—something was going on whether we were ready or not. And I wasn't sure I wanted to know what the end of it looked like.

Because for the first time in a long while, I felt a little alive. The barbs in my chest weren't the prettiest, but I knew they were there. I'd stepped on the platform.

I didn't need to step back off now. But the idea of telling Hadrian about the items Aunt Cadence found made my stomach churn.

Would he be excited about them? Try to find them? Should I be happy for him?

I didn't know.

I sealed the envelope, tucked it into the center console, and drove home.

Chapter Twenty-Two

Emma texted the following night, saying she might be coming back a day early, only to text again, unsure. When I asked why, she said she had to go to the office that afternoon and considered staying at her apartment because of the late hour. The drive from her apartment to Harthwait wasn't terrible, but Emma always went to bed early, and the thought of late-night driving didn't appeal to her.

EMMA: doubt will make it until morning

I sat on the couch in the living room, moving images around on my mood board. Four color-coded sticky notes ran along the arm of the couch. One for base colors, one to write item aesthetics, a third for the story they wanted to tell in their home, and the last for miscellaneous. I took a screenshot of what I had so far and sent it to a client.

Should I text her back? Would she care? Or was she just letting me know?

I frowned.

LANDRY: That's fine, don't want you to drive too late. I'll be here either way

I stared at my text. The glow from my tablet burned, so I turned it face down as I thought about my next words. Days had passed since Mom showed up. Still, not a word from Emma about Penny and Vince.

Quickly, I tapped out another message. I hit send before I lost my nerve. I probably should have waited to talk to her about it in person.

LANDRY: Did you know about Penny and Dad?

Bubbles appeared. Stopped. Appeared again.

EMMA: Walked in on her leaving, actually. Will tell you later?

I gave her message a little heart, then set my phone on the armrest of the couch.

Penny and Vince separating didn't need to impact my ability to talk to him. I shouldn't have felt guilt for not reaching out to him. When had he taken anything else into consideration when he'd deigned a moment worthy of speaking to me? He'd made his bed, and part of that bed was my mother.

Again, the platform. The train station I stood in. Would I step on the car, when given the chance? Or watch it roll by?

I pinched the bridge of my nose with a wince. Did I really want to do this right now? I'd already texted him once with no response. He probably wouldn't answer. But leaving a message was easier than hearing his voice. And it was only a matter of time before my mom's patience expired.

If there was anyone that could handle my mother, it would be Dad. And only because she was desperate to gain his good graces again, even though I highly doubted they'd existed in the first place. If they had, he wouldn't have cheated.

I corralled my nerve and dialed. As it rang, I pinched my eyes shut and whispered, "Please go to voice mail, please go to voice mail."

"Vince Frederick. Leave a message, I'll get back to you."

A beep.

I inhaled. "Hey, Dad. It's Landry." Using Mom as the reason for calling wouldn't work, so I tried another angle, which wasn't a complete lie. "I need a good estate lawyer. I figured you might be able to help. Call me back."

I hung up. Short, sweet, to the point. Dad might not have worked in estate planning, but he likely had someone at his firm that did. And if I wanted to handle this correctly, especially with Mom snooping and scrounging, I would need someone with experience to help.

Still, it was disheartening to know you were someone else's pawn and not their treasure.

I turned back to my tablet, cheek in my palm, a blanket tangled around my legs. Shuffled through Pantone palettes and sketches I'd made for layout ideas. A serene idle screen dissolved in and out on the TV while one of my playlists hummed.

Montell Fish came on. My entire body loosened at the familiar first chords. No matter where I was, I always stopped to listen to this. Always made a moment of space for it.

I let the tablet cover fall shut and dropped my head back, my eyes drifting closed. I hummed along with the music. Whimsical. So, so sad and hopeful for a possible love. Of something that could have been.

Like Hadrian.

How he liked to listen to the birds sing.

How his mouth felt on mine.

How my words shanked the moment in two.

I sunk into the couch. Maybe, just maybe, it would swallow me whole.

It wasn't until my breathing slowed that I realized the song had played for almost fifteen minutes—the final notes bled easy enough into the first, so instead of a gradual fade, it looped in an endless croon when left on repeat. But I'd put everything on shuffle.

Invisible fingers traced the length of my forearm.

"Long face, dearest," Hadrian said over my shoulder.

My eyes popped open with a jerk. "Been a long day," I admitted.

The floorboards creaked. He rounded the recliner before stopping to stand at the edge of the rug. His burnished shoes toed the fringe. All human this time, just like in the library.

I searched his face. Found nothing but a placid smile and slitted eyes, still stuck in yellow from before. There were so many things I wanted to say; I felt the familiar scratch of shame in the back of my throat, that I knew what happened to his father in detail. A pregnant moment settled between us.

"You are tired," he said, matter-of-fact.

Not anymore. Now I felt very, very alive, and the room was extremely small.

"A little," I whispered.

"I wanted to apologize for the things that were said on my part," he murmured. He knotted his hands behind his back. "And for what I didn't say."

I sat my tablet on the end table. The reflection of his back in the window behind him enamored me: the way his fingers fiddled together, uneasy. The breadth of his shoulders. The baby-fine hairs at the nape of his trimmed hair, something I took wonder in. It was amazing how people from different eras were still connected by the simple things—hair trims and schedules and smiles.

Slowly, I stood, and found myself clasping my hands together, sweatshirt crooked on my shoulders. This was it.

"Hadrian . . ." My mouth pressed to a line.

"I should have told you everything," he whispered. "You shared things with me through the night. Not all, but some. And I did not return the sentiment—and I wanted to."

I nodded. "I know. I was unnecessarily mean because of things I'm dealing with. That have nothing to do with you. And I'm sorry." I stomped that wriggle of doubt, the voice that said he only wanted to get my help. I needed to trust someone—to take a chance, trust that they meant well, especially when I felt in my gut that Hadrian was a good person.

Because when I looked at him, I saw something burned. I saw a child that grew up and did the only thing he knew to do in order to stop a bad man.

One side of his mouth twitched, stuck in a grimace. It revealed the line of sharp upper molars—as if he'd tried to shift into his beastly form, but couldn't.

"You left today. For a while," he said. He ran a hand over the back of his neck. The other found its way into his pocket.

"I went to see if Meredith could help me." I couldn't meet his eyes, but still, his voice reeled me in.

He nodded. "Remind me who she is?"

I told him about Aunt Cadence's donation habits. About my mother showing up, assuming he'd heard our first exchange in great detail when she'd appeared the first time.

His brow furrowed to cover the spark in his eye. "And was she? Help, I mean?"

My lips parted. Then pressed shut.

What good was it to keep something from him? I'd just gotten upset with him for doing that to me. And here I was, debating on doing the same, just because I didn't want to lose the possibility of him being here a while longer.

I reached for the letter I'd tucked in my laptop case. Offered it to him.

"She left me this. Meredith found it in a rooster."

His brow crinkled. Eyes danced to me, the letter, and back.

"You can read it," I whispered. "Please."

A careful nod. He stepped closer. The room shrunk twice in size. He sank down beside me on the couch, elbows on his knees, expression tight with thought. I picked at a hangnail while he read.

When he was finished, he folded it back up, but didn't speak.

"She did not mention the toy train," he said, gruff. He handed it back to me. Already, a cold sweat started at the back of my neck. "What came of it."

I sat forward. Our elbows nearly touched. So much body heat in one space.

"I haven't seen it while going through things. I'm sorry," I whispered.

"It may still be somewhere. We can look," he said. Cleared his throat. "If you wish, that is."

"Of course I do." I put the letter back in the case and scooted against the couch arm. "It's what we agreed on. Do you think the train could be something that—"

"Yes, but—Landry. Please."

"You said you wanted to break this. If the train or something else is keeping you here—if it's really a remains thing—then we need to find it," I said, more forceful. I tried to erect the shield, piece by piece, as I went on. Pushing him away. Pushing the feelings back. "We can go look right now—" I started to stand.

He grabbed my wrist. "Landry, enough."

I tugged. "I'm serious. If it's something she found, then we can look. Right now."

His eyes turned pleading. He stood, not once breaking my gaze. "No. Right now I just want to talk to you."

He didn't. He was stalling. He had to be. Pushing back the inevitable. Reeling me in from a cliff.

"About what?" I said, breathy. He hadn't let go of my wrist, his palm hot and electric on my bare skin.

"You had a heated conversation, if I remember correctly." His eyebrows rose. "That man you spoke with. Who you refused the listing to."

"Ivan." My heart ratcheted.

His personal space was suddenly my personal space. It made my body hum. He tilted his head, throat tight, just like he did when he was the creature, but this time it was thoughtful. "The things you said to him. What happened between the two of you."

I searched his expression. His pulse fluttered in his temple. The way his hair fell in soft, slight curls in places. The strong swoop of his jaw.

He was asking me. *No more secrets.*

"Ivan and I dated before," I started.

A shadow passed over his face. "Courting?"

I offered a gentle smile. "Yes, courting. I was, I don't know? Eighteen, nineteen? Maybe twenty the last time we spoke?" I shrugged. "I never . . . told him how I'd felt before."

"Did he . . . hurt you?"

"Some ways, yes."

His eyes narrowed. "I should have taken his fear to my advantage, then," he said, gravelly.

"Hurting someone for me isn't necessary, Hadrian."

"There is more than one way to injure a man's soul, dearest. And sometimes, it's more than what they deserve. It's what they need."

Time to show my hand. "You say it like you know from experience."

He nodded, contemplated for a second. His hand slipped a bit farther up my sleeve until he encircled my forearm. "I . . . felt it. When you went to the room. I heard it. Everything."

I stared at a point on his throat. I couldn't tell if the room had a looser hold on Hadrian, was giving him more liberties, or if whatever was inside it was seeping out. Becoming a bit more unruly.

Like he heard my thoughts, he said, "I think something is changing, Landry. Do you remember how I said the house felt different? When I first came out of the room?"

"Yes."

"I couldn't place it then. Everything was disorienting. Like wading through silty water. But now I believe it was like this *before,* in my time. Harthwait, I mean. It had a feel that made your skin prickle. Your aunt mentioned it getting worse, and I remember something similar as a child, though it would come and go."

A thought came to mind—the feeling I'd had when I'd gone back to the room, the energy around me, like it had built itself up. As if it wasn't contained and bled *out* now. The same kind of energy Irene had mentioned, that my aunt mentioned.

"You think the house was being contained? In that room?"

He shook his head before I could go on.

"Fall in Love with You" started to hum from the TV. Hadrian offered his hand, low at his side. "Care to dance with me?"

That hummingbird jerked in my chest at the sudden pivot. "Dance with you?"

"Do I have an echo in here? Maybe if I say yes, it will answer it back to me?" A brief but devastating smile appeared. "We can talk as I lead."

I dipped my chin. "Yes, but I'll warn you, I'm not any good."

"I'm poor enough at it for the both of us," he teased. His hand slipped down my arm, then captured my right hand. I stepped forward at the same time he tugged. My hip hit the top of his thigh, my other hand landing on his shoulder. He cinched me at the waist. Two stacks of blank pages, pressed together by a book binder. Something told me the glue was already setting between us.

And it terrified me.

Because I couldn't keep this man.

"Poor in love from a father, maybe," I said. I meant it as a tease, but there was something sad in my words. I tilted my head back and watched his eyes drift over the living room. Soaked up the feel of him being this close. *We could give each other that missing piece, though,* is what I didn't say.

"Poor in love does not mean rich in life."

My throat burned. "You never loved your wife, then?"

"Arranged. Her father was one of the first migrants to strike oil. Maybe I would have grown to love her as a friend, if we'd had enough time." His sincerity was refreshing.

"No one came into your life after she passed?"

"I traveled too much to settle. I took over everything after my father died. Made a few poor choices, to say the least. Decided to go west for a while. I made a few connections with Cora's father, which kept the shipping port afloat, and . . ." He shook his head. "I became jaded. Arrogant."

I chuckled. "You, arrogant? Never."

"You tease," he breathed. He squeezed the low of my back. Then, his expression hardened. "I would search these brothels for the men my father worked with and I would wait to see what they would do. I would see if they—took part in acts with children. And women without the woman's consent."

"What?" My feet tangled with his.

He met my gaze. "My father was a monster, Landry. The only way monsters stop eating is if they die."

The dots connected, one by one; my hand gripped his shoulder so hard, there would likely be crescent marks beneath the fabric of his shirt. Children. A port. Multiple, not just him. Could it have been a trafficking situation?

"Did they—did you—" I couldn't ask. The words died on my tongue, hugged by the taste of vomit.

"Kill them? Yes."

My cheek fell against his chest. The wild beat of his heart in my ear matched my own. I thought I was going to be sick.

Hadrian's father—I couldn't ask, but I couldn't *not*. I needed the full picture, and the thought of not knowing what happened to him as a child would eat me alive.

"Did he ever do things to you?" I whispered against his shirt. He was so warm, so *alive*.

We swayed in a slowly unraveling silence. I let him marinate in his thoughts, while I sorted through my own. While trying to navigate the dread in my gut.

And Hadrian had been in that room for over one hundred years? Knowing everything his father had done? Reliving past memories, and who knows what other kinds of figments, as they'd appeared?

"He attempted. Once," he said after a while. "I was perhaps seven, maybe eight. Bunny walked in on accident." He paused. "I remember little of what he said after. If he defended himself to her. He'd been in a foul mood the majority of the month, and this was the . . . pinnacle." He took a calming breath; it rushed through my ear, vibrated against my jaw. "I just remember this baby rabbit I found outside while she was drying clothes that week. I'd begged her to let me stay outside and watch it. Out of pity, I suppose, she allowed me to feed it, morning and night for the following month with excess goat's milk. Really, I wanted an excuse to keep out of the house. And he never attempted again."

I couldn't help but imagine it. That moment. That feeling, that visceral wrongness of knowing that something was happening that wasn't supposed to and there was nothing he could have done about it. That innocence, teetering into oblivion with gnashing teeth snapping below.

I gripped Hadrian tighter. As if I could shield him from the world.

"I'm so sorry," I choked. I could see it clearly—the hatred he'd had for Bertie, the butler. The insinuations that Bertie had known, had aided. And then Hadrian, an adult, ending the line.

Then Bunny, trapping him within the house.

A coil of hatred emerged. How could she have subjected him to the house if she'd known what it would show him?

"You relived it because of the curse keeping you in that room," I murmured. "How could she do that to you? After helping you?" Tears threatened my vision.

"You do not understand, dearest. I think that is the issue we have at hand."

I dug my fingers into his hand, his shoulder. "Don't I?" I asked vehemently. "That's—disgusting to subject you to those—memories a-and—"

"Landry," he said, firm. "She likely did not know how the house, the curse, would treat me. I was in a different place when it happened."

"But that's *torture.*"

"You do not realize what I turned into as an adult." He swallowed. "I remember when I came back from Fort McKavett. Hot, muggy month. Late August. God, I was . . ." He shook his head. I lost myself in the sway, the smell of him, how we bent together in all the right ways.

"I was inconsolable. I was—ruined. Imagine, I killed my father. Lost my wife. I traveled west for years, leaving my affairs in such disarray. I *wanted* it to fail. I wanted everyone to suffer like I had. And finally, a man I was chasing took me toward Stetson. I decided to stop for the night. And there I was, consumed with hatred for . . . everything. I was still wildly upset with my father, with myself for putting up with him for so many years, and I was angry that no one did anything to help me but Bunny. A part of me snapped. I ruined the front parlor. The office. Planned to burn the place to the ground and kill myself."

I pictured it, his voice rumbling in my ear, and stepped on his foot on accident. *Kill myself.* Those two words.

His mouth settled against my hair, right at my temple. "Oh, yes. Our stableman, Revley, heard Bunny screaming at me, and tried to stop me. I knocked his ears clean back. Bunny caught my attention long enough to keep me from—but I,"—he shrugged, lost—"I came to pieces. I was mad at what my father had built. I was mad at myself. I hated everyone and everything, and if I'm being honest with myself, I am not so sure I wouldn't have taken Revley and Bunny's life had she not done what she did. I wanted everything to end that badly."

My lip quivered. "Hadrian, I—"

"Do not pity who I was. *I* was wrong. I know this. Pitying only romanticizes the things I did, and I deserved every last bit of what I got in that room. I was running, and running only ever makes for a coward."

I slid both hands away until I encircled his waist and hugged him to me. And here I was, ungrateful for the circumstances I had been dealt, with the parents I had been given?

"All I remember is Bunny stopping me. I don't remember how or with what, because the screaming—she loved me. She was my mother from the time I was born, nursemaid or not, biological or not. From my infant years until I was thirty-five. No matter what version of myself I was, I was hers, and she was protecting me. Do not hate her for what she did." His thumb found my cheek. Brushed away a lone tear that raced down to my chin.

Maybe he was right. If Bunny hadn't stopped him, how would things have ended? What lengths would he have gone to end it all?

Suddenly I saw Aunt Cadence, turning me away as a child. Telling me that Mommy's home was better. The thought made me shiver. She knew something was wrong here and chose to push me away. Was it the same? To choose the lesser of two evils?

"All of that to say, as a child, I remember Bunny being vehement about the house. Keeping things clean. She never liked the things my father brought into the house. Granted, I was too young to know what she might mean." He stepped closer, his presence nearly enveloping me. "She briefly had help from a friend of mine's mother. I remember something similar to what your aunt mentioned—a cleansing, that is, but Mrs. Haste passed not long after." The corners of his eyes crinkled as he gave me a pointed look. "Bunny could have messed something up. The curse, when she went to stop me. The feeling that had been in the house, that she'd tried to get rid of, and then keep me from doing what I intended—it could have culminated."

"So it could be anything keeping you here. Something with an emotional tie . . . or remains." The last two words felt like a pebble tossed in a rushing river. I didn't like the idea of finding his grave.

"If they followed tradition, the grave is not on the property. I would have been buried near the river with the rest of the family plots. No bodily remains on house grounds."

A tension knot uncurled in my gut. That was good. Good, because I wouldn't be searching for a grave, but also good because that left us at another dead end.

A pause.

Then, "Do you hate me? For the decisions I made?" he asked.

I shook my head. His shirt was plush against my cheek. "No. I don't hate you for what you did."

"Nor I, you," he whispered, and this time, those three words were intoxicatingly gentle, not laced with malice.

We swayed for a while. The playlist shifted to something a little more passionate. My feet and hips found rhythm with his; I matched his step, anticipated the weight shift of his body.

"I haven't heard you talking in the middle of the night," he said.

I managed a smile.

"I've missed your voice."

"My endless ramblings?"

"Just you talking. I like it."

"Really?"

"Your words give me traces of color, Landry. It makes me feel like I might live again, listening to your stories. So yes, I really do miss you talking."

And for a split second, I thought maybe, just maybe, he wasn't in a rush to figure this out because he wanted to stay a while longer, too.

Chapter Twenty-Three

We danced.

He asked me about my childhood. I asked him about his. Easy, simpler questions. *Did you ever lay out on the lawn at night? Did you ever get in trouble for something absolutely ridiculous?*

"At least I know the answer to one question," I said. The mood had lightened, worries forgotten. I tipped my head back to look at him. What a concept—that I would be here, dancing in the middle of the living room at night. It felt good.

His mouth curved in a grin, still pointed angles. I stifled a shiver. "Enlighten me, Miss Frederick." He gave me a spin. Tendrils of hair fanned around me. I came dangerously close to hitting the coffee table.

I laughed, the sound chest-deep. "You don't know how to drive a car and I do."

He yanked me back in. Our bodies collided, his grip playful, fervent. Both his hands on my waist now. My fingers tangled around his neck.

"Of all the things you hold over me, you choose this? At least I have no obsession with tiny screens, like you do." He pressed his face into the crook of my throat and swung me into a dip. There, at the bottom, he pressed a kiss to my skin. I shrieked with laughter.

"I have to hold something over you, don't I? Here you are, all handsome with good social standing. Besides—what are you going to do about it?" I giggled, breathy. His touch tickled. I tried to pinch my shoulder and chin together.

"Kiss you," he said, mouth moving to the soft place beneath my ear. "If you would let me."

Fluttering wings erupted throughout my ribcage. Moments like this didn't feel real. Like any second, the room would dissolve around us, and I'd wake up.

"You're asking." My eyebrows pinched in. I didn't mean to say that. Not really. It was more of a thought that came to the surface without my consent.

Right then, our gazes *snagged*. Like a hangnail between the teeth, ready to pull it away. To expose the sensitive, raw skin around it and below with one swift tug. That's what he was doing to me. Peeling that layer. Letting air hit it.

The thought made my blood burn—in gratitude.

"I would never not ask you," he murmured. A bated breath hung between us.

I tried to smile. To muster up that teasing thread that had somehow vanished. I couldn't find it. Instead, I answered honestly.

My breath brushed his cheek. The hollow place just before his ear. His hair fluttered with it. "For you," I said, swallowed, "always."

I felt the smile before he pulled back, before he kissed me. Warm, inviting, happy.

Happy.

I took his face in my hands and deepened the kiss. His tongue touched mine, until he drew my bottom lip between his teeth. The music came to a murmur in the background, crickets chirped from an open window, and in that breadth of a moment, I lived in an infinity. An infinity where everything was okay, where each gasp was perfect, and I couldn't get enough.

Because his hands didn't move with force. They were languid and urgent all at once, nearly floating over my arms and around my low back, like I might drift away if he weren't careful. I was the last clothespin holding a shirt on the line, ready to whip away in the breeze.

And I couldn't help but wonder if this could grow into something *else* if it were given the chance.

The thought made me falter. I shoved it away, far down into the barrel of my chest. I needed to stay in the now. But deep down, I loved that he'd grown not just into a nail that kept me pinned to the earth, but an anchor.

And the last thing I wanted was to let him go.

He walked me back. I let him. The air tasted crisper, the house grew closer, the night pressing inside toward us, urging us, farther, farther, faster. My calf scraped the coffee table.

Hadrian's mouth gravitated to my neck again. "Should I have met you," he said against my skin, "I would have run into you on accident." He said it like a lie. An *accident*. "I would have asked who your family was."

His hands gripped both sides of my waist. His voice turned rich, painting a picture with each breath.

His hair smelled of smoke, soil, and musk. Arms encircled me. Chest to chest, breath to breath. His shoes whispered over the rug.

"I would have come to your front door and knocked. Brought something I thought you might like. I would have spoken to your father and searched for you in the other room when he turned his back to me. I would have asked to take you for dinner or a walk."

I squeezed my eyes shut. Why was he telling me this? And why did it hurt so badly?

I backed into the arm of the sofa. He stepped between my legs, bent down, right there, the bridge of his nose lined up against mine, and suddenly the world felt smaller than it ever had before.

"I would have known before the night was over that I would be back within a fortnight, and I would have returned every night after until you grew tired of me," he whispered.

"I wouldn't have gotten tired of you," I said against his lips.

"You lie."

The irony in his words made me smile, just a little. My hands drifted from around his neck, into his hair. A fluttering against my breastbone caught my attention. I glanced down.

His button shirt had grown damp—a maroon, nearly black spot the size of a fist—right where his heart should have been. It was like he heard my thoughts.

"Do you wish to see it?"

I met his gaze. He spoke as if it had changed, so I nodded.

He pulled his shirt out of his trousers and made quick work of the buttons. I expected it to be opened and oozing like before, but instead found raw skin—purpled, raised scars around the edges, nearly an inch or so in width, while the center remained split open. I started to pull back, worried that I had hurt the wound, but he held me fast.

He took my hand and flattened it against his chest. Quick, persistent flutters. Like a flag snapping in the wind. His breath brushed my cheekbone when he said, "It's never looked like that before."

"Oh." The word was broken. Like a part of me had chipped.

Because of course it had changed, too. It wasn't just him anymore, it was parts of him, the gnarled edges that smoothed. Clotted and healed, as if they would all collectively vanish soon.

I frowned. "But that's good, right?" Tried to keep my voice light.

His eyes softened, thoughtful. "Perhaps."

The palm of his hand pressed against my cheek. "Don't do that. Please."

"Do what?"

"Look like I'm breaking your heart."

I didn't push against his palm, didn't blink, just stared at that point on his neck. Could he see it? Did he know, without me having to say anything? Did he think I was delusional for catching feelings?

He licked his bottom teeth, tongue briefly running along the empty sockets—then his body locked. Joint by joint. Even his hand twitched.

"My teeth." The two words were no more than a whisper. "When I killed him, I found them in the family safe inside a box." His nostrils flared. "I kept them."

My heart fluttered like a wet fish at the base of my throat.

I knew without meeting his gaze what he meant: *remains.*

"Where?"

"I hid them in"—his throat bobbed—"the floors."

At first, I didn't speak. He could be right.

Teeth didn't decay like tissue and flesh. If they'd been in the box Aunt Cadence found—

"Okay." I gave a tight, single nod. That was that, then. Problem solved. His hand dropped, leaving a print of fire on my cheek in its wake.

"That look," he said. He leaned back in, his nose close to mine. I leaned away. "Tell me what you're thinking."

"There's your answer," I whispered. I blinked, hard, and met his gaze. "We should find your teeth. Then you can—you can—"

"Landry, if you—"

"Don't argue with me, Hadrian," I cut in, but my voice was too high, too thin.

"I'm not. I'm trying to discuss this with you because I care."

"But this is what you wanted," I said, persistent. "This is what we agreed to. Now you can just—"

"—you know little of what I want—"

"—*leave*, just like everyone else."

There. I'd said it. The words hung between us like a dead corpse on a hook, bleeding and fresh and rank. It felt like I'd stripped open two halves of my chest and let him look. Like I should have been the one with the bleeding heart and not him.

"Don't say that," he murmured. "I'm not leaving."

"Aren't you? That's what we agreed on. We fix this for you—we break whatever is holding you here, and that's it."

"That's not it, we don't even know if my teeth are the answer," he urged. "Why are you putting me in the same box as everyone else? Why haven't you asked me what I want?"

I stood from the couch, but our faces were already so close, and I couldn't help it, I grabbed his face in my hands and I wanted to scream. "Because."

"Because *why*," he snarled, that gritty, earthy hint seeping into his words.

A cold sweat bloomed along my brow. A sick sense of dread enveloped me, hugged me, squeezed. If I didn't say it now, I didn't think I ever would.

"Because I care what you think," I said. "And I want to help you." *Tell me how we need to do it. Tell me you don't feel this.*

Tell me you want to leave.

Gray. All I saw was gray. Wilted, rainy, storming gray, with a flash of yellow lightening.

"You think that's it? All of this, done? Is that how you feel about it?" His voice turned to a growl.

"It's all you've wanted."

"It's all you *think* I've wanted."

"Then tell me what you want, Hadrian," I blurted.

He straightened, but he looked down at me, our bodies so close, his skin near feverish. Every part of me wanted to slip around, to walk away first, to settle it. To let him go. But my heels remained locked in place, the pressure in the room lapping higher, higher until it hit my elbows.

"I—you are not selling the house."

"That's not what I asked—"

"I want—*this*."

I flinched like he'd hit me.

He chewed the inside of his cheek. "For a little while. Here, with you. Just . . . don't search for them. Wait." He raked his fingers through his hair, sending streaks of blond in all directions. He didn't look nervous or unkempt. Somehow, even his uncertainty looked steady.

My question came out reedy. "Why?"

His eyes shuttered. This time, when he leaned in, I didn't sit back on the couch arm. His open shirt waved, the muscle in his chest flickered like he was straining or unsure. He captured my mouth with a certainty, an urgency, both hands grabbing either side of my face and holding me there. A groan slipped from his chest, and he was everywhere. We were everywhere.

He pulled back just enough for his lips to whisper against mine, and said, "Because I don't want to let you go ye—"

The front door opened. "Landry!"

It happened so quick the room spun.

Hadrian and I shot upright at the same time. He grabbed both of my shoulders and dragged me in front of him so my head blocked the opened part of his chest. He wrapped his arms around my shoulders, tight, steady, as if we did this every day. As if this were normal.

His chin rested on the crown of my head.

Emma rounded the corner to the living room and looked up. "Hey! You're—"

Everyone froze. Stared at each other. Embarrassment surged in a red heat over my skin.

"Oh my God," she gasped, wide eyed. The TV, dreadfully and embarrassingly, still hummed in the background. Like we were two frantic teenagers before a parent got home.

I could only imagine how we looked right then. Hadrian, shirt open. Me, eyes wide, face hot. And then there was Emma: mouth agape, purse dangling at her side and the front door still open.

"I will . . . step . . ." She jerked a thumb over her shoulder. "Out . . . side."

I nodded, mute.

Hadrian cleared his throat. When the front door clicked shut, I turned. Not an ounce of blush heated his cheeks.

"She saw you," I murmured, stepping close. His shoulder brushed my cheek. "She *saw* you, Hadrian."

His Adam's apple bobbed when he nodded. I couldn't help the sense of dread that filled my stomach when he said, "That she did, dearest. That she did."

Chapter Twenty-Four

After six minutes of pacing and texting furiously while she walked, I'd managed to wrangle Emma back into the house. Now, both hands were splayed as we sat on the couch, like she'd been trying to keep a child from eating a battery they'd found lying on the floor.

"I'm not mad," Emma said. "I just wanna know."

She also kept talking in partial sentences. I could almost see the smoke billowing out of her ears. Granted, I understood. At the very least, Hadrian had looked completely human tonight—which was a blessing, because explaining horns and teeth would have been difficult.

"Who that man is," Another pause. She puckered her mouth into duck-lips, tilted her head, and raised one eyebrow. Then, she held up a finger. "For one. Two," another finger went up. "Why is he so attractive. Three. Where did he come from?"

I sat with my hands pinned between my knees. A low vibrating sound came from her pocket. She retrieved her phone, texted in quick, snapping taps. "Um. Would you believe me if I told you he just kind of fell out of the closet one day—"

"I am not joking! Landry May Frederick! Focus!" She faced her screen away from me. It buzzed again.

"Yes, Mom!" I exclaimed with just as much enthusiasm.

She pointed a finger at me. The morning sun did wonders for her eyes. Almost burnt auburn with a gold ring around the outside. "You were dry humping a hot man in our living room."

"My living room." I didn't say it with venom. Just to poke her.

"As far as I'm concerned, I'm not sure you're *cognitively able* to own a home when you have men like *that* hiding in your life. You never told me!" She flung her arms wide. One hand smacked the window frame. I knew she was serious, because she didn't so much as wince.

"Like—WHY? How? Where did you meet him?" She leaned across the table, eyebrows so high they nearly blended with her hairline. "I swear on our dad's grave, if he's a serial killer—no, scratch that, even something as low as not putting his own shopping cart away, I'm going to bury him in the backyard and plant squash over his plot before fall."

"They would have actually needed to be planted about two months ago—"

"You get the point!"

"I don't think it's that serious, Em." I kept my tone gentle. Now I was using the placating hands. She trembled like Donald The Chihuahua used to. "He's not—"

My throat clogged. *He's not a bad guy* insinuated he had not, in fact, killed someone. Or multiple someones.

"—going to hurt me," is what I settled on instead.

"Hurt is subjective." A flash behind her eyes, something to hide.

My posture softened. I leaned my elbows onto the table. As if making myself smaller would allow Emma to open up.

"Is this about, you know. Your mom?" I asked.

The room grew so quiet, I heard the air settle around us. The question hung like a swaying chandelier—any moment, that final wire holding it in place would snap and it would crash to the floor.

"No," she breathed. Her pointer finger traced an idle path around the edges of her hand, where tan met porcelain. "I just want to make sure you're making good choices and not going out and picking up a random off the street—"

"You're changing the subject." I reached out and started tracing a path, too. When we were young, we would use our fingers as racecars and see which of us could complete as many laps as possible on her macules before the other. I'd take a thigh, she'd take the other thigh. We'd end in a fit of giggles and start over again.

A sigh. "My mom should have left Vince a long time ago."

"He'll get the house," I muttered. My finger stopped tracing. Instead, I glared at the table. "He'll get the cars. The kids are all gone. No child support. She'll be kicked."

Emma nodded. "I stopped by before I left."

"How was she?"

"Terrible. Looked like she'd gotten stung by a bee and had an allergic reaction. For every bag she packed, she wrote down something on a list. I read it." Emma leaned back in her chair and smiled. "One said, 'Pour instant potatoes in front yard.' Another, 'Slash three tires, not all four, insurance won't cover it.'"

"A revenge list?"

"A very *long* revenge list."

"Sounds like she's handling it a little better than my mom did." I thought of the bottles that had slowly piled up in the corner of her bedroom after my father left. "Is there anything I can do?"

She shook her head. "Not a thing. I offered to let her stay at my place. She agreed to one week and that's it. Said she needed to do this on her own."

"Well—"

The front door slammed open. The rattle of the stained-glass sheets made both Emma and I swivel in our seats. I really needed to start locking the front door.

Sayer stomped into the living room, a basket in his arms. A single tasseled kazoo poked out, lined with four bags of candy and a sign, taped to a popsicle stick, that read, *Congratulations!* in arching, rainbowed font.

"Surprise!" He held the basket in the air. His glasses slid down his nose. He walked to the island and dropped his present in the center of it. "I thought this would be fitting."

"I thought—y-you aren't supposed to be here?" I stuttered. I stood and examined the basket. Confetti lined the bottom. "What is this?"

Sayer removed his glasses, wiped them on his shirt, then pushed them back into place. "For you. Who else?"

I looked back to Emma. She smiled.

It clicked.

"You didn't," I muttered. "Did you tell him? It's been thirty minutes."

"Of course. I told him as soon as I went outside." She got up and hugged me from behind, nuzzling her chin into my shoulder. "I knew you wouldn't. Thankfully, he was already on the way."

"Let go of me, traitor."

"What's he look like?" Sayer asked. He squinted, lips puckered. He leaned against the island and propped his chin in his hand. "Tall? Brooding? Does he smolder?" Sayer proceeded to smolder.

I covered my eyes. "This is excessive."

"Did you have sex?"

"No! We did not!"

"Have you?"

"What are we, high schoolers?"

"Adults can gossip, too, Landry. Besides. I need to know what this man's like. It's not often I see you flush *so pink*."

I pulled my shirt neck up immediately and glared at him. Then Emma. "You two are insufferable." All I could think about was how Hadrian was probably eavesdropping and basking in my embarrassment.

I spotted a bag of peanut butter–filled pretzels in the basket.

Eyeing both of them, I snatched it up, then walked to the living room. "I will tell you about him on one condition."

Sayer gasped. "Yes. Whatever it is." He strode after me. "You would have told me anyway, but I like to humor you. I hope you know that."

"You help me with the office and tell me why you're here when you said you wouldn't be." Now, it was my turn to give an expectant look. "I'll pay you both extra, of course. For listening to my woes."

"My companionship is free. Off with the money."

I ripped the bag open. Emma had trailed me, hand extended. She shoveled what I offered into her mouth. Crunched loudly. "I don't need your money, either, Frederick. We help because we love you. And you let me use your Wi-Fi because mine sucks."

"Fine," I conceded.

Over Sayer's shoulder, in the kitchen hallway to the left, a flicker of movement. Like a shoulder hiding behind a wall.

Before, I'd have felt a swell of discomfort. Or even dread. Now, it was only a warmth that started in my toes and buried itself in my blood before riding all the way to my chest.

I didn't want to get used to the idea of him being here.

But I was starting to.

* * *

The next few days passed in a quiet calm—so much so, that I was starting to get nervous. One, because Hadrian had visited at night, each night, at his normal hour. The second reason made my skin itch.

My dad still hadn't called me back. And Mom's time limit was looming.

"Are you waiting for the Pentagon to call you?" Sayer heaved. "I heard they're hiring. They would pay a lot more than—pulling—bushes." He yanked at a dead rosebush in the front yard.

I suppose I was attached to my phone like Velcro this morning.

"You offered to help and wouldn't take money. It's not my fault." I set my phone on the porch railing.

"I regret my choices." Sayer pulled again—this time, the roots gave way. He teetered. The dead bush fell apart in his hand. "I hate gardening."

"You heartless peasant," I said in my best British accent. I started to lean against the porch railing. "How dare you disgrace these beautiful—ouch." I hissed and yanked my arm back. Blood welled around an embedded splinter.

"I told you," Sayer muttered. "Dangerous work."

Just then, my phone vibrated twice. I hurried to catch it before it buzzed right off the porch railing. I swiped without looking at the caller ID, already walking away from Sayer for privacy.

"Hello?"

"Landry. How are you?"

I paused mid-step. "You got my message."

"Of course I did." Dad's words were somehow cushioned and hurried all at once. Busy. I swallowed against a dry tongue. Waited for him to continue.

"You mentioned an estate lawyer," he began. Shuffling in the background, similar to papers over a desk, and I imagined him in his office in Charleston, looking out at the tapered skyline. Which direction would he look today? Out toward sea or inland, where I would be?

"Um, yes," I said. I kept my voice even. "I figured you would know someone."

He cleared his throat. From the garden, Sayer looked up. Shielded his eyes from the sun and mouthed, *Is it Vince?*

I gave a pinched nod.

Sayer started taking his gloves off, but didn't come closer. A car whispered by.

"I assumed another lawyer might do, yes, unless you want me to handle your affairs?" he assumed. As if he wanted me to admit I didn't want him, when it was he that never wanted me. The thought soured as soon as it appeared.

"It would be a conflict of interest." I straightened, feeling the drying sweat along the waistband of my shorts, only for it to be melted by a new rush of heat. I didn't want to say it. But I didn't know legal ramifications like my father did.

He'd never exploited her. He'd never gossiped about her. He'd disrespected her and their marriage, he'd left me behind, but he'd never once denied the alimony she'd requested. His only downfall was abandonment.

He was my father. Not a good father, but my father. A father that knew law.

"Is something wrong?" I heard him sit up. The plastic click of a pen being set atop a table. Then the snick of a laptop being shut.

"You know Aunt Cadence died." I inhaled through my nose.

He swallowed. Deadpan, he said, "Yes."

I ignored that needle of pain, the affirmation that he'd never once called to offer condolences. *Focus.* "Have you spoken to Mom since she died?"

"I haven't spoken to anyone, Landry."

"She left everything to me. The house. The trusts. Life insurance money. All of it." I blinked away a sudden burn of tears.

Silence.

Sayer paused on the front step. Concern laced every inch of his face.

I leaned against the tree and let my head fall back against its trunk. "Mom is pissed. She showed up a few days ago and says I'm keeping things from her. I'd planned on selling the house but—"

I don't know what's best.

I don't know what I should do.

Help me.

"I don't know where to go from here," I said, flat. I walked away from the tree, closer to the edge of the property. It butted up against a fence of bramble and ivy, tangled over an old wire fence that looked nearly completely camouflaged by the foliage. Somewhere, miles up the street, another house stood. I wondered if they could hear my voice travel on the wind.

"I see." More rustling, like a harsh palm running over beard stubble. "So she came to you because she was upset you were selling things?"

I squeezed the bridge of my nose. He needed to know, whether or not anything would come of it. "And she heard that you and Penny split up."

A long, heavy breath. "God."

"She wanted me to get in touch with you."

He cursed, low. "*Did she* now." It wasn't even a question.

"She's out of money. She's looking for a place to stay. She said she could stay with me while I get in contact with you." And the Airbnb I set her up with, which was due to end soon.

He gave a brittle, viperous laugh. "*Did* she."

I nodded even though he couldn't see me. It was like he heard it, because he went on, "Tell her she has no room at my house. She can figure it out on her own."

A spark of anger. "So what am I supposed to do about her? She's been circling and I know she wants to go through Cadence's things and—"

"Why not let her?"

"Because they aren't her things, Dad. They're mine. Aunt Cadence left them for me." I hated how much of a child I sounded in the moment. "What do I do?"

"Landry. Listen. Your mother is going to get something whether you like it or not."

"She's a grown woman. She didn't even show up to her funeral," I bit, blood starting to bubble. "Why should she get anything when she only cares about filling her pockets so she can spend it at the ABC store and get wasted in the middle of the road downtown? Why should I enable her any more than I already have?"

"Because she won't—"

"Do you not see what I'm saying?" I cut in.

The line went silent. For a moment, I thought he hung up. Then I realized why it was quiet. From the corner of my eye, even Sayer stood by the dead rosebush, frozen, staring at me.

I couldn't remember the last time I'd cut my dad off.

A whistling breath. "I see what you're saying, Lan. I'm asking you to see what *I'm* saying."

I ground my teeth. I wanted to be petty. I wanted to ask, "Why should I when you weren't here when she left me for three days and bounced off to some casino in Virginia and left me to eat stale ramen and curdled milk?" but I didn't.

I'd called him. I'd asked for this. I was an adult. Being combative would get me nowhere.

"What I'm saying," he started again, "is that your mother doesn't just need money. She needs a clinic, but she won't take it. Giving her a roof is the only thing that can help right now unless—"

"She is not living with me."

"Then admit her, Lan."

My eyes narrowed. "Why, so you don't have to?" Not just pay for it, but wipe himself of responsibility?

"I tried," he snapped. "*Twice.* She did the time, she got out, and relapsed. Both times in the last four years."

I stared at a particularly tall blade of grass. "You had her admitted to a clinic?"

"Yes. And she will only get help if she wants it. I've tried to help her, I have paid her more than enough alimony over the last however many years, I've paid her bills, I've paid every *collection* she accrued, *everything.* The rent, the water, the insurance—every last dingy bit of that hellhole she picked, I paid for. She's had enough opportunity, and I refuse to give her another."

My cheeks started to tingle.

I'd always thought—Mom never said anything about her not paying the bills. Then again, I wasn't surprised by that. Just surprised that Dad still paid for it all. That he'd known where I lived this whole time and never once stopped by.

Why would he pay to keep our lights on, knowing she had a problem, but then leave me behind at the end of the day? Return to Penny, continue his sideways love affairs, and turn his back on the person that needed him the most?

Why would he help her, but he never helped me?

Vomit ate at my lungs. I shook my head. Closed my eyes. The birds singing mitigated the anger only so much.

What more of an answer did I need?

"I'll figure it out," I whispered. "Thanks for your help, Vince."

"Landry—"

I hung up. Almost immediately, his caller ID blinked on-screen, but I declined it. Below the declined call appeared a text message bubble—this one not from my father.

My heart leaped into my mouth; immediately, I wiped sweat from my eyes and beelined back to the house. She'd seen it.

"What did your dad want?" Sayer asked, cautious.

"More of the same. Just a bunch of excuses." I picked up a hand trowel and an extra set of gloves. "I can clean this up."

"Where are you going?" Sayer picked up the dead rosebush and tossed it into the bramble. It floated on the live bushes, but he left it, then balled up his gardening gloves and trailed after me.

"I need to meet someone in town really quick. I can pick up lunch, though."

"Emma said she'd bring something back. She went to The Blue Corduroy to finish her work." Sayer followed me into the living room. I grabbed a water and a protein shake out of the fridge, chugged one, then sipped the other.

He made careful work of not touching the couch. Instead, he peeled his shirt from his body. "Well. If you're leaving, can I borrow your shower?"

"Sure."

"As long as there's no hot blond guy hiding in there somewhere." Sayer tilted his head with a heavy squint.

"Hadrian is not hiding in the shower."

"Mm. A ghost, then?"

"No." If only he knew.

"Says the girl that told Emma about a book nook turning on and off by itself."

Chapter Twenty-Five

I didn't think she'd actually meet with me.

Hemlock had one Italian bistro that sat nestled between an upholstery store and a nail salon. I missed the little red, white, and green sign the first time; after a second trip around the block, I managed to snag a parking spot.

I hated having to find people in restaurants. It reminded me of Whack-A-Mole as a kid—I'd stand like a pillar in the middle of a rushing river, waiting for the right head to pop up, all while the rest of the patrons watched with curiosity as to who I was looking for.

"How many?" the hostess greeted me. She chewed her gum with unbridled aggression.

"Two. I'm looking for an Irene? She might be here already?" I held onto my bag strap. The bistro was brighter than I'd expected; the far wall was blanketed in faux dangling ivy. A neon pink sign hung in the middle that said, *Italy wishes you were here.*

"I don't know any Irenes," the girl said. She gathered two menus. Then rolled her eyes and muttered, "Follow me."

She sat me in a corner booth, big enough for a family of eight, right next to the ivy wall. As soon as she left, I touched it. Definitely fake.

Irene bounced from another booth toward me, something tucked under her armpit. "I can't believe she put you at a different table," she muttered as she plopped into the seat across from me. She shot a look to where the hostess had disappeared. "Can't find good help these days."

I forced a smile. "I'm sorry, I didn't see you."

"You're fine, you're fine," she said. She gave a small headshake, forehead creased. "I'm so glad you texted me, though. I wanted to know how your issue was going." She said the word *issue* in a whisper, like she didn't want anyone to overhear.

"Oh, it's going." I rubbed my hands on my thighs. My answer wasn't enough: She seemed to lean in a bit, her eyes attached to my hands, how I sat, my expression. Too observant.

So I said the only thing I could think of. And it was honest.

"Good, actually. Things have calmed down. I think it's stopped, at least for now."

Her eyes brightened. "That's good! What did you do? Or did it just—"

"I think it was a culmination of things, like you'd mentioned. Briefly. Bad things brought through the house, attached to items, and I found some of them, I think. Got rid of them." I forced a smile, willed the truth to my eyes. Because when I'd thought about it, Sayer had been the one to go through the attic, and Meredith said everything had sold. So everything likely *was* gone. And the teeth—out of sight, out of mind.

"That's great, I'm so glad. I felt horrible for not getting you those things sooner. And at least you didn't open the door, so whatever that's for, it can just be left."

"Exactly." Little did she know.

An awkward bubble lifted between us. In the back, voices and clatters from the kitchen echoed around the otherwise empty dining area. Thankfully, a young man with braces and slicked back hair appeared out of thin air a moment later.

Irene ordered garlic bread. As soon as he walked away, she unfolded her menu. "To share, if you want."

I nodded.

She nodded.

Then we both chuckled.

"I'm sorry," I offered. I took a long sip of my water. "I just don't know . . ."

"What to say?"

"Right."

The text I'd sent hadn't been specific—just that I wanted to talk. To ask questions, more for my own peace of mind than anything, but how did you bring up an ex without sounding too forward? My brain hummed like an air conditioning unit in the middle of summer.

"About Cadence—" she started, just as I said, "I was wondering if you knew—"

The tension cracked. Pieces rained down on the table. Another chuckle, this time a deep one from both of us.

I tried a different angle. "Can you tell me about it? About my aunt, I mean? What exactly did she tell you about the house?"

Irene's brow crinkled, thoughtful. "Not much. Each time she talked about it less. I did the digging on my own time after I went to see what she was talking about, but . . ." She gave a shrug. "She didn't lose interest, but she seemed kind of—defensive about it. I'm not sure."

"Oh." I tried to hide my disappointment.

Irene sucked on her bottom teeth. "She did talk about you, though. All the time."

"She did?" My stomach bottomed out. Here it was: the moment of truth. Had she been upset I hadn't visited? I wanted to bury my face in my hands.

Instead, I braced myself, ready for the guilt to resurface.

"She always showed me pictures of the houses you'd redecorated. You do, like, interior design?"

I nodded.

A shred of sadness crept into her eyes when she looked at me. "She always said you would make it into *Home Living* or something one day. She tried to show me your website but couldn't figure out how to get the newsletter pop-up screen to go away."

A small smile pulled at my lips. "That sounds like her."

The waiter came back with the garlic bread. We both gave plastic smiles, our orders, and thanked him before waiting for him to walk out of earshot.

"She said you grew up here?" she asked. "In Stetson, I mean?"

"I did," I said, then launched into my abbreviated life story, similar to the one I gave Hadrian that one night, while skimming the painful parts. When I took a sip of my drink and asked, "And you?" I felt it.

Irene's eyes were thoughtful.

Knowing.

Our waiter returned with our orders and centered a basket of fried pickles between us. I'd just gathered enough courage to beat around the bush, when she said, "You know Ivan Kenneth, right?"

I paused. Glanced up.

"Why?" Hundreds of bees came alive in the center of my throat. There was only one reason she would be bringing him into the conversation. "Did he say something about me?"

Was she still in his good graces? Surely, she wasn't if she'd removed his pictures. But the towns were small, and it seemed like the circles were even smaller, which meant it was only a matter of time before he started sputtering on about what I'd said to him in the foyer, right?

What if he'd told people I was giving him the listing, only to back out? To flake? Use him for clout or attention or whatever—just like before?

She sighed. Her cushioned lips parted, closed, then parted again. A pink glow cast over her cheekbones, her nose, from the neon sign to my left.

"No, it's just—you sent this to me." She flipped her phone around.

My mouth opened in surprise.

A photograph of Ivan and I, together from years ago, had been sent from my phone to hers *before* the text message I'd sent asking her to meet for lunch.

But I didn't send that picture.

Fire crawled up my spine, curled around my chest cavity, hissed along my heart. I wanted to push my plate aside and smack my head into the table in embarrassment.

"Oh," was all I managed. I knotted my hands in my lap.

Irene locked her phone and set it back on the table. She made quick work of splitting her wrap in two halves and dipping one in sauce. She took a small bite, chewed, swallowed.

I wanted to melt into the seat. I thought of all the times my phone had turned on by itself. Maybe . . . Maybe it hadn't really been me. Maybe it had been someone else.

Or something else. Maybe for the same reason the doors closed, the lights turned on. The things I'd seen as a child that I didn't remember.

"I didn't know if you wanted to talk about it?"

I found myself shaking my head. "I must have sent that on accident. I didn't mean . . ." My words fell away.

Where was this coming from? Yes, I wanted to talk about it.

Before I could talk myself off the ledge, I jumped—right into the railcar this time. Not just a step on the platform.

This was the reason I'd texted her. And I needed to take the jump.

"Ivan Kenneth assaulted me while we were dating," I whispered. "Multiple times. And I never said anything." The words felt like arrows being ripped from my skin. From the disk in my spine, from the hinge of my jaw. Everywhere, bleeding. "He told me things I only realized later was manipulation. And I'm having a really, really hard time forgiving myself for putting up with it for so long and I thought maybe since you two dated that—"

I shook my head.

"I wondered if maybe it happened to you, too," I breathed. And I realized then how terrible that sounded. How someone might take it as me asking, or wishing, my own ill will onto them. My skin splotched at my neck, burned, and my nails found themselves at a semi-healed scab at my wrist. I started to pick it off. "It's wrong to assume, and I don't want to put you on the spot or anything, and you don't have to—"

"You're not alone," Irene whispered. Her syllables cracked.

"It sounds terrible, and I'm sorry, I don't mean that I wished—"

She stood from her seat. Then I found her scooting into my side of the booth. She didn't touch me, only existed three inches away. Her shoulder the same height as mine, her lashes curled to her browbone, wispy and beautiful. Glittering with tears.

"You're not, Landry," she choked.

You're not.

My lip started to wobble. I didn't remember leaning in—I wasn't so sure she realized she did, either.

Her arms wrapped around my neck, mine went around her back. Her body, so slight, somehow felt like a life raft. Like she would take me to shore eventually. I didn't know how; I just knew she would.

A sob broke my chest.

"I promise," she whispered. "You aren't alone. You are never, *ever* alone."

Chapter Twenty-Six

The driveway danced with fireflies by the time I got home. I'd driven back in silence, my thoughts racing while the world around me remained quiet. So much at once.

Numb, I shifted into park and stared at the vines crowding the edge of the drive. Down to the freshly pulled landscaping, in desperate need of mulch and a new set of marigolds. It ran all the way to the shed. The door was cocked at an angle, the lock in the loop but not shut.

I stepped out of the car. My shoes hissed on cracked pavement and gravel. There was time to fix that now, too. Another thing on my never-ending list.

The list would never be finished. I could feel it. Like the house loomed over me.

Home, home, home, it whispered.

I patted my hands on both cheeks. Still warm; I'd tried to wait until the puffiness settled—Emma would demand for me to explain why I was crying, and the thought of explaining why I'd met with Irene again wasn't something I was ready to unravel. I'd been so close to sticking my head out the window while I drove down the road to see if the cold air would calm the redness. Now, I'd just have to deal with it.

I took in the house as I walked up the cobble path. The streaked maroon and blue skies. The half-lit windows, curtains open. Emma's silhouette in the living room. The main door hung ajar behind the screen door. Laughter echoed from inside. Maybe that voice was right.

Home.

The music stopped when I opened the front door. Someone cursed. Then a groan.

"I don't get it," Sayer said from the kitchen. I rounded the corner to find him unraveling a sour strip. He waved it around like a lasso. "She doesn't sound any better than she did, like, four years ago? What's the obsession?"

Emma stood in the middle of the living room, arms wide. "How can you say that? Have you no taste?" She gestured wildly to the TV. "*Everyone* loves Marion Blanchet. How do you not?"

Sayer gave her an exasperated look. He swung the sour strip toward the pantry and asked, "Why do you think?" Then he spotted me. He gave me a wicked grin. "Oh, Landry! You're back!"

Emma whirled. "Tell him Marion Blanchet is not a tone-deaf walrus."

"I mean—" but my words died.

Hadrian leaned out of the pantry, two bags in his fists. One, an assorted bag of Reese's, the second a bag of cheese puffs. He wore his same button-down shirt and trousers and shoes as always.

His skin looked a bit more sunned, though, his cheeks flushed, and his eyes—completely gray.

They could see him. They spoke to him. Breathed the same air, existed on the same plane as he did.

For a split second, I saw it: a possibility. An alternate reality where this was normal. Maybe Hadrian came by after work to eat dinner with everyone. Emma and Sayer would bicker, just like they were now. We would be up through the late hours, Emma would trickle up to bed early, and Sayer would fall asleep on the couch. Hadrian and I would be on the front porch, he would say he had to leave because of work in the morning, I would complain about sanding floors, and he would say it would be okay. That he'd see me tomorrow and he would help, because that's just the kind of person he was.

And then I would watch him leave. He wouldn't vanish into the humid air or fold himself into darkness. He would just walk away, and he would come back tomorrow.

Already, my phone was in my hand. While all eyes were turned, that moment between movements when someone *almost* locked eyes, I started to take a picture. The three of them, together, in one space, proof that Hadrian had been here with us—with me. He eyed the phone before he set the bags down. I manage to catch a look at the pictures before they disappeared into their folder.

Only Sayer and Emma stood in frame. Hadrian didn't, like he didn't exist.

I swallowed a sudden knot of tears. I stuffed my phone away.

"Landry," Hadrian greeted, then turned his head. At just the right angle, his eyes flitted yellow like a cat's. Sayer wagged his eyebrows while Emma continued on her stint, oblivious.

"—haven't listened to her sophomore album," she insisted. "You don't know the story she's painting until you've at least listened to that one."

"I didn't realize there'd be a party when I got back," I said, suddenly very, very aware of the undereye bags I'd accrued.

"I stopped by," Hadrian said. He rounded the couch, brushed his hands on his pants. "You know. Figured I'd say hi." His Lowcountry accent seemed thicker than before. Like I could drown in it. So *human*.

"That's okay." I pulled my purse off and sat it on the back of the couch.

"We've enjoyed his company," Sayer said. He handed Emma the bag of cheese puffs. Immediately, she stopped talking and ripped it open. Another wolfish grin. "You didn't tell us he lived nearby."

"She didn't tell us about him, period," Emma muttered. She held up three cheese puffs. "Not that I'm mad. I'm not. Just hurt." She popped the cheese puffs into her mouth by the handful. "But free food does help."

I glanced at Hadrian. His eyes glittered.

"Are you okay?" he whispered. He shifted to stand slightly between Sayer, Emma, and I.

"Of course." I noticed the balloons Sayer had gifted me still floating in the corner of the breakfast nook. "Just a long day."

He searched my mouth, my eyes, then back again. "Mm. Liar."

I nudged him. "Rude."

"I need a poll," Sayer announced. He took the bag of cheese puffs from Emma when she started to wander toward the TV.

"I wasn't finished with those," she shot back.

"All eyes for thirty seconds." He set the bag on the counter. "Dinner, a movie, SNL reruns, or we attempt a fire in the firepit outside."

Hadrian did a decent job at looking ambiguous when Sayer made a scan of the room—but I thought of his comment once about hating the TV, so I blurted, "I vote firepit. We can use those metal tongs Emma found."

Emma snapped her fingers in approval. "Yes, okay, I've got this. Marshmallows. Graham crackers. Chocolate." She rounded the island for the pantry, ready to gather supplies. She passed off bags to Sayer before emerging with three sets of long toasting forks.

"Sorry, Hadrian." She gave me a quick glance, devious. "You'll have to share with Lan."

She slipped into the hall, Sayer hot after her. The two of us brought up the rear. The screen door that led out from the sunroom had just managed to slam shut when he leaned forward, his mouth at the soft part of my neck, and whispered, "We've been conspired against, haven't we?"

I suppressed a smile, but failed. "I fear we have."

"Do I want to know what *S-N-L* means? Or *movie*?"

He held the door for me. I made a point to walk close, close enough to brush against his shirt, and said in my best spooky voice, "It involves that horrid little box with the moving pictures."

A look of torture split his face. "Dear God, please, no."

I laughed, low, as we trekked down the back steps, over the steppingstones, and down to the back patio. Sayer and Emma already had the accoutrements spread out, as if it were a feast. Sayer attempted to dig a lighter out of his pants, while Emma whipped a box of matches out of hers. Then it was a race to see who could light the starter the fastest.

Hadrian pulled a chair out for me. Instead, I motioned for him to sit instead.

His mouth flattened. "Ladies sit first."

I stood on my toes. "Thank you, but I'd rather sit with you than alone. You sit first."

After a seconds-long stalemate, he narrowed his eyes and sat down. I held back a smile when he spread his knees, back still straight, in a partial man-spread. It wasn't as casual as men's today posture tended to be, but it was there.

I couldn't lie. Something about him, being here with Emma and Sayer, made me brave.

I sat down on the footrest in front of his chair, right between his knees. He shot me a look. I settled my hand on his knee and scooted closer.

"It's okay. Calm down." A grin played on my lips.

He jerked his chin to Sayer and Emma, a silent question. *And them?* he seemed to say, not so much out of fear of disapproval, but his eyes questioned comfortability. From me.

Emma tried to bat the lighter out of Sayer's hand. He snatched her match and broke it in two.

"That's rude," she spat.

"Not everything has to be a competition," he shot back.

Her eyes went beady. She grabbed the lighter, threw the matches toward me, and shoved her shoulder into his chest. They skittered across the rocks surrounding the pit and stopped a few inches from my feet.

"Let me show you how a real survivalist starts a fire, *Sayer*," she said.

Sayer didn't blink when he turned to me. "Do you see the abuse I put up with?"

"Now you feel my pain," I said.

I leaned back, my side against Hadrian's leg. Little by little, the tension in his body loosened. While Sayer and Emma continued to bicker, he shifted from my peripheral. Reached out like he might approach a skittish animal—and let his arm drape across my back. His fingers made idle circles over my shirt.

The fire made a *wooft* sound. The starter blazed to life, which only sent Emma's ego higher than it already was.

"See." She stood and smacked the lighter against Sayer's chest. "I told you."

He took his glasses off and pointed them at her. "No couth. Whatsoever."

Emma only arched her eyebrows and ventured to the table.

It wasn't until the marshmallows were roasting over the fire, the smell of smoke had seeped into my hair, dried my eyes, and heated my toes, that I realized I could do this: life, with the three of them.

My marshmallow caught fire when I drifted in thought. I gasped, wrenched it out of the flames, and huffed on it so hard I saw stars.

"No! That was a good one," I whined. I'd gotten just enough crisp to it that it would've melted the chocolate.

"Here." Hadrian dug another marshmallow out of the bag that Sayer had stolen. "I'll eat that one."

Emma had given me a secret, wicked grin. Sayer saw. Glanced at me. Wiggled his eyebrows.

I'd rolled my eyes, but inside, my chest warmed.

And I very well thought, if he'd let me, I might have floated away right then out of happiness.

Chapter Twenty-Seven

"Do you worry about what'll happen? If things progress, I mean?" I asked, trying to ignore how Hadrian's body radiated heat.

Darkness had nearly fallen, leaving us with lightening bugs drifting in and out of the tree line. Emma had ventured back inside to retrieve another bag of marshmallows, to which I'd said I was good. Sayer said something about using the bathroom, but I wondered if they wanted to leave Hadrian and I alone for a minute.

Hadrian eyed the last of my s'mores. I offered it to him. I'd ended up in the chair with him. A thin layer of sweat dotted his neck and chest, with one arm looped around my back. He brushed his fingers over my arm.

"You don't want it?"

I shook my head. "I'm good."

I was trying. But trying didn't mean the roadblock was gone.

He gave my arm a squeeze. "Are you sure? You are all right?"

I nodded. Without words, I knew that he knew. Of course he knew.

He polished off the last of mine, licked his fingers. I watched. Then he pulled me into his side and whispered, "I'm proud of you, you know."

"For what?"

A half shrug. His hand went back to making idle trails along my arm. "For being you." Then, after a second, "For trying."

I suppressed the sudden knot in my throat. My only answer was a nod.

And that, somehow, meant more than any string of words could have ever meant.

I'm proud of you for trying.

An old wound itched at his words. "You don't think I'm too—"

Skinny.

"Do not finish that sentence." His voice went hard. "You are not too much of anything, Landry."

I frowned at him. The seriousness in his expression made the tears well up—stupid, persistent tears. "Why did you say that?" I asked with a wet chuckle. This was so embarrassing.

"Say what?"

"Something—so—" I used my shirt's neckline to dab the tears. "You're making me cry. Stop it."

"I hope I've never *made* you do anything." He gave a soft smile. "It's all those years of experience you teased me about before."

Inside the house, Marion Blanchet started playing again. Above, a single bat swooped down from the treetops before twirling back up after a bug.

"For what it's worth," I said, taking his free hand and tracing the lines of his palm, "I'm glad that Bunny locked you in that room."

His expression turned thoughtful. Mouth softened. "I thank her every day for giving me the chance to meet you."

I clutched his hand with both of mine. "So."

"Mm?"

"You never answered my question."

"Ah, you're trying to ruin the moment. I see."

I wiggled his hand until his fingers laced with mine. "I'm serious."

He sucked on his bottom lip, nodded, expression faltering. "It might change. With time. We will have to see. I feel like the house—the energy, I suppose—is changing with me. Or maybe I'm changing it. And eventually, maybe . . ." He didn't finish.

Maybe I'll vanish, is what he didn't say.

"Until then, I'm okay with lurking in your corners." He brought our knotted hands to his mouth and placed a gentle kiss on the back of my hand. "One day at a time. Who knows. It worked for your aunt for a while. If we stick our heads in the sand, perhaps we will have years."

Sadness threatened to weigh the corners of my smile down. I saw the moment he noticed: He made a noise in the back of his throat and drew me in until my face tucked in the crook of his neck. He rocked, gentle, from side to side in the chair, the soft sounds from the woods behind us. A perfect, quiet infinity, just as I'd had once before.

And like fate, it couldn't last.

Ever so faint, I heard a voice from the house. No—a shout.

"Get out!" a voice screamed. "I said get out!"

I pulled back. Glanced up to the kitchen window. It had been too loud to come from inside, anyway. No, the voices came from the front lawn.

"What was that?" I started to untangle myself.

"They are not in the house anymore. In the front." His neck strained—I'd forgotten that he said he was able to hear everything. His jaw set. "Someone's here."

Hadrian steadied me as I started for the sunroom door, but then I thought better of it and rounded the back of the house to come out in the front. I felt the whisper of Hadrian's presence as he followed. The front lawn was highlighted in the remains of nightfall, the only light coming from the front porch.

The back of Sayer's head was the first thing I saw. My legs burned as I walked faster.

"You don't live here, Carla," Sayer said. His voice steady.

My mother held a key in her hand, the butter yellow of the porch light making her hair look honeyed instead of fiery. Her car sat parked, crooked, in the middle of the lawn instead of the driveway.

"I should!" She stalked closer, a single finger in Sayer's face. "I *should* be here! You two didn't so much as say hello to Cadence when she was still alive. But here *you* are."

Not right now—this couldn't be happening right now.

"*Mom*," I started. But no one so much as blinked.

I hurried to wedge myself between my mom and Sayer. His glasses dangled, pinched, in his hand. Emma barged out the front door, phone in hand.

"I will call the police, Carla," Emma said, stern.

"You poor thing," Mom crooned. She only squinted one eye, expression foggy, when she pointed at Emma next. "You're mad your momma found out what it's really like to be with Vince, aren't you? Welcome to the club."

"What's going on?" I asked. Hadrian's steps halted in the house's shadow.

"I see how it is." Mom turned to me now, her mouth pulled in a sunken frown. "You bring all your little friends, gloat about what you have all day, and then leave me out on the street, huh?"

Heat flooded my skin. Hadrian's presence suddenly felt overwhelmingly wide and cavernous behind me. Was this how he felt when I'd gone up the steps and seen the memory of his father? Ashamed? Embarrassed?

I held my tongue. "Mom, I paid for you to have a room for *days*."

She scoffed. Started to make her way back to her old Neon. She popped the passenger side and started rummaging through it.

"Why aren't you there?" I dared a single step closer. The inside of her car was ravaged with trash, used Styrofoam cups and piles of dirty—assumed—laundry. Between the back windshield and upholstered speaker set, a sliver of silver glinted.

My tongue went dry.

The spoon's bottom was burnt in the middle. She wasn't just drinking. She was using.

"I'm *your mother*, Landry. That's not how this works." Her voice was muffled.

I caught Emma's eye and mouthed, *Call the police.*

She nodded and slipped back inside. Her shadow remained in the foyer, her eyes peeking every few seconds through the stained-glass overhangs.

Hadrian's hand landed on my shoulder. "Do you need me to—"

"—serves them right, ungrateful sons of—" Mom snarled under her breath. She hauled a red canister from the passenger seat. Liquid sloshed out the bent, dingy spout.

"Hey!" Sayer pushed Hadrian and I aside. "Drop that!"

Like she was a disobedient dog. She only huffed.

"Mom, no. Stop." I wrenched away from Hadrian, but he grabbed my arm at the last second. Sayer tried to take the can from her, but the spout was already unplugged. She swung it at him. Gasoline sprayed him from shirt to shoes—and the porch.

"Mom!" I shrieked. "Stop! Emma's calling the police—you can't—"

"Shoulda done it while you were at that stupid funeral!" she howled. Her eyes were blotchy, her skin peppered with red marks. Sayer grabbed the can just as she yanked the nozzle out of the top completely. Gasoline poured over the porch, the bushes, both my mother and Sayer. He ripped the can away and tossed it in my direction. Before I reached it, Hadrian scooped the canister up and tossed it far on the other side of the driveway.

"Nothing but a bunch of spoiled brats!" she shrieked as Sayer caught her by the waist. He hauled her up the front porch, careful to keep her away from the puddle of gasoline.

"Mom, stop it," I bit. My teeth ground together until dust was sure to fall out of my mouth. The fight, ever so little, seeped from my body. Until I stood at the foot of the steps and she struggled against Sayer, her hair sticking up at all angles.

I looked at the tracks over her forearm. The blown veins that looked like little spiderwebs under the skin. Again. Just like Dad had said.

She has to want to help herself.

"Get inside, please," Hadrian whispered against my hair. "I can help Sayer with her."

I shook my head. His words bounced off my skin, fell onto the ground, melded with the gasoline. One wrong light, and we'd all go up in flames.

"I talked to Dad," I said, broken. I tried to grab her hands, but she swung at me.

"Of course you did," she spat, all venom. "He called me. You wanna know what he told me about his little girl?"

I braced myself.

"He said to leave you alone, that I doing nothing but ruining your chances. You poor, deprived little thing." She stopped struggling for a moment. "You get it *all*. He threatened me with lawyers, he threatened me with money, with a treatment program—all of it! Are you *happy* now? You got my sister, my husband, the house! Did you get everything you wanted? Can't have *just* Vince keeping tabs on you through Cadence. You've gotta have him wrapped around every finger you've got!"

I reeled at her words. Dad had been keeping tabs on me through Aunt Cadence? Since when? For how long?

A hole, bottomless and gaping, yawned open at the center of my heart. Not an ounce of fight reared inside of me. I was done fighting with her. I couldn't do this anymore. The only person it was hurting, at the end of the day, was myself.

"No, Mom," I whispered. "Because the only thing I wanted as a child was you. And I accepted I'll never get that a long, long time ago."

She stilled. Stared at me. Her watering eyes trembled; for a split second, I thought she might speak. As if Sayer felt her relax, he relaxed, too—and then she lunged.

She wrenched herself from Sayer's arms. She elbowed him in the neck and pulled a lighter out of her pocket. Sayer bent forward, coughing; Emma started shouting from inside the house. Panicked, I raced after her.

"Don't deserve *none of* it," she shouted. But her hands weren't steady, and I stumbled into her. Grabbed her wrists while she used both hands to try and light the Zippo.

"Stop it," I demanded, eyes blurred. But it was useless. We wrestled over the lighter, the sound of hurried feet after us as we careened closer to the porch. Hadrian appeared at my right, just as Mom tripped on the first porch step. He grabbed for her upper arm at the same time we went down. The lighter went skidding across the porch. She struggled to go after it, and I saw the split-second decision: If she got the lighter and flipped it—

Hadrian gave chase.

She cursed and kicked under me. I tried to shift my weight. My knee shoved awkwardly on the second step, and I attempted to brace myself with my left hand—right when she elbowed me in the jaw. "Let me go!"

Stars burst into my vision. I let go out of reflex. Hadrian's blurred silhouette came into view right as I heard her footfalls barge into the house.

"What did she leave you?" she shouted. Something crashed. "You owe me money after keeping all her good stuff."

I scrambled after her. A tantrum—that's what this was.

She'd already turned over the foyer table by the time I shoved the front door open. Emma held the phone to her ear, eyes wide, relaying everything to the operator.

"Where's her jewelry then, huh?" Mom shouted. She moved to the office, tearing anything and everything off the shelves—the book nook, encyclopedias, the journals—and heaved them onto the floor. She wrenched every drawer open with so much force they tried to bang shut.

"There's no jewelry," I said, voice rising. I went behind her and tried to close the desk drawers. Surely, the police would be here soon.

"Landry." Hadrian said my name like a demand—urgent. The hairs along the back of my neck rose. A sinking feeling grew in my gut.

Something wasn't right. But I couldn't let her out of my sight.

"She has to have something in here," she snapped. I tried to round on her and block her way to the hall, which led to the sunroom and library, but she clambered through quicker than I could move.

"Yes, as quickly as possible," Emma said into the phone. Hadrian pushed by her, after me, eyes hard.

He took me by the arm. "Let me handle her."

I tried to slip away as I heard books hitting the floor, splaying open, *thump, thump, thump*. I gave him a pleading look.

"She's my mother," I whispered.

"She is not—"

I jerked away, already crossing the hall. A tight ball of frustration rose in my throat. He didn't know my mother—*I* needed to handle her, to stop this, but I felt like I was six years old again, trailing after her as she swayed in the hall, cursing and pointing at me.

"Look what you did, Landry," she'd spat. Now, in an almost identical fashion, she whirled when I entered the library, Hadrian tight on my heels.

"All of this, for *you*? Really, Landry?" Mom muttered under her breath as she continued her search. Her pupils were blown, her breath smelled rancid, and her teeth—the roots were grayed. "Can't even—"

She swayed.

I didn't reach out, I didn't grab her shirt, I didn't try and get her back to the front of the house where there were witnesses, I didn't do anything. *I didn't. I didn't. I didn't.*

Because when push came to shove, I couldn't. I froze.

She upturned books and boxes and portraits I'd hung on the walls. Then she stopped at the mantel, checked the bottoms of all the little elephants and roosters I'd found in Aunt Cadence's things. And started pocketing them.

My father's voice held me back. *Why not let her? Your mother is going to get something whether you like it or not.*

Hadrian slammed the door shut and brushed around me.

Something inside of me broke. I couldn't let him do it—he couldn't be the one—

Take, take, take, just like she always had when I was a child. But this time—I'd furnished this place. I'd fixed it, I'd polished and painted. Fissures in my heart started to crack wider until it split in two.

She reached for a blown-glass hummingbird just as I grabbed his elbow. He froze, eyes darting between me and my mother. I gave a tight headshake as she moved to the candleholder.

Please, I mouthed, forehead creased, face flushed with embarrassment.

His jaw clenched, nostrils flared, with the faintest flash of yellow over his eyes. But he didn't move.

I turned to Mom. Eased closer. She swayed again. Whatever she'd taken was starting to hit, hard, and there I was, the truth molding itself to my lips: "Mom—I know where the jewel—"

I tried to grab her wrists, but she swung an empty candleholder. I hissed when it clipped my cheekbone; immediately, a heady iron scent filled the room, my skin on fire.

I held my hand to my burning cheek as she filled her pockets with anything she considered valuable.

When she reached for the new mirror I'd bought for the mantel, something overtook me.

"Landry—" Hadrian started.

"Mom, that's enough." I tried to grab her waist, but she had a hold on the bottom of the frame. It jerked forward, sending all the decor to the floor. She tried to bat my hands away, but I held fast. The two of us stumbled against the closest chair.

I heard the crunch before I felt the grind of a box under my foot. I glanced down—the wooden box I'd set on the mantel lay partially shattered, it's latch now broken, contents spilled around Hadrian's feet.

Three teeth had fallen on the floor—and I'd just stepped on two.

Chapter Twenty-Eight

Mom slumped against me. I staggered and grabbed for the chair—kicking the last tooth across the room. Hadrian's arms wound between us, wrestling my mother away from me with a firm grasp. The remnants of shattered teeth crunched under my heel, stuck to my shoe.

"Let me go!" Mom screeched. Her words slurred, the sudden, narrow-minded focus she'd been grasping starting to slip. Outside, the distant sound of police sirens grew louder.

"Stop fighting," Hadrian growled, mouth curved in a pained frown. The veins in his arms protruded the longer he held her still.

"You," Mom snapped. She flung her head back. Narrowly missed Hadrian's nose. He jutted his chin up, keeping the fragile parts of his face away. "You're why she ain't with Ivan, aren't you?"

Hadrian's jaw feathered but he didn't speak.

She mumbled under her breath, limbs calming, only to shove and claw again.

My hands shook. I picked up a few of the sharper items she'd tried to pocket, careful where I stepped, while Mom struggled against Hadrian. He ground his teeth and held fast while she kicked and scratched, but nothing broke his composure.

I couldn't tell if it was me, the room, or if it was Mom's screaming, but my blood sizzled in my veins. *We'd found the teeth.* And here Mom was, in the house, falling apart.

This was everything I'd never wanted.

Everything had just been perfect.

Tears welled in my eyes. I bit my lip hard enough to taste blood and gathered the trinkets into my shirt, then picked up the broken teeth parts and the box and stuffed them into my pocket. I trembled from head to foot. Where was the last one?

Mom groaned, slumped out of my peripheral. She used her weight against Hadrian, dropping limp, but he held her up anyway. Her shirt road higher, higher, until a sliver of skin shown around her midriff. Her hipbones poked out over her belt loops.

I stilled. The skin was bruised, almost translucent. Little marks all over her skin.

It hit me, then. She wasn't just my mother. She was struggling. She was human, and she'd made choices, and those choices were wrong, sure. But she was no different from me or Hadrian or Emma or Sayer.

Her choices were bad choices, and they had consequences. But seeing her, as an outsider, slowly inhaling the whole picture instead of just the section of life where she'd failed me—she'd probably been failed somewhere, too. And she was hurting.

It wasn't just people that hurt people.

Hurt people hurt people.

Dad was right. She needed to help herself. I couldn't expect someone that couldn't take care of themselves to feel sorry for never taking care of me. As a child, I was failed, but as an adult, I knew Mom was broken, and I couldn't change that.

She'd have to.

Sharp, firm voices from the front door. "Colleton County Police Department."

"Mom, they're here to help you," I said, low. Hadrian grunted when she slapped a heel on his foot.

"No!" she spat. "You just wanna get rid of me! That's all you've ever wanted, Landry, is everything for *yourself*!"

Her words bounced off me, one by one, and sunk into the floor.

The next thirty minutes were a blur.

One of the officers removed my mom from the house with Hadrian's help while Emma and Sayer's voices murmured from the front. Once the officers documented the items Mom tried to take, one of them spoke to me. One of them took pictures of my injuries while another took notes, another mentioned a restraining order—or maybe it was Emma, because she floated in and out a few times—another asked about us coming down to the station in the morning.

And still, like a gnat circling my head, all I could think about was the tooth. Here, in the room, on the floor, *somewhere*.

By the time everyone was questioned, statements given, and contact information collected, it was pitch black outside, not a star in sight. All the lights on the first floor were on. Sayer's nose was crusted with blood. My cheek was swollen. The lone remaining officer scribbled in a notepad, forehead creased.

"I'm going to go get a pizza. We need it," Emma murmured.

I wilted. It felt so long ago that I'd come home to the three of them in the living room.

Emma pointed to Sayer, then Hadrian. "Cheese? Pepperoni?"

"I'll go with you. We'll get a few, so it'll be a surprise," Sayer said. His glasses sat crooked, the frames cracked. A red welt had spread over the side of his neck where he'd been elbowed. "You good here?"

I hugged myself, closest to where the teeth had dropped. "I'm good."

Sayer pointed to Hadrian. His only answer was a nod.

"All right, we'll return." Sayer gave a two-finger salute and followed Emma out into the hallway, leaving Hadrian and I with the officer. Their voices faded like a lantern in the night, followed by the click of the front door.

"Good people," the last cop murmured. He scratched something else on his notepad. Hadrian rubbed his palm over his chin while the officer jotted down the last of his notes. He was my height, stocky, with kind eyes. I tried not to think about the little piece of history in my possession, burning a hole in my pocket.

"Think that should be all, for right now." He gave a soft smile.

"Thank you," I whispered.

"Much thanks," Hadrian said at the same time.

The officer turned to leave and rounded one of the covered end tables that I'd set to the side maybe a week ago. "I'll get out of y'all's hair, then. Just holler if you need anything, all right? We'll keep you in the loop if she posts bail and—"

A crunch.

My hand covered my mouth.

The pit in my stomach turned into an open maw, unhinging wide, and dropped straight to my toes.

The officer paused, bent down. "Shoot. Done stepped on something. Sorry 'bout that."

I wiped my hand down my neck. Glanced to Hadrian, who had turned still. He didn't so much as inhale as the officer excused himself and left the room.

No one spoke. The front door opened with a light gust of wind. It rustled the strewn items in the foyer before a heavy click came, and the officer's footsteps echoed down the front steps.

"Hadrian," I whispered, hesitant. "We found the teeth."

He grunted—again. A pained noise. I turned when the first chime came—as if the grandfather clock was ready and waiting. Midnight already.

I slipped around the furniture and bent to the floor. Sure enough, right by the floor-to- ceiling bookcase, was a broken tooth. A fully developed adult molar, all four points crushed and ground into the wide floorboards.

Tears welled again, but this time, they slid down my cheeks. Dripped from my chin. Pressure built from the base of my spine, all the way up and around my lungs. Something was wrong—I knew it, just like I knew it when I followed Mom into the house—

"Landry," Hadrian choked.

I stood and whirled. He grabbed the back of the closest chair with one hand, the other grabbing at his chest. Right over his heart.

"Wait—No, sit down. What's wrong? What hurts?" *Heart attack*, my first thought blared, just like Aunt Denny, but I knew better.

The blood around his chest bloomed like an opening morning glory. It was thick, soaked through the fabric before I scrambled over to him, that's how much there was. It painted his shirt, turned the ivory cotton to a thick maroon. I started with the buttons at his neck, ripped the tail of his shirt from his trousers. A few buttons popped away.

"What a time to undress me," he said, pained. Both hands grasped the back of the chair.

"This isn't funny." My voice wavered. This wasn't funny at all.

It was happening—I knew it. The air turned heady, sharp with the scent of blood as I yanked the shirt off his arms, down his back. Earth tangled with it, soil, musk. *Dust.*

The smell of an old house.

"It hurts," he choked.

I balled up the shirt and tried to turn him. Blood streaked his skin, my fingers, seeped into the beds of my nails and the crevices of my palms. It trickled down to his trousers, soaked into the heavy fabric of his pants.

"Sit," I whispered. My words grew soggy, like I was drowning. Maybe I was drowning. "Let me try and stop it—I can use your shirt—"

"There's no point, Landry, and you know it," he urged. He didn't sit, no matter how I pushed at his shoulders. He just stood there, bent over the back of the chair as if it pained him to straighten. He was too tall, and my hands shook too much. I was like a fluttering moth around a dying animal, a mere nuisance and nothing more.

I was a faint blip in his decades of existence—because it was ending. The remains were here, broken, in my pockets.

A moth couldn't save a beast. All it could do was watch.

I wedged myself between him and the chair, shirt balled at the ready anyway. The scar that had looked so healed before, purpled and raised, had flattened—but the center of his scar had changed. It hung open, revealing the thickest sliver of heart beneath. And so, so much blood. It poured in streams, and any other time I might have balked, might have stepped away when I saw it drip to the floor, but I didn't.

Because the blood wasn't evaporating like it had before.

It hit the floor in rhythmic splats. A sink left on, dripping into the basin. *Tap, tap, tap.*

The last of the grandfather clock chimes echoed through the house. That urgency I'd felt the night I'd heard him crying, like a pressure on my sternum, filled the room, like water rising in a flood. Soon, it would reach my neck, my mouth, cover my nose and my ears. It would wash everything away.

"At least let me try," I muttered. Tears trickled over my mouth. Salt coated my tongue. "*Please.* The blood is—"

"Real," he gasped. Hot air rushed over my cheek. "It's real. I cannot—there is a pain—" He twitched. His shoulder hiked to his ear, his head bent in. He hissed. "Don't. Don't touch me."

I hesitated a moment too long.

His jaw cracked open. A monstrous sound rumbled from his chest. I pressed the shirt to his wound anyway, spittle bubbling around my lips.

"Hadrian, please. *Please.*"

What was I asking him to do? What *could* he do?

His shoulders rolled to straighten. He released the chair, taking his body heat with it—too hot. A flush rose up his neck, over his cheeks. The lively warmth that once made him look healthy now turned feverish.

My eyes widened in horror as his neck rolled. Lumps, like bones changing, emerged beneath his skin. Rose and fell with sickening, wet sounds. I stepped back, straight into the chair behind me.

"I think"—he winced as he opened his mouth, the teeth along his bottom jaw lengthening, sharpening, shifting—"my time is up."

I reached forward. Stopped. Started again. "I need to help you—f-find s-s-something."

"*No.*"

He snarled at my words, all creature. He blinked and his eyes clicked to a ghastly yellow, so bright it reminded me of melted sunlight.

The single word sent me into a tailspin. I grabbed for him, my reflection wild in the window over his shoulder.

He let me grab his forearms, pull him in. Forehead to forehead. The bones his face snapped into place. Sharper, harder, his skin shifting between flushed and grayed. The pressure hit my knees, rose up to my waist. The room felt muffled, concentrated.

"—we haven't had enough time and I just—" *I'm not ready for you to go yet, I wanted you to stay, I wanted more months with you, I wanted, I wanted, I wanted.*

"Dearest—"

"You're not listening to me! I wanted you to stay, I wanted you to be here, with me, I don't want you to leave, what if you don't exist anymore—"

"Lan, dearest, please—"

I cut in, more forceful. "I wanted—"

"*Landry!*" he roared.

"I need to fix you!" I shouted back, blood rushing up my neck. My hands pushed at his chest, around the wound, but the bleeding wasn't slowing, wasn't growing black and clotting, his heart pumping too strong to keep the blood where it needed to be—inside his body. "I can f-fix it!"

"You can't fix me," he growled. He captured both of my wrists with his single palm. "*Stop.*"

My teeth chattered in my skull. Spittle dripped down my chin. "No! It doesn't end like this! You can't just—this isn't how it's supposed to happen—"

"How do you know that?" he asked, voice softening.

"Because you can't leave!" I shouted, tears streaking my cheeks. Why did I feel like *I was ending*?

He pulled my hands against his neck. Kept them knotted there in an ironclad grasp.

"We both knew I could never stay." His mouth quirked to the side. Red tinged his teeth. A slight shake of his head. All those angles I once thought so terrifying, now they looked too beautiful to simply cease existing. "What did I say? The train." A shallow breath. His big body swayed. "Sometimes you have to get off at the next stop."

I wriggled my wrists from his grasp. "Don't get off at this stop. Stay with me at Harthwait for a while—just don't—not yet."

A tightness strangled my heart.

Force someone to stay, and that is not love, a little voice murmured.

"Landry, dearest," he whispered. My eyes met Hadrian's. Even his horns had started to curl up, away. I pressed one bloodied hand to his cheek, the other to his shoulder. As if I wanted to hold him together, hold him up like he had me in the living room, our feet moving in tandem, his smile with mine.

"Do not be angry," he hissed. Then his neck snapped to one side.

I *felt* the vibration through my palm, up the entirety of my arm. The crack of his trachea and thyroid cartilage.

For the first time, the fragile flutters in his chest stopped.

His head slumped against my palm, but he was too heavy for me to hold. He hit the floor in a heap, so hard that one of his horns snapped at the end.

I dropped, knees first, in a keening scream.

"No, no, no, no, you can't do this yet. We didn't—I'm not *ready*, Hadrian, don't you dare *do this to me*!"

My hands touched his neck, his chest, his wrist. I clutched him for dear life. He was too heavy to keep upright. So I leaned close, I aligned my nose with his, I cried at him, because I needed him. I needed his body, that warmth, I needed him to move, but he wasn't moving.

Sweat slithered between my shoulder blades, down my temple. Over and over, my fingers found his neck. There was no pulse.

No pulse.

"Hadrian," I panted. "Hadrian. Wake up." I patted his cheek, desperate in disbelief. "Hadrian, please, wake up. Wake up, Hadrian, please, please, *please*."

I rolled him onto his back, grabbed his face in my hands. The lines of his jaw blurred. His hair, soft to the touch, fell to the floor around his pointed ears. I pressed my forehead to his again, whispering prayers and wishes and hopes and cries into his skin, as if that would will him to blink. Will him to wake.

I love you, I hadn't said.

I love you, I thought, because I was scared; he might still be able to hear it, if I said it out loud. Could he hear me still?

The room exhaled in a rush of air, so profound that the curtains fluttered against the walls. The sheet over one of the chairs slipped off the back. As if the house were sighing. *Letting go.*

And with it, Hadrian's body. He fell apart in my fingers like smoke. Like the dust on a moth's wings in the wind, never to be seen again.

Chapter Twenty-Nine

I waited eight days before I found myself at the county office. This time, it wasn't for a restraining order against my mother.

The same woman with a chain on her glasses glanced up from a stack of papers on her desk. I ground my teeth together, breath leaden.

"I need to find a burial plot," I said. "You have those here. With death certificates."

She stared at me. Snapped her gum. I didn't bother to look at the clock—I had over an hour this time, and Emma was sitting in my car with the AC blowing at full speed. The final summer weeks were upon us, when it was debatable if hell had risen from the depths of the earth to scorch us one last time. Then by a miracle, we'd wake up one morning and realize there was a chill in the air and a smidge of humidity had been shaved away.

Soon. It meant time was passing.

I didn't want time to pass. Not yet.

She shifted her stack of papers. "Name."

I swallowed. "Hadrian Belfaunte."

She turned in her swivel chair. Today, she wore a blue floral dress that swished with each step. My jaw remained locked as she rounded the corner.

When I'd searched Colleton County's death record office, I should have guessed it would be kept here.

She returned moments later. This time, only two papers. She smacked them into the copier and punched a button. The machine coughed, whirred, then spit the papers back out.

She returned to her seat. Stamped them with a signature stamp, then handed them to me.

"Here."

I walked away before she could close the curtains on me.

* * *

"Where are we going, again?" Emma asked. She unwrapped a stick of gum before offering me one. I shook my head. "Suit yourself."

"A plot," I said. Because I didn't know what else to tell her. I just knew I needed her with me when I went.

"Did you murder someone?" She chewed her gum much gentler than the woman at the county office. "I didn't bring my gloves."

I clutched the steering wheel at ten and two. Dust kicked up behind us as I followed the GPS off the main road until we met an entrance ramp for the highway. Soon enough, we were on the straight stretch back to Stetson, and the hour and a half slowly morphed into forty minutes, then thirty, then twenty.

When I'd mapped the gravesite, I hadn't paid much attention to the direction or the distance. Only that I needed to get there.

Questions burned in my chest. Nothing had happened at the house since Hadrian had vanished. I waited up every night until a quarter past midnight, but no cries came. My dreams were nonexistent—I fell asleep, then woke up. Wash, rinse, repeat. The house renovation was coming along, but Sayer came over more often than not to sleep on my couch, and Emma had mentioned moving to Stetson when her lease was up. "I'm hybrid," she'd said. "What are they going to do, fire me?"

They didn't fire her. They gave her a stipend to move to a different office—one thirty minutes south of Stetson, a lot smaller, but with only one in-office day a week. "A family emergency" she'd called it, when her supervisor asked. "I need to be close to my sister," was her only reasoning.

"Have you heard from that hottie yet?" she asked.

I gave a hollow head shake. "No."

I felt her eyes on me. I didn't meet them.

Going through the restraining order process was another headache. But I did it. Because it was best. Especially when I had no plans to sell the house anytime soon.

Even if I did, I wasn't so sure my heart could take it. There was something cathartic about waiting every night. A little ounce of hope that a shadow would move out of the corner of my eye, that I'd hear something that couldn't be explained. But I hadn't seen so much as a curtain out of place, and neither had Emma.

I hadn't gotten the courage to message Irene yet. I wanted to ask her about a reversal—if maybe she could ask that forum writer if he knew the curse that might have created the door in the first place. But our last conversation was too raw, and there was a deep, guttural feeling that the forum writer wouldn't know any more than I did. Because, now, the house felt like a one-way street: I was driving in the right lane and no one was at my left anymore. The sense of dread wasn't there at all.

Once or twice, I'd thought I'd felt the pressure from before, but it never lingered long enough for me to tell. I truly felt like whatever had kept Hadrian in the house had broken when his remains had been ruined.

I can fix it.

You can't fix me.

He was right. I couldn't.

Hadrian hadn't needed fixing. Because loved ones didn't need to be fixed. They simply *were.*

Maybe Mom would reach that point one day, too. Where she found the solace she needed to heal from the inside out.

Emma and I finally pulled onto another dirt road—nothing more than two paths for tires, long since dried to nothing but dust and pebbles. The sea oats were high and packed on either side of the SUV, brushing up against us like fingertips, and I thought we might be close to a shore or marsh.

"Isn't the Uroahs' farm back that way?" Emma pointed off to the right, straight to a tree line that grew inland. We'd gone to school with the Uroahs' youngest, Melony.

"Maybe," I whispered.

We bumped over a small hill. Emma held onto the handle above her door, while I craned my neck to see over the wheel. The grasses broke apart into a flattened area, and sure enough—the soggy glint of marsh dissolved into a river just beyond.

The flattened area was trimmed, though not recently. A little wrought-iron fence, eaten with rust, guarded the plot.

I eased to a stop. The plastic bag in my pocket felt unnaturally heavy.

I glanced to the papers stuffed between my console and my seat. Then the GPS, just to make sure.

This was it.

"This . . . is not far out of the way," Emma said, cautious. She turned to me. Her white tank slipped off a shoulder, exposing her bralette. "How did we not know this was so close to the house?"

It was about four miles up the road.

"Because it used to be part of the property a long time ago," I said. Emotion clogged my throat. "I'm sure someone's responsible for keeping it mowed." There was no telling who'd taken ownership of the family cemetery. For all I knew, it could be the county, since the house was a registered landmark.

Emma watched from the passenger seat as I climbed out first. I pulled the little box where Hadrian's teeth had been stored out of my pocket and clutched it in my fist, so hard it pressed against the bones in my hand. Finally.

Warm, welcoming air swirled around me.

This was him.

"What are you doing?" Emma scrambled out after me. I already reached the little gate by the time she caught up, my hands gliding over the arrowed points of the fence. I wiped away a few cobwebs. The grass hissed around us in welcome, but the slow gurgle of water in the distance calmed it, calmed me.

"I need to find someone," I whispered.

"Uh . . . okay?" She shielded her eyes from the sun and swiped her hair off her neck. "Who are we looking for?"

The gate screeched as it swung. I propped it against a weed cluster so it stood open for us. I didn't say anything as I started scanning headstones—starting closest to us, then row by row, working my way back. The most recent years were up front, and grew older the farther back I wove. One after another, I scanned the names.

"I'll know it when I see it," I said, soft. My hands grew sweaty, slick.

In the very back, off to the right, a little square marker, shaped like a brick, lay hugged with weeds. The date caught my attention first.

1855.

I paid no attention to the other plots. Only this one.

Only ever this one.

I knelt down in front of it. Pulled the weeds away with pops and rips until the name was visible. Some of the letters were muddled, eroded with time. Moss had found homes within the divots of the small headstone.

My breath shuttered.

Emma stepped up behind me. "Who are you—" She stilled.

I ran my fingers over the name.

Hadrian Belfaunte

Son—Friend—Husband

April 23 1855–August 8 1890

A long, swollen pause.

"Landry," Emma whispered, her voice barely audible. "Whose grave is this?"

I blinked at the dates. His time of death hadn't changed. The article in the paper had said 1890 of natural causes. Of course, I only had the photocopy, which I hadn't dared to look at. It was still too painful.

Maybe there was a part of me that thought his date of death might have changed. But all it did was settle like rocks in my gut. Because if it hadn't changed, that meant he was well and truly gone. No tangled threads left behind.

Similar to how I felt looking at Aunt Cadence's urn, which had found its rightful place in the library on top of the mantel my mother had raided, I felt a presence. Even if he wasn't really here. He was.

Just not really. But it was as close as I'd ever get to him again.

"You know . . . Hadrian?" At the time, I'd made up an excuse. I'd said he'd had a family emergency and had to leave. Both Emma and Sayer had asked what happened, if he was okay, and I'd been vague.

But now—I needed to tell her the truth. I needed to be honest.

I squinted; glanced up at her.

"What, did something else happen?" Her expression twisted, earnest. "His mom's okay, right? Or . . . ?"

I nodded. Took a deep breath. If I told her, there were no more secrets. No more holding my own baggage.

I needed to ask for help, even if it meant opening up a bit. Not all the way, but enough.

Tears slipped down my cheeks. The thoughts had plagued me since Hadrian left—what would have happened if I'd never come across the door? If Aunt Cadence hadn't passed when she did, would I have ever found him? Would he have been left in there for another decade or two, or until Aunt Cadence sold the house for something a bit smaller when her knees didn't love the stairs anymore? Or would she have eventually let curiosity get the best of her, as she'd mentioned in the safety deposit box letters? Would he have found me anyway?

Or would we have never crossed paths at all?

A swell of emotion bubbled from the darkest parts of my soul.

"Em, sit," I urged. She immediately knelt beside me in the grass and tucked her legs like we used to as children, facing me.

"I'm a little confused and you're scaring me," she said, attempting a tease.

I tried to smile. "I'm going to start from the beginning and you need to promise you're going to believe me," I said.

She nodded. "Don't I always?"

"I mean it."

"So do I!" She laughed. "Stop crying, you're making me nervous."

I rubbed the heels of my palms against my eyes. Gathered myself with an inhale, and said, "Do you remember when that book nook turned on and off by itself?"

Her expression became wary. "Yes?" She drew out the word to three syllables.

Those stupid tears started welling again. I wiped them away angrily. How could I have cried more in the last summer than I had in my whole life?

"Landry?" she urged. "What's wrong?"

What were the words for what I was feeling? What was I supposed to say? How could I explain—anything?

All this time, everyone had left. I'd stepped back and boxed myself into this one square, waiting for the day that people decided to stand beside me. It hadn't worked. Because I was always pushing people away.

Out of what? Fear that they'd see my insides and leave anyway?

But Emma—she hadn't left. Sayer hadn't left. Hadrian hadn't had a choice. I hadn't, either. And at the end of the day, life offered cards and paths I didn't want. That didn't mean I could refuse them.

This was a card I needed to keep. I needed to forgive myself for the things I'd held onto in the fear of being alone, of being left. Just like Emma and Sayer hadn't left me.

The words bubbled over. "He's gone, Emma. Hadrian's gone."

Emma's expression softened. She leaned her head on my shoulder, then wrapped her arms around me in a bear hug. My bones pinched, but I didn't care. I let my cheek fall on her head with a sigh.

"What? Like he dumped you?" she gasped, eyes going wide. Then, they narrowed. "What did he do? Have someone on the side? Do I need to find a house and set it on fire?"

I offered a watery chuckle. "No. No fires." Because if she set his house on fire, we'd have been homeless.

She didn't pull back. Instead, she only rocked with me. "Then what happened?"

I kept one hand on the headstone. "Would you believe me if I told you the house was haunted?"

She bolted upright. "There was a ghost? And you didn't *tell* me?" Her eyes went wide with offense.

"Not a ghost," I said. "Hadrian."

I told her everything.

Chapter Thirty

At least it got to keep the girl for a while longer. There was something about being heard that warmed a heart—any heart. She'd heard it, hadn't ignored it, not like the ones before.

Harthwait relaxed at the thought. Yes, that would work. Borrowed time while the knot inside of its foundation settled.

It knew—it *knew*—as soon as Cadence had ushered the girl out during the day that she'd be able to hear the house, feel it, and that Cadence had known it, too. That the girl would come back to Harthwait, slowly but surely.

And now, it felt different. The air a bit lighter. The gnarled, jagged feeling inside of its walls smoother, less hungry.

He was gone, at least—that poor boy that had the atrocious father. Always a bad sore, that one, drawing in that darkness, or whatever his guardian had done to keep the boy anchored here. Harthwait never had minded him. He made it feel alive in a different way, but maybe now it was time to sleep. One day, Harthwait might miss that feeling. The starvation for attention, for life, for someone to give to it. If it ever gained that ability again.

Yes, that sounded like a nice idea.

Now, Harthwait felt their feet on the front porch steps. They'd been with Landry quite often the last few weeks. The sister, Emma, talked with her hands, hair bobbing as she spoke. The mourning doves called; the sky wasn't quite dark, but near. In the driveway, the man with taped glasses attempted to gather bags in both arms and close the car door with his shoe.

Landry jogged back. He shook his head, but she took a bag or two anyway. Emma still talked, eyes wide.

A family. It was nice to have a family.

"And then," Emma exclaimed, "he said my PTO days were included. Guess how many that left me? None. So you wanna know what I emailed back?"

Landry eased up the steps. What a familiar picture: her expression weary, lips parted, hands fisted at her sides, but with shopping bags this time. Her eyebrow quirked. Except now she was grown, her mother wasn't in the driveway, and Cadence was gone.

Sayer waddled up behind them. Groaned. Closed his eyes.

"What?" he wheezed. "Hurry up before I drop something. You're both in my way."

Landry stepped aside. Suppressed a little smile.

"I said 'I hope this email finds you before I do.'" Emma smirked.

Landry's eyes widened, her mouth formed an O. Sayer froze midstep.

"Emma, you didn't," Landry breathed.

"Oh, but I did."

"So that's how you got fired." Sayer pushed around both of them, knocking the doorway when he entered. "I shouldn't be surprised." He fumbled through the living room, straight to the kitchen.

Harthwait strained—just for a second.

The light over the sink flickered on.

Sayer froze. Glanced about. Carefully, slowly, began unloading the bags with a gradual urgency.

If Harthwait could have smiled, it would have. But it didn't have the energy for much else. Not with him gone—not anymore.

"Hey, Lan?" He tossed the milk in the fridge and beelined back to the foyer.

". . . so he didn't fire you—"

"—a promotion, is what I was getting at—"

"*Hey,*" Sayer blurted. His knuckles whitened as he clutched the doorframe.

Emma stopped in the foyer, the front door open. A country silence, the type that felt cushioned with swaying grass, chirping crickets, and cicadas, filled the room.

"What's wrong?" Landry glanced up the steps out of habit.

It made Harthwait shrink in shame. Just a little.

"I swear the kitchen light just came on by itself."

Emma's eyes went wide. She gasped. "Really? Do you think it's—"

"I replaced the bulb today," Landry cut in. She deflated. Brought her bags into the kitchen while the other two trailed behind her like chickens after their mother. "I'm sure it's a bad circuit."

A bad circuit. Yes, that's what it was.

And after that, Harthwait worried that's all it ever would be: a house with a thousand possibilities, where one day it would be left, with no family that could hear it. Where Landry might leave and take her sister and friend with her.

Her family. *Its* family.

So until it couldn't anymore, Harthwait might let them know that it was still there. Somehow. Until what little festering life drained away completely.

Then it would be as if the boy had never been, the house had never felt, and Landry had never heard anything—anything at all.

Chapter Thirty-One

One Year Later

"No, Mom. Please don't paint the kitchen without asking the landlord," Emma groaned. She pushed her pointer finger into her temple, squinting into the high sun. I took a seat beside her on the last porch step, Harthwait's new FOR SALE sign wobbling from where I'd just stuck it into the front lawn. It was hot outside—the muggy kind of hot that came with humid inhales and sticky shirts.

"Tell her she needs to ask him on a date," I whispered, just loud enough for Penny to hear on the other end.

"See!" I heard her screech. Emma held the phone away from her ear. "Landry thinks he's cute, too. It's not just me."

"Please stop screaming," Emma said. "I'll be deaf by thirty-five."

Penny started to ramble, this time at a better volume. A pre-wrapped ice cream cone dribbled over Emma's free hand. She chased the drips with her tongue. After a second, she turned to me. "She wants to know about the Beetle. Did Sayer decide to buy it?"

"It drove good the other day, but he didn't say. Why?"

"Mom wants to buy that hunk of metal."

My mouth formed an O. "Aunt Cadence would roll over in her grave if she heard you say that."

"Sure, sure." She waved me away with a grin. I unwrapped my own ice cream cone—this one had pecan bits on the top—and examined the front yard as Penny and Emma said their goodbyes. The trim around the flower beds had been our focus the last couple of weeks. Sayer had helped me with the mulch and laying the brick—Dad had offered, but I'd refused.

"At least let me buy the mulch for you," he'd said.

I'd let him.

As far as I knew, he was doing okay. He'd helped me get the estate affairs in better order after the new year, but I didn't push it.

The only one we pushed was Penny. She'd taken over Emma's lease soon after the separation. I'd asked Emma to move in with me, we'd squabbled over it a bit, Emma said it was too much, before I'd said I'd charge her rent.

I liked having someone else in the house. It didn't feel as empty that way.

The first month had been a fever dream. I'd found myself following Emma, or Sayer, around a lot, not quite ready to be left in a quiet room for too long, mostly out of fear that my mind would make up sounds that weren't real—that I'd convince myself I heard Hadrian moving around, even when I knew he wasn't there.

At one point around the holidays, Emma had a come-to moment with me.

"I know you love me," she'd said, "and I'm flattered you think I know everything, but I think it's best if you talk to someone qualified, Lan." She'd squished my face in her palms. "Maybe not about the house stuff. Or the ghostly-boyfriend thing. I just really, *really* think it'd be a good idea for you to talk to someone. Especially after what your mom did and—other things."

The eating, is what she didn't say.

At first, I'd been offended—how dare Emma tell me to go talk to a therapist? I was an adult, I could make my own choices—but days turned to a week, and when I sat and stared at my half-eaten lunch, in tears, I knew she was right. I could only carry myself so far.

Since I'd been seeing someone regularly, things had improved—thoughts still hung at the back of my mind like vultures, but I could manage them now. I was, at the very least, happy I didn't need to wear a hoodie during hot weather anymore.

"I know we talked about this before," Emma said as I finished off the bottom of my cone, "but I think we should get a guard dog."

I rolled my eyes. "You have allergies."

"To shellfish."

"And dogs," I said, incredulous.

"Still, you can get immunotherapy shots—"

A sound came from inside the house.

Emma's words died.

The hairs along my nape stood at attention. The faintest of flutters rummaged through my chest. It couldn't be.

A year, I'd waited. I'd stop by the closet and stand in it for a moment or two. Emma never said anything, and I never said I was trying. That I was checking. Then, slowly, the nights fell away. I started going to bed. I'd turn out all the lights. Weeks came and went. Eventually, I hung coats and linens in the closet. Nothing came of it.

Neither Eleanora or Ivan had gotten the listing. As of last week, I'd started searching again, but Penny had given me a good recommendation with someone she'd worked with before. She said Vinnie was a gem, and I'd known on the first meeting that he would be a good fit for Harthwait.

Now, the thoughts of selling wavered, if only barely. If the right buyer came along, I would sell, but I wasn't in a rush.

"I think I left the broom propped in the hall," I said. A poor excuse. If I looked her in the eye, she'd be able to tell the nervous anticipation sparkling in my expression. But I knew she already knew.

"I'll be right back." I pushed up from the step and brushed my shorts off.

She rolled her lips together before nodding, wary. "Okay."

The foyer hadn't changed after the renovations finished. I'd kept the stained-glass coverings on the front door and windows, the floor runners, the catch-all entryway table, and the wallpaper. I'd painted the baseboards, but left everything else, because it felt almost cynical to remove every part of Aunt Cadence. And what better way to greet people than by ivory-colored beadboard?

The front door creaked shut behind me. I waited until the latch snicked into place.

Harthwait had been silent for a year. Countless midnights, a death anniversary, and the anniversary of Hadrian's leaving.

But now, almost a year to the day—

"Hello?" I whispered. I cupped the base of my throat. Waited.

The sound of squeaky hinges answered me. Upstairs.

I hurried to the staircase and took the steps two at a time. My heart thundered in my ears, pounded like a drum against my skull, as I swung onto the landing and stopped dead in my tracks.

The half closet hung open—only an inch. But within it—

I exhaled a shaky breath. Pried the door open farther, and froze.

On the other side of the door, a mirror image of Harthwait greeted me. Except this time, the furniture was not burned and watered down from rain. The lawn didn't fall into a maze on the other side of the windowpanes. The air didn't hang with dust and smoke. It was whole.

Real.

Sunlight spilled through heavy crushed-velvet curtains. Sitting chairs flanked a love seat, hardened with antique pillows. The floorboards shined, darker in some places and lighter in others, as if the rugs had been rolled up and put away for warmer months. Netting covered a chandelier in the center of the room to keep gnats and flies away.

I held my breath, lips parted.

I inched forward. My hands shook so hard, I barely caught the doorframe as I stepped through. The air was hot, still slightly dry like an early summer day.

"Is that supposed to happen?" a deep, unfamiliar voice asked. I leaned through the doorway and looked to my left. A hardened, crystalline set of blue eyes stared back at me. I'd seen this man before—on the lawn at Hadrian's wedding. I couldn't explain how, but I felt it. This was the man who'd taken over Hadrian's affairs after his death: Haste.

My resolve started to crumble.

There, just over his shoulder, a woman stood in the middle of the room, sweat beading over her forehead. Behind her, a writing desk. I recognized it all from a memory.

Once upon a time, she'd rushed down a hallway for a little boy.

A shadow emerged from behind the blue-eyed man, this one a bit taller, sharper, one eye gray, the other yellow.

A sob broke from my lips as I covered my mouth. Tears blurred my vision. His voice, rich and thick, split the air.

"Dearest," the yellow-eyed man said. "You came back."

Acknowledgements

We made it to the end and, if I'm being honest, I wasn't quite so sure I'd ever make it this far.

Writing a book is hard—editing is even harder—and then coming to realize that people might read it one day is (gasp) terrifying.

If you know me, you know this book began forming a long time ago. It started as a different idea entirely, where Hadrian's backstory was never flushed to the reader; it focused on the monsters in your head that follow you. Even then, I knew that Hadrian had his own journey, so I'm glad that I've finally gotten to tell it.

This version of *A Heart So Haunted* was already being drafted when my own aunt suddenly passed in June of 2023. To say that made finishing this book a challenge is an understatement. Landry's story became one of the hardest things I've tackled, because I desperately felt inadequate in telling it. Here I was, trying to build Landry's pivotal moments of growth while I'd been tossed backward in my own—this then made writing Hadrian's guidance almost bittersweet. In the end, I hope I managed to tell both of their stories in a way that touches someone.

All of that to say, it takes a village to bring a book to life. To my agent, Joanna Rasheed—I would literally be curled in a corner debating my life if you weren't my guide. I still marvel at how you plucked me from your inbox at the time that you did. To everyone at Ultra Literary for also going to bat for me in so many ways.

To my editor, Melissa Rechter—you *also* picked me, and I can't thank you enough for the notes, ideas, and suggestions ("Hollie, you forgot *this*") to keeps my distracted mind in line. To the team at Alcove, thank you for the endless guidance and enthusiasm. To Colin Verdi, for the beautiful cover art.

Before there were agents and publishers, there were English teachers. Mrs. Robinson, Ms. Petty, Mrs. Weeks-Gardner, and my MFA advisor, Mrs. Smith: you ladies developed me before I realized what was happening. Thank you.

To my family, because you all let me talk to the people in my head. To my cats, for being the sweetest constant companions and following me, quite literally, everywhere.

To my husband, Hunter, for being my biggest cheerleader. You keep me grounded and encourage my book hoarding. You put a hand at my back and push me when I need it, but you also sit me down and keep the demons away.

Speaking of demon-like-things—Hadrian, you jerk, you've been with me for years. You've been so many different iterations of the same creature, I've lost count. Thank you for making me grow. You've always been in a shadowed corner, whispering things I can't forget. I'm grateful you've pushed me as a writer and as a person. I think the hardest part of this however-many-year journey with you is seeing *this* version of you come to a close.

And thank *you*, dearest reader, for picking up this book.

Last but not least, I want to thank the One who pulled me out of that dark corner years ago and washed His blood over my imperfections. I'm not perfect, never will be, but You saved me. I think that's why I like the scary—the things that can't be explained. Because when everyone else says only evil is there, I still walk back to You.

Deus ubique est.